HIGHLAND HARVEST

INDIAN SUMMER

Stuart Edgar

Grosvenor House
Publishing Limited

This book is published by
Grosvenor House Publishing Ltd
Link House
140 The Broadway, Tolworth, Surrey, KT6 7HT.
www.grosvenorhousepublishing.co.uk

This book is a work of fiction. Any resemblance to
people or events, past or present, is purely coincidental.

A CIP record for this book
is available from the British Library

ISBN 978-1-83975-859-1

Dedication

To Carol my first and last editor and
my constant support - with love.

Note from the Author

Though many place names in this novel are real, others are imaginary and I have, I am afraid played somewhat fast and loose with Scottish Highland geography for convenience sake. I have tried to suggest the Highland vernacular in speech for the sake of realism and included Gaelic words and phrases where I believe them necessary or appropriate to the story and apologise profusely for any errors or unintentional abominations of use - they are entirely a result of my ignorance of those two beautiful languages. All the characters and institutions in this novel are fictitious and any similarity to any person or place, living or dead is entirely coincidental.

I would like to express my gratitude to the people of the Highlands and Islands of Western Scotland, whether indiginous or incomers, who, on my frequent visits over the years have treated me with unfailing kindness and for whom I have a great respect and admiration. Lastly, I would like to express my deep love of the Highlands and Islands of Western Scotland whose wild beauty never fails to inspire and astound me. I hope, however inadequately, to have expressed something of their magical nature and ferocity of their seasons in these pages, both as a living, constant and formative presence for the characters of the story, and as a presence in themselves. I hope I have been able to breathe something of the life of this remarkable land and its people into the following pages.

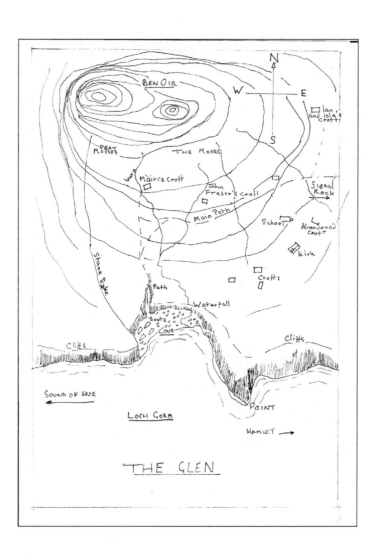

THE GLEN

CHAPTER 1

STORM CHILD

Callum was born in 1921 at one o'clock in the morning during a fierce October gale. The force of the storm threatened to strip the wet turfs from the roof of the squat, brooding croft house. The storm, so common on these West Highland coasts, tore up the glen, straight off an iron-grey sea, funnelling spume into the air where, spittle-like, it rolled off rooftops amid torrents of black rain. The neighbouring burn had swollen into a crashing, peat-brown flood, which promised to uproot the rocky foundations of the brooding old black-house from where it stood in its sheltered hollow.

Hamish, Callum's father, fed more peat turfs on the fire and coughed as the dark, bitter smoke caught at the back of his throat. A bent, gnarled, dark man, Hamish, though still only thirty, had the deeply ingrained creases around the eyes and face which told of ever squinting into biting sea winds and flying surf. An educated son of a Scottish parson he had come to the glen as a young man to preach to the ragged crofting community, had met Màiri, a crofter's daughter, taken her for a wife and turned his back on the church. He had become a fisher and farmer and was useless at both; success eluded him, drained away through his fingers, a bitter ooze of failure. Although a tall man he had become bowed over from straining, not just against the fierce sea winds but against the bitter blows of misfortune that he ever anticipated striking him full in the face. Disappointment and bitterness had drained his youth, lined his face and turned his heart sour. He had come to see his lot as a just punishment from an abandoned, jealous, Calvinist God.

His face impassive, his gaze swept the corner bed where Màiri, his exhausted wife, lay clutching the pale, white infant. It had been a fierce struggle after a long labour to give birth to this thin scrap of a babe. Old Mrs McCrimmon, acting as midwife, as she did for all the women of the little community, clucked over the mewling child.

The old woman drew her ragged shawl more tightly around her bony shoulders as protection against the cruel draughts that pierced every nook and crack of the little cottage and then she helped the child to the mother's swollen breast. It greedily hung on, sucking warmth and life into itself with the desperation of a creature on the edge of survival. The raven like Mrs McCrimmon, in her black widow's weeds, talked softly to the mother, comforting her and reassuring her, telling her that the boy would live. Màiri had lost her first child at birth, she had been too weak from hunger and privation to provide the baby with much sustenance in the womb: it had perished almost at the moment of birth. She couldn't bear another loss.

Màiri had tried to feed herself up on potatoes from a patch she had grown at the back of the house and had begged milk from a neighbour's cow instead of relying on the poor fare that Hamish could provide from his wasted efforts. For once though, he had had a reasonably successful harvest of oats and barley, and had improved his catches from the loch. She had eaten moderately well, if with little variety, in the last stages of her pregnancy and that, along with the tenacity that little Callum had inherited from her, had resulted in a successful, if difficult, birth.

She caught Hamish's gaze and went to lift the child for him to see, but it was too raw a moment. He was too used to perceiving a look of contempt or pity in his wife's eyes. He tore his gaze away and stumbled for the door. The guilt and contempt he could bear as his due for his failures, though they pressed hard down on his shoulders and threatened to buckle his knees with the terrible weight of it; that he would bear, but he was not strong enough for her kindnesses.

His self-recrimination and brooding fed him and watered him. The moment he married he began to shrivel up inside; the failure of his mission, the betrayal of his father's trust and the bile he had imbibed with his Calvinist porridge as a boy gnawed away at his guts. Beaten and prayed over by his father with no intimation of mercy or humanity, Hamish had been left with a great capacity for self-recrimination and self-loathing and precious little room for self-forgiveness.

Màiri had been fascinated by this educated young man with his refined manners and respectful tone towards her when he had first appeared in the glen to hold services, and to preach in their meagre stone chapel. He was so different from the rough young fishermen she had grown up with and gone to school with. His fine manners and careful dress, his ardour in the pulpit and his passion for justice for the crofters and fishermen in their struggle with over-mighty landlords had impressed her and won her over to his side. She took his part in his struggle to win over the villagers to regular churchgoing and even joined him when he strode round the neighbouring glens smashing illicit whisky stills and promising damnation if the fisher folk didn't change their ways. He was just as fierce in berating a greedy factor who tried to break those villagers who did not have protected crofting leases with exorbitant rents, and who then tried to foreclose on them when they couldn't pay. A young firebrand with passion in his belly and a jealous God to drive him, he had burned with an energy that overcame all resistance.

But then he settled down amongst these Highland people and tried to live their life and it was one for which he was ill-prepared. The fierce sea frightened him; he perceived it as malevolent and wilful, the thin soil refused to yield to his will and even his cow recognised his ineptitude and refused to obey him. For three years now he had struggled in this way, gradually being worn down in mind and spirit. The loss of his first child, for which he blamed himself, had just confirmed in him his own uselessness.

Gradually the sheer, grinding struggle for existence, his failure to bend this land to his will and the hostility of the environment wore down his resolve and sapped his physical and spiritual strength and, when his prayers failed to bring any relief to his situation, he abandoned his God altogether and gave up hope of salvation.

Màiri, with an ever-increasing sense of helplessness, saw the gradual strangling of Hamish's spirit and its replacement by a corrosive bitterness. Over the years he became defeated and irascible: whatever she said he took as veiled criticism; encouragement was seen as goading, support as undue interference and kindness seen as pity.

To a proud, rigid man, driven by a neurosis engendered by his father's scorn and beatings, the failure of his crofting life was unbearable. His struggle to succeed became, at first desperate and then, by stages, a weary daily grind against seemingly impossible odds. Sisyphus-like Hamish got up, weary to the bone each morning, to push that rock up the hill and he returned each evening in heartbreak to find the rock back at the bottom of the slope.

In the end though, through sheer persistence, he managed to make some sort of living for them, although it was never enough, hunger kept them company throughout the long, lean winter months and summer was never bountiful, they were only ever just getting by, Hamish spent every waking hour working and despairing.

Màiri bore it all with stoical, quiet grace, despite her frustration at not being able to reach the man she had married, not ever being able to sit him down and explain that it was all right, that she understood and appreciated his efforts, recognised that the life didn't come easily to him. She tried desperately but he had closed himself off to her; with each new failure he set his sights more resolutely against happiness. He simply didn't deserve it, in his eyes he stood defeated and condemned for being weak enough to fall in love with her and he began to resent and then to hate her for it.

They began to live parallel lives within the little croft cottage. She would carry on with her chores without reference or acknowledgement to Hamish while he fled the house each morning as soon as he could. He came back exhausted at night, when he would eat in brooding silence whatever Màiri had managed to scrape together, before slumping into a chair by the peat fire and dozing until bedtime. In the summer, when the sun barely dipped below the horizon before, a couple of hours later, rising again, he would sometimes stay out all night; tending his few ragged sheep, coaxing some life from the poor soil, or casting his nets out in the loch. He struggled on, isolated in a semi-torpor of clumsy, exhausted activity.

Eventually, through sheer persistence, he found a sort of peace in these physical activities, a way of keeping busy rather than of thinking, of doing rather than feeling. His hands learnt a kind of rhythm as he went about familiar tasks, even the cow began to trust him after a fashion. He still struggled with the life, was still never able to produce a plentiful harvest nor relax his grip lest he fall behind and lose everything, but he simply got used to it. He began to inhabit the life as he would an ill-fitting suit.

The Scots have a way of identifying somebody with their place rather than the other way round. Hamish belonged to the croft, just as his neighbour John Fraser belonged to his. The scrap of coarse land on this fierce coast on which the crofts lay was all that was left to the inland villagers once they had been cleared out of their fertile valleys generations before by a greedy, absent landlord. It had, in time, taken possession of them and their children, and in turn, it had taken ownership of the reluctant and incompetent Hamish. Finally reconciled, after a fashion, to the land, Hamish found it more difficult to become reconciled to his wife.

Màiri had gradually developed a life apart from her husband while sharing a house and a bed. She spent time with the women of the village as they helped each other with chores and, if she had any social life at all, it was with these tough, uncomplaining women going about their joint tasks; collecting seaweed from the stony shore of the little cove at the foot of the glen where the open fishing boats were hauled out, helping to dig potatoes on each other's plots or exchanging a few eggs for dried or salted herrings, stored in wooden casks against the bare, hungry winter.

Over the years Màiri brought load after load of seaweed up the precipitous, stony track to the croft, it would lay heavy and wet as she carried it on her back in rough hessian sacks. She would leave it in a heap for Hamish to use to enrich the unproductive land. Without acknowledgement he would take the seaweed and fork it over raised ridges of the poor, thin, stony soil. The work of creating these misnamed "lazy beds" was

7

back-breakingly hard. With nothing but a spade and a mattock, for the community could not afford a horse, Hamish would work his way along the strip of land, digging out soil from between the beds to start a ridge, as often as not hitting stones beneath the surface with a shoulder jarring 'thunk'! Having started the ridge with soil he would build it up, layer by layer, with seaweed and cowdung, ready for the next year's planting. He would pile the larger stones to one side of the plot, later using them to build a rough wall round the planting area to keep his ragged, hungry sheep off the crops. Over the years he gradually, painfully, built up the fertility of his hard earned plot.

After each storm Màiri and the other women would make their way down the stony path, worn smooth by three generations of sure-footed, boot-shod feet and share the spoils of the storm: a harvest of seaweed, flotsam and jetsam. Sometimes this bounty proved to be valuable, driftwood especially was always welcome in this relatively treeless landscape, the smaller pieces for kindling, the larger for fencing or for patching up buildings. Màiri collected enough silver-washed planks to make a passable chicken house and a picket fence to keep the hens in and the fox out.

Unlike Hamish Màiri fiercely held on to her outdoor role and enjoyed the hard work. She had worked the croft since she was a small girl, firstly with her mother and father and then, when they had both tragically and separately died; he in a boating accident, she, a year later of septicaemia, she had continued to work the twenty acre croft. She struggled on, managing to the best of her ability, from age sixteen until aged twenty one when she had married Hamish and allowed him to take over most of the outdoor work,which was his proper place. At first she had tried to work with him but, as estrangement intensified, and especially after she had lost their first baby, more and more they worked separately. She still, however, got up most days eager to tackle her tasks with energy and long practised skill.

She was popular amongst the taciturn, reserved crofting people. She had grown up with them, they were her own and had given comfort and practical help when first her father, then her mother, had so cruelly died. Taller than most of her contemporaries at five-foot-eight she stood straight and moved her statuesque, heavy-boned but graceful frame with effortless ease. She had dark good looks, a train of black curls which tumbled down her back and deep, dark brown eyes that shone with energy and intelligence and crinkled at the edges with a subtle humour. She was bright and quick-witted and as easy in the company of these Highland people as Hamish was distant and awkward.

After Callum was born she was up on the second day, making Hamish an early morning bowl of home-ground porridge and, as an extra treat, a spoon of precious Tate & Lyle's Golden Syrup on top. She breakfasted on fresh milk and home-made oatcakes. Today, she was determined to get hens for her newly built chicken run. There were three of them to feed now and she needed a means of exchange with neighbours other than the occasional catch of ubiquitous herrings that Hamish brought home, and of which there was often a surfeit in the glen. Like most subsistence farmers and fishers, the glen had either feast or famine and there was always plenty of the latter. As well as a good source of nutrition for her small family eggs were a currency more useful than money, which anyway was scarce to be seen in this impoverished community.

After breakfast, dressed in a long, black, rough dress, pulled in at the waist by a homemade plaited belt and wearing a thick, long plaid shawl across her shoulders, she picked her way, more slowly and delicately than usual, over the familiar stepping stones to the main path that led through the centre of the village and which also branched steeply off down to the cove.

Unlike Hamish, who hated the harshness of the glen, Màiri loved it for its wild beauty. At the junction with the main path she stopped to take in the view, as if seeing it anew after her claustrophobic confinement in their small, dark cottage. The little glen lay in a natural bowl or amphitheatre at her feet, overlooking Loch Gorm, the Blue Loch, a sea-loch that cut deep into the surrounding hills. The hillsides above shone brown and orange with dead bracken in the pale autumn sun, lighter patches of emerald green grass still poked through here and there, not yet desiccated by winter winds. Some of the heather growth on the slopes was still a deep viridian where it coated their flanks but was slowly turning to black as the bare stems were revealed. Beinn Oir, head in hazy clouds, towered and brooded over the loch-side, pale ochre and umber igneous rock, its head rounded with age from uncountable millions of winters.

The Beinn rose high up behind the croft, the browny-yellow and green slopes tilting ever more sharply as they rose to meet the bare rock at the summit. Màiri found the great hill behind their house a comfort, a presence that seemed to offer protection to the little community, to stand guard, a constant sentinel in her life. She knew all its moods and colours, she loved its bright white top on a winter's day. She was fascinated by the hares and ptarmigan in frosty winter coat which haunted its sides, little friendly ghosts picking their way through snowflakes to find a few rough green shoots of vegetation or scraping a little lichen from the rocks. In summer the lower slopes would glow deep purple, dressed in their cloak of flowering heather.

Looking out towards the sea, round the headland, shadowy in the morning mist, she saw the perky little profile of a motorised fishing boat, out from Kyle of Lochalsh to try its nets in the deep channel down the centre of the loch. It buffeted a gently rolling bow wave, white against the dark of the loch waters. The gentle putt-putt of its motor drifted down the loch and up the hill towards her on a gentle breeze of softly moving, morning air. She spotted movement down on the shingly shoreline of the cove. She could see one of the women picking her way along the strand line, but from way up here at was impossible to work out who it was, just a small, bent black figure against the white stones, an early riser, even earlier than she.

Her view down to the lower end of the loch was restricted, though she knew that was where the little, nameless sister community lay, a couple of miles away.

It was made up of just a few crofts and a couple of cottages for estate workers. Between her and them lay a great headland of soaring basalt; grey-brown cliffs, striated pillars of solidified lava. Black chuffs played on its upper rim, dancing in the light breeze and catching the updrafts, their bright red legs flashing in the sun, crying out their name all the while, 'cheeough!', 'cheeough!'. Their sounds drifted on the wind towards her, familiar and welcoming.

She heard the plaintive, haunting cry of a curlew bubbling and piping up on the moors, above the cliffs where they nested in springtime, amongst the bobbing cotton-grass, blowing and sighing in the wind, an unruly regiment of nodding white tufts. Soon the moors would be silent again until the spring; just the odd bark of a surprised, grazing ewe or the 'raark!' of the great golden eagle that sailed the spaces above the glen; frightening the hares and making stags and hinds from the estate lands raise their heads warily.

Màiri spoke quietly to Callum, strapped to her chest in a roughly made papoose. She carried him in front of her where he could feel her heartbeat through her soft chest, could see her face and where she could readily communicate with him. He was so unbearably precious to her, this hard-won little scrap, she wanted him to know her glen and to love it as she did. She described to him what she saw in soft-voiced Gaelic, whispering lest Hamish hear her from higher up the hill and disapprove. The Church, just as the rest of establishment Scotland, detested and was intent on suppressing the language of the independent-minded Highlanders and Islanders, and

Hamish, though he had cut himself off from the Church, still retained his old prejudices. It was just another barrier between him and the other villagers.

She turned to look back up the hill to where the squat, turf-thatched croft house peeped out from its hollow higher up the glen, at the foot of the great beinn. She pointed to their home, supporting Callum on her arm and lifting him so he could see, though she knew he was still only aware of close-up shapes and blurred light patterns;

-"There's yer hame wee Callum, the place ye'll always belong tae and the place ye'll always come back tae. I jest ken ye're goin tae grow tae love it and respect it as I dae". Her hushed voice was softly sibilant and in tune with the low shush of the breeze on the morning air.

-"I'll make it happy and safe fer ye my beautiful son and ye'll grow up to know this glen as I dae and be at peace here." And she added to no one in particular;

-"And maybe yer athair will be able tae find a little peace too now that we have ye here with us!"

Then she turned her gaze to the little cove far below them, circled by large wave-rounded rocks, secure in a bowl made by the sheer cliffs that curved round the headland protecting the tiny looking upturned boats which were hauled out on a shingle bank. Circling gulls called out their piping cries in the bright morning air,

-"See Callum, they're welcoming ye!" she whispered, chuckling softly at their antics. Their voices were thin and quavering in the soft updraft that was the only remnant from the fierce storm of two days ago. Màiri turned her face to the sky, her curls fanning out behind her; it felt so good to be alive on this clear autumn morning, with this new life in her arms. Callum convulsively sneezed and snuffled at her by way of reply before burying his head again into the soft warmth of her breast.

She could see the translucent, clear waters of the loch gently lapping the stones of the cove in a rhythmic swell; greeny-turquoise at the edge and so transparent that the pale stones could be seen rippling under the surface for quite a way out, where the water turned first deeper and deeper blue-green and then became a softly, rippling sheet of slate blue. Further out still the sea loch was patched with silver, the watery sun shimmering in dappled, reflective islands across to the far shore.

A cry caught her attention, she saw Maggie Fraser, their neighbour John Fraser's gauche young daughter, bounding up the "Main Street" towards her, black skirts flying. Her cheerful, bright, red jersey was a stark contrast to the natural colours of the glen and clashed with the dark silhouettes of the crofting cottages, which were dotted here and there along the stony, mud track that passed for a communal thoroughfare.

-"Màiri, the babe, is it a bòidean or is it a suaineag?" she pleaded, and then, breathlessly; -"Oh Màiri, may I see, please?"

The villagers, especially the younger ones used a broken form of Gaelic-English to each other, easily substituting one for the other at random. Màiri felt sad that many of the youngest were beginning to lose the Gaelic altogether, having it beaten out of them by the "tawse" when they went up to the big school at Kyle.

Young Maggie was glowing, red-cheeked with running and excitement.

"Fàilte na maidne dhut Maggie!" greeted Màiri.

The young Maggie, not yet sixteen, was a pretty child if a bit ungainly and uncoordinated in her movements. She tended to lurch from side to side as she ran in a muddle of arms and legs, her scuffed boots sliding, her metal shoe studs sparking on cobbles. She was suddenly shy now that she came close and drew up a yard or two from Màiri.

"Please Màiri can I see?" She repeated quietly.

She treated Màiri rather more like a big sister than a neighbour and worshipped her for her cleverness and good looks.

Nellie Fraser, Maggie's mother, had kept an eye on Màiri after her parents had died, acting as substitute mother when needed, quietly reassuring her and comforting her in the understated, undemonstrative manner of Highland women. She offered practical help when needed without seeming to interfere, inviting Màiri in to "share a bite" with the rest of her family when she sensed she was lonely and making sure that Màiri always had something in the house to eat. John Fraser, Maggie's father, had likewise quietly offered and given practical help on running the croft without any fuss or seeming to interfere and took the cow once a year to the old Aberdeen Angus bull the two villages shared between them, in order to make sure she continued to produce milk and a calf for Màiri.

So Màiri felt like a member of the Fraser family and enjoyed the easy familiarity Maggie usually showed towards her. She was very fond of this skinny, gangly young girl who otherwise only had two big, rough brothers for companionship and she sensed the shyness that had come over her.

-"It's alright Maggie of course ye can. He's a bòidean called Callum, a lovely, bonnie wee mannie with the most beautiful little face!"

She felt the excitement more even than Maggie, showing off her precious new baby, so hard gained and so yearned for, yearned for over many long, soulless nights waiting for Hamish to finally return in silence from his work while she grieved for the loss of her firstborn and ached for a new life to come out of her.

Maggie crept up quietly, peering in at the little bundle on Màiri's chest. Màiri pulled back the corner of the rough blanket tucked under Callum's chin to give Maggie a good view of his squashed, wrinkled little face; red and shiny and with long, black eyelashes. Streaks of wispy, thin, black hair peered out from under a tiny, faded, woollen cap, given to Màiri before his birth by a neighbour, along with many other gifts of blankets and baby clothes. People in her community didn't have much but they shared what they had and then it was passed on. Callum blew tiny bubbles and gurgled and gave another little sneeze and poor Maggie nearly swooned in delight.

Maggie was desperate to stay and admire Callum but reluctant to risk the wrath of Nellie, her mother, if she didn't return to her chores straight away. She tore herself away with a quick,

-"I have tae gae Màiri!"

before taking off again up the main track the way she had come, in a whirl of skirts and arms and legs, the hobnails and heel-caps on her boots again sparking on cobbles and stones. She tried to look back over her shoulder as she went but her coordination wasn't up to the task and she barely stayed upright as she lurched first to one side then to the other as she tried desperately to regain some sort of forward momentum without actually falling flat.

Màiri smiled as she carefully set off again, down to the cove. By the time she had reached the stony shore Callum was showing the first signs of irritation, opening his miniature pink mouth, showing minute gums and issuing the beginnings of a sob; he was clearly hungry. She settled herself on some large stones piled up near the upturned boats and began to feed Callum. He sucked greedily and noisily, gurgling and huffing as Màiri held her breast for him and cradled him in her plaid to keep him covered. She felt a deep warmth flood through her. She had learnt enough from watching ewes with their lambs and the calf with her cow to know it was a natural bonding process which flooded both mother and baby with strong feelings of attachment: just part of the survival process for the infant. But she hadn't been prepared for the overwhelming emotions she had experienced when she had first fed Callum and held him close and which she felt again now, and every time she held him and fed him.

The woman she had seen earlier was now at the far end of the strandline, where the little beach narrowed as it reached the great towering headland. The woman turned and didn't notice Màiri at first, so intent was she in studying the wave-edge. When she did look up and notice Màiri she raised her arm in greeting and headed towards her. Even then Màiri didn't recognise her for a moment. The small, neatly dressed figure was all in black with a shawl which covered her head and which she held together at the waist in a tightly bound white fist. It was Mollie McClelland, a widow whose husband, like many on this coast, had been taken by the sea some years ago.

She was a small, upright woman with a white drift of hair tucked under her shawl. Only in her late fifties, her tight, pointed face nevertheless was deeply lined, incised with hardship and harsh weather. She smiled a toothless grin at Màiri as she came closer. Like a lot of men and women of her generation she had taken the opportunity, when in town one market day, of paying a visiting dentist to take all her teeth out in one go in order to save later unplanned for bills and to have to suffer the scourge of toothache.

She greeted Màiri in Gaelic and came and sat on the pile of stones next to her. Mollie had a thin, reedy voice with the slow tuneful lilt of the Western Highlands. She asked after Màiri's health and advised her to eat plenty of fresh herring, especially the livers for their iron. She said that she would make her a rich broth which would help to give her strength. She would bring it over later in the week when she had collected some local herbs which would have a restorative effect. Màiri didn't question the woman's expertise in such matters, it was just accepted; Mollie had learned herbalism from her mother, who had learnt it from hers and so on. At a time when doctors were not widely available or affordable, traditional healing was still much used and respected. It was a part of the self-help attitude of these little self-sufficient communities who had virtually no external support to aid them in their daily lives.

Mollie stayed for a while, chatting about the storm and about the business of her neighbours which Màiri had missed since being confined at home for Callum's birth. Finally she asked about the baby in an almost casual, offhand manner. Màiri was disappointed in this lack of interest in her new baby, so unlike Maggie Fraser's excited curiosity, but she understood nevertheless.

At a time when many infants were lost at or soon after birth, or in their first few years, the wider community couldn't afford to invest the emotional and physical energy required to bring up a young child that may well not live. Most communities would celebrate a child's fourth or fifth birthday as if welcoming them into the world for the first time, unspokenly acknowledging that they had survived long enough to stand a good chance of making it to adulthood. It was a conspiracy of silence; the community watched and waited and hoped and maybe prayed but never admitted that they were watching the dance with death that was a young child's early years.

Màiri sensed this and knew it deep down but she was not going to admit to it, even though it nagged at the edge of her consciousness, this terrible possibility that she might still lose Callum. Seeing the look in Mollie's eyes, a look of hope mixed with anguish and sadness, caused a chill to run through her. She looked away and clutched Callum more tightly. This unspoken interplay drifted through their conversation, as Mollie continued chattering about the trivial doings of her neighbours and Màiri clung on to Callum, her stomach knotted with fear.

Her unease was transmitted to Callum who was becoming restless. He was complaining in tiny open-mouthed "ach!, ach!" sounds. Màiri rose, chastened by the meeting and took her leave of Mollie, thanking her for her offer of the broth and then heading back towards the steep path up to the village.

When she arrived back at the main track she turned east towards Isla McDonald's croft. Isla was not much older than Màiri, they had been at school together. She had helped to teach the young Màiri to read. Màiri shared almost everything with Isla, her grief when her parents had died, her worries about Hamish and the small everyday trials and pleasures of crofting life.

Isla and Ian McDonald lived half a mile off the main track, around which the rest of the croft houses were dotted. Their croft was the last one at the opposite end of the village to Màiri, on the way to the little community at the end of the loch. Their small, square, white-painted croft house, the only one in the community with a slate roof, lay in a small grassed enclosure, surrounded by a chain-link fence to keep the sheep off Isla's little flower garden. Ian McDonald was a carpenter. He had been apprenticed at fourteen to a craftsman in Aberdeen, an uncle on his mother's side. He had inherited the lease on his grandparents' croft when they had retired and gone to live with their son, Ian's father. Most crofters didn't get to retire, worn out with hard work and hardship many died in residence continuing to care as best they could for their much cherished croft.

The descendants of the current generation of crofters, like Màiri and Ian, had been the eventual beneficiaries of an attempt to turn back the clock on the injustices suffered by the Highlanders and Islanders in the previous two centuries. The '45 Rebellion of Bonnie Prince Charlie which led to the harrying of the Highlanders by 'Butcher' Cumberland's soldiers and militia; men, women and children were slaughtered as they fled, their homes put to the torch: the bloodiest slaughter ever to take place on Scottish soil. In destroying old clan loyalties it established a semi-feudal system of land ownership on the part of the sons of loyalist clan chiefs and absentee Englishmen. They exploited the people and their lands and replaced most of them with more profitable sheep.

From Oban to Sutherland, Arran to Lewis, across the Highlands and Islands, land had been seized and people cleared; there were mass emigrations, willing or not. The Crofting Act of 1886 was an attempt at redress after so much injustice for people like Màiri's and Ian's grandparents and gave secure tenure and the right to a fair rent to tens of thousands of Highland and Island households, with a right to bequeath the crofting tenancy to a family member. Crofts were on small parcels of land, and averaged about thirty acres, but fewer than that for some in the glen, with community rights to a larger area of rough grazing; which comprised around three hundred acres of high pasture and moorland in the glen. Ian McDonald's grandparents had been one of the first families to benefit and they had worked their croft for thirty years.

Ian McDonald was a big man with large strong hands, a shock of red hair and deep blue eyes. He was everything that Hamish wasn't, outgoing, optimistic and with an enormous generosity of spirit, he loved the crofting life and thrived on physical hard work and the outdoors. Constrained and uncomfortable indoors his huge frame seemed to expand in the open air as he moved around his croft with an unexpectedly easy motion for such a big man. In an earlier age he may well have been mistaken for a Viking raider, like those who plundered the Islands and coastline for centuries.

Right now he was in the process of manhandling a recalcitrant, black Highland cow, not one of the pretty longhorns beloved of the Victorians and shortbread tin manufacturers but the traditional tough, stocky, black-coated cows of the Scottish hills. The cow, wide-eyed with frantic fear and excitement, was trying to escape down the track that Màiri was following to the croft, but it was no match for Ian McDonald.

He had expertly grasped the great black neck in one of his huge arms, and then, using his great strength and the leverage of his powerful legs, he bowed the cow's head and turned its front legs into the gate to the paddock. The cow had no option but to follow and bellowed an ear-thumping roar in protest as it swung its rump in a last attempt to escape. But Ian had it beaten and met the rump with his full body weight, refusing to budge an inch. The cow kicked up its back heels and, as Ian released it, cantered into the field, still bellowing a protest and shaking its stocky head and neck from side to side in puzzled annoyance.

Ian smiled and greeted Màiri warmly. Though Màiri was tall for a woman of her time, Ian towered a good six inches over her. He grasped her between those massive arms and hugged her close, being careful not to squash little Callum in the process, He immediately asked after the baby. Màiri noted this lack of caution, clearly he had no reservations about the future of this child. She felt immediately better in the face of Ian's enormous goodwill and optimism.

-"Màiri McDonald will ye put that man doon and come away inside!"

Isla had seen Màiri coming up the track and had rushed out to greet her. She was beaming widely, obviously pleased to see her. Isla was as striking in her own way as Ian, her almost white blond hair, unusual amongst the dark-haired, swarthy Highlanders, streamed behind her in the breeze. She had pale green eyes and a clear, pale skin. Like Ian, she was probably a throwback to fierce Viking raiders, followers of the Norseman Somerled who conquered most of the West Coast and took the Lordship of the Isles for himself.

Isla clasped Màiri by the elbow and steered her towards the neat, white croft house. When they were inside the cosy, comfortably furnished cottage Isla settled her in a large, overstuffed armchair. Màiri found herself sitting in front of the soft peat glow of the cast-iron range that filled the large fireplace. The doors to the stove, inlaid with small, smoky, crystal windows, radiated a fierce red heat. Màiri felt the sting of the heat on her cheeks and smelt the glowing peats. She eased herself back in the armchair away from the heat as Isla dragged a heavy, blackened kettle across the cast-iron top of the range and placed it with a dull, metallic clang on the round hotplate above the fire.

Isla said how grieved she had been at not being able to be with Màiri, her best friend, at the birth, but they both knew that Mrs McCrimmon would allow nobody to 'clutter the place up' while she acted as midwife, and nobody, not even the self-confident Isla, argued with Mrs McCrimmon. This prohibition applied especially to the father, Hamish had had to busy himself outside during the labour, until eventually being let in to eat his supper. He was then only allowed to stay quietly in the background so long as he didn't interfere. Not that he could have brought himself to do otherwise anyway. It would not begin to occur to a man to be with his wife at such a time, this was strictly women's business, he was not welcome. Isla, however, who so desperately wished to have children of her own, had felt a keen sense of responsibility for Màiri and had been distraught at not being able to attend her. Now she lavished praise and attention on little Callum and, when Màiri handed him over for her to hold. was almost as overjoyed and overwhelmed with emotion as Maggie had been.

Màiri relaxed into the chair, feeling a warm and comfortable weariness seep into her. She felt more at ease here than in her own home. It was a retreat, a haven, a place where she could allow herself a little happiness. If she were truthful, it was an escape from Hamish and from the dull weariness of his life, which, when she was at home, crept into her like a grey sea mist and soured her mood, dragging her, inch by inch, towards the dark gloom that was Hamish's constant temperament.

Isla was enthralled at this privileged contact with Callum, feeling this "wee baggage" so close, warm and alive. For Màiri to share this gift of life with her was important, a sacrament to their friendship and an act of emotional significance for them both. Isla sighed with a deep longing and Màiri, knowing how painful such longing was, was keen to reassure her about her own prospects of pregnancy.

Màiri stayed chatting for over an hour over cups of tea and one of Isla's delicious golden oatcakes with home produced, pale honey; Isla's cooking always shamed her own efforts. Màiri asked Isla if she would stand as godparent to young Callum. Though Màiri attended the kirk only intermittently she was still a Christian by conviction and wouldn't have dreamt of not having Callum baptised. It was important to have this naming ceremony done as quickly as possible in a society and time where many children didn't survive their first few weeks. Her first baby, stillborn, had been buried outside and alongside the cemetery wall, unnamed and unrecognised by the Kirk and in an unmarked grave, forgotten by everyone but Màiri, and of course Hamish, who would never have been able to share such memories with anyone. She remembered her every day with a twist of her heart that was an intense physical pain.

Eventually, Màiri had to leave, she was worried she would not be back in time to make Hamish's midday meal. Isla, still enthralled with little Callum, was reluctant to hand him over and followed Màiri outside. Màiri still had to check on her way home if John Fraser had any spare chicks with which to start off her flock and she was aware she could only walk at a fairly gentle pace just now.

As she walked down the grassy track, now a stale green and browning off as autumn's age increased, she studied the sedges and grasses and the remaining plants, those that had not withdrawn into the ground to lie dormant and protected over winter. She knew that much also now existed only as seed, annuals full of potential that would burst from the ground when the seasons and the earth turned again towards the sun. This far north the summers were brief and the winters long, she yearned for spring to return and spread its green optimism over a somnolent land. But she also loved the stormy, rain soaked brown and gold of autumn, so moody and misty. Between storms it was a pensive, crackle-leaved, quiet time of thoughtfulness; sombre and contemplative, it was a prelude to the sharp, white sparkle of a hoar frosted, snowy, winter when the wind shrieked up amongst the bare peaks and all was still below.

As she walked she studied the ground with a naturalist's eye. She grazed the verge with her eyes, examining the border between the track and the stone-walled, wire-posted, raised grassy bank of the field boundary. Between the browning, seed-headed sedges and grasses nestled ferns and stoneworts, mosses and delicate fading asphodels. She recognised the tiny leaves of violets and birdsfoot trefoil, the remains of delicate orchids and sticky cleavers and she spotted a tiny, grassy tunnel, evidence of the regular run of a secretive vole or shrew.

Ever since her early childhood she had been fascinated and enthralled by this natural backdrop in all its guises. Her much-loved mother had also been in love with this wild world and had shown her its hidden places and mysteries and explained its wild, open spaces, its secretive, shy creatures and the unvisited nooks, crannies, glens and bays of her small wilderness world of coast and hills. Her mother had put names to its plants and animals in Gaelic and Scots, vernacular of biological labels and ecologies of wonder, understood and valued and magicked in a way that only a child's mind can do. She knew much of the folklore and healing lore that surrounded this natural orbit in which she and the others of her community carried out their lives.

In a slow rhythm with her walking she named and described this quiet, intimate world to the squeezed up little face of Callum as he peered, unseeing from out of the covered-in, snuggled, comfy space between the warm mounds of her chest, alert to her voice and soothed by its sounds.

Autumn seemed to her an odd time to be born into the world, fast closing down for its winter rest. But autumn had other faces too, wild, stormy and full of energy or gently meditative in hues of orange and yellow, its moods subtle or furious by turns.

She turned off the main path towards John and Nellie Fraser's croft. Maggie came out to meet her and escorted her up the path to the traditional turf-roofed crofting house. The house stood squat and part of the landscape, the turfs were secured with a lattice of ropes, as were those on her own small cottage, held firm against strong winds by being tied at their ends to heavy boulders which hung over the edge and which were now gently swaying in the breeze.

Màiri stooped as she entered under the low, heavy beamed entrance, designed to minimise draughts and keep in the heat. Nellie greeted her warmly and asked solicitously about her health, immediately scraping out a cane-back chair for her from under the large, well-worn table that half-filled the room. The floor was uneven and made up of hard earth, packed down by many feet over many years and embedded with large round pebbles in the areas of heaviest use such as near the stove or around the table.

Maggie hung around impatiently, moving from one foot to another with pent-up frustration, hoping to be able to see more of the baby, who was now contentedly asleep against Màiri's chest.

-"Away with ye lass, ye've enough chores tae be getting on with without standing there gawping and bothering Màiri!" said Nellie sharply.

Maggie's face dropped and her shoulders sagged in disappointment, and, as Màiri tried to protest on Maggie's part, Nellie impatiently waved Maggie away:

-"Off with ye lass ye've chores tae dae!"

As Maggie dejectedly slumped out of the room with a sigh Nellie relented a little and said to Maggie:

-"Ye can gae visitin' Màiri later in the week if she'll have ye, ye might be some use tae her. Now off with ye, go!" then more softly with a hint of a smile,

-"Gae on! Off with ye now lass!"

Màiri called out a reassurance to Maggie's departing back:

-"Of course ye can Maggie, I'd love tae see ye whenever ye can come up!"

Nellie clearly wanted Màiri on her own so she could talk to her about important women's matters. She was concerned about Màiri's health and wanted to ensure there was nothing untoward,

-"Daes everything doon there work fine now Màiri, after the birth, it's only two days or sae?"

Màiri nearly spluttered at the directness, but that was Nellie, always practical and sensible, always got straight to the point. Màiri had no need to be embarrassed or hold back where Nellie was concerned, she was direct but caring, she took her duties as surrogate mother seriously and since she first took Màiri into her care, with no fuss or bother or hint of interfering, there had been no secrets.

-"Was everything done properly? She is no as fussy as she should be that Iris McCrimmon!" she said sharply "I should hae been there. She had nae right!" Nellie was a little tearful now. She, like Isla, had been hurt at not being allowed to look after Màiri during labour. Màiri, in a small, intimate, placating gesture gently placed her hand over Nellie's where she had grasped the table edge. She quietly reassured her.

-"I'm fine Nellie, just a little sore. After last tame I did nae want anyone there" she explained "I could nae hae borne the pity. I just wanted tae get it over with without any fuss. If it was tae be another dead baby --" she gasped a little and sucked in her breath to stall a sob.

-"Sae I'm sorry, I did nae try tae argue with Mrs McCrimmon. I hope ye can forgive me?" She looked up at Nellie, pleading silently, not wishing this to come between them.

Nellie paused to take it in and then took a deep breath while she digested it.

-"Nae lass" she said quietly "I think I understand. If it had been me I might've done the same. Dinna worry yersel' lass, there's nothin' tae forgive". Then she brightened and said,

-"Noo if ye're sure ye're all right let's hae' a look at the bonny wee mannie!"

The tense moment was resolved. Màiri was relieved, she would have hated to have hurt a woman who had given her so much care and affection and whom she was so fond of in return.

While they were inspecting the squashed up little face and gurgling contentment that was young Callum, John Fraser banged the door open with a foot and entered the room with a flourish. He ducked under the lintel, carrying a shallow, wooden fish-box in his arms. He was a dark, taciturn man, very much in the Victorian Highland tradition, bearded and dressed in a black "pilgrim's" hat and dark, subdued working suit. He looked every inch the sober, god-fearing puritan he was.

-"Aye, if it's wimmin's talk ye're at I'll away til ye've finished! I cannae be doing with ony gossip. I dae hope it's no idle gossip, is it Nellie?" He wheezed in a narrow-eyed, reproachful tone.

Nellie and John Fraser were as different as peas from raspberries. She was a generously proportioned, cheerful and easygoing homemaker, she liked nothing more than a cup of strong tea and a lengthy spell with a neighbour and confidant with whom she could explore the foibles and shortcomings of the rest of the village: he was reserved, dutiful to a fault, intolerant of perceived weaknesses and wickedness in others and short in temper. Her generous proportions echoed her generosity of spirit; he was as narrow as a rake and his sternness echoed his upright bearing.

Nellie clearly however was in charge,
    -"John Fraser! Wipe the grime off yer boots afore ye come in here, and take that damned hat off! And we'll have none of yer nonsense about gossipin! We're talking important women's talk. Sae hold yer tongue if ye've nothing helpful tae say"!
    John Fraser "harumphed" but otherwise held his peace. He knew better than to argue with Nellie in her own home. He wiped his boots on the home-made, rag rug at the door and took off his hat while trying to juggle the box he was holding to prevent it from falling.
    -"Ah Màiri, tis fine tae see ye oot, how are ye feeling?" he soothed as he came towards the table.
    Màiri turned to acknowledge him. She was always reserved where John Fraser was concerned. Although he had been very neighbourly and helpful, understanding even, when her parents had died, she still found it hard

to warm to him. And, since she had married Hamish three years ago, there was even more of a distance between them. He deeply disapproved of Hamish giving up his ministry and his faith and denigrated his efforts at crofting and fishing in hints and asides that Màiri resented. She said evenly,

-"Guid morning Mr Fraser, I'm feeling fine thank ye very much"

-"And how is the wee bairn if I might be sae bold as tae ask?" he questioned solicitously.

-"He's bonny thank ye, and as fit as a flea with a healthy appetite tae match"! she replied, perhaps a little too assuredly given the fears that lurked so poignantly in her mind.

-"It would make it easier if that sinner of a husband of yers were a bit mair fortunate in his chosen calling", said John Fraser in an exasperated tone.

Màiri bit her tongue to save her from snapping back. Instead she said, firmly and quietly:

-"Hamish is the hardest working man in the glen Mr Fraser, nae one can deny that. We've had a guid harvest and the fishin' has no been tae bad either. Hamish is a good husband and a god-fearing man who holds God's commands for charity and sacrifice a sight more seriously than some in this glen. I've nae complaints and nor should anyone else!" she said pointedly.

-"Aye I'll give ye that, that man of yours works hard enough lass, I'll no fault him there. But the man who gives up the kirk sacrifices his soul and there's a fact". expostulated John Fraser reproachfully.

-"There's mair ways tae God than ever dreamt of in the catechism of the Scottish Free Kirk Mr Fraser!" Màiri retorted, spiritedly but politely.

-"Ye're right there Màiri"! added Nellie in support., "Now wisht yer preachin' John Fraser, ye're no in the pulpit just now". She added "And what the hell have ye got in that filthy old box anyway"?

-"Language woman"! Retorted John Fraser "How I came tae marry sich an ungodly woman I'll niver know!" he wailed.

-"Ah wisht man, ye ken nae one else would've had ye ye miserable old skinflint! Noo what's in the damned box"! Nellie demanded impatiently.

John Fraser raised his eyes and tutted and then laid the box carefully and ceremoniously on the tabletop. It was covered with a piece of grubby, hessian sacking. Nellie made a disagreeable face, turning up her lip and sniffing but said nothing. John Fraser lifted off the sacking with a magician's flourish:

-"There ye are!" he said turning to Màiri, "I heared that ye were lookin' for some wee chicks to bring on - and here they are"! and he stood back to receive the admiration of his audience.

Inside the box were a dozen fluffed up, yellow chicks, some just beginning to develop to the more leggy stage with traces of dark feathering beginning to appear. Now that the covering was removed they cheeped crazily, clambering over each other and flapping vestigial wings, giving something of the impression of a box of indoor fireworks going off.

-"Oh ma God"! cried Nellie "What the hell are ye daein puttin' them filthy creatures on ma meal table man"!

John Fraser theatrically raised his eyes to the ceiling again, held his hat in both hands in a supplicating gesture and sighed deeply;

-"Oh casual blasphemer, thou wilt be judged by thy maker on the day of repentance!" he announced dramatically in an Old Testament voice.

-"The guid Lord will recognise that I'm tried beyond endurance by the fat-head of a husband I married and will most likely gie me a special pair of wings and ma own cloud fae showing such forbearance!" Nellie retorted sharply.

Màiri wondered if this banter between them ever stopped, whether there was ever a moment during the day when they might sit in companionable silence; he reading his Bible maybe, the only book he ever read, and she, maybe quietly knitting or sewing. She doubted it, she knew though that they were a devoted couple for all their differences, and for all his foibles and argumentative nature, John Fraser was a dedicated husband and father who loved Nellie dearly. Nellie in turn would have been lost without him.

Màiri was delighted at the sight of the chicks and carefully laid Callum down on the table wrapped in his rough blanket so that she could stand and lean over the box to inspect them. They tried to huddle in the corner of the box as she quietly cooed, gently stroking one on the head with a finger as it cautiously stretched its neck towards her in response and half closed its eyes in what looked suspiciously like sheer pleasure.

-"Oh! That one there has something wrong with its leg puir thing" she pointed to one of the young chicks that had a gnarled lump on its twiggy, backward-facing knee. It limped a little as it followed after the others as they shuffled about the box but otherwise seemed unconcerned.

-"Ah, sorry lass I had nae noticed that one!" said John Fraser as he reached out a bony, calloused, hand towards it.

-"No!" Màiri cried out, grabbing his wrist quickly to stop him. She had immediately realised he was about to dispatch the bird with the usual pull and quick twist of the neck once he had hold of it. She had seen it before with chicks and other creatures on the crofts. A misshapen or poorly beast might fail to thrive; the runt of the litter or an injured animal that would need much tending with no sure promise of success was a burden on a crofter who lived pretty much hand-to-mouth. The wasted feed and effort for a poor or non-existent return didn't make sense.

Nevertheless, she had experienced too often the cruel or casual indifference in dispatching an animal or bird with no more consideration than if it were a patch of stony, unproductive land or a poorly-yielding stook of autumn barley.

-"I'll give it a chance Mr Fraser if I may. If it suffers or becomes poorly I'll take care of it as needs be."

She knew she was capable of dispatching a suffering animal if she had to, cleanly and quickly before it knew what was happening. She had had to do it before, though it sickened her and always haunted her for days afterwards but she would do it only if humanity, not economic need were the cause. She also knew she wasn't the only crofter who felt that way but perhaps she was one of the few who would admit it. Hard life as it was, living on the edge of just enough or too little, these people nonetheless depended on their stock, were close to them physically and often in sympathy with their hardships in a tough environment and they cared for them accordingly. John Fraser himself might be more hard-headed or hard-hearted than her but she knew him for a fine husbandman who cared well for his stock and treated them with respect. A man in this glen, or any other she knew of, who showed deliberate cruelty to any of his beasts would be ostracised by most. It was despicable in the eyes of the great majority of them, though that didn't mean that it didn't go on. Sadly, Màiri knew that the same consideration was not often shown to the wild creatures who also lived side by side with them.

Màiri opened the bartering;

-"How about the first two dozen eggs when they start layin' Mr Fraser"?

Most crofters enjoyed bartering and bargaining. To get a good deal in exchange for their goods and a good return on their investment of time and effort was at the heart of a successful crofting life. However, in this case the exchange would be a more tricky and delicate business. Màiri was very aware of the fact that she owed Nellie and John Fraser a great deal. And they in turn still saw themselves as having some responsibility for Màiri who they treated as near enough one of the family. This was not the customary cut and thrust of hard bargaining with the neighbours that was the normal pattern. Màiri had deliberately offered high: after all the chicks were newly hatched, anything could happen to them and they could get through a lot of feed before they started laying. Mr Fraser poo-pooed the offer and waved it away dismissively.

-"Nae lass, I'll no be wanting onythin' fer them, ye'll be takin' them off ma hands. I've got mair than enough and they're just spares. Besides I dinna ken if they're layers or no, ye've probably got some cocks in there mind."

Màiri knew he would have checked, in as far as was possible at this stage, to ensure they were mostly female chicks but she must play along for the sake of his feelings.

-"I'll tak' that chance Mr Fraser. If they're cocks I'll fatten them up for broilers. They'll be about ready to make a guid broth for Callum when he's ready".

-"Alright, a dozen eggs and I'll throw in a bag of feed". Mr Fraser offered archly. He was enjoying a little largesse for once.

This was outrageous, even more generous than giving them away. Màiri was touched. It couldn't have been easy for him to make such a generous offer against his usual hard bargaining instincts. She played along.

-"Now ye're jest playin with me Mr Fraser, this is a serious business. I cannae have ye giving me stock at a loss! Ane and a half dozen eggs, the first ane and a half laid and ye'll no' be givin' me any feed, that's final". She spat on her hand and held it out, palm upwards.

It was a final gambit, he had lost, there was no going back now without him losing face, she had beaten him at his own game. Nellie laughed, John Fraser gave a mock grimace and said;

-"Ye're mad woman! Right, ye leave me nae choice." 'Slap!' his hand came down, palm to palm.

Màiri smiled warmly. Even John Fraser almost grinned, and that didn't happen very often.

-"I'll call Maggie tae carry the box up tae the hoose fae ye Màiri", said Nellie.

Màiri readjusted her papoose to accommodate Callum, who all this time had been enjoying himself, lying on the table, staring blindly at the ceiling and kicking his tiny legs in the air while chewing a fist with pinky-white gums. Màiri gave Nellie a quick hug and peck on the cheek. She shook hands with a now delighted John Fraser, who was showing that delight by scowling like a silent movie villain, but nevertheless, couldn't prevent his eyes crinkling at the edges while doing so. She then waited at the door for Maggie who rushed in to collect the box before escorting Màiri up to her croft house high on the hill.

It was good to be out in the fresh air again after being in the cosy but stuffy Fraser cottage. Maggie chatted excitedly while Màiri mostly listened, feeling tired now. It was a ten-minute walk and Màiri was not relishing the last steep push up their narrow path. She was stunned to see Hamish striding down to meet them. He never came to meet her like this, especially if she had someone with her, even if it was only Maggie who was friendly to everyone without distinction.

-"Hello Mr McDonald" Maggie trilled brightly. For a moment Màiri felt a quick start of panic "What was wrong"? But Hamish just quietly and politely said,

-"Good day Miss Fraser, shall I take that for you" he gestured towards the box. Hamish spoke with the cultured Scottish accent of Edinburgh, soft but well enunciated. Maggie loved it. It sounded so cultivated to her ears compared with the more vernacular, soft, burr of the West Highlands.

-"No thank you Mr McDonald" Maggie said, as poshly as she could manage,

-"It weighs hardly a thing you know".

Màiri nearly sniggered but kept a straight face so as not to hurt Maggie's feelings.

-"I'll tell ye what Hamish, ye can take wee Callum, I'm feeling a little tired", said Màiri brightly. He was standing above them on the steep path looking down at Màiri in a concerned manner.

-"Are you all right Màiri" he almost never called her by name "You've been out a long time. I was getting a wee bit worried".

-"No I'm fine. It was good tae get out". She unstrapped Callum and handed him over to Hamish. Hamish stood dumbfounded, he hadn't yet held Callum and he had had no intention of doing so. He didn't know what to do but he could hardly refuse now and Màiri knew it.

-"Here!" Màiri helped him to fold his arms around Callum, supporting him in the crook of his elbow with his arm under his bottom and cradling his head in his large, slightly grubby hand.

-"My hands are dirty Màiri, I'll --" he started to protest nervously, looking for an excuse.

-"He'll be fine Hamish, dinna worry, ye'll no break him". She smiled, speaking softly, encouraging him.

Looking up at him, she caught the emotions that passed across his face, from tortured anguish to anxiety at being given responsibility for holding his son, through to something gentler, warmer trying to break through. The struggle of his childhood, the whole of his life was revealed there, in that moment. Her whole being went out to him, she could have wept on the spot from the pain and the doubt she saw there, all the years of suffering and confusion over his feelings which were exposed in that fleeting moment.

He straightened up, his face impassive again. He led the way, carefully and awkwardly, cradling Callum all the way back to the house like some precious, fragile object. The moment had passed but it had affected Màiri deeply. She felt filled with a deep sadness and something else, something she couldn't place but it disturbed her.

CHAPTER 2

WINTER'S SOLITUDE

When Màiri got back to the house she thanked Maggie and placed the box with its bustling, chirping contents in front of the warm range. She was astonished to find that Hamish had made her a meal. Two fresh, prepared and cooked herring, coated in rough oatmeal, were sitting golden on a plate keeping warm on the hob. He had explained that a neighbour had brought the freshly caught fish for her. It was usually 'a neighbour', Hamish had got to know few of the villagers in his three years living in the glen. He had cooked the fish, prepared her a cup of warm milk and cut a chunk of dry barley bread which he had placed on a wooden board with a small bowl of home-made butter.

She was deeply touched, almost to tears, at so unusual a gesture from Hamish. He stood awkwardly, looking a little embarrassed, waiting for her to take a seat. She realised he must have been looking out for her, had seen her leave the Frasers' when he had quickly cooked the fish and then come to meet her. She felt sorry she had been so long now, he must have worried, but he was usually still up in the fields at this time.

As he pulled out a chair for her she lightly touched his hand in a small, intimate gesture and thanked him for his kindness. He almost withdrew his hand, reflex-like, but then steeled himself to let it rest there. They hardly ever touched during the daytime, unless accidentally in brushing past one another. He shrank from any sign of intimacy or tenderness, he just didn't know how to deal with it, he had never experienced it before they were married, had never known the tender touch or clasp of another human being.

After they had married she had, rather näively and optimistically, thought he would gradually come round, that it might just be shyness, but slowly she discovered the depth of deprivation he had suffered in growing up. From odd comments, from her own observations and from occasional confidences she realised, disclosure by disclosure, just how badly damaged he had been by a malevolent father. His mother had died in childbirth so he had never known the touch of her hand; wet-nursed until weaned, his father had been solely responsible for the damage inflicted, perhaps in part as revenge for the loss of the mother. Who knows? Hamish certainly didn't.

The only physical intimacy Màiri and Hamish usually shared was the rare and desperate thrusting and clutching in the dark when Hamish's physical feelings overwhelmed him and he could no longer hold back. Afterwards, spent, physically and emotionally, he would recoil from her, repelled and disgusted with himself and flee first thing in the morning, to return shamefaced at last light.

On these rare occasions of desperate, thrashing emotion she would try and hold on to him, draw him to her with soothing words and stroking gestures in the hope of taming his frantic, furious, physical grasping into a more extended coming together. Sometimes, he managed to relax just enough to give and receive some tenderness, easier in the dark when he could try to imagine himself as someone else, someone deserving and worthy of the affection of another human being.

In the morning though he would again be dejected and self-censorial, and silently censorious of her for putting up with such treatment, while all the time realising he was being unfair to both himself and to her, and knowing that she genuinely felt deeply for him. And in such emotional confusion and turmoil he would again escape to the fields and lose himself in the exhaustion of physical activity.

Hamish had already eaten and while Màiri completed her meal he prepared to leave. Before he turned to the door to go Mairi again said;

-"Thank you Hamish!" She looked him full in the face, smiled and tried to communicate the affection she felt. His mouth pursed in a straight line and he gave an almost imperceptible nod of acknowledgement. It was little enough but she knew she had touched him for once. As he turned and stepped out of the door his head was held just a little higher. That small motion all but broke her heart.

After her meal Màiri placed another peat turf on the fire and sank into her mother's wooden rocker in front of the glowing peats. She was exhausted from the morning's physical exertion so soon after the birth and she felt emotionally drained. She gently swayed to and fro as she fed Callum who, when full and content, dozed off at her breast. She was so tired after her first day out that, later on, she lay on the bed in the corner, dozing for an hour or two with her new-found love, before getting on with her chores. She reflected that for once she was content, despite her feelings and her fears about Hamish, and she felt a deep inner warmth. The uncomplicated love she felt for this new human being was sufficient for now to consume her fears.

In the succeeding days and weeks Màiri and Hamish continued much as before; Hamish going about his crofting tasks, at times bitterly cold and exhausted, at others more content now to busy his way through the day in routines which, though not mastered, were now familiar. Màiri, with Callum as her constant companion in his makeshift sling, went about her own well established routine of domestic and outdoor chores as well as feeding and caring for her baby: feeding Hamish, caring for her new chicks and taking her turn milking the cow, preparing and salting down herrings caught by Hamish, and fixing and repairing the fabric of her home and their clothing in preparation for the cold, dark days ahead.

As winter drew on daylight became more valuable. Hamish would rise in the dark and carry out indoor tasks like mucking out the cow's byre and feeding her hay, repairing tools and milking with the aid of a glowing hurricane lamp. When the sun finally rose it followed its short track low on the horizon and then, once into December, disappeared again a few precious hours later.

Crofting life slowed down to bare essentials. During daylight hours Hamish would take hay out to the lower fields, the in-bye land, on the slopes nearer the croft, for the sheep who could find little to eat and precious little comfort from the wind and cold on the upper slopes. The flocks of sheep on the crofting lands and common land would be reduced to a minimum at summer and autumn market sales. Only the breeding ewes, served by the tup in October and, hopefully, pregnant as far as the crofter could tell, were carefully husbanded over winter, ready for lambing in spring.

The hills were a quiet, secluded place in winter where few people went because no-one needed to. Life focussed around the croft house and fishing: the hills were left to brood in silence.

One evening in early December, when Callum was nearly two months old, as the invisible sun dropped below a grey horizon, Màiri felt the need to escape. Cooped up all day in the house, with only the thin, pale shafts that penetrated the small, low windows for light, she was feeling claustrophobic. She placed Callum near to the softly glowing, peat-fired range, well wrapped up in his cradle, a brown, wooden, Victorian, boat-shaped box on rockers, and she fled the house.

Outside a storm was brewing; dark, ragged, bat-wing clouds swept across a purple-grey sky, obscuring the moon as it rose behind her. She headed for the path, noting the warm, yellow glow coming from the lean-to abutting the gable end of the house, where Hamish silently mended his nets by the hissing, blue-yellow flare of a paraffin lamp. When she reached the main path, standing at the rim of the great bowl which encircled the glen, she stopped and breathed in deeply and took in the view. She wrapped her shawl round her shoulders, and clutched her arms around herself in a tight embrace against the chill of the evening.

Rain blew this way and that in the cool air, stinging her face, cold and wet. The natural amphitheatre was alive with a wild energy, forbidding and invigorating. A late solitary gull, blown crazily in the mounting, contrary winds, squealed overhead as it headed for shelter to join its colleagues on the rain-soaked clifftops. It would be too rough for the gulls to sit out the night bobbing on the sea as they usually did.

The little croft houses, spread around the main path as if dropped randomly from a height across the lower slopes of the upper glen, peeped, yellow-eyed from pale, glowing windows, winking on and off in the breeze-blown spray. The low-slung houses hugged the ground, protected from the worst of the weather, like dark, cowering beasts hunched up in their sheltered lairs.

Màiri found the glow of lights in windows comforting. In the creeping, crepuscular gloom they gave reassurance, familiar outposts of crofting neighbours. She knew that in too many of them tonight and every night solitary and lonely women mourned long-dead men and that too many of the blind, dark cottages lay deserted and uncared for, now abandoned by those left behind. Death had reached a whitened, bony hand into the glen and plucked out its young men. Twelve of the glen's sons, fathers, brothers and cousins from just twenty families lay as shattered, flesh-scoured bones, beneath the cloying mud of Flanders Field or the Somme's dank, marshy soil, or interred in the shell-ploughed landscape around Ypres or Cambrai. Six men; Hamish, Ian McDonald, John Fraser and his two sons, who had been too young to fight and were now married to local girls, and one grandfather were all that remained of the menfolk of the glen. 1918 had left behind a glen full of soulsick women. Of all those who went to war Ian McDonald was the only one to return. The community of the glen had paid a heavy price for a pyrrhic victory.

Màiri pulled her shawl closer and looked out over the dark loch below. White horses danced on the waves, the crests, piled up by the wind were collapsing in on themselves, blown over or torn way by the rising gusts. The waters of the loch, were being fretfully funnelled between the steep, dark cliffs. Driven on by the westerly winds the waves would be piling up at the far end of the loch, where it narrowed to a low exposed shore. The waters were already sucking and crashing unevenly on the shoreline of the cove. Màiri could hear the grinding and crashing of the large, wave-rounded stones far below her and she heard the rising and falling hollow moan of the wind on cliff faces. It sounded to her like the lament of drowned sailors come to warn the village of what was on the way.

The deep, dark waters of the loch had their own wild dynamic; complex and dangerous in a storm, placid and mirror-like on a calm summer's day. Tonight was no night to be trifling with the sea. Any fishing boat caught out beyond the Inner Sound would be racing for home and Màiri felt a sudden, cold shard of fear and shuddered for any who might not make it to Kyle or Portree before the storm struck. She saw in her mind's eye the strained white faces of the men and boys at sea as they fretted to stretch every sinew of their small boats to beat the wind and waves to a safe harbour ahead of the tempest to come.

The black, oily waters of the loch, laced with white ribbons of broken wave-crests, were swelling into humps and eddies as Màiri watched, awed and fascinated. The sea seemed to sigh dolefully as it pulsed in and out on the long Atlantic swells that forced their way into the loch's mouth, open to the angry ocean.

Despite the coming turmoil Màiri knew from the tales of fishermen that the waters beneath the waves of the loch would quietly flow to their own drumbeat. Cold, dark currents circulated in the deep waters below her. The seabed, scoured out by glaciers, spawned by an ice shield a mile or more thick which covered the Scottish uplands during the last ice age, had rasped a channel fifty or more metres deep at its centre. Here, in the darkest reaches of the loch, currents and tides operated on a different timescale, sucking down unwary souls and holding them in their cold embrace, sometimes for years, sometimes forever. She shuddered and turned back towards the yellow glow of the croft, refreshed by the energy of the coming storm but also disturbed by her insights.

The long, dark winter was punctuated by the Christmas service, administered by a hell-fire and brimstone preacher who berated this outcast little flock in these the furthest reaches of his parochial grasp. Winter, rather like the service, seemed interminable, Hogmanay came as a blessed release. The point when the year turned and began to start the slide downhill into spring was welcomed with gusto.

Hogmanay was one of the two main festivals which provided the opportunity for a riotous ceilidh in the glen, the other being 'Hairst Hame' in the autumn. Ian and Isla McDonald had turned over their lambing barn for the occasion, there was no other suitable meeting place in the village. Ian played the pipes and Isla was an experienced fiddle player, it was one of the things that had brought them together. One of Nellie Fraser's sons, Murdo, played the penny whistle with huge bravura. All of the village and many from more isolated crofts round about were there, even John Fraser, who enjoyed himself hugely by sitting scowling, harumphing and complaining loud and long to anyone who would listen, decrying the frivolity of the occasion. The only person absent, as always, was Hamish.

Màiri sang laments in Gaelic in a pure, clear voice which brought tears to her own eyes as well as many others. All had someone to remember, some loss to bear. She also sang Gaelic work songs and dancing songs, which are easily substituted for each other, so there was plenty of opportunity for group dancing, ably directed by the young Maggie. Maggie knew all of the traditional dances and often taught the young girls and sometimes, rather reluctant young boys, of the district. Though oddly uncoordinated at other times, when dancing she excelled herself with grace and rhythm. Isla and Ian also played jaunty sea shanties and jigs which, with the help of a "wee dram" and plenty of home-made heather and barley ale, led to a lively occasion for everyone. It was an ideal opportunity to bring light and laughter, emotion and friendship, to the darkest and grimmest time of the year.

Màiri sang and danced and laughed and talked, and young Callum, now healthy, fat and pink, gurgled and chuckled and charmed everyone, especially Isla who, now pregnant herself as Màiri had predicted, swung Callum round and round and danced with him in a jig, holding him high and whooping with delight while he shrieked with pleasure.

1921 dragged slowly into 1922, cold, dark, rain and wind an almost constant accompaniment. Fishing was poor and the cow dried up with only dry hay to eat and her calf long weaned. Oats, barley, winter kale, a few potatoes and salted mutton and herring provided the daily fare for Hamish and Màiri but, for once, they had just enough to last until the fishing picked up and the cow calved and started to produce milk again. By then they would be into lambing at the start of their crofting year. Hamish began to relax a little as he sat mending nets in the lean-to, or sometimes he just sat in the yellow glow of quiet solitude with only the hissing and gentle popping of the lamp for company, finding his own kind of peace for a while.

In late February they received their first heavy snow. The tops around them had been white for months, the estate lands were regularly snowed in but, up to now, the little glen, in its favoured position, had escaped any heavy snowfall. They had had flurries and biting cold but their situation usually saved them from the worst.

A towering shoulder of the beinn shielded them from the bitter cold easterlies which brought snow and ice across from the North Sea. They had the benefit of the warm Gulf Stream to keep the worst of the frosts at bay and which helped turn snow flurries to rain, but, when the northerlies brought the cold arctic air, they shivered and looked to their suffering sheep.

On a day that began clear and bright with sparkling icicles hanging from their eaves Hamish and Màiri set out separately looking for lost, straying or suffering ewes. Màiri set off up the lower slopes of the beinn, the fresh snow squeaking and scrunching underfoot as she placed her feet carefully, leaning on her father's shepherd's crook to deliver extra purchase. Màiri loved the feel and sight of new snowfalls: everything was so fresh, clean and still, sounds were dulled and quickly cut off by the dampening effect of the snow layer. Snowflakes sparkled and twinkled in the low shafts of sunlight which probed between dark clouds as she slowly made her way upwards, scanning the slopes for any signs of the yellowy, off-white humps of sheep against the brilliant white, snowy background.

Higher up the slope she saw a small mound in the snow that she didn't recognise. Màiri knew the whole hillside so well that, even covered in snow, she could tell if anything were out of place or untoward. She headed towards it, heather and dead bracken beneath the snow providing an uneven footing and doubling the effort needed to reach it. By the time she approached the hummock she was breathing heavily, her breath trailing out in smoky wisps in the cold air.

She could see now that the hump was a sheep that had lain down in the lee of a boulder and was now covered with snow. She brushed the snow from its fleece with her hands, feeling the cold wetness between her fingers. The crofters never wore gloves, they just made you clumsy, got in the way, and taking them off and putting them on all the time in order to do a job just wasn't practical. She had knitted Hamish a pair for his first winter but he had soon lost them, his hands becoming cracked and chafed with the cold, bleeding and sore. It was just an occupational reality, your hands suffered and became tougher.

She worked her way to the ewe's nose and mouth, clearing the snow as best she could as she went, the fleece was clotted with frozen lumps which clung to the wool. When she got to the nostrils she could feel it was still breathing, its eyelids flickering open and shut.

-"You foolish beast, get up!" she called, giving it a shove on its backside. The ewe unfolded her legs from under her and stiffly made it to her feet. Màiri gave it an extra shove on its rear end with her foot and it seemed to wake up suddenly and scrambled its way downhill. Màiri smiled, relieved. She was a young ewe, this was her first winter on the lower slopes. Unlike the other, more experienced sheep, she wouldn't know to move down into the lee of the croft when the snow came. If Màiri hadn't found her she would have sat it out where she was, got wet and cold and gradually frozen to death. With only thirty breeding ewes each and every one was valuable. The youngster was too young to be pregnant but Màiri was pleased and relieved all the same at having found her in time.

She pushed on up the slope but found no more sheep and sat down on a small boulder rather like that which had been so inadequately shielding the sheep. It had been hard work gaining this height ploughing through the deep snow layer. She was now a couple of hundred feet above the croft. She tried to make out the other croft houses but most had disappeared into the landscape under their cover of snow. In the summer their roofs, turned green with rain and sun made them look like little drumlins, now they looked like so many snowdrifts. Only the melting patches around chimneys and puffs of smoke gave away those where fires and ranges had been lit. The houses had an organic feel, as if they had grown out of the landscape.

Ian and Isla MacDonald's house off to the east showed hints of the blue-grey slate roof where snow had slipped off the edges in small avalanches. She knew Isla would be preparing a morning broth for Ian who would be out in the fields checking his sheep and precious black Highland cattle. Soon she would need to go down and prepare something similar for Hamish.

She had checked the whole slope from her vantage point and could be pretty sure there were no more sheep in need of help, unless of course, blinded by snow, any had blundered into the deep ravines and water-cut gullies that incised the hill at frequent intervals. She could leave that to Hamish this afternoon, he would check all those nearest the croft, just as other crofters would do near their crofts, for their own or anyone else's sheep.

Before heading down Màiri took a moment to breathe in the cold air and look for signs in the snow. A fresh snowfall was a great time to explore signs of wildlife even up here in the clear air of the beinn's upper slopes. She had a keen and practised eye. Scanning the fresh surface of the snow she first saw the unmistakable tracks of a snowy hare and a small depression where it had nestled itself into the snow, perhaps to freeze while an eagle or a raven passed over. The tracks led downhill to where the hare might more easily find a few fresh shoots of heather under the layer of snow. Then, further off she spotted the feathery-footed tracks of a ptarmigan, elusive and mystical mountain bird, whose plumage turned pure white in winter in order to provide camouflage from predators.

She sat silently for a little longer. She had the patience needed of an amateur naturalist and knew if she sat still long enough the wildlife was likely to come to her. She enjoyed the stillness, the cold, sharp air as she breathed in, the hush of a snowy landscape and the almost imperceptible creak of snow layers, contracting and slowly sliding. There was almost a crackle in the air, an electrical potential of static that made her feel more alive.

From her vantage point the whole community was spread out below her mapping her whole world. She could see the main track, delineated by irregular footprints of people going to and fro about their daily business. The steep track down to the cove had disappeared, blended into the rest of the slope where it plunged to the shore. The upturned fishing boats on the beach were not needed now that the fishing was so poor, each had a hummock of snow covering its tortoise-like shell. Paddocks, homes and sheep fanks were all written in shadow-lines on the bright undulating surface. Even the soaring cliffs and towering headlands were diminished from up here.

Her gaze followed where she knew the main track lay under the snow, out of the village and away to the West. Her gaze stopped as it reached the outcrop of dark rock known to the villagers as the Devil's Nose, no one knew why any more, the nickname was lost in folk history. Further on, the path, completely obliterated by snow, passed over a shoulder of the great hill on its way out of the glen. Here there was another promontory of rock, a small, natural platform beside the path known as Signal Rock.

The rocky platform had a special place in the mythology of the glen. Long before the present population's ancestors had been forced out to these marginal lands, a small community of fishermen and cattle herders had inhabited the glen. The rock had provided both lookout and warning post against cattle raiders trying to carry out a surprise attack via the only path into the glen. As often as not the raiders were clansmen looking to recover their own stolen beasts. The position of the rock and the acoustics of the glen and surrounding hills allowed the sound to echo and reverberate around the village. At one time the children of the village had used to use it to call from, impressed with the power of their voices.

Ian McDonald had stood there on his return home from the war, head bowed with emotion and played a lament, the 'Soldier's Return' on his pipes, both to announce his homecoming and as a memorial to all those who had left the glen for war never to return.

Màiri remembered that day, just over three years ago now, when he had come home and had stood on the rock, the notes from the pipes echoing painfully, achingly, around the glen. It was his tribute to friends and neighbours, young men swallowed up in the service of a faraway king and country of which they knew little, for reasons they couldn't comprehend. She remembered that Isla had broken down then, with emotions of joy and relief at the return home of her man but so strained and anguished with pain and sorrow at the loss of schoolfriends and young men she had thought of as family. It had been a bittersweet sound for the whole glen. The rock had stood empty ever since, eschewed by children who had lost fathers, brothers or uncles and for the community as a whole for whom it had taken on the role of memorial. Occasionally someone would lay few wild flowers at it's foot but no-one climbed up there anymore.

With a sigh her gaze turned to the loch far below her, a long, wide strand of deep, dark water. It looked black against the glaring white of snow all around. Màiri thought it strange that a fall of snow should bleach the colour out of everything and turn the landscape into a black-and-white photograph.

She had been sitting for about a quarter of an hour, becoming content, still, no longer conscious of the cold or the pressure of the hard boulder she sat on. Suddenly a fluttering movement in the corner of her eye brought her back to the present. A little flock of pale, white and brown birds were alighting and leapfrogging each other as their faces dipped in and out of the snow, searching for seeds. The flock called out short musical notes to each other 'eeu!', 'eeu!', as they bustled and scurried across the snow, their pale underbellies reflecting the whiteness, speckled backs breaking up their fluffed out profiles. It was a flock of snow bunting in winter coat. She hoped this little flock would stay over the summer. They were birds of northern moorlands and coasts and most would return to Scandinavia to breed but she knew some stayed on over the summer in these north western, rocky hills. They were a real treat and she studied them closely as they busied themselves, like fat, pale, upland sparrows spread out across the slope, their feathers puffed out against the cold.

When they were gone, the bustling little flock swallowed up by the white hillside, she stiffly raised herself from her hard seat and rubbed her cold arms, stamping her numb feet before setting off downhill. She headed back home to prepare Hamish's and her own warming meal and to feed Callum, now lying fretting in his cradle by the warm fire.

Winter produced more snow and ice, more biting northerly winds and torrential rain, wet westerlies and north-westerlies clung on until well into spring as so often happened.

But finally April arrived, seed potatoes went in to Màiri's plot behind the house, some bare-rooted raspberry and current bushes were planted out, optimistically to start a fruit patch, and the last of the winter kale was eaten. Spring was just round the corner, the sun had gradually traced a higher arc in the sky week by week and the days imperceptibly lengthened, until first the length of day and night were equal, and then, at last, there was more daylight than darkness. They had survived another winter. The pantry was just about bare but, with the change in the weather, relief wouldn't be too long in coming.

When relief arrived eventually it was with a return of the silver fish to the loch and shore crabs to the rocky crevices in the cove. Mussels could be collected and cooked in seaweed and the occasional rabbit was caught. Màiri hated the practice of catching rabbits in snares, she thought it a cruel and dishonourable way to hunt. Rabbits, and sometimes other creatures, would be caught by the leg, sometimes for hours, thin wire biting into flesh. Often an animal would attempt to chew through its leg, desperate to try and escape, exhausting itself with pain. She would never accept a gift of a rabbit caught in such a way and none of the young men from round about who used such a method would bring one to her. She would though, accept gratefully a rabbit caught by a net and ferret and killed quickly with a wooden "priest", a cosh formed from heavy wood that put a quick end to a rabbit's life or that of a line-caught fish. Such a rabbit would make a welcome change to the pot, though once into May, with breeding in full swing, hunting rabbits ceased for a while.

If they weren't hunted though they became too numerous, the deprivation of crops could be prodigious with only the eagles and occasionally a raven and, of course the fox to keep their numbers down. Màiri was the only person she knew in the whole district who had any time for the fox; to everyone else the fox was a reviled enemy, despite its avid predation of rabbits. She failed to understand why other people were so vindictive or casually cruel to creatures who, like them, were going about their business just as they had before people had inhabited the glen.

Hamish had started relaxing a little more recently and, when Màiri wasn't watching, he would take an interest in little Callum. Callum was now six months old and was becoming more vocal, he would lie in his cradle gurgling, talking to himself in a nonsense language all of his own and then would start shrieking in amazement at some real or imagined sight. Sometimes, when Màiri was busy ironing or mending while sitting at the table by the lamp and Hamish came in a little earlier than usual, he would stand warming himself by the fire. When he thought she wasn't looking he would lean over Callum's cradle and pull faces or hold out his finger while Callum grasped it tightly and kicked his legs in the air, chuckling with pleasure. Màiri would pretend that she hadn't noticed and smile to herself, relieved and pleased at this new aspect of Hamish's complex character.

But then slowly Hamish sunk into despondency again, only this time it was worse than before. He seemed much more reluctant than usual to get up in the morning. He didn't bother to eat any breakfast and hardly touched his midday meal or his supper when he finally came in from work. He would sit at the table, staring, wide-eyed into emptiness. He had a look of infinite misery. Apart from washing his hands before he sat down for a meal, which he seemed to do with terrible slowness, the normally very fastidious Hamish stopped washing or shaving.

He began to move with a slowness that frustrated Màiri as he went about his daily tasks. She would have to chase round after him completing his jobs, doing the things that he missed. She tried talking to him, demanding to know if he was alright, begging him to tell her what was wrong. She was desperately worried about him. Finally, in sheer frustration, she shouted at him, but there was little reaction, only a huge, doleful sigh as he shuffled off, in a world of his own misery. At night he would toss and turn, unable to sleep. When he finally dozed off he would groan and whimper, sometimes waking with a start and waking Màiri with him. She would try and sooth him, telling him he was safe, smoothing his hair and shushing him the way she did when Callum cried. He would lie still, making no sound, expressionless and then drop off only to start whimpering in his sleep again.

This continued until well into April. Then one day Hamish rose in the morning, washed, dressed and shaved, took a long look at Callum in his cradle, which Màiri always placed beside the bed at night where she could reach out and comfort him if he woke, and he went out to work. He came in for breakfast and Màiri could see he had a more normal look to him. He paid attention to what he was doing, no more shuffling to the door, no more looking into the middle distance as if in a trance. He still didn't speak much, still seemed to have nightmares, but less so.

They gradually returned to some sort of normality; Hamish would disappear after breakfast and lose himself in the work of the croft. Màiri wouldn't see him until the mid-day meal, or he might take with him a hunk of bread and cheese wrapped in a cloth for his 'piece' and drink spring water in cupped hands to wash it down with. His stooped, solitary figure, only his own thoughts for company, laboured on amongst the sights and sounds of the croft and the high pasture or on the lonely moors until he returned, exhausted in the pale glow of evening.

Màiri perpetually feared for a return of his illness when he would again be abandoned by his senses as his dark thoughts and demons overwhelmed him. She daren't talk to him about it openly lest such an approach push him away and cause him to flee out to the fields again to dwell on his fears alone.

Nonetheless, over the months the mutual anxiety in the household slowly diminished to a gnawing memory that both, in their own ways, learned to live with. But still Màiri watched and waited and prayed.

Then, one sunny, blustery, ice-cold morning in late April Hamish did something completely uncharacteristic. Having disappeared outdoors as usual while an early-morning mist still enwrapped the little croft in its soft cocoon he suddenly reappeared, mid-morning, while Màiri was finishing her chores before heading outdoors herself.

She had just made herself a mug of tea, the steam curling greyly and invitingly up towards the cold air cloaking the boarded ceiling. Blackened with soot and cobwebs in the corners, that ceiling had cost her parents dear but held far more warmth than the open, leaky thatch of turf.

Hamish bent his back low under the door lintel. As he entered and took off his grubby cap which he twisted nervously between his gnarled and bleeding fingers, cracked by the cold but unnoticed now, scarred over with much use. He moved with a slow hesitant step to the large deal table that had now served several generations of McDonalds. He pulled out a chair and sat down so slowly and deliberately that he barely disturbed the dust motes drifting in the narrow shafts of sun-bright air which shone through the small casement windows.

Màiri watched him wordlessly and then poured him out a hot, strong tea before placing it carefully on the scrubbed white wood by his right hand. She took a seat herself and gently sipped from her steaming mug, hands cupped around it to steal its warmth. The only sound was the gentle creak of her chair as she breathed in deeply, betraying her anxiety. She feared that this untoward behaviour on Hamish's part might signal a return of his melancholy, reinforced by his neglect of the mug sitting, steaming in front of him. He stared, impassive and expressionless into the near distance.

"Drink yer tea Hamish or it'll grow cold" Màiri risked quietly reminding him, desperate to break the heavy, trembling silence.

Hamish's blue-grey eyes flickered and he looked towards her, as if seeing her there for the first time and he slowly took the cup and raised the hot brew to his lips.

He held onto the mug for a short while, allowing the heat to sting the cold from his palms and fingers. And then he quietly, nervously started to speak. His long gaze resumed, it was as if he were watching pictures roll by on the wall, fearful pictures of a childhood of sorrow and anger. Màiri had to stretch across the scarred, white table top to hear Hamish's barely whispered words as the hard remembered fears seeped from his half open lips.

He told Màiri that, from the time he was a small boy, he would have to rise early from his bed, fear acting as his alarm clock, and wash in cold water in a small china bowl, resting on a battered dresser, the only furniture in his room save the bed and a catechism in copperplate tacked onto the wall. He would then have to dress in his school clothes and make his way downstairs, tiptoeing carefully lest he prematurely wake his father.

He was expected to scrub last night's pans and then rake out and clear the fire grates in the kitchen and dining room; never the parlour; that was forbidden, reserved for group prayer and parish meetings; a holy of holies. Then he would shine all the boots and shoes to a reflecting, deep shine. At the finish he would stand on his appointed flagstone by the cold, empty, kitchen fire, awaiting his father in dread.

The minister would stride into the kitchen at his self-appointed moment, head high, face sour. He was a tall, square jawed, grim-faced man and always wore a high, starched, clerical collar and bottom-shined, pinstripe trousers with a dark waistcoat; the chain of a pocket watch would be stretched across his ample stomach. He held himself tight, back broom-handle straight and he would glower down his nose at the small boy who would quietly tremble, feeling the hard, cold, gritty surface of the rough slate on his stockinged soles but not daring to shift his feet.

The minister would silently inspect each pan, plate, knife, fork and spoon and each cup and saucer, all lying carefully aligned on the wooden draining board. He would inspect the fire grates for cleanliness and the boots for specks of dust.

"I fair shook with fear all this time' whispered Hamish "my cold, empty belly would turn and turn in anticipation of the suspended punishment and of the quiet, threatening air of that room and I could feel the cold of those slates numbing my toes". Hamish's face had by now taken on a look that Màiri could only interpret as that of a hunted fox or of a scolded, whipped collie.

He then confirmed what Màiri had fearfully expected as she had imagined herself into the cold feet and shivering body of that young boy. He described the inevitable outcome. At any point, a flaw found, the minister would draw in his breath; the prelude to restrained fury, all the more fearful for the holding back.

-"I would try so hard to get it right, to please him, just once, but I never did -- never did ...." . Hamish's voice drifted off, his lined, red-chafed face a mask of misery'
    -"Sae hard!"
His voice, expelled in a rush of air, was almost the wail of an injured creature and was cut off as quickly as it came. Màiri shivered as she felt something of what that small boy had felt. Her heart cold she knew what would follow.

Hamish sucked in his breath sorrowfully,
    -"There was always something, always!" he said quietly.
He then told how his father would stand silent and still for a moment: not a sound penetrated that cold, dark house from the outside world. The house was devoid of ornament, except for a carriage clock in the next room which audibly tortured out the minutes. The young Hamish would hear the slight sounds of the minister removing his belt; first the metallic unbuckling and the smooth whip of leather on cloth as he unleashed the belt from its loops, then the thick

polished leather creaking slightly as he gathered it in his hands. A heart stopping 'Snap!' would break the desperate silence as he doubled the belt over and experimentally slapped his own hand: always the same routine, the same order, no variation, no intimation of compassion creeping in.

The young boy would hear the gravelled crunch as the minister turned on his heel towards him, shoes grinding the rough, cast flagstones. Màiri watched Hamish's expression transfixed as he haltingly described the scene; his face was that of the small boy back in the cold kitchen again all those years ago. He was feeling the terror prod his inner core again.

He haltingly recounted how the minister would utter his only words of the whole exchange;
    -"Hands boy!"
    The harsh-voiced order would split the silence and the minister would take two strides towards him. Daring not to look up the young Hamish would feel the brooding presence, just in front and slightly to one side; stale candle wax, perfumed shaving oil and acrid, stale sweat pervaded the air. The small boy would raise his pink, scrubbed hands, flat in front of his chin and hold in his breath. The first bitter, deafening slash of leather was always a shock, the waves of stinging fire always an awful surprise.

Màiri, listened appalled and terribly saddened. She realised that for Hamish these memories were living fears; they constantly returned, infesting his waking and sleeping hours with a malodorous air of fear, He relived the experiences over and over but still struggled to find the words to describe them to her.

By the finish of the week the palms of his hands would be red and bloated, livid weals beginning to seep: only the Sabbath and the minister's early duties in the kirk gave a weekly respite. Never once during his ordeal would the young Hamish let a tear escape an eyelid nor or a sound pass his lips less the beating give satisfaction to the man and encourage more.

Afterwards the man would briskly leave. Hamish would somehow fumble the thick square of cold breakfast porridge into his jacket pocket with his stinging, bloated hands and, looking up for the first time carefully unlatch the back door and breathe in the open air before setting off to school, relieved to be out of that house.

Màiri watched Hamish wince as he relived his childhood experience, his face a mask of pain. Her heart ached for that young boy standing shivering in his father's kitchen. She could see the black-leaded range, the cold, stone flagged floor and the bare scrubbed furniture. She could feel his pain and misery as he heard that rush of air and experienced that savage cut of leather stinging the bare flesh. He had looked away and shuddered and she had shuddered with him.

Màiri could hardly breathe now so strained were her feelings. She knew there ware more, much more that Hamish wasn't telling her and she sensed that the rest was somehow worse, but she also knew she couldn't rush him. He would have to tell her what he could in his own time. And she somehow knew that there were things he would never tell her or anyone else. For a moment she felt she knew what it was to experience absolute despair.

For a while they returned to some sort of normality, or at least what stood in for normality for them. Then, one rare, sunny day, as April turned to May, Hamish picked a small bunch of early primroses for Màiri. She was overjoyed at the unfamiliar gesture of affection. That evening, when their meal was cleared away, he haltingly recounted another memory from childhood, the last he would ever describe to her.

He told her that, when he was around seven or eight, his father had employed a maid. She was a young girl of fourteen when she came to them, barely out of childhood herself; thin and pale she looked half-starved and probably was. Her father had died of consumption and had left the mother with five children and no income. The mother took in washing, scrubbed floors and sold clothes pegs from door-to-door; anything to keep herself and her children out of the dreaded workhouse. The girl, Lizzie, had left school at ten years old and had helped her mother look after the younger children and the older boys. She was loaned out to better-off neighbours to clean their houses for a few pence. She had, at the age of ten in other words, begun a career as a skivvy that would last until she somehow found someone to marry her.

Hamish's father had taken her on as a full-time maid on the recommendation of a parishioner. She worked from first thing in the morning until seven or eight at night with no complaint and was given no thanks and a meagre wage. The minister barely spoke to her except to berate her for her imperfect work and to brusquely spell out her orders for the day.

Hamish always felt sorry for this poor, pale and skeletal girl whom he wasn't allowed to talk to because she was a servant. One day he remembered, when he was about nine he picked a small bunch of summer flowers for her from the grassy verges on his walk home from school. The bright little bunch of yellow primroses he had brought Màiri had summoned the memory back. He had hoped to cheer Lizzie up after a particularly scathing dressing down from his father.

As he entered through the heavy front door of the parsonage his father happened to be coming out of the parlour. He spotted him holding the bunch of flowers and demanded to know what he thought he was doing with them. When Hamish told him they were for Lizzie his father had demanded he hand them over. He then threw them on the floor and ground them to a pulp under his foot and then ordered Hamish to clear up the mess. The young Hamish obediently did as he had been told as always; scraping up the smashed stems and the once colourful petals, blue, pink and gold now smeared on the stone passage floor.

As he swept the sorry mess into a dustpan he had realised with a visceral spasm, that he hated that man. The thought had both shocked and secretly pleased him. It had somehow helped to arm him against the worst of his father's treatment from then on. He still feared and dreaded him and he still recoiled from the violence and mental torment the man inflicted on him, but now he held a secret against him. He nurtured it and it gave him the strength to perpetrate small defiances.

The first of these had followed immediately. He noticed a stem that had escaped destruction, a small purple dog violet. Once the minister had gone he carefully carried the bright purple flower to the kitchen where Lizzie, sweat plastering her hair to her forehead, was struggling to the kitchen range with a heavy potful of stew. He helped her to carry it and, when they had done, he had handed her the flower and smiled. She had beamed with the sudden and nervous delight of someone rarely shown any kindness. From then on the secret knowledge that he hated his father and his small defiant acts, albeit unbeknownst to his father, gave him some succour, even though he still lived in constant dread.

During the account Hamish's expression had become one of barely restrained rage. In referring to his father he had hissed out the words of hatred with barely suppressed bitterness at the injustice done to both him and to the unfortunate Lizzie. When he came to the part where he had given the flower to Lizzie he had smiled, his expression had softened and taken on a look that Màiri couldn't fathom. It was a look of both resignation and tenderness with, as she saw so often, something defeated and darker underneath.

Hamish had told her that this fearful life had dragged on into his teenage years when he was sent to a biblical college for preparation for ordination. He hated these years of discipline and repetition of Bible readings, catechism and prayers but gloried in the freedom from his father's bullying and in the peace he found in meditation. He was not however, cut out to be a parson. He was naturally painfully shy and, except when preaching which he had found he had a passion for, he could not socialise and felt no connection with his fellow trainee ministers. In the end he decided on missionary work and had come to the Highlands to gain preaching experience, in part to distance himself from his father but also because he had thought he had had a clear vocation. Severing his ties with the church, and therefore his father, had come as an unexpected but blessed release, though leavened with a corrosive guilt. Without him saying so in so many words Màiri was made to realise that without his love for her and her clear love and respect for him he wouldn't have had the courage to break so effectively with his past. It was something for her to hold on to.

Hamish had clearly agonised about speaking to Màiri about his early life and feelings Doing so stirred up his emotions and gave him a burning, anxious sensation in his chest which made him feel restless. He felt the need to do it nonetheless; it was a way of driving out some of his demons, a way of dissipating some of the anger and grief he felt for his lost and wasted childhood. But afterwards he needed to get out and do something. Movement displaced some of the pervasive and enervating despair he felt buried deep within.

After he left for the open air and the relief that activity brought him Màiri had sat and eased out her breath, relaxing her tight muscles. She realised that she had become tense and was bursting with restraint: she had sucked in her breath along with her feelings and had held on to them. She had tried to reach out physically to Hamish in an instinctive action after he had finished telling her of his hatred for his father and of the misery of his life before they had met. She couldn't bear to see him struggling with emotions that were written in the lines of his face. But he had risen quickly, avoiding her touch, and had left the house, leaving a pregnant vacuum of pent-up feelings.

Màiri was confused, sad and angry, she couldn't understand any parent treating a child in the way in which Hamish's father had treated him. She was distraught and confused about her own feelings and at Hamish's confused feelings for her. She looked at young Callum lying in his cradle blowing bubbles and talking to himself and she rose and picked him up and hugged him, holding him tight and swaying slowly as she quietly sobbed to herself and he snuggled his head into the crook of her neck, playing with her loose curls.

The next day saw the beginning of spring lambing and the start of a new farming year. Frantic activity filled their minds and drove away thoughts of the past for now.

CHAPTER 3

LIFE RETURNS TO THE GLEN

Spring comes late to the Highlands. This year it was later still, there had been snow flurries almost up to the end of April and what sun there was had little heat in it. But finally, in the first week of May, the sun began to blaze out in all its glory and the ewes started to give birth. Because of the altitude and northern location of the croft lambing was always later than elsewhere in Scotland.

Màiri was excited, lambing was her favourite time in the farming calendar, albeit an exhausting one. Every year she watched and participated in awe as the tough little hill sheep brought new life into the world.

The morning of the first lambs was fresh with cold air being blown off the snow-covered tops by a gentle breeze. But the wind no longer held a winter chill. Out of the breeze the sun warmed pale skin unused to its touch. The grasslands on the lower slopes were taking on a new, fresh green and leaves were bursting out on furze. The heather was putting up urgent new growth and goat willow was showing rabbits-foot tufts of silver grey, furry catkins. Loch Gorm sparkled in the sunshine, fishermen were rowing out to the fishing grounds, half hidden in the wispy clouds of morning mist coming off the loch. Further out, they were standing in their boats to cast their nets, silhouettes, dark against the shimmering loch waters.

House martins twittered in the early morning sunlight as they dashed in and out of the eaves of the house and barn, white rumps flashing. They were hawking for insects across the fields, competing with swallows who were gracefully swooping so low they seemed in danger of crashing into the grass as they twisted and turned in order to pluck insects out of the air, flying with breathtaking speed and agility. Màiri was always astonished that all these tiny birds travelled thousands of miles to the far north, all the way back from sun baked Africa every spring. She could see more migrants darting between the newly green bushes and dry stone walls and from the budding green furze: small, brown insignificant birds bringing their cheerful sounds back to the Highlands; the onomatopoeic chiff-chaff and the subtle little stonechat, whose call sounded like two pebbles being struck together; "chip, chip!" They were all dashing about building nests or foraging for food for newly born, hungry chicks. Màiri was bewitched, just as she had been every year since her mother had first shown her these little creatures and named them for her. She realised that the naming of a creature, recognised by sight or sound, invested it with a distinct personality and invested her with the knowledge and intimacy with it that made it a friend, a familiar, something that could not be unknown ever again and which gave her endless fascination and delight.

Those household familiars, the house sparrows, were nesting in the turf roof, squabbling and chirping; the sergeant-major male with the largest black bib bossed all of the others about; while the shrill, unmusical cheeping provided a continual, cheerful backdrop to the crofters lives, even after all the migrant, summer birds had fled. Màiri loved these cheeky little brown and grey birds and always put out crumbs for them to squabble over.

Further up the slopes the black stems of the heather were slowly turning the slopes a dark green as summer foliage clothed their branches, spreading up the hill day by day like a slow motion tide. Looking up she saw a dark shadow patrolling the sky, smaller than an eagle or buzzard. She recognised it as some sort of hawk and hoped it wouldn't carry off any of 'her' birds, even though she realised that it probably had hungry chicks to feed too. It is the naturalist's dilemma, as an observer of the struggle for life: should she be more concerned about the young of the predator or the death of their prey. Màiri knew that sudden death was the corollary to the new life that pulsed all around her.

She wondered whether this knowledge, the knowledge of the life and death struggle going on right now, and the consciousness to understand its meaning, was itself the "knowledge" the serpent in the Garden of Eden passed first to Eve and thence to Adam. To understand life and death, to know that the end is coming to every living thing, including ourselves, and that it will be the end, was that, rather than the realisation of our nakedness and shame which the puritan preachers seemed so obsessed with, the real "felix culpa", the happy sin, the fortunate fault of banished humans? Was our consciousness the most accursed blessing for listening to the snake's hissing tones. And was the realisation of our eventual death the price we pay for the wonder that we are shown in this abundant natural world. A bird could only know the fear of the moment, we knew the fear of the future. Màiri found it hard to believe that the glen on this sunny morning wasn't itself some sort of Garden of Eden and that the consciousness to appreciate it was not some sort of fortunate gift, albeit one with a fatal sting to its tail.

Her attention was taken by the quavering bleating of the firstborn lamb. The sound that rang in the crofter's year, the archetypal sound of spring that shepherds beyond history had heard with gratification and joy and more than a little trepidation lest things go badly awry.

Hamish was in the temporary lean-to he had constructed against the old stone walls of the sheep fank, built to give extra shelter to the newborn, vulnerable lambs. The ground was strewn with a deep litter of barley straw and separate pens which he had constructed with willow hurdles tied at the corners. The first of these pens was now occupied by the proud ewe and the newborn lamb that Màiri had heard calling. She let Hamish go in and have some breakfast while she filled the roughly constructed, wooden mangers in each pen with some hay, saved from the previous harvest ready for the mothers to feed up on while their lambs had the first few draughts of rich suckling milk.

The rest of the flock of little blackface ewes were in the surrounding paddock where Màiri watched for signs of imminent birth or difficulties from any of them. She was sitting, sheltered by the lean-to, on a rough bench of flat stones surrounded by the warm smell of sheep; lanolin, grassy breath and the sharp tang of their dung and by the smell of the dusty straw and grassy hay. It was so much a part of her life since early childhood that it felt deeply comforting and reassuring, a yearly ritual of life starting up again. One or two of the ewes were becoming restless, constantly shifting position and trying to find a space away from the rest of the flock who were standing or laying chewing the cud.

These tough, little blackface ewes with their large curling horns were independent beasts. Those who were somehow missed in the roundup to bring them down off the hill, as occasionally happened, were quite capable of giving birth in the open. The lambs were resilient enough to survive rough and cold weather from birth, but there were also many risks. A ewe on the hill over winter would have trouble foraging and there could be problems with the birth, much safer to gather them all in and supervise them in a sheltered spot where problems could be dealt with and the lambs given peace and shelter to bond and feed up before being turned out on spring grass. Hamish and Màiri between them had managed to get all thirty of their ewes off the hill and a couple of their neighbours ewes as well, which had been duly returned to their proper place, identified by the nicks clipped in their ears soon after birth.

The morning turned out to be busy: eight lambs in all, including a pair of twins. One lamb had tried to come out backwards and had been manipulated by Màiri so that it could come out the right way, front feet forwards followed by the head. One lamb was born still inside the placental sac. Now separated from the oxygen giving process of the womb it would have quickly drowned in placental fluid if Màiri hadn't intervened to break open the sac and clear its airway.

The feeling of satisfaction and renewal lambing brought with it never failed to surprise Màiri. Every year she expected that experience and repetition over the years would diminish the wonder but, as each lamb was born, she gazed anew at the mystifying miracle that brought life from a straining ewe; this year particularly so. She had great sympathy for these little, hardy sheep who had so tough a life up on the hill, feisty and quick to startle at a potential threat, they nonetheless got on with birthing and accepted her presence with a purposeful calm, getting on with the business of producing lambs.

As each lamb, or pair of lambs, was born Màiri would rub them vigorously with a handful of straw to stir life into them, after having first cleared their throats with her fingers and tickled the nostrils with a straw to make them sneeze. She would place them in front of the mother for her to lick off the slimy remains of the fluid that had cocooned the lamb in the womb and they would begin to bond with each other. All the while Màiri would keep a wary eye out for the other ewes to ensure the lambs didn't accidentally bond with the wrong ewe or weren't hijacked by another pregnant ewe who would then abandon them when her own lamb arrived. Fortunately none of the ewes had rejected their lambs so far which sometimes happened, especially to first-time mothers, so hopefully no pet lambs this year, although there was opportunity enough yet. A pet lamb would need feeding regularly from the bottle and keeping warm by the range. In other years Màiri had been pleased enough to care for a pet lamb but now she had Callum, and one dependent baby was enough to cope with alongside her busy working life.

When the lambs had had their first suckle of the vital colostrum, the first extra rich, life-giving milk which helped build the lamb's resistance to disease, Màiri would then carry the lamb, or twin lambs, to an empty pen, coaxing the mother to follow and leave them alone to continue bonding. For the lambs and mothers to create strong bonds early on was important, recognition by sight and smell, and soon by the sound of their mother's voice was vital, especially for hill sheep. The lamb's survival up on the hill where all sorts of dangers threatened was dependent on the lamb's ability to call for and identify their mother when lost or frightened and to seek her protection and sustenance. The lambs were prey to eagles, foxes and ravens and also, so far as their mothers were concerned, wolves. The ewes ancestral memories told them that wolves were still waiting out there on the hill ready to ambush them or their lambs and they behaved accordingly.

They had lost no lambs on Màiri's watch and she was deeply relieved: the lambs were not just their livelihood but so much more. To see one of her lambs born dead or for one to die while still very young, as many did, affected Màiri deeply, especially after the devastating blow of losing her first baby, her daughter that never was. The first lambing after that loss had been almost unbearable for her, each birth had torn at her insides. When a lamb had been stillborn she had broken down and she had wept until she had felt she was empty of feelings.

Lambing was still an emotionally turbulent time for her, but there was joy as well, she could be almost overwhelmed with happiness at a successful birth while just as easily made tearful by a death. It was something she never really got used to, this roller-coaster of lambing time. Even Hamish, distracted as he was, seemed to find the birth of the new lambs a mystifying and deeply gratifying experience. After the highs and lows of lambing Màiri would feel emotionally spent and physically exhausted from lack of sleep. She nonetheless carried around a feeling of euphoria for some time afterwards.

After three days of lambing she was in need of a break from the relentless pace and Callum was getting tetchy and fractious at being left so often for long periods alone. Màiri and Hamish had each taken turns at lambing duty while the other had a rest, slept or got on with their other essential chores. So far everything had gone reasonably smoothly, with fifteen lambs born and only one lost and no rejected lambs, good fortune indeed. She had decided to take Callum with her on her next spell of lambing, but before she did she took him for a walk up the hill.

She had missed the constant physical contact of Callum strapped to her breast. He had grown considerably and was now a lot heavier, but seeing and feeling him contentedly snuggled up to her in his familiar sling was so satisfying that it gave her a boost of energy as she headed off up the hill. She had set her sights on a familiar outcrop about two hundred and fifty feet above the croft. She struggled through the stems of freshly growing heather and tussocks of tough, moorland grasses to a familiar path, used by sheep and stray red deer from the estate lands on the other side of the hill. The smell of a night-time, patrolling fox was still strong in the air.

She breathlessly climbed the steep slope, taking smaller and smaller steps to accommodate the increasing steepness. Callum was feeling heavier as she climbed. Her calves were stretched tight and she winced at the pull on her muscles and the tight pain of aching thighs as the angle became yet more acute. She had to work hard to keep her balance and to keep an upward thrust to her strenuous walk pushing her knees ever upwards with her strong legs. By the time she reached the outcrop and perched on a familiar ledge she was breathing heavily, her body tingled and twitched with the effort. It had been a while since she had had the chance of a strenuous walk and she felt refreshed by it.

She was now over three hundred feet above the loch and the air was cool and fresh. The sun was peering through fluffy clouds and the water was an azure slash through the browns and fresh variegated greens of the surrounding hills. Dappled silver light shimmered like a shoal of gilded fish across the loch, a shifting tapestry of nature's watery subtle colours of deep blue and emerald melted into soft greys and sparkling silver-white, a supreme artist's palette of fresh spring shades.

Màiri drank in the sights and sounds while Callum played with her loose hanging curls and chuckled and hiccupped, all the time carrying on a soft burbled conversation with himself. She let out her breath in a deep sigh of contentment, happy to feel the sights and sounds wash over her. Hamish had released the first few lambs into the lower paddock with their mothers and she could see them prancing across the fresh green pasture while their mothers enjoyed the new, succulent grass and the aromatic herbs that grew amongst it.

From up here the lambs looked like tiny white puffs of fluff caught up on the skirts of a bright, green cloak. They were bounding this way and that, leaping and butting each other, playing with complete abandon and then springing into the air like jack-in-a-boxes; then losing their mothers and calling frantically until their mothers called back, when they would dash back in panic for a suckle of reassurance. Màiri could hear the fading bleats of the lambs drifting up and away across the hillside and the faint, gruff replies of the ewes straggling up to her on a gentle sea breeze and fading away into the empty air above the moors. The gentle, buffeted air held the smell of new grown pasture on its cool herby breath; the essence of spring. Callum gently murmured to her and she fed him, feeling a close bond with the instinctively protective ewes far below.

By the time she had to head back down to give Hamish a break she felt refreshed and ready to spend another four hours or so on lambing duty before going in and getting the midday meal and then rushing through the other household chores. Hamish had another stillborn lamb to report and her mood slumped but she had to accept it as part of the balancing lows and highs of crofting life and she busied herself by checking each of the remaining ewes for signs of imminent birth with a heavier heart. She began the grisly business of skinning the dead lamb with a sharp knife in the hopes that a ewe would give birth to twins or perhaps that a rejected lamb from another ewe could be paired with the mother of the dead lamb. The dejected, lambless mother called softly for a lamb that wasn't there and was turning round and round looking for it in vain and becoming increasingly distressed, tugging painfully at Màiri's emotions.

Two more lambs were delivered easily and with no fuss by their now attentive mothers before a young ewe began to struggle. She had only taken ten minutes or so straining to give birth but was obviously distressed and confused about what was happening to her. Màiri recognised her as a first-time mother and intervened.

She rolled up her sleeve and pushed her hand deep inside the animal, carefully sensing with her fingers. First she found a foot, then what felt like a knee with the lower leg bent backwards. She knew she had to try and straighten the leg and pull it forwards so that she could grasp both front legs and pull.

The ewe had by now rolled on to its side and Màiri had to go with it, lying face down in the straw and sheep droppings, stretched out, legs braced against the dry stone wall. She reflected, not for the first time, on the indignities of crofting life and smiled wryly to herself. All this time she was talking softly to the ewe in a low voice, trying to reassure her. The spasms from the ewe were getting weaker; Màiri could tell she was about ready to give up pushing. She didn't want another dead lamb.

She grasped the unborn lamb's bent leg and pulled it with as much strength and care as she could muster. She had done it! She felt for the second leg, came into contact with a muzzle and felt movement. Now she knew the lamb was still alive she was desperate to get it out before it suffocated in the birth canal. She had both legs in her hand now and she pulled with a steady strength, the ewe gave a last, weak push and the lamb was out in a sticky wet rush. Màiri fell flat on her back, legs in the air but she didn't mind, she had at least saved the ewe and, hopefully, the lamb.

The limp, wet body of the lamb lay apparently lifeless on the ground. Màiri had tried to clear the airway, tickled at the nostrils with a straw and rubbed the lamb vigorously, but there was no sign of life. It looked as though all that struggle on the part of Màiri and the ewe was going to be in vain. She took the lamb by its back legs and swung it high from side to side, nothing, again, no reaction from the limp creature, then again and there was a tiny splutter. She quickly placed it back carefully on the straw covered ground and rubbed its whole body vigorously, a little sneeze and the lamb took its first breath. Màiri gave a little yelp of relief and joy and took in a deep breath; she had almost forgotten to breathe herself during her anxious struggle to get the lamb out,

-"Well, no' a very propitious start tae life little one - ye had me worried there fer a wee while!" she said to the now struggling lamb.

It was trying to get to its feet, its legs still too weak, collapsing back onto the straw and shaking and shivering. She scooped it up and placed it in front of the mother who was standing looking around bemused, apparently wondering what had happened. Màiri stood back, the ewe sniffed the lamb, backed away and turned away from it. Màiri manhandled the ewe back towards the lamb and lifted the lamb for the ewe to smell, then backed away after placing the lamb in front of the ewe again. The lamb wobbled to its feet only to be butted away by the confused mother before she walked away, leaving the sprawling lamb altogether. It was no good; she had seen rejections before and this one was definite, the ewe just didn't recognise the lamb as her own.

The young ewe had wandered off and was looking for something to eat, completely unaware for now of having given birth. It was her first lamb and she obviously didn't have a clue what was going on; her fear and confusion had overridden her instincts, not yet reinforced by experience. Unless Màiri did something quickly all her struggle to save the lamb would be wasted, though she knew that by getting it out she had at least saved the ewe from an otherwise painful and lingering death with a dead lamb still inside her.

Màiri carried the lamb to where she had placed the skin from the lamb who had died earlier and wrapped the now stiffening skin carefully round the little creature who was too weak to resist the indignity. She tied the skin loosely onto the lamb's body with a piece of string and placed the lamb in the pen where the dead lamb's mother was still restlessly pining for it. She stood back and waited, holding her breath.

The ewe sniffed, nervously backed away and then sniffed again and tentatively licked the lamb, recognising the familiar smell on the false skin. Màiri held her breath anxiously. The tiny lamb rose pluckily to its feet, its now adoptive mother licked it again and the lamb's legs gave way and it fell over. It got up again, more licking and mutual sniffing and the lamb tottered round to the ewe's teats. It shakily reached for the teat, fell over, tried again and again and eventually made it, its instinct for life strong. The ewe shifted slightly and the lamb was over again. Finally, after much struggle and a helping hand from Màiri it suckled greedily on the teat, another new life had begun on the croft after the desperate struggle of birth.

Màiri removed the old skin, it had served its purpose; the ewe had recognised its scent and had now marked the lamb as her own with her saliva and sheepy breath. Màiri backed away and secured the hurdle of the pen with a length of twine. She gave a deep sigh of relief as she watched the homely scene of the lamb suckling, the new-found mother now looking completely content, gently calling and snickering to the lamb, Màiri smiled; a little victory.

She turned her attention to Callum. She had laid him on a pile of straw next to the stone bench. He was surrounded by curious ewes. She thought they would have ignored him but two of them seemed to have taken up station either side of him, as if to take possession of this odd looking lamb. One was trying to lick him and he chuckled and then shrieked with laughter. His small, plump arms flapped in the air and struck the ewe on the nose, though she seemed completely unconcerned. Màiri reclaimed her baby, much to the chagrin of the disappointed ewes who complained loudly.

The rest of her spell of lambing was uneventful and she was relieved when Hamish took over. By the time the lambing season was finished two weeks later they had lost one more lamb but could be pleased with twenty-seven healthy lambs. Two ewes had not been impregnated by the tup and were grazing unconcerned, waiting to be released onto their high pasture. A few days after the last lamb had been released into the paddock with its mother the grass in the paddock was exhausted and they were running out of hay. It was time to release the ewes with all the young lambs to the mercies of the high pastures to spend the summer months cooled by soft mountain breezes, in the freedom of the moors.

After breakfast Màiri followed Hamish out to the lambing paddock, carrying Callum in her arms. Hamish untied the gate to the paddock. The season's wheel had turned, the excitement of lambing over, farming life turned to other concerns.

The more experienced ewes were already waiting restlessly by the gate, they knew what was coming and, as Hamish stood swiftly back they pushed their way forward and headed off up the slope. Lambs trailed behind, calling their mothers to try and keep in touch. The enthusiasm of these half wild sheep for their territory up on the hills was infectious, the pull of the mountain pastures strong. All the ewes started leaping and running, stragglers hurrying to catch up as bleating lambs panicked and fell behind. A small, straggling river of off-white sheep streamed up the hill, calling to each other in a cacophony of bleating; lambs calling to mothers, mothers calling back and ewes calling to each other; some were just shouting with joy, others impatiently encouraging their young to keep up.

Their fading voices echoed off the beinn and back down to the croft, embroidering the early morning hillside with their cries. Eventually calm returned, the ewes spread out, each finding their own patch of succulent green grass and herbs. All the lambs finally located their own mother and then dashed off to play with a crazy exuberance, adapting quickly to their new mountain home.

In the next few days crofters who had not already released their sheep did so. The different herds settled down beside each other, largely staying within their own territories. Hill sheep, being hefted know their patch on the hill which they learn from their mothers or from the other sheep. They know their way down to the croft and their way back up the hill, the herds on either side keep them within their own patch, although a few still wander from time to time. If there is no herd on one side a sturdy barrier is needed.

Màiri and Hamish had the last croft on the hill before the estate lands and the wild coast began so they had to maintain a dry stone wall running right up to where the grass and heather ran out and the bare rock at the top of the hill began. Their allowance, the number and type of stock they were allowed, including a share of the common grazing, the 'souming', was up to forty-five mature sheep and up to ten head of cattle, which they couldn't yet afford.

The sheep began to settle into their summer pattern of grazing and the lambs grew. Hamish sowed barley and oats and Màiri turned her attention to growing vegetables and attending to her flock of hens and she went back to collecting seaweed and other bounty brought in on high tides and summer storms. She created a vegetable patch, foraged for herbs and natural foods, helped Hamish on their tiny fields and ran the house and she milked the cow when it was her turn, tended the new calf and fed her growing chicks. Summer brought its own cares and demands, life quickened.

May was the time to begin cutting peats to leave them plenty of time to dry out ready to use as fuel when current stocks ran out. Peat cutting was an art, something else that Hamish struggled with. Whereas

Hamish found it so hard Màiri had been doing it since she had been old enough to help her athair and màthair and looked forward to it every year. With Callum in his papoose, now seven months old and too heavy to carry far without a break, she trekked up to the moors with her peat iron which she used as a staff on the steeper slopes.

The marshy moorside was half-hidden under the cover of cotton grass, bustling and waving in a steady, drizzling breeze. Bog asphodels and the carnivorous, star-shaped sundews, which suck the life from captured insects, proliferated and lady's smock grew on the sheltered streamside looking like unruly peals of delicate, miniature bells. A curlew mourned tunefully, sounding its bubbling, rising and falling song, the moody songster tailing off in nostalgic liquid fluting, the sound of the high moorland. An oyster catcher sitting on eggs started up at her presence and broke cover, presenting its chevroned, startling, black-and-white back as it banked away on the warm, humid air, wings clapping, disappearing into the drizzle. Màiri felt that intimacy of wild places when the mist comes down and cocoons everything in a grey muting cloak. The moor felt mystical. She felt the presence of ghosts just beyond the grey curtain of steadily falling fine rain, as if walking outside time. Even Callum became subdued, perhaps he too felt the mysterious presence of the mist; he lay still and silent, wide-eyed and watchful, listening.

The ground itself moved under Màiri's feet, gently undulating and sinking beneath her weight and adding to the strangeness of the place: sphagnum bog is ninety percent water. It was no wonder an allocated site for peat cutting was known as a "moss". A moss was one of a number of sites in different locations, allocated to each family and divided up so as to ensure everyone got a variety of the best and least good peat cuttings.

Both Hamish and Màiri spent time at the peat mosses, cutting, stacking, drying and then carrying home fuel in shouldered, heavy basket loads for cooking and for heat in the cold, dark winter. In a relatively treeless landscape peat was a natural alternative. Màiri enjoyed the process of extracting it, hard, wet, cold, physical work but deeply rewarding in its results. It gave her a reason to spend time on the sparse, deserted moor; a beguiling wilderness.

The rich, dark, wet peat, composed of compressed sphagnum moss and other vegetation was built up over many thousands of years, spongey, more water than substance. It was now many feet deep; when dried it made a wonderful brown-black fuel, glowing hot and smoky, with a richly evocative aroma. The process of harvesting peat was long established, going back to prehistory, ever since people had inhabited these dark, wet lands. Peat allowed year-round occupation, even after most of the trees had been felled back in the bronze ages. Peat was a natural fuel, a dark bounty that repaid the effort made in its harvesting tenfold.

Hamish had already begun a new row at the edge of the three-foot deep cutting at the most accessible of the mosses. He had scraped off the turf surface to begin a new row of peats. Màiri placed the long, flat bladed iron ready for the next cut and placed her foot on the top of the blade before pushing down on the long, wooden handle for the full length of the blade. She repeated the exercise, removing the first peat "turf" and throwing it behind her to the side of the trench. She worked on steadily and smoothly, well practised, allowing her mind to wander. It took her over an hour before she reached the end of the trench, by which time she was puffing with the effort.

She took a breather and leaned on her iron in a stance that would have been familiar to any Highland or Island dweller down the ages. In her dark, three-quarter length frock and plaid shawl, standing on the moor with a background of the hills all around and the islands across the silver sea beyond the Inner Sound, she could have been a figure from history. She could have been the subject of a black ink study by Landseer or a sketch by a passing Victorian gentleman, exploring these strange northern lands: "Woman at the peat cuttings on Highland moor".

So still was the scene on the dark moor that she seemed frozen in time, ghosts of her ancestors all around her; her mother, her grandfather, the people of the glen before her own people had been driven there, the cattle reivers. Few people lived out their history so clearly and so wholly as the people of the Highlands and Islands. She placed her peat iron ready for the next turf and began cutting at the beginning of the row again.

When she had finished she began to stack the peats into tall pyramids, like a tepee built out of black, wet logs, so that they could drain off over the next few months; the rain would run harmlessly down the sides of the pyramid. She stood back and looked on the results with satisfaction, her two pyramids completed a row of three started by Hamish. They would fuel many meals and warm many dark nights. She found a dry hillock to sit on and laid the long handle of her peat iron across her knees to use as an armrest in another timeless gesture. Callum, who had been lying on a small dry patch of rough moorland grass while she worked, rolled about on his belly and practised crawling.

Màiri felt dreamily disembodied, her mind drifting. She remembered trips to the peat mosses with her athair. They would laugh at the antics of the lambs and he would gently tease her and she would run like the wind itself through the waving cotton grass; white, bobbing wisps of wool brushing her bare legs, careless and carefree, her athair looking on astonished at her youth and energy. When her màthair was ill she had run up here puffing and panting to escape the close, foetid atmosphere of the dark croft house, and when her mother had died she had come up here on her own to remember happier times and to weep her heart out and rage at the dark, scudding clouds, cursing the loss of her dearest mother and of being orphaned so young.

The drizzling mist had lifted while she had been working and her gaze now seemed to rise above the moor and the peat mosses and she imagined her soul soaring up over the surrounding hills. She was looking down on herself, on the dark moor and across the shoulder of the beinn, over to the wide estate lands and then back across the moor, following the small burns that drained it. Down the glen she passed in her mindsight, off the moor where a more powerful stream picked up, bubbling and splashing, white foam crashing over rocks and sweeping down to a V-shaped gorge cut deep in the cliffs, where it poured over the edge in a spectacular, white waterfall, crashing two hundred feet onto the shore below and thundering into the loch. Her mind's gaze, on beating gull's wings, soared out over the loch, seawards towards the wild bays and coves she knew so well and out over the sea, to the Inner Sound and on to the Outer Hebrides, Harris and Lewis, a massive distant landmass of extraordinarily ancient rocks, brooding and misty, low-down on the horizon. She wished to live nowhere else, she gloried in the beauty of her ancient Highland world.

Màiri was startled from her reverie by a cry from Callum. She looked to where she had left him and he was gone. She immediately panicked, visions of eagles or foxes snatched at her mind but she immediately dismissed them as ridiculous. She turned and turned again, searching across the empty, solitary moor, but no sign. She was frantic, her heart pounding, mind dizzy with anxiety; it was as if the dark peaty ground had swallowed him up. The most precious person in her life had suddenly gone, she was completely beside herself, her legs turned to jelly and she shook with fear. If she lost Callum she lost everything. She was in the instinctive panic of a mother for her lost young.

She tried to calm herself, to think rationally. He couldn't possibly be far away, all her senses were alerted, fine tuned, stretched out. She was calling and calling his name, she stopped and listened for a moment. All she heard was the gentle susurration as the wind stirred the cotton grass, the sound rising and then falling away.

The faint, high-pitched, cry of a bird echoed off the beinn, then silence as the soft breeze faded. She listened acutely until she could hear the individual drips of peaty water dropping from the lip of the peat trench into the puddles below. She listened to the sound of all her hopes slipping away.

It was a possible turning point in her life she realised: if Callum was found her hopes were still alive; if he was lost, she was lost too. It wasn't an hysterical thought, just a fleeting, reasoned assessment; if he were gone then everything else became meaningless. The enormity of having given birth to this child struck her. From now on her happiness was bound up in his.

The thought terrified her, anything could happen, may already have happened, and the rest of her life was attached to this vulnerable child who, as he got older and more independent would be less and less under her protection. Motherhood suddenly seemed a terrible weight. Wherever he was in the world in the future she would always be aware of him and concerned for him. The dark fears at the edges of her nightmares picked away at her sanity.

She heard the cry again; now she could identify it as coming from the peat workings. She hurried to the edge of the trench only to see Callum, quietly whimpering in the bottom of the watery trench. His clothing was streaked with black, peaty stains as he held his hands up in a supplicating gesture. He lay on his back in a dark brown puddle, his plump small face crinkled up in misery and making "pup-pup" sounds as his tiny lips pouted out sobs.

Màiri was so relieved she almost collapsed to her knees. She leapt into the bottom of the trench, sending water and oozing black, peaty divots cascading with her feet. She scooped Callum up and scrambled back out of the trench and then stripped his clothes from him before wrapping him in her long plaid shawl. She wiped his smutty face and crooned to him.

-"Oh my poor wee bairn! So ye found out how tae crawl did ye, well ye could have waited till we were safe hame!"

She beamed at him, so desperately relieved to have him back safe that she still trembled with emotion. She held him tight in her arms, clucking to soothe his sobs, which now seemed to be more about feeling sorry for himself than about fear or hurt.

-"Come on my wee adventurer, let's get ye back in the warm and dry"

She could see dark clouds rolling in from the sea and knew they were both in for a drenching unless they got down from the high moorland and back home pretty soon.

She softly, breathlessly hushed a Gaelic lullaby to Callum as she hurried down the steep slope back to the croft. By the time Hamish came in for his evening meal she was ready to laugh with relief about the incident, even Hamish smiled a little at her description of little Callum lying miserably in the trench and feeling so sorry for himself.

She didn't forget that incident though and once Callum became more proficient at crawling, and then tottering about on his short, plump legs, she became ever more aware of his scope for calamity. She had had to construct a fireguard out of odd pieces of chicken wire and would have to ask Ian McDonald to build her something more permanent to keep Callum away from the ever-glowing fire to which he seemed drawn. She also had to be careful about leaving the front door open, having once found him out in the garden and heading for the steep path. She began to watch him out of one eye as she got on with her daily tasks. Now she had been so cruelly alerted to the dangers she carried them with her at the back of her mind. Becoming a mother had, she realised, made her a true hostage to fortune.

Màiri also had Hamish to worry about. He continued to have periods of deep melancholy when he was virtually incapable of working. They could last up to two or three weeks and placed a heavy load on Màiri, emotionally and physically. These black moods would strike overnight and Màiri would do her best to coax Hamish out of them, but nothing really worked. They passed in their own time. But Hamish never again spoke of his childhood, if Màiri asked he would simply close down and escape outside: never again would such intimate and awful secrets pass between them as they had that spring.

Callum became Màiri's escape and her hopes, she took him everywhere with her, played with him, carried him and suckled him and loved him more than anything or anyone with a renewed intensity she found breathtaking and consuming.

In the autumn the community had a celebratory service at the kirk for Harvest Home or "Hairst Hame" at which the grudging minister had seen fit to remind them that, as such lowly and unfaithful sinners, they had hardly deserved the good fortune that the year's harvest had brought them. It had indeed been a good harvest and even Màiri and Hamish had had sufficient to send a couple of surplus sacks of barley to the market at Dingwall to the east, the old capital of the Highlands, travelling from Kyle via the railway with the rest of the surplus of the little township and its surrounding areas. They had also managed to send off fifteen lambs to be sold to lowland farmers for fattening up. They had kept a few back to fatten for the local market and to cover losses of their own ewes over the year, one to an accident, and two to disease. A fine black calf was similarly sold at Dingwall. It was their best year by far and they had obtained good prices owing to a severe drought across England which had meant better rewards for Scottish farmers. After paying rent and buying in essential supplies they had made twenty-one pounds ten shillings, a small fortune for a crofter and more money than Màiri and Hamish had ever had. Half of that was kept back for expenses and the rest secreted in a biscuit tin in Màiri's larder. She called it her insurance fund.

In order to get their beasts to market they had to be driven by cart to the railhead at Kyle of Lochalsh. Màiri and Hamish had both taken the pony cart into Kyle with the calf tethered behind, bellowing all the way. The driver had charged them sixpence and tuppence extra for the well grown calf, even though it had walked the five miles. From there it would join other beasts going by railway cattle truck to the community's agent at Dingwall.

Usually John Fraser would act on behalf of the whole community: representing them with the auctioneers and helping to show the beasts in the sale ring and making sure they all got the best price. When that year's surplus sheep and lambs had set off for market John Fraser had led with his two sons, the young men with their dogs dashing this way and that, frantically trying to keep the excitable herd together.

If cattle were going in any number, especially if they were his own, Ian McDonald would also go, having both the strength and the expertise to deal with a recalcitrant heifer or bullock. They would drive the mixed herd all the way over difficult terrain and stony trackways until they got to the railhead and then coax, coerce, shove and bribe the sheep and cattle with choice titbits until they had all the animals in the cattle trucks ready for the rail journey. When they all got to Dingwall they would unload the animals, drive them to the market and look forward to a good price and a refreshing pint or two as a reward. All that is except John Fraser, who would stand about harumphing and disapproving of their consumption of alcohol and at the rough, bawdy behaviour of other farmers with drink taken.

A railway journey in a third class compartment on a wooden bench, then an expensive proposition, was a real treat. When she had been a small girl Màiri had occasionally gone with her father and mother to Dingwall by train on market day. They had set off at dawn to walk the five miles to Kyle. Waiting for the train when they arrived she would be bursting with excitement. When the steam train came in, huffing and puffing in great steamy, white clouds, with the unique smoky, nutty smell of boiler coal smoke she was thrilled by the sights, sounds and smells: she had never seen anything so big, so frightening and so beautiful. The noise was deafening and the loud whistle made the train sound so important, but joyful at the same time. The whole experience had filled the head of the young girl and had almost overwhelmed her.

Dingwall too had appeared to her as big and noisy and enchanting; a bustling cityscape. She was so completely agog at so many people and fine houses and shops that she hadn't known what to do or where to look first. The thought that she would now be able to take Callum there one day made her feel so grown-up that it was daunting.

The small family were able to go into the winter of 1922 feeling more confident than they could ever have hoped. They had a well-stocked larder and something to spare and, as an extra treat, a large leg of salt cured pork hanging on a hook in the chimney, smoking and slowly turning into golden-rinded, juicy, fatty bacon. Màiri would eke it out over the long hard winter; an occasional treat, fatty fuel against the cold for Hamish, and occasionally for her too.

The "Hairst Hame" celebration in the autumn had been uproarious, with Ian and Isla McDonald, helped by James Fraser, John Fraser's youngest son, providing the music and Màiri and Isla providing most of the singing. Isla now had a newborn bairn of her own to take care of, a girl called Flora Màiri McDonald. Her first name was in memory of Flora MacDonald who had rescued Bonnie Prince Charlie from the redcoats and spirited him away to Skye, and thence to France forever and thus poked the English in the eye. The Highlanders had suffered in his stead but none had betrayed him to the hated English. Her second name of course was after Isla's best friend. Màiri was delighted to have someone else to share her experiences as a young mother and the community was pleased to see life coming back to the glen after their terrible losses during the war.

The war had deprived them of so many men folk and so much promise, now left abandoned in empty crofts as wives and sweethearts had moved away, unable to cope on their own and many of the old folk had now gone to the graveyard, disheartened and heartbroken at so many losses.

But for now, with a good harvest, both of crops and of bairns for all to celebrate the riotous ceiledh had gone on until well into the night. Over the next few years there would be a dozen youngsters to swell the numbers of the crofting community and the nearby areas and a new small schoolhouse would be urgently needed; a new beginning for the glen.

As the year drew to a close a bitter winter set in, and those extra supplies everyone had put by were thankfully available and desperately needed.

CHAPTER 4

WIND IN THE COTTON GRASS

By the time Callum was five the McDonald family had grown by one more. The stout, freckled, fair-haired baby called Dougal was the result of a brief respite in Hamish's relentless melancholy and isolation from Màiri. Dougal was now four months old, good-natured and easygoing but lacked any particular qualities as a plaything and was therefore an object of supreme indifference to young Callum.

The family and the community as a whole had gained enormously from the long-term loan of two large Clydesdales from the neighbouring estate which was now becoming more mechanised. The estate were not keen on continuing to feed and care for the surplus horses. These two massive beasts, great powerhouses; beautiful and full of energy, had allowed the community to plough up a greater area of arable land; to harrow and prepare it and to transport crops, hay and straw from the fields and people and goods to the town. Màiri and Hamish now had ten acres of land on which to grow barley and oats and enough potatoes to last most of the year round. It wasn't the best or most productive of soils but they made the most of it and in any case, extra horse manure always helped.

The community had also invested in a tough, feisty little Shetland pony to carry the peats back from the mosses and to carry small loads along the steep rocky paths of the glen.

The great, friendly Clydesdales and the spirited little 'Hero', as well as serving the community as a whole, would come to provide Callum with great fascination and companionship over the coming years. For now though, Callum had the delight of a new yearling sheepdog called Jess, who turned out to be too boisterous to work with the sheep and too timid either for shepherding or cattle handling. She was relegated to family pet and revelled in her appointed role.

The family had also added, year by year to their herds: they now had two milking cows and five cows grazing on the hills and had built up their flock of sheep to near the maximum allowance of their grazing rights or "souming" with forty breeding ewes.

For Màiri this had all meant both a boon and much greater demands on her time and energy. But good fortune smiled on the harvests in Callum's early years and all should have been well, even if life was still a demanding daily grind for his parents.

But Hamish's black moods of despair were gradually becoming deeper and more extended. At times he would be barely able to rise from his and Màiri's shared bed.

Màiri would coax and sooth him and encourage and talk to him gently with the infinite patience she accorded the man she loved and feared for. Often though, he would simply be incapable of responding being almost emotionally flat and virtually unable to communicate.

At these times of dark despondency he would slouch and stoop, mumbling and sighing and neglecting his appearance and cleanliness, rarely washing and becoming rank and stale with sweat. He would move with a terrible slowness and reluctance, as if his physical self had become a burden to be borne only with the greatest of efforts. He would neglect his work, missing important tasks that Màiri would then have to chase round after him to complete. She would become exhausted with having to take on much of his work as well as her own. She never complained, never gave in, never abandoned hope of recovery, always supported him, never quite despairing. She would become so tired at times she could hardly stand and she would pray fervently for Hamish to recover his will and his wits. And, in the end, sometimes after weeks, he would gradually become his usual, lugubrious self again.

They never spoke about it afterwards, acting as if to do so would be to conjure up a relapse at the very least. Then, for a month or two, they would return to some sort of normality and the little household would settle into a sort of routine again.

But all the time Màiri would be on edge; she would watch and listen to Hamish breathing at night, waiting for that disturbed pattern that presaged his nightmares and demons and for another bout of despair and absolute dejection that would draw a cloak of darkness over his mind.

Apart from the extra load she had to take on when Hamish was struck down by these bouts Màiri already had more to do than ever and perhaps that busyness was her salvation, that and Callum. Callum would watch; his bright, shining, dark eyes taking in his father's suffering and he, like Màiri would hope and wish and he would try and make himself useful. Sometimes he would follow his father, just to be near him, not saying anything, just letting him know he was about. It seemed to the small boy that his Pa needed the quietness of his company when he was poorly.

To a small boy's mind much of what surrounded him was a mystery; not just the adults in his life; his Ma and Pa and his uncle Ian and Aunt Isla and Auntie Nellie, they were mystery enough, but the world surrounding his home provided the greatest mystery of all and gave endless fascination. The vast open spaces of the moors and high pasture, the deep, broad, greeny-blue loch and the soaring cliffs, all surrounded him with an air of mysterious wonder.

From the age of three or four Callum had followed his Ma, tottering across the foot-baked earth yard behind her or led by her chapped, pink hand to the cow byre. He would sit on a milking pail or a pile of straw and take in the peace and dreamy warmth. The closeness of the cows breath and their warmth was somnambulent. While he looked on Màiri would be tucked into the flank of a ruminating, black cow, the cow gently lowing spouting creamy milk ringing the sides of the bucket like a bell; breath made visible in the half light of a high window, streaming sunshine.

Callum also played with the chickens when Màiri went to feed them and handled the warm, fresh-laid eggs, magicked from fluffy hens into his mother's basket, and he was astonished and enthralled by it all.

And he wondered at the greatness and the fury and the terrible quietness and loneliness of the wildness around him. As he grew he explored and as he explored he wondered. On thrashing, thundering nights when the Atlantic gales crashed ashore from a boiling loch, flinging spume and rain at the slopes above the tall cliffs, he would push his head and shoulders out of the little window of his bedroom to feel the wildness on his face, to feel the noise and the fury, exciting and frightening, the thumping thunder buffeting his eardrums and the wet wind stinging his eyes. The flash of blue lightning always shocked him and caught him unawares. The energy of the storm made it good to get back into bed and consider monsters rolling boulders around the dark mountains.

But what wasn't a mystery to Callum, even from his earliest age, were his fellow creatures of the glen, not just Jess, his new companion, but his parents sheep and cows, the smelly fox, the prancing, roaring stags of autumn and the skittish hinds and the browny-grey mice and shrews hiding in the waving meadows nor his mother's bees and the shiny, black beetles as they plied their trade among towering grass stalks: these were his firm friends. The birds that shared the thatch of turf became as familiar to him as the human residents of the house; as did the bank voles and harvest mice who scuttled over the rafters and who he could hear on the other side of the ceiling at nights.

These animals rewarded his attentions with trust and with glimpses into their secret lives. Their closeness and familiarity and his understanding of the commonsense of their lives and their actions seemed to offer him some hope of one day understanding the apparent strangeness of people too.

Meanwhile Màiri was frantically busy; apart from looking after her new baby she now had two milking cows which allowed her to make cheese and butter from the surplus raw milk, for the family and for sale. She would take her excess butter and cheese on the wagon to Kyle once a month to be sold to local grocers, along with a couple of dozen eggs from her expanding flock of hens. She would pack the eggs carefully in barley straw in a cardboard box and tie it securely to prevent breakages on the rough cart track.

Callum, when he was not exploring the local wildlife, did his best to help his mother. He became Màiri's helpmate and did his best to make her life a little easier. Every morning he would make his own breakfast of brose while Màiri attended to Dougal. He would then fetch a bucket of water from the burn with which to top up the deep-bowled, copper boiler that Mairi kept bubbling all morning in her little, stone-flagged scullery. Along with heaping up the permanent fire in the old cast-iron range Màiri would build a peat fire in the brick grate underneath the 'copper' in the scullery every day when she first got up. Each morning Callum would stagger back from the burn with a heavy bucket of water clutched in both small hands with which to top up the copper, his legs buckling with the strain, often with Jess the young sheepdog running in circles around his legs wanting him to play, while Callum scolded her for getting in the way.

From the age of five onwards he was given what he considered to be his favourite job; feeding the chickens, which he did after breakfast every morning and again in the afternoon. He loved the way they strutted round with a purposeful and self-important gait, "chuurking" to each other as they went about their business, then frantically clucking and squawking as a couple of them would have a spat; the constant business of establishing a pecking order in a flock of twenty-five birds. But most of all he loved the rooster, the browny-red dandy of the flock who strutted around bossing everybody about, pecking at any rebellious hens as he passed. He would flap noisily onto the roof of the coop where he would pose, his chest pushed out, shining black and brown, iridescent, his bright red comb glowing like a bonfire's embers and give out his cock-a-doodle-doo call, just to let everybody know how important he was.

Callum would squat down in the dusty, clawed up earth of the chicken run, observing the hens closely, laughing when they came up to him and pecked him to see what he was and whether he was good to eat or not. He would watch as they pecked about on the ground for the individual creamy, golden grains he had turned out on the ground for them, and they would pick up tiny pieces of grit or sometimes gravel or small stones to keep in their gizzards to help grind up the corn before digesting it. They would chase after beetles or snap at passing flies or tug at turnip tops or the weed leaves that he collected for them.

After this entertainment he would open the flaps to each of the raised laying boxes on the side of the wooden coop and collect the smooth brown and white, porcelain like eggs, often still warm amongst the straw.

If a hen was sitting on the eggs he would gently slide his hand under her, feeling the warm, fluffy down on her feathers as she murmured disapproval with an indignant "chuurrk, chuurk"! He would gently remove and place the eggs in an oval basket woven by his mother from reeds and willow withies, and then carefully carry his haul indoors to show proudly to his Ma. Màiri always praised him highly for his efforts, rewarding him with an, increasingly less well-regarded, kiss on the cheek and sometimes a much preferred oatcake plastered in Màiri's home-produced golden, sweet honey.

One of his favourite pastimes after he had finished his chores was the study of Màiri's bees. She had set up two, white-painted, wooden hives in her little garden behind the house. The beautifully crafted hives had been made for her by Ian McDonald in exchange for a regular supply of eggs.

Callum would sit in front of the hives for hours watching the busy, little striped insects flying this way and that. He would try his best to track them down by running after them and trying to keep up but would fall over things in his rush and couldn't see where he was going for watching the bee. When he couldn't keep up any more he would carry on in the same direction as the bee's flight, negotiating all sorts of objects, searching for the bee at work on a flower.

The problem was, when he found one on a flower, he couldn't know whether it was from one of his mother's hives or not. He could identify it as a typical slim, dark bottomed, honey bee, as opposed to any other kind of bee, but not identify where it came from. It was all very frustrating. He would sit, squatting on the ground with his chin in his hands scrutinising the bee with a frown and sigh of frustration. Jess would lie down next to him also studying the bee with what seemed an equal degree of interest and frustration. But then she would lose patience and leap up, barking at Callum to do something more active, like leaping across the fast flowing burn without getting their paws wet.

Callum had grown into a fit, stocky boy with a mop of black hair that defeated any attempt to tidy it. He wore short, grey, serge trousers, he had two pairs plus one pair for best. The seats of his everyday trousers were always patched and darned where he tore them and wore them out sliding down rocks and grassy slopes, much to Màiri's displeasure. He always managed to be dirty, even within five minutes of being scrubbed from top to toe by Màiri, and somehow apparently, without even moving from the spot. He was a bundle of energy, bright, cheeky and full of fun, a small box of perpetually exploding fireworks, with a keen sense of justice, especially towards other creatures: like his mother he couldn't abide the idea of any creature being hurt or treated cruelly. He could, unusually for a small boy, be still for long periods, just watching; watching the sea or the bobbing cotton grass, studying an insect crawling up a blade of grass or a marsh spider creating a trap of gossamer, or watching the sheep clambering over the high rocks to a juicy patch of alpine meadow. At such times Jess would despair of him, sitting on her haunches and whining in protest.

Callum was a very private boy; he didn't often show his feelings or say what was going on behind his dark brown eyes but he was deeply thoughtful. He spent long hours just pondering on an idea and then ask Màiri "damn fool questions" as she teasingly put it. Occasionally he would sit and intently watch Dougal in his cradle, and then poke him and watch him to see if he moved or reacted in some way and then ask his mother why Dougal didn't do very much, just sleep all day or cry and shout. Her explanation that he was just a baby didn't seem adequate, surely he must have a purpose. Then he would lose interest and dash outside, closely followed by Jess furiously wagging her tail, off on another adventure. He brightened up Màiri's life considerably.

Callum spent his mornings helping his mother and doing his own appointed chores and then, after a midday meal of bread and cheese, or bread and jam, he was free to do whatever he wanted until teatime. He had learnt early on, after a few tumbles and scraped knees, how to negotiate the steep, rocky path down to the cove and he would trek down to the lochside and throw stones into the sea or watch the men going fishing; launching their boats and setting their lobster pots round the deep water near the headland or running out to the deeper waters to cast nets.

Occasionally he would see the magical sparkle of silver out on the loch while keeping vigil on the shore as the fishermen's nets were hauled in and flashing fish spilled out. He would immediately dash up the steep pathways to home and burst in on Màiri announcing; "Silver fishes for tea!" His favourite meal.

Callum, like most of the villagers, was keen on searching the strandline for what the sea brought in, except that he was much easier to please. He marvelled at the empty crab cases and seashells and "shepherd's purses"; the small, black purse-shaped egg cases with curly horns on each corner that drifted, empty and mysterious to the seashore. He sometimes waded into the sea, usually forgetting to take his shoes and socks off, trying to catch the little fishes that swam about in the clear water, though they were always too quick for him. Jess would leap into the water and splash about trying to get him to join her in paddling out into deeper water but Callum couldn't swim and was frightened of the sea beyond the shallow edge. He had nightmares about being dragged down into the deep, dark currents that his mother had warned him about and of never being seen again.

Most of all though, Callum liked to scramble about up on the moors and the slopes above the glen, climbing over dry stone walls and exploring. He would travel as far from the croft as his short, stocky legs would carry him. When he was exhausted he would find a patch of long, dry grass and lay flat on his back in it, gazing up through the stems of waving grasses and wild flowers at the sky. He loved to study the billowing clouds in a blue sky and imagine shapes in them while Jess lay, paws on his chest, panting over him.

Many days though were grey and wet and so he knew all the best places for hiding from the rain. He knew all the overhangs of rock on the lower slopes of the beinn, and if they were caught in the open he knew to rush for shelter and squat behind a dry stone wall on the lee side or dash into one of the little gulleys which ran down the hills and which, protected from browsing sheep, held small trees and bushes for them to crouch under while cuddling up to Jess.

Jess hated rain, she didn't mind getting soaked in the sea and then shaking water over anyone standing nearby, but she hated rain and she would huddle under a bush or behind a wall with Callum, looking up at him beseeching him to make it stop and whining, shivering and looking miserable while Callum told her to stop being so soft. Callum, however didn't mind rain at all and often came home soaking wet to a good scolding from Màiri. Jess meanwhile was usually dry as a bone from dashing off and finding shelter at the first cold drop on her black, shiny nose which, when shelter was found, she would protect with both paws like a pantomime, performing dog.

But Callum's freedom, were he but to know it, was about to be severely curtailed. Now there were two children of school age in the village, Flora was just coming up to five, and the issue of providing schooling was raised amongst the villagers. With more children on the way, and more young children from the other little hamlet down the loch also needing schooling, action was needed and so a meeting was held in the kirk. The old school house, a one-room building of stone and slate, had fallen into disrepair, neglected for the want of pupils and needed rebuilding. Otherwise a new building must be found. John Fraser made clear that the kirk must not be expected to be offered as an alternative, the church fathers would not put up with 'noisy children cluttering up the place, soiling the pews and running up and down the nave', but he did agree to speak to the church authorities and to the new Laird about providing a teacher.

Callum eventually of course heard rumours of the place called "school". He had caught the odd sentence from neighbours speaking in hushed tones round Màiri's dining table and looking over at him in what he thought was a rather strange way. He had begun to understand that "school" was somewhere that grown-ups "sent children" in order to be "educated". He had seen such places in his picture books of course but never realised that *he* might one day be expected to go to one. He wasn't at all sure he even wanted to be "educated". It didn't seem to be much fun in the pictures.

For the next few weeks he tried to be really well behaved and helpful in a vain effort to make himself appear indispensable; so much so that Màiri eventually felt compelled to ask suspiciously;

-"What's wrong with ye Callum, why are ye trying to be so guid? Have ye done something awful that ye're trying tae make up fer?"

-"I dinnae want tae be sent tae that school place, I want tae stay here!" he blurted out suddenly and tearfully, hoping that emotion might win the day.

"Oh Callum! Ye poor wee boy! I did nae ken ye'd picked up anything tae dae with it. We should hae explained it all tae ye. We're going tae build a new school, right here in the village fer all the children. Ye'll gae there every weekday and learn all sorts of useful and interesting things." Màiri said brightly

-"But I already know lots of things' said Callum, 'like how tae feed the chickens an look after them and I know about the insects and bees and -"

-"No not those sorts of things Callum! Things like reading and doing sums and history and geography and the like".

-"But I *can* read, ye showed me all the letters and I dinna need tae dae sums or those other things. I want tae stay here with ye and help oot and take Jess up the hill and -"

-"Well ye can still dae those things Callum but ye can gae tae school as well. Ye'll really like it."

Callum had heard before from adults about what he would and wouldn't like and it seemed to him that adults didn't seem to have the same ideas at all as children did about what was likeable and what was most definitely not.

-"Other children will be there, including Flora' Màiri said, playing her ace card. She knew Callum liked Flora.

-"But I can play with Flora when we go tae Aunt Isla's, I don't need tae go tae a horrible old school tae dae it" he wheedled.

-"It will be a very nice school Callum, and ye'll have a very nice teacher tae look after ye. Now are ye goin tae help me make some oatcakes? Ye like that dae ye no?"

But Callum wasn't to be distracted.

-"Aw Ma, please don't make me gae tae school!" he pleaded "I'll be very good and dae lots of jobs on the croft."

-"Callum!" Màiri said sternly "it's tame ye went tae school. Ye're a big boy now and ye're goin' and that's that!" she finished emphatically, having failed with persuasion and having resorted to parental authority.

Callum knew when his Ma put on her stern face that there was no moving her, so he tried to look really miserable for the rest of the day in the hope that she would feel sufficiently sorry for him and change her mind, which of course she didn't.

The next day he had nearly forgotten about school and he carried on as usual, and the next day, and the next and, after a week, when neither his father nor mother had referred to it, he began to think everybody had forgotten about the whole idea after all. Of course they hadn't, adults aren't like that he was beginning to find. They couldn't see you having fun for too long without putting a stop to it by getting you to do something less enjoyable. So he wasn't too surprised when the subject was raised again.

Màiri said rather pointedly to Hamish one night when they were all having their evening meal;

-"Well, the school's very nearly ready! Ian and the others hae done a really good job."

Callum pretended he hadn't heard and determinedly studied the tabletop. He had decided to ignore any further mention of school and pretend it wasn't happening in the hope it would go away.

Ian McDonald, as village carpenter, had taken on the building of the school with the help of other men from the two villages, notably John Fraser's two sons and two young fishermen from 'doon the loch'. The estate had provided building materials which had been transported in the village's cart, pulled by the two great Clydesdales. Local stone was collected from around the village to build the walls and, within three months, the village had a two-roomed school with a smaller room attached for the schoolteacher to use to store all her materials and as a small study.

Simple desks and benches for the pupils to sit on had been made under Ian McDonald's instruction and a fine chair and desk for the schoolteacher had been brought in from the estate's offices. Some of the women from both villages had made and hung curtains at the windows and had provided a cushion stuffed with sheep's wool for the schoolteacher's comfort. The church provided schoolbooks; and paper, pencils and other materials along with a blackboard and, lastly, the estate provided a schoolteacher who would reside at a cottage on the estate.

The schoolteacher was a young lady called Miss Pargeter who was the daughter of a shopkeeper in Kyle of Lochalsh. She had been trained as a schoolteacher in Edinburgh and had returned to work in the little town as an assistant teacher in the town's primary school. She was attractive in a rather elegant and severe way, tall and slim with long dark-hair which was always held up in a bun or drawn up onto the top of her head. She was a strongly independent woman and, as Callum was soon to discover, was also very strict. She always wore a dark grey or navy blue suit to school with a crisp, white, high button-collared blouse and thick dark stockings.

On Monday, the sixth of September 1926 Miss Pargeter stood outside her new little school at five to nine waiting proudly for the schoolchildren to arrive. Callum's school-life was about to begin. Each of the children brought to the new school by their mothers had been scrubbed and tidied up, dressed in their Sunday best clothes and told to behave themselves at the new school or there would be trouble. The mothers of the unfortunate children had led them by the hand to the school from their various locations. Three children were coming from the little hamlet at the end of the loch. Callum and Flora, both protesting loudly, were led along the main path to the little school which was at the far end of the village from Callum's home.

On arrival, Isla and Màiri stood by the little cropped green in front of the schoolhouse which would serve as a playground, each holding the hand of their child. There had been tantrums and tears when Callum had discovered, with outrage and disbelief that, not only was he being made to go to school but that he couldn't take Jess to school with him. He simply couldn't believe it. "Why?" he had demanded in a genuinely mystified and affronted tone. Màiri had tried to explain as simply as she could why dogs didn't go to school with their children and why the schoolteacher wouldn't allow it. Callum was appalled; his already low opinion of school was now also applied to the teacher: someone who didn't allow dogs to go to school with their children companions had to be an ogre. He tried everything; tantrums, sulking, tears and pleading but Màiri, feeling more and more fraught and unsettled about sending her beloved first child to school, had just had to remain firm and try not to show how upsetting she found it all. When they arrived at the school he was still sulking belligerently; chin out, eyes sparking with righteous anger, lower lip protruding, arms defiantly folded, deliberately looking straight ahead, wordless and radiating indignation.

Small, plump Flora didn't look any happier. Short for her age, stocky, with her mother's blonde hair, which, like Callum's defied any attempt to tidy it, she looked as defiant and truculent as Callum. Màiri could see that Isla had also had a hard time of it this morning. They looked at each other and sighed, both were close to tears and doing their best to hide it. The upset of having to make their reluctant children go to school and the prospect of leaving them there, separated from them for the first time in their short lives, made them both feel as if they were somehow abandoning them. The three mothers from the other hamlet down at the end of the loch came into view, past Signal Rock and the Devil's

Nose, walking briskly, children trailing miserably behind; two boys and a girl.

Màiri knew that the little sister community at the other end of the loch lived in real poverty but nonetheless was shocked at the extent to which that was now made so visible. The land there was even poorer than in the glen and they had less of it. They had a few sheep and cows and grew a few crops, but mainly survived through fishing. The only money they made was when they took a lamb or calf to market which wasn't very often, and by selling dried or salted fish at rock-bottom prices. By the time they had paid the carter there usually wasn't much left.

The mothers were dressed simply in their best clothes which, nonetheless had clearly been mended a few times, and one of the women had only a thin, ragged shawl around her shoulders rather than a coat, despite the chill of the morning. The women had thin, pinched, white faces, lined with worry, worn down by hard toil and not enough to eat: Màiri was shaken. They rarely saw these people nowadays, the war had upset their previous pattern of neighbourliness. The other community mainly kept themselves to themselves and, as they were Catholics, didn't attend the kirk. The last time Màiri had seen them was a few years ago and they had looked a lot healthier and better off. She knew they had suffered the awful tragedy of losing a couple of boats at sea and, even worse, the men in them, and their grievous loss was telling. She berated herself for her neglect and ignorance of their predicament.

She smiled in greeting and called out;

-"Deagh là!"

One of the group called back;

-"Guid morning Màiri!"

Màiri didn't recognise her at first, but then realised that it was Moira McGregor; she had been to school with her but she looked more like forty than in her late twenties. Màiri was taken aback at how the young woman had aged so quickly: things must be harder than she thought down at the end of the loch. She was suddenly ashamed, she should have known; they had lost three of their fittest men from an already reduced population as a a result of the war, and they had lost half their boats, their main means of making a living, albeit a poor one. She resolved to try and help but she knew it wouldn't be easy. The communities were far more distant in many ways other than the few miles between them suggested, especially in terms of religion which was a live issue in these parts and of course they were proud people, sensitive to their own poverty and to others reactions to their state.

The religious issue could present Màiri with a real barrier to re-establishing co-operation with this neighbouring community. Many protestants still looked on Catholics as being idolaters and traitorous atheists and many catholics looked on Protestants with enmity in return. John Fraser had had real problems persuading the church authorities to accept these Catholic children at school, and it was a testimony to his generosity and his powers of persuasion that they had been allowed at the school at all.

The three children looked clean and tidy but their clothes were well darned and patched and their shoes were well worn and most likely had holes in the soles. The little girl was obviously the youngest of the three, she had dark hair tied in pigtails and a little dark bonnet on her head, her face was fixed in a sulk and she was dressed in a cut-down, home-made skirt, cheap blouse and home knitted jumper, that had faded over time and had clearly been passed on by another mother. The two boys both looked about six years old, they also had dark hair, one black, one red, roughly cut and both wore cut-down adult suits in black serge that were too large for them. They both wore large flat caps with greasy rims and worn peaks.

They looked awkward and stiff and were shuffling their feet, and the larger boy spat on the floor and immediately got a hard slap on the head and a sharp reproach from his mother. Màiri and Isla winced. The woman seemed to be the oldest of the group and her face was deeply lined and had a sour look; her mouth set in a tight, grim line. All three women had the pale pallor and dark rings round the eyes that told of grinding poverty and perennial weariness. Moira's boy was thinner and shorter than the beefy, tough looking one who had spat on the ground. He had short, reddish, curly hair and, though sulking like the rest. His sharp, intelligent eyes darted this way and that showing a quick interest in everything that was going on. His mop of curly hair and blue eyes gave him a cheeky look somehow. Màiri thought he was probably quite a handful. He was standing in front of Moira who was affectionately and lightly resting an arm across his chest as he peered shyly out at Màiri and Callum.

-"I see ye've a new bairn now Màiri!" Moira observed.

Màiri had little Dougal strapped to her front, the way she used to carry Callum.

-"Aye, he's a bonny wee lad, nae trouble at all" said Màiri.

-"I wish I could say the same for this one" said Moira, whipping off the boy's cap and ruffling his hair affectionately. The boy looked up at his mother and smirked, then remembered he was supposed to be sulking and adjusted his face accordingly.

-"How are ye managin' now Moira? It must have been a bitter blow losing yer menfolk like that!" said Màiri, then immediately regretted it, thinking it too direct a question and knew it would sound as if she were prying or worse.

-"We're managin' Mrs!" abruptly cut in the older woman, mother of the big, surly looking boy.

Màiri felt a stab of remorse at the rebuke, for rebuke it surely was.

-"Oh I'm sorry Màiri, forgive me, I've no introduced ma friends!" Moira intervened, trying to change the direction of the conversation and forestall a confrontation.

-"This is Morag McLennan!" She indicated the older woman, and then, in turn, pointed to the mother of the little girl who seemed to be a shy, unconfident young woman;

-"This is Lizzie, Lizzie Robertson!"

Lizzie gave a shy little smile before looking down at her shoes again, her small girl was standing in front of her, acting as a sort of defensive screen.

-"Perhaps ye'll all come up fer tea afterwards?" suggested Màiri tentatively, trying to make amends and again attempting to make some connection with the women.

-"We need tae be gettin back thank ye very much!" said Morag shortly, in a tone which made clear to Màiri that the invitation was unwelcome.

-"Mebbe another time thanks Màiri" said Moira rather sheepishly.

Isla decided that she would also try to extend the hand of friendship, despite Morag's obvious hostility.

-"Morag McLennan? Isn't yer older sister married tae ma uncle Hughie McDonald, over in Applecross?" she asked, looking perhaps to establish some distant kinship with the woman.

-"Aye, she is. I did nae realise he had a relative in these pairts though. He's a good enough husband I'll gie him that. And nae damn Proddy either!" and then, realising she had overstepped the mark in raising religion so openly she said,

-"Forgive me, I did nae wish tae sound ruid!" She was at least trying now to be a little conciliatory.

-"Ach! We're all the same under the skin Morag are we not?" asked Isla, boldly, green fire sparking in her eyes momentarily, challenging Morag, who clearly thought no such thing but couldn't really say so now without sounding as if she were being churlish.

-"Aye, mebbe" she said in an unconvincing manner.

-"We'll be having a Hairst Hame next month -- perhaps ye and the rest of yer people will join us? It'd be good to get together again, like the two communities used tae. Unless ye've already planned something yersels?" Màiri asked hopefully.

She was referring to a time before the war when both communities would come together once a year for a celebration, usually at harvest time, but occasionally at Hogmanay too. It was a time when they had also co-operated by working together at key times during the farming year, such as when gathering the sheep in off the hills and in bringing the crops in. With most of the men being away in the services during the war the celebrations and working co-operation had petered out and by then, people had moved on, men were lost in the war, connections lost. Nonetheless, the offer was difficult to refuse outright, given that there was an established tradition of coming together not too long ago.

-"That would be grand wouldn't it?" Moira replied quickly, before Morag could think of a reason to turn down the offer.

-"Aye weel, we'll see what the others in the village think furst. But thank ye fer the offer Mrs MacDonald" Morag said circumspectly. "Jest now I think the teacher is waiting fer the bairns" she added quickly, trying to cut off the conversation.

-"I'll come up tae see ye and let ye know Màiri; when we've managed tae talk with the others" said Moira, determined not to let the offer be forgotten.

She too it was clear wished to reach out to the other community and she smiled warmly at Màiri and Isla. Then the women escorted the children over to the teacher who was waiting by the little porchway to the school.

-"Good morning ladies! I'm Miss Pargeter the teacher" she greeted them "It's lovely to meet you all."

Each woman in turn introduced herself and her child, with Màiri and Isla following the others.

-"Thank you ladies" Miss Pargeter said when she had met everyone.

After a moment she said;

-"I'll take the children now if I may!" in a polite and cheerful manner to the still lingering parents and very reluctant children.

-"Come on children!" she said brightly, beckoning the children and then reaching out a welcoming hand to the small, dark little girl who was shyly clinging to her mother's skirt.

-"Now put your hats and scarves and any other outdoor clothing on the hooks in the lobby please children! She indicated the porch, forestalling any extended goodbyes from the mothers. She knew what a fraught situation it was for them all.

Except for Morag McLennan the mothers all looked apprehensive and tearful as they said their goodbyes to their children. Callum quickly spun away as his mother went to kiss him goodbye. It would be embarrassing to be seen being kissed by his Ma in front of the other boys. Flora just gave an exaggerated, theatrical sigh and shrugged her shoulders as her mother kissed her and then turned to Callum and raised her eyes in a look of patient resignation. He shrugged as well and sighed audibly and the two shuffled into school for the very first time. Màiri and Isla held out until they reached Isla's croft and then sat down to tea before they both shed tears.

Miss Pargeter explained to the children that they should call her "Miss" or "Miss Pargeter" and always to use either of them if they wished to address her. She explained where the toilets were, one for the boys and one for the girls and told them that they must raise a hand and ask her if they wished to go during lessons but that they should make sure they go at break times. At the end of break time when she rang the bell they must all stop still and be silent. When she told them to they must all form a queue and enter the school in a quiet and "orderly fashion". They must not talk in class unless she gave them permission. Callum thought that school didn't at all sound as if he would enjoy it very much.

Next Miss Pargeter took the register and they all had to call out their full names. Callum discovered that the big boy was called William but he said it was really Billy; the little girl was called Fiona and the curly, red-headed boy was called Alistair.

-"Now!" said Miss Pargeter "were all going to do letters!" and she wrote the alphabet in chalk on the blackboard in big capital letters, sounding out each one carefully as she did so, and then asked the children to say them after her as she pointed to each in turn. Then she told them to copy them with the paper and pencils she handed out to them. Callum was soon bored and started playing with his pencil. He already knew his letters; his Ma had shown him how to do them. He began tapping the pencil on the desk and poking the blunt end up his nose, at which point he was told off severely by the teacher and decided that he liked school even less. It looked as though it was going to be a long day for everybody.

The classroom smelt of wax polish and newly sawn wood and an indefinable sense of stale air. Callum gazed longingly out of the windows at the soaring clifftops, the dull grey sky and scudding clouds and imagined himself running through the cotton grass up on the high moors with Jess cantering beside him.

After what seemed an age, and what Callum thought were more very boring tasks, Miss Pargeter said;

-"Now put your things away in your nice new desks children and you may go outside for a quarter of an hour's break!" At which there was a clattering of desks lids and the children rushed to the door with a thundering of boots and shoes and audible sighs of relief.

-"Mind you stay in the play area!" called out Miss Pargeter to their departing backs and she followed them out in order to supervise their first playtime.

The children didn't know what to do at first and stood around, gaze lowered, shy and awkward in this new situation, but then Alistair suggested they play horses and they all followed him in galloping around the large patch of well-mown grass in that odd, loping sort of trot that children seemed to universally understand passes for the motion of a horse. Fiona couldn't quite manage the motion and tripped herself up after a while. Alistair then deliberately fell down as well and rolled around on the grass and, for want of something better to do, all the other children followed him.

-"Let's make a daisy chain!" suggested Flora and dropped down on the grass to begin earnestly picking daisies.

-"That's a lass's game!" said Billy contemptuously and Callum, who had been about to join Flora, turned away and faced the two boys instead, he didn't want to mocked for playing a girl's game and instinctively realised that he needed to establish his position with the other boys.

-"What shall we dae Billy?" asked Alastair.

Billy didn't know so the boys stood around and kicked the ground with their toecaps while Fiona and Flora carried on making daisy chains, chatting brightly to each other.

-"We'll play sodjers" said Billy after a few minutes

-"Alright!" said Callum, not really knowing what a soldiers game was.

-"We'll be Highlanders an ye be a red coat!" said Billy pointing to Callum; the shadow of Culloden still hung heavily over the Highlands.

-"I dinnae want tae be nae red coat" said Callum defiantly.

-"Ye will tae!" said Billy emphatically

-"Wont!" said Callum,

"Will!" said Billy "or I'll punch ya!" Billy pushed his chin out and sniffed defiantly at Callum.

-"Won't" said Callum hesitantly, a little less sure of himself now.

-"Will!" said Billy, and he punched Callum on the chest, hard, screwing his eyes up and taking up an aggressive, boxing stance as if preparing for a contest.

Callum was astonished "Why should Billy punch him?" he mused. Seeing no reaction Billy punched him again, on the chin this time, though he almost missed and the blow glanced harmlessly off.

Callum thought hard, his Ma had always said he mustn't hit people, but if he didn't do anything he presumed that Billy would probably carry on hitting him.

-"Won't!" said Callum and screwed up his courage to punch Billy on the nose, to show he meant business.

By now Miss Pargeter, who was squatting down making daisy chains having joined the two little girls, had noticed the aggressive turn of events.

-"Boys!" She said crossly "Stop that at once!" She stood up and advanced on them, looking very cross.

-"I will not have fighting at my school! Do you understand?" she said angrily. She was now towering over the two boys, looking from one to the other and held a firm hand on each boys shoulder to prevent any more aggression.

-"Yes Miss!" They both said reluctantly and sulkily.

-"Now, Callum MacDonald, say sorry to Billy!" said Miss Pargeter.

Callum was beginning to understand that when adults called him by his full name it meant they were pretty cross with him.

-"But Miss it --." He started to say that it was Billy who had started it but Miss Pargeter didn't give him the chance to finish.

-"I don't want any excuses! You were fighting and I won't have it! Now say sorry!"

Callum sighed and said sorry to Billy.

-"Now Billy, you say sorry to Callum" demanded Miss Pargeter.

-"Sorry Callum" mumbled Billy in that dull, formulaic voice children adopt for acquiescing to teachers demands.

-"Good! Now shake hands and be friends again!" she said firmly.

Callum held his hand out and Billy took it and they shook hands vigorously as boys are supposed to do. Callum noticed Billy had a sticky hand.

-"Good, now play nicely!" she said "and the next time I find either of you fighting I will spank you and tell your mothers".

Callum thought he had a good idea what spanking was and he didn't fancy that. As for telling his Ma, he knew that could only lead to a lot of grief for him, so he resolved not to be caught doing it again; which was slightly different from not actually doing it again.

After Miss Pargeter had gone back to the little girls Billy's nose started to bleed. Callum was horrified, "Had he done that?" Billy didn't seem too concerned and put his finger in his nostril to stop it. Callum pulled out the square of torn sheet from his pocket that his mother had given him for a handkerchief and offered it to Billy.

-"Thanks Cal" Billy said snuffily and rubbed his nose with it.

-"Don't let teacher see!" whispered Alistair loudly.

Billy and Callum turned away from the teacher and nonchalantly wandered off to the edge of the grass.

-"That was a guid punch Cal!" said Billy admiringly to Callum.

-"Thanks, they were pretty good punches you gave me too Billy!" said Callum, who didn't have any previous experience to go on.

-"Teacher was really cross!" said Alistair breathlessly.

But Billy said in a worldly sort of way; - "That's the way teachers are Ali, ma uncle Hughie says they're cross all the tame!"

Callum and Alistair nodded in a sage sort of way, recognising the wisdom inherent in the statement.

Miss Pargeter had gone indoors and collected a large, shiny, silver bell which she was now ringing enthusiastically.

-"Silence children, stand still!" she ordered "Stop what you're doing now!'

The children froze at the teacher's natural command of authority. Then they dutifully filed back indoors, heads lowered, any previous expectations of an extended freedom curtailed.

-"Well done children! said Miss Pargeter when they were all seated quietly.

-"Now we are going to do some numbers!"

Billy groaned, Callum put his hands on his head in a despairing gesture and pulled a grimacing kind of face.

-"Callum, stop pulling faces, if the wind changes you'll be stuck like that!"

Callum was mystified, there wasn't any wind indoors!

-"And Billy, that's enough groaning from you!" the teacher said sharply.

The long day crawled on. At lunchtime the three children from the other village were allowed to eat the lunches they had brought with them while sitting at their desks while Callum and Flora went home for theirs. Callum held Flora's hand on their way home, as the other boys weren't around to see, just until she got to the path up to her croft and then he ran all way back to his house: halfway there he was greeted by a racing ball of black and white fluff, tail wagging furiously and barking crazily.

-"Hello Jess!" He greeted her joyfully burying his face in her fur and stroking her roughly. The two ran back to the croft and burst through the front door noisily.

Màiri, who had been miserably fretting about Callum all morning, greeted him warmly and gave him a big hug.

-"Hello Callum, did you enjoy your first morning at school?" she asked.

-"No, it was horrible!" he said firmly.

-"Oh dear!" She said "didn't you do anything interesting?" she said sympathetically.

-"Nope!" He said off-handedly.

-"What did you do then? she asked, trying to sound interested.

-"Just sums and letters an things" he said dismissively "boring things like that" he added.

-"Oh well, they are very important but perhaps you'll do something that's more fun this afternoon" she said helpfully.

-"Don't 'spect so!" He said dismissively.

He held out no expectations of school ever actually being fun.

-"Well wash your hands and then eat your meal" she said, changing the subject despairingly with a sigh.

In the afternoon the children spent time painting and drawing and Miss Pargeter praised Callum's painting of Jess chasing a rabbit in a field, although she'd had to ask what the round blob was and anyone could see it was a rabbit. Billy had painted a big round, pink and black blob standing next to what was supposed to be a house.

-"And who's this Billy?" Miss Pargeter asked him.

-"It's me ma" he said.

-"And what's this she's holding -- is it her broom? Miss Pargeter asked brightly.

"Naw it's her bum-stick!" he said, as if that were obvious.

Callum sniggered.

-"Callum, stop sniggering!" ordered Miss Pargeter sharply; "Now Billy that is a naughty word, don't ever let me hear it again!" she said sternly.

-"Now, what's the stick for Billy?" she asked again, rather unwisely.

-"I told you miss it's a --"

But Miss Pargeter stopped him abruptly, "Don't say it again Billy!" she snapped, despairingly, "It's a very nice picture Billy!" she said and moved on swiftly to Flora, who seemed to have covered herself in brightly coloured, powder paint in the process of doing a very red painting.

When Callum got home that afternoon he claimed to be "tired out" and declared school even more horrible than he had at first thought. Màiri sighed and sympathised and pointed out that everybody had to go to school, and that she had gone to the old school in the village when she was his age and she had got to quite enjoy it. None of which of course convinced Callum to like it any more or to feel any the less put out at having been made to go.

Nevertheless, against his will, Callum gradually did begin to enjoy school. He enjoyed the company of Alistair and Fiona and of course Flora and even, most of the time Billy, and, against his better instincts, he began to like Miss Pargeter. She made some school subjects seem interesting and rewarded the pupils with fulsome praise and gave them all lots of encouragement, even if she was a bit strict. Alongside the more academic lessons and the lessons he didn't enjoy very much they played interesting games and did PE outside, even if it was in their underwear; which Callum found a bit embarrassing at first but as it got them out of the classroom he soon forgot about it. Most of all though she taught them about nature and about the world around them which she made them see with a completely different eye.

Each afternoon, while the children were still small, they would be encouraged to have a short sleep. Miss Pargeter would pull the pretty curtains that had been made and hung by the women of the village and the children would be told not to talk and to fold their arms on their desks and to lay their heads on their arms and have a rest. Miss Pargeter would sit at the front and quietly do whatever she did with her pen and pieces of paper while they all slept for half an hour. Callum noticed that Billy snored a lot but mostly he fell asleep too.

Best of all from Callum's point of view the children were taken by Miss Pargeter once a week for a nature walk: Callum particularly enjoyed these walks, especially since he was able to point things out to Miss Pargeter which made him feel knowledgeable and important.

If it wasn't raining, winter or summer, snow on the ground or not, Miss Pargeter would take the children out into the glen and the surrounding area and this continued for all the time Callum was at the school. If the weather was too bad they would stay in the classroom and Miss Pargeter would hand round found objects for them all to study and discuss; objects like crumbly leaves from the trees, or spiky pine cones or colourful flowers in a little vase, which Billy would sometimes spill because he was a bit clumsy. She would ask the children if they could identify the object and what they knew of it and then she would tell them all she knew about it. Sometimes she would also show them pictures of animals, including those from far away like lions and elephants and exotic birds and tell them all about them as well. Callum was quite good at identifying the flowers and birds and animals but not so good at trees because they didn't have that many in the glen.

Best of all though were the nature walks. As the school filled up over the next few years Miss Pargeter would take as many as a dozen children into the fields or down to the cove, or follow the paths up the hills or over the moors. She always made their finds interesting and communicated her enthusiasm for nature to all of them. She used nature as a way of teaching them about the world and the way it worked; about life and death when they found a dead animal or bird and how the tides worked when they were on the seashore, or about the age of the rocks when they studied the cliffs and the stones on the shoreline. In summer she told them about the golden sun and how, as a ball of gas and fire, it worked to warm the world, and in the winter when it was dark before they went home and, when the sky was cloudless, she taught them about the moon and the stars shining bright and clear in the crackling, velvet black skies of the glen. She coloured a world of wonder and mystery for them all.

Many years later Callum would look back on these times and still marvel at the wonder of the world about them and the world beyond the glen that Miss Pargeter had so strongly inculcated in him and all of the children while on these walks. And he would remember it as being amongst the happiest and most absorbing of all his times while living in this very special place.

They also collected objects while on these walks; things which they found interesting or beautiful and every week Miss Pargeter or the children themselves would bring in objects to put on the nature table which she had set up at the side of the classroom, by the windows. Soon the table was overflowing onto the windowsills. There were dried flowers; pretty stones, different shaped leaves, the whitened bones of small, dead animals, colourful seashells, empty red-brown crab shells and the shiny black, mysterious shepherds purses.

Once Billy had brought in a rotting rabbit carcase which he had found on the walk to school. Callum wasn't sure whether he had done it as a prank to shock the teacher or whether he was serious, but Miss Pargeter was unperturbed. She called his bluff, if bluff it were; she asked Callum to ask his Daddy's permission for him to bring a spade to school when he went home for his lunch, or "luncheon" as she called it in her polite Edinburgh educated accent. That afternoon she buried the rabbit with the children watching and she said they would dig it up in a few weeks when the worms and other creatures in the soil had stripped the bones so that they could study the skeleton and keep it for their nature table. There was much mock disgust and pretend shuddering from the children. The attitude which she showed towards this event gained Miss Pargeter a great deal of respect from the children, not once had she shown any squeamishness, just a lively curiosity and sympathy the dead creature.

When Callum got home that evening he said to his mother,

-"Flippin' heck! Miss says I've got to take that heavy old spade back again in a few weeks!" Callum quite liked the phrase 'flippin' heck!' it sounded good, Billy had taught it to him along with a few other words and phrases, some of which he had discovered were definitely not allowed; his mother had banned him in no uncertain terms from ever using them again. He had asked her why but all she would say was that they were "bad words" and that he would find himself with "a thick ear" if he repeated them. Callum didn't know what a "thick ear" was but he was pretty sure he wouldn't like it. Màiri had wanted to know why he had to take a spade back to school in a few weeks time, and when Callum told her what it was for, it was a tribute to her respect for the teacher and of Màiri 's broadmindedness that her reaction was only a slightly shocked surprise.

Of course the children wouldn't let the rabbit lie. After a week their impatience to see what was happening to the rabbit under the ground was greater than the fear of any reprimand if "Miss" found out. Billy, the oldest of the children was of course the first to try. He picked up a stick on the way to school one day, the children from the little hamlet were now allowed to walk to school unaccompanied, and he had saved it to use as a digging stick in order to disinter the rabbit. The stick was about a foot long with peeling bark and about an inch thick, where it had broken off at one end it was jagged and pointed; just right for digging. When he got to school he hid the stick to use later. Billy, the oldest of the children, wasn't very bright for his age but he was always canny.

At break time the children rushed to the corner of their little playing field where the rabbit had been buried and, while the others kept an eye out for "Miss", Billy started scratching at the ground with the retrieved stick. It didn't take him long to disinter the unfortunate rabbit as it had only been lightly covered. The body was heaving with maggots; the carcass moved in some terrible mockery of life as tiny, shiny white creatures swarmed inside and out: worms and insects joined in the feeding frenzy. The fur coat was still largely intact, stiffened with age and sloughed off the bones. What remained of the rotting flesh which had become dark brown and a sour, livid scarlet where it had been prised away from the ivory white bones. The children looked on in fascination, squatting down over the crawling mass;

-"Oooh look at the maggits!" cried Fiona

-"And the 'sects and worms!" trilled Flora

Billy poked the carcass with the stick, maggots and black, shiny-cased beetles spilled out in a rush.

-"Eugh!" exclaimed Alastair.

Callum thought it was sad for the poor rabbit to end up this way. It somehow felt wrong to be poring over it so ghoulishly,

-"It's 'scustin!" said Billy.

The children were revolted but fascinated and excited by their grisly find.

Callum noticed the empty eye socket, the eye had already gone, "It's bin 'et" Billy had said. A black beetle poked around in the centre of the dark socket, looking like a glinting, horrific parody of a pupil. It flipped over on to its round back, all six legs frantically wriggling to right itself.

-"How long d'ye think it'll be before only the skellington is left?" asked Billy.

But before anyone could hazard a guess, Alistair, who was keeping an eye out the teacher hissed hoarsley;

-"Miss is coming, quick!"

The children's scuffed the soil back over the carcass with their feet as they stood up, and then tried to look innocent.

-"Children, move away from there, leave that rabbit alone! It's not time to disinter it yet." Miss Pargeter called out.

The children wandered away, trying to feign indifference but bursting with excitement and frustration and some of them a little disturbed by what they had seen. Alistair tried to whistle nonchalantly, pretending innocence but he wasn't very good at whistling as he had lost some of his front teeth and it came out as a blow rather than a note. Callum still saw that eye socket and he shuddered. It was something he wouldn't forget easily.

School-life continued as it had begun, excitement and interest filling in between the tedium of learning basic knowledge and rehearsing basic skills. Callum nonetheless found himself, almost against his will gaining a thirst for knowledge and his fascination with a wider world deepened. The years passed, Callum became more involved with the work of the croft as he became older.

His father started taking him with him when he went up the hill to check the sheep. His father wouldn't say that much to him but it was a comfortable silence between them, punctuated by occasional work-focused comments:

-"That young hog's looking a wee bit lame Pa!"

-"Aye son let's have a look at him, you take the head" and they would go about the well-practised business of holding and checking the ewes and the lambs. Or they would milk the cows together and clean out the byre; take hay out to the in-bye fields in winter or sow barley and oats in the dark soil together in spring.

Callum also carried on with his own chores; looking after the chickens, collecting the eggs, fetching water for his Ma and, when necessary, looking after little Dougal. The last was his least favourite task. He would always do it sulkily and reluctantly;

-"Aw Ma, not agin, he does nae dae anything, he jest sits there an' wails!"

-"He would no wail if ye kept him amused Cal!" Màiri would say in return.

When Dougal was learning to walk Jess was fascinated by him. She would nuzzle him and lick his face and Dougal would shriek with pleasure and throw his small plump arms around her and Jess would support him as the two staggered round the floor. Jess was a lot more patient and tolerant of Dougal than Callum.

Hamish however was all this time developing ever blacker moods; he was having deeper, dark periodic slumps into a world of misery, anxiety and self-loathing. At such times Callum, like Màiri, had learnt to be patient and sympathetic and wait, sometimes weeks, until the moods finally left him. Callum didn't understand why his father would suddenly become like this. It saddened and confused him and he worried about it, despite Màiri telling him not to; but then she worried terribly about Hamish as well. And she worried about Callum and the affect his father's suffering would have on his childhood. But Callum still saw his father through a child's eyes and had a young child's enormous capacity to adapt to most things given enough love and understanding, and he still had an enormous capacity for forgiveness and for the acceptance of flaws in others.

Despite, or maybe because of all this, Màiri still found time to trek out into the wild surroundings within whose shadows and lightness their lives ebbed and flowed. Sometimes she would carry Dougal with her, sometimes she was alone and sometimes with Callum. Callum loved these walks together, spending this time alone with his mother. He was fascinated by what he found around him and by the things his mother pointed out. He was at an age when everything was still new and held a special magic. That magic would inevitably fray and fragment as he became older and experience took the gloss of freshness and suspended disbelief off his perceptions, as it did for everyone. But for now, even the suffering of his father, though it saddened him greatly, couldn't take away the wonder at his highland world and his joy of small things. Perhaps later he would become older and wiser and learn not to trust such magic, as most do, perhaps have to do. But for now the world was still a special place to be explored with all his senses at full tilt, thin-skinned and full-blasted.

When he was eight he experienced with his mother, a place that, forever afterwards, wherever he was in the world, he could return to in his mind's eye; whenever he was low or in crisis he could summon it up, a nourishing and calming presence. It was as if, along with the love of his mother and his belonging to the glen and to those who lived there, this special place anchored him, gave him a core of serenity and certainty which would always be there for him, even in the deepest, bitterest chasms of despair.

In her most terrible days: when her athair had died and again when her màthair died and when, heartbreakingly, her daughter, who never was, died, Màiri had gone to this place, not to mourn them but to remember them. Days or weeks after the event she would find herself there. And, when Hamish began to experience his periods of dark gloom she had come here to think about it and to seek comfort, which she always found. Now she sensed it was time for Callum to know it and that she should act as his guide.

It lay a hard two hour's walk along the lochside, towards the sea, a direction rarely taken by anyone else, beyond the end of the road, beyond the last glen on the road, their glen. With Màiri leading, they followed a track, lightly worn but distinct at first; away from the croft and the little village. The track kept them about a hundred and fifty feet above the water most of the way. It took them over rocky outcrops and tough, sparse grassy patches, then over hillside folds whose green slopes swept towards low cliffs; wildflowers and startled birds claimed their attention as they went. The path quickly became more and more barely discernible. It was mostly made by wild animals; by red deer or badgers, foxes or martens, and occasional gillies tracking the deer, or else by night-time poachers on moonless nights, trekking out to streams where they knew the salmon ran. Sometimes the path disappeared altogether, but Màiri knew the way so well that she could find it in heavy mist or darkness if need be, having visited often since the time when, as a small girl, her mother used to take her there. Now, taking Callum there for his first time, she again felt a little of that first excitement, that small girl's sweet memory of a place out of time.

To their right, in the distance, lay the hills of Wester Ross and ahead lay the sparkling Inner Sound, for now hidden amongst rocky outcrops and the morning's pale, soft mist. It was about half past eight in the morning on a late spring day, the slight sea breeze fanning down the loch kept the first swarms of Scottish midgies at bay, hidden down in the grass. The black, vicious, biting flies were the myriad torturing imps of a Highland summer and reached plague proportions most years. But for now the sun and the breeze were beginning to disperse the sea fret and it drifted in ragged tufts down off the hills and settled towards the loch where it lingered awhile, casting deep, wide shadows over the clear, shimmering waters peeping through.

After an hour or so the sun was high and becoming strong. Climbing and scrambling up the path became hard, hot work. They stopped at a spring that burst out of the flanks of a rocky outcrop and tumbled across their path in a gully, before it careered down the hillside towards the cliffs in a bubbling, frothy stream. Cupping their hands they drank deeply of the sweet, cold, sharp water, numbing their lips and the tips of their tongues. They relished the refreshingly cold taste and stood awhile looking out over the glittering loch which now shone silver-blue in the bright sunshine. Màiri adjusted the canvas bag on her shoulder that carried their lunch; a roast chicken leg each from one of Callum's pullets, the death of which, along with the death of any other farm animal grown for food, Callum accepted philosophically but with sadness. They also had a chunk of barley bread and cheese and a hard-boiled egg, also a gift from Callum's hens. The rest Màiri would forage for when they reached their destination.

With renewed energy they headed off up the path and past a rocky outcrop that the now almost non-existent path skirted around. As they climbed sharply they reached the highest point on their trek. At about five hundred feet they were met by a broad panorama of land and sea dropping away and opening out in front of them. Ahead of them they could see a vast circle of dark, rocky land where it met a deep, cobalt blue and emerald sea, beyond which were pools of mists and rocky islands in glittering sunshine and then another enormous expenses of shining sea stretching as far as the Outer Hebrides and beyond. Islands dotted the entire seascape, shimmering in a heat haze, bathed in sun, the whole scene transported them out into the soft morning air. For a moment they felt like gods or eagles perched atop a high eyrie. They stood awestruck;

-"I never cease thirsting after that view Cal; storm or mist, sun or gloom, even dreich it looks like another world!" Màiri whispered, the wonder sounding in her voice.

Callum stood quietly, drinking it in, he had never seen so much sky, so much sea, he let it seep into him: it tasted in his mind of a glinting, sweet, golden liquid, filling his senses.

They trekked on for another hour, gradually coming back downhill, coming closer to the level of the loch, but still a couple of hundred feet above it. The path drew near a barbed-wire fence marking the boundary of the estate. Nearly two hours of walking Màiri thought and still within reach of the damned estate,

-"How much of Scotland dae these people want tae own?" demanded Màiri angrily, kicking a fence post as she said it.

The whole estate was a vast acreage, tens of thousands of acres, a sizeable bite out of the Scottish Highland, hereditary lands that only the Scottish Crown and the clans had once owned, much of it had belonged to no one at all. And this damned Englishman, a rich Sassenach, rarely visited the place. It was held and looked after by his local servants, the rightful owners, for his occasional pleasure and that of his wealthy, spoiled friends. The injustice and appalling greed made her furious, she could feel the sour taste of it in her mouth.

She stomped on angrily, Callum struggling to keep up. After a couple of hundred yards later she called out.

-"Stop Callum! I see something on the fence."

She could see a dark brown flapping shape in the distance, hanging down against a fence post. She sincerely hoped it wasn't what she thought it was and she swallowed nervously. She hurried up to it, telling Callum to stay back, but he followed out of curiosity. As she approached she slowed down and walked more carefully and quietly: it was as she had feared.

A large, brown and pale tan bird was fluttering upside down. Its wings were flapping weakly and spasmodically and it was clearly in great distress. She recognised it as a buzzard, a mature male, slightly smaller than the female but still a big powerful bird: except this one wasn't very powerful any more. She slid her bag carefully and slowly off the shoulder, so as not to startle the bird. She could see it was caught in a vicious pole-trap, a ghastly, cast-iron, sprung trap with toothed jaws and a sensitive touch plate that was secured to the top of a post, waiting for a bird to alight, especially a buzzard, which were fond of post-sitting. When the bird touched down it would be caught viciously and firmly by the legs. The force of the trap closing would spring it off the post and the bird, along with the heavy trap biting into its legs, would hang, helpless on a chain linked to an attachment fitted round the post.

Màiri cursed viciously in Gaelic under her breath but Callum still caught the gist of it and it drove in the gravity of the situation. She forced off the fitting that attached the trap to the fence post using one hand while holding the chain in the other hand to make sure she didn't disturb the bird too much. She laid the bird gently on the ground but it tried to flap wildly and she was afraid it would hurt itself even more. She tucked the bird's wings under one arm and asked Callum to come round and take the bird from her, which he did with practised ease having done the same many times with the chickens. He could feel its tiny heart beating frantically fast and he shushed it and stroked it and Màiri was surprised to see that the bird began to relax and calm a little.

-"Now gently hold its legs Cal while I release this evil thing!"

Callum held the bird facing away from Màiri so that that its head was shielded by his arm from seeing what was going on. He held the scaly legs, with their fluffy, feathered breeches firmly with just enough pressure to ensure they didn't move. The bird was caught by a single toe; it must have made a desperate leap to avoid the snapping trap and had almost made it.

Its lightning reactions had at least made it possible for it to be returned to the wild if it lived. Normally both legs would have been caught the moment it touched down and they would have been instantly snapped by the cruel, rusty jaws of the trap, as surely as snapping straws. No bird could live after that, the shock alone would weaken it too much even to struggle. It would hang uselessly, dying slowly in agony and fear, a glorious, predatory prince of the air brought low by the callous act of a far more destructive species. As Màiri eased back the crushing, rusted jaws with her strong, toughened hands she swore again as she saw that the mess of the partially severed toe which was still bleeding. It could soon heal though with a little quick treatment although it would never function properly again. She would find what she wanted to treat it where they were going.

-"Keep hold of the bird Cal, I'll just get rid of this foul thing!" She said.

She stood up grasping the cruel trap in one hand, swinging it by the chain.

-"I'll have that bird -- and the trap!" demanded a strident, grating voice.

Màiri, momentarily shocked by the unexpected intrusion, spun round to see a skinny, ragbag of a man standing a few yards off; a short, heavy looking club in one hand, and a dead hoodie crow hanging limply down from the other. She hadn't heard him coming, he had a poacher's step.

-"Cm'on missus, hand them over; the bounty on that there bird is mane fair an' square!" he spat the words out in a threatening, wheezy growl.

He clearly thought that Màiri was after cheating him out of the prize from the estate for catching the bird and killing it.

-"Sae this is yer dirty work is it?" she demanded, spitting the words back at him.

-"Come on now missus, a'm jist doin ma job?" He said in a wheedling tone, sensing her disapproval, "There's sixpence fer that bird missus and I'll nae be doon oot o' it!" He sensed he was about to lose his prize from the estate factor and he was getting truculent.

She sized up the short, stooping figure. He was a type she knew and detested, a chancer who schemed his way from one day's drink to the next and had few if any scruples about how it was achieved.

-"Sae ye want this filthy trap dae ye?" Màiri demanded mockingly.

She stepped forward, turned towards the loch and, holding the swinging metal trap above her head, flung it high and far out down the slope. It soared out over the grassy slope and right over the cliff. She turned to the man, her whole body taut and sprung, ready to advance on him. Her eyes sparked as she threatened him in a furious tone,

-"And the next tame I see ye round here setting those evil things ye'll gae the same way!" she bellowed, rolling up her sleeves. She stood astride the path long legs braced, and staring down at the unsavoury looking figure from a couple of feet away. He was only about five foot three and Màiri seemed to tower over him.

She studied the man, she thought she recognised him; he had a narrow, rat like face and deep red cheeks and nose, covered in broken veins from an excess of strong drink. Now that he had threateningly moved closer to her Màiri could smell cheap, stale whisky on his breath.

His thin nose ended in a point, not unlike a hawk's bill and he wore a faded, torn, tweed jacket, greasy with dirt at the cuffs and pockets, and he had on grubby brown serge trousers, shiny from age and use. He was glowering and his lips were wet and flecked with spittle. As he opened his mouth to speak she caught a blast of his stale, rancid breath, but she held her ground despite the revulsion she felt for this man.

He fingered his club threateningly but Màiri was more than a match for him and furiously angry and he knew it. He looked desperately about him, not knowing how to react, whether to attack or flee, to try to claim his prize by force or beat a hasty retreat. It was clear Màiri wasn't going to back down.

-"I ken ye" she said "ye're Hughie McLennon, nephew of widow McLennon frae the village. Ye always were a nasty wee piece o' work!" and then she swore at him, fierce and long in Scots and Gaelic, cursing him in language and in ways he had rarely heard from another man let alone a woman.

The man backed off a little, his face contorted with anger and resentment but too afraid now to challenge her outright. Then Màiri reached into her dress pocket and found some change amongst the pieces of string, nappy pins and odds and ends. She pulled out a sixpence, wiped it, then spat on it before contemptuously flinging it at his feet.

-"There's yer blood money ye dirty little crow-strangler. Now get oot of here or I'll throttle ye with ma bare hands!" Her dark eyes blazed anger and contempt at the man and, as she advanced towards him, he decided he had had enough and, snatching up the silver coin from the ground, he slipped it quickly into his pocket as he turned tail and half ran, half stumbled back up the path.

Throughout the whole exchange Callum had remiained stock still, shocked and rigid in aweful fascination at a side of his mother's personality he hadn't imagined. He held onto the buzzard defensively as he had stared, wide-eyed and open mouthed, astonished at the fierceness of his mother and by her dispay of power. The raw energy of her and the strength and her fury had clearly overwhelmed the little man. Callum had kept the bird close, screening its eyes from the angry scene, instinctively protecting it.

Màiri turned and picked up her bag and shouldered it. She smiled grimly at Callum, relaxing a little and said,
    -"A guid morning's work eh Cal! Come on, let's get on I'm getting hungry" and she carried on up the path in the direction they were previously heading, wanting to put distance between them and that horrible man. Callum followed mutely with a renewed respect and pride for his mother and more than a little overawed by her.

Just a short stride further on they reached a small jumble of tumbled boulders and Màiri sat down on one and said,
    -"Here, let's stop a minute and have a wee look at that bird!"
    Callum held out the bird carefully as she gently checked the foot and then studied the bird's head and the rest of the beautiful, glossy-feathered body.

He was a beautiful bird; she had never seen a buzzard so close before, let alone held one. He was a glorious, glossy, brown and buff prince of the sky. She shook her head to see him in such a state, feeling his fear and trembling. He felt soft and vulnerable but still with a muscular power. His eyes appeared glazed over as he peered mournfully up at her and looked apathetic. She felt his racing heartbeat under his fine, glossy feathers. Màiri knew that the make-up of a bird was finely balanced; it wouldn't take much to send him into terminal decline. It was a pact birds had made with the powers of evolution: their delicacy was the sacrifice for the gift of flight.

-"We need tae get something intae him Cal, tae give him energy and he'll have a fierce thirst" Màiri explained.

She shushed and cooed the bird, stroking his head tenderly with a finger and felt an infinite sadness for his state and for his fear and for the knowledge that it was one of her species that had caused this. She reached into one of the pockets of her pale, fawn, canvas bag.

-"I was saving this as a treat for ye Cal", she said sadly "I hope ye don't mind? Yer Uncle Ian picked up a few in Dingwall when he was there last" she said by way of explanation.

She pulled out a green and gold-flecked pear. It would have been stored carefully since the autumn before being sold in the market. Getting hold of fruit was difficult in the village, especially at this time of year. They had to wait for someone to go into Kyle or even to go by train all the way to Dingwall and have the money to buy it. She looked at Callum, enquiring.

-"Of course I dinna mind, he needs it mair than me" he said, sighing.

A juicy, succulent pear was a treat he would have drooled over given the chance.

-"Thanks Cal, ye're a fine generous lad and I'm proud of ye". She looked at him and he smiled and blushed pink, turning away.

She took a small penknife from her pocket; it was small and well-worn with a white, pearly shell handle. She recalled that she had bought it in Dingwall at an iron-mongers with the little pocket money her Ma could afford for her when she was a small girl, not much older than Callum was now. She also recalled that she had recently bought Hamish a large multi-bladed knife, with extra little tools on it, from a little shop in Kyle. It had a black, Bakelite handle with a diamond-cut pattern and a steel ring onto which he had tied a long piece of string so he didn't lose it. He had tied the string to his belt and then slipped the knife in his pocket. He always carried it now, it was a token of something that remained unspoken between them.

She cut off small pieces of pear with the knife and held them out towards the buzzard's sharp, downturned beak, while Callum held on to him. He held the large bird confidently, as if he was one of his chickens. The wary, rich, chestnut brown bird looked at the small piece of pear, hesitated, then pecked lightly, looked again, turning his head on one side to get a better look; a bird of prey's nearsight is not that good. He nibbled a piece of the juicy, white pear, grasping it with his small, pink, pointed tongue, and then swallowed it. Then he tried another piece and another. Màiri fed him half the pear and then thought he had probably had enough for now. The sugar in the pear should give him a little energy and the juice would help reduce his thirst but she supposed he needed some water as well; he would be badly dehydrated.

She knew there was a little spring that spouted from a rockface further along the path. When they got there Callum held him up to the silver, sparkling stream that caressed and tickled it way over the rounded rocks, the grey-brown rock turned dark green where algae grew in its wake. The bird carefully leant forwards and delicately placed its beak in the stream of water, lapping with his tongue and tipping his head back to let the cool, clear water wash over his tongue and down his pulsing throat.

Màiri watched mesmerised as Callum carefully held the bird steady. She had never seen anyone have such an intuitive understanding and connection with a wild creature as Callum did with the bird. He murmured softly to it in a low-pitched, slightly lyrical voice that seemed to come automatically to him. The bird appeared to trust him and to feel confident enough to drink. She had seen his remarkable connection with the cows and ewes on the croft, and he did seem to have a very intuitive understanding with Jess, but they were domestic animals, used to being handled; this was a wild creature. Nonetheless the bird seemed to feel confident that he meant him well. The large, young bird of prey was beginning to look more alert now, beginning to look about him at Màiri and Callum; swivelling his head round, first one way and then the other, and he was beginning to try his wings though clearly was too weak to fly yet. Callum gently placed him back under his arm and they set off again.

Within a few minutes Màiri announced that they had arrived.

-"Here?" questioned Callum, mystified.

All he could see were the same slopes and hills to the right and, to the left, a rocky, rough-shaped natural wall about fifteen feet high which sloped upwards, creating a barrier between the path and the loch below. Màiri stepped off the path and walked straight through the rock wall. She had stepped into what seemed like a vertical fault line in the dark rock but which Callum could now see was a barely visible, narrow gap.

He followed her, still carefully clutching the buzzard close to him, which astonishingly, still seemed to be relatively relaxed. He seemed to sense their protective intentions towards him, although he was still also subdued by his trauma. His passivity was as much a symptom of shock Callum realised as any confidence in his rescuers.

They were standing on a rough, green pathway through the tall, waving grass on the other side of the gap. It looked as if the gap was used by deer and foxes; there were no sheep on this land and it was well trodden and flattened by sizeable feet. The grass had been parted by the passage of the animals, showing up as a darker shadow against the pallid, summer green. Perhaps even a secretive badger made use of it Màiri thought judging by the way the grass had been trampled here and there and pushed aside.

Callum had to watch where he placed his feet as the path was uneven. To his right the rocky outcrop faded into thick woodland which tumbled down over a long curving ridge that became sheer cliff faces in places. Scrubby growth swept upwards and met the woodland in a crashing green wave. To his left were more scrubby bushes; hawthorn and gorse, grown over towards him, bent by onshore winds so that he needed to shove his way through, protecting the bird as his mother held back overhanging branches.

-"This is more overgrown than I remember, I've not been here for a while" she said "we should hae come doon further along, there's good paths through the woods."

They came out from behind the bushes and the scene took Callum's breath away. As a small boy he was constantly being astonished at the glory and beauty of the place where he lived. Laid out beneath him was a Hebridean bay of exquisite beauty and isolation, sweeping away towards the Inner Sound. To his left the rocks continued to roll and bowl their way steeply downhill; smooth igneous basalt and gabbro which had been rolled out in fat, toffee strands in the time of chaos, when the last great spasm of creation had made these wild, rocky lands; hot lava spewing out of the tortured planet's surface; the land born in fire and smoke.

Where the smooth, weathered rock reached the shore it spread out in little rocky, wavecut islets and rock pools, seaweedy and barnacle covered, running out through the smooth green and blue waters, lapping the rocky, seaweed-stained, brown flanks.

Callum took in the broad, sweeping bay that stretched away for miles in front and below him. It was a great curving, shallow sickle of white, shell sand, sparkling far below them in the bright sun. The white sands extended for three or four miles to a rocky promontory in the distance. Beyond, the loch opened out into a wide estuary before flowing into the shimmering sea; the Inner Sound which swallowed up the gentle waters of the loch in its choppy, swirling currents. They had walked almost to the end of the great loch.

He had never been this far from home before. It was a magical, mystical place, secret and unvisited by all but wild creatures, where nature played free from man. Where the pure white sand line faded into the sea it flushed first greeny-white, then azure and emerald before disappearing beneath the broad, shallow waves that lapped in lazy, white curls onto the shoreline. Gentle white horses danced on the wavetops, contrasting sharply with the Mediterranean hues of the quiet sea.

Towards the end of the bay lay the wrecked, dark hull of a rounded, tub-ended fishing boat, caught out in some terrible Atlantic storm. It had failed to make it home and was flung up on the beach at the entrance to the loch, high on the strandline: a soft landing for the fishermen but a sorry end for the boat, which lay like a beached whale, flesh stripped and its ribs showing. Its jaunty little deckhouse was tilted at a crazy angle, open to the sea. The boat was collapsing in on itself, the sea gradually taking it; stealing the man-made object jealously to itself, the great giver and taker, today benign and beautiful, but fierce and dark in anger.

Nearer the white sand, grassy slopes took over from the scrub line. The scrub petered out to become a fine mown lawn, a close-browsed, natural pasture for rabbits and deer. Scattered as far as the eye could see, across the base of the sloping cliffs lay a tapestry of colour; wildflowers grew in profusion; purple vetch and yellow birds-foot trefoil, white-flowered chickweed and bright green, wild sorrel, celandine grew in drifts of yellow stars and the curled leaved patches of pale, yellow primrose hidden in shady damp spots.

In the Highlands and Islands, where spring comes late and crashes into summer, the two seasons flowers come together, producing a glorious spectacle of colour in a grand riot. Swathes of bluebells carpeted slopes in a bluey-purple, a mat of woodland flowers where the ancient woodland have long disappeared. Fluffed-up, fresh looking spring rabbits browsed, brown and white, half hidden in the blue carpet, chewing on mouthfuls of succulent bluebell stalks and flowers, thinking themselves invisible to the interlopers amongst their succulent stems.

Statuesque stalks of tall, delicate cow parsley waved green and pregnant in the breeze; their creamy, white umbrels ready to burst open in early summer alongside elegant, spiky stems of thistle which poked up like barbed, green saplings above clouds of spring colour.

Skylarks hovered high, proclaiming ownership of their particular patch of wild pasture, their piping notes floating down the air. Barn swallows swooped low across the slopes, catching insects which darted from daisy head to poppy flower. Màiri wondered where they roosted and nested in this wilderness, perhaps along cliffs or stone escarpments, as they would have done before humans came along to name them as creatures of their outbuildings and house roofs. She wondered what the "old ones" had called them. Bees buzzed in the grass, laden and lazy with nectar and dusted with pollen. The warm air was heavy with scent and green, grassy smells, buzzing and dozily somnambulant, drugging the newcomers into sleepy languor.

-"This is called Selkie Bay" said Màiri softly, as if to raise her voice would disturb the otherness of this place; she saw the wonder on Callum's face and smiled to herself. She was so pleased he too seemed to see in it what she did, its very special quality, a secret, true Hebridean shoreline.

As they made their way carefully down the grassy slopes Callum tried hard not to slip and frighten the injured bird. The creature was beginning to look more lively now, darting his eyes about with interest; no longer glazed over, the brightness had returned to his yellow, glowing eyes. His sharp, predatory intelligence was being stirred by the abundance of the surrounding prey; memories of rabbits and insects and small birds taken for his hungry chicks. His nature was beginning to reassert itself; the bird twitched with impatience.

Where it reached the bottom of the slope the grassy soil was fragmented into grass covered, rain moulded islets. Runoff had worked on cracks and depressions and intruded its way through the soil to create dark gullies in an intricate mesh of many tiny islands and dry waterways, down through the earth to the bedrock.

Away from the probing waves freshwater pools lay, cool and dark amongst the grass, some of large size, swollen by recent rain, protected from sea salt spray in their hollows. The dark, still pools were ringed with bog-loving cotton grass, ragged robin and the green, gladius bladed leaves of flag iris which grew around the water's edges and whose buds would soon burst into joyful, bright yellow pennants. Long, collapsed grass stems floated on the pond's surfaces and pond skaters and water boatman busied themselves on the meniscus. Meadow pipits and thrushes and blackbirds and tits were all busily chasing and seeking food for greedy nestlings, and dipping down to sip from the ponds in between feeds.

Màiri selected a large grassy mound, mown short and spiky by nibbling rabbits and peppered with their droppings. Cushions of pale, pink sea thrift danced in the light sea breeze all around them, their pom-pom heads bobbing and trembling. Callum squatted down and lightly placed the buzzard on its feet. Màiri went off in search of stitchwort and purple-flowered marsh woundwort with which to heal the buzzard's foot.

After a short while she returned with what she needed in her bag and with greens for their meal; a salad of chickweed and sorrel and tender, bitter, young dandelion leaves. First, she took a clump of the spiky grass and soaked it in a rock-pool and gently bathed the torn foot in seawater, despite protestations from the bird who complained noisily; it was a nasty open wound. Then she masticated the leaves of stitchwort and woundwort, tore off a small piece of the mushy mixture and spread a smooth, sticky layer all around the toe. She delicately bound it in a small sorrel leaf and neatly held it all together with a binding of tough, dry grass stem. It was incredibly delicate work. All the time the buzzard tried to peck at it, but each time she tapped his beak lightly until he learnt to leave it alone. When she had finished the bird looked up at her as if to say, "Is that it?"

Callum let him stand without holding him. The binding on his toe didn't seem to bother him. He took a few steps, ignoring it and Màiri was pleased that the dressing held; it would last at least a few hours or even a day or two if he didn't tear it off. It would give the wound a chance to begin to seal over and start to heal. The toe wouldn't work properly ever again but it shouldn't prevent him from perching or grasping prey and more importantly, it shouldn't now become infected. Then Màiri said;

-"Hold on tae him again Cal while I have a good look at him before we let him go". A stab of apprehension pulled at Callum's stomach at the thought of letting the bird go.

She carefully splayed out the long, broad, wings, delicately checking the bones for breaks, as she had done occasionally for smaller birds which she had found injured around the croft. He complained and Màiri felt the power in his wings as he tried to escape. Callum calmed him and she expertly felt both wings and stretched them out to their full, impressive span; then she checked his chest by feeling his keelbone for fat. He was in good condition, muscular and with good fat storage to keep him going.

-"He'll be fine now I think Cal, I'm sure." She said with relief and satisfaction.Callum smiled wistfully, he had become attached to this handsome, noble bird; but he knew they would have to let him go. He opened his hands, carefully letting the buzzard try his wings. He began to stretch them and walk about with a tentative, strutting movement, opening and closing the wings as if to feel the familiarity of their power again. The bird flapped his wings with a cracking of the air and he rose a few inches, before closing them again and beginning to study the ground. He began poking about with his beak for insects, he was hungry now: he needed energy before he could fly.

Màiri opened her bag and unpacked their lunch; she took the skin off one of the chicken legs and handed it to Callum to give to the bird. Callum held the white-fleshed leg close to its beak and it looked at it suspiciously, nibbled gently at it, and picked a little of it off, tearing the meat away gently. It clearly liked it and snatched the whole leg from Callum's grasp in its strong beak and then jealously turned its back on them, cloaking its food with part opened wings and sneaking a look round at them as if expecting them to try and snatch it back from him. He took it from his beak with his good foot and held it in his talons while he delicately tore up the soft flesh.

-"I hope this does nae gie him a taste fer chicken eh Cal!" joked Màiri;

Callum looked a little alarmed.

They ate the fresh salad leaves Màiri had foraged and wolfed down thir barley bread and cheese and boiled eggs, they were both famished. Their morning's efforts and the excitement of the rescue of the buzzard had sharpened both their appetites. Màiri gave the second chicken leg to the buzzard and then she took out a battered enamel cup and went to fill it from a stream which bubbled its way down the grassy slope. Callum watched the buzzard finish eating and then watched it playing with a bone, relaxed and quite confident, ignoring the humans for now.

Màiri and Callum greedily drank down the cool, fresh water and then took off their shoes and socks and bathed their tired feet while paddling in the creamy, sea water. Callum searched in rock pools while keeping an eye on the buzzard, who was hopping about on the grass happily searching for grubs, and snapping at passing flies but making sure he kept close to his human protectors for now.

When they returned for their socks and shoes the buzzard was flapping his wings furiously and looking skyward agitated and distracted. Màiri's attention was caught by a sound high above them and looked up and saw the cause of the buzzard's distress;

-"There's his mate Cal, come lookin fer him" she paused as she watched the balletic manouvres of the large bird high above them.

-"He'll find it hard to take off from here; he's still not quite strong enough fer that," She looked at Callum;

-"He'll need a hand" she said.

They could hear the evocative and urgent 'kiiieee!' cries drifting down from the circling female. She was circling out to the shoreline, catching a thermal, searching for her mate and he was softly whistling wistfully up at her, his beak pointing skywards.

-"Ye'll need tae take him high up the slope Callum and launch him intae a breeze when he's ready. Can ye dae that?" she asked quietly looking at him. She knew it would be a real wrench for him to let the bird go.

-"Aye Ma, I can dae it!" replied Callum sadly. "Come on big bird, tame tae fly hame!" He sighed, a heavy feeling in his stomach, the sadness of parting, and he gently took up the buzzard by its legs in one hand while supporting its body with the other. The bird reacted calmly, looking up at Callum with unblinking, golden eyes, allowing him to carry him up the slope without complaint, gently flapping his wings to keep his balance and still looking up, searching for his mate from time to time.

The bird became impatient and more and more agitated as they climbed higher, as if knowing what Callum was intending. Callum reached the edge of the grass slope, before it became scrub, high up on the escarpment. He was about fifty feet up now with plenty of air to launch the bird into. He gazed one last time into the bird's bright yellow, eager eyes and he suddenly realised that the look there was alien to him; the bird gazed back with no connection nor affection, no fear nor hatred, it was simply other. It seemed to trust that he meant it no harm and that he was about to release it to the air; all else was disinterest. The bird returned his gaze, constant and inscrutable, this was a truly wild creature from an unknowable element. Callum couldn't begin to see into his world, his mind, couldn't ever share the intimacy of this creature's life; it belonged and was part of an unfathomable wilderness that Callum had merely touched for a moment.

Callum sighed sadly and held the bird high, like a hunting falcon, letting him curl his sharp talons round his small fist, biting into the flesh. The bird sensed the air currents, feeling with his wings, trying it with his feather tips, feeling the ways of a medium that Callum couldn't even begin to understand. The bird could go any time it wished now. Callum gently stroked its head with a curled finger one last time. A light breeze was ruffling the dark, strong, flight feathers. The big bird's nature had fully returned and its keen eyes were taking in the scene, searching the sky for his mate. Turning his head to one side to listen intently, his sharp gaze catching something beyond Callum's vision.

The air filled his great wings as he spread them fully, his wing tips ruffled like whiffled stalks of dancing cotton grass. He was ready to take flight and with a single, powerful beat of those fully extended wings he launched himself into space; the great wings clapped the air as if in delight and applause at his own magnificence. Callum felt the draft of displaced air from the beating limbs and watched spellbound and ever earthbound as the bird soared out into the midday summer space. It banked and circled and gained height, exultant in its freedom and magnificence, crying out to his mate above, a mournful and haunting 'kieee! kieee!"

The great buzzard circled and swooped down towards Callum in a last farewell;

-"Bye big bird, fly! Fly to your mate!" Callum called out, breathless, tears filling his eyes. He felt joy and elation and a stab of pain, felt the loss of the creature's going. He felt wonder for this glorious bird as it climbed in great circles on an upthrusting thermal between land and sea and his mate swooped down to meet him. They danced in the air for a moment, re-establishing their bonds and Callum felt just for an instant as if he were with up there with them as they sheared off, high up, away to their home wood, nobility in flight.

Callum sighed again as he came back down the slope to his mother, who hugged him and wiped away the tears.

-"Ye've done a guid thing today Callum" was all she said softly, and then "Come on, we'll gae and meet the Selkies!"

She picked up her bag, collected her things together and led him off up the beach, her arm over his shoulders. They took off their shoes and socks again and felt the warm sand between their toes. She set off up to the high dunes that lay back from the beach, where fierce winds and storm breakers had piled up magnificent, sandy peaks.

CHAPTER 5

INDIAN SUMMER

They found themselves further along the beach, amongst the machair on top of the dunes, feeling the spiky grass on the bare skin of their feet. Machair occurs nowhere else except in the North-west Isles of Scotland and a few special places on the North-west Highland coast. Brilliant, white shell sand provides a unique limy medium for rare plants. It builds up in massive dunes which become a battleground for wind, rainwater, waves and disturbance; ever shifting along the beach. Beyond the storm surges the sand becomes more stabilised as marram grass and other pioneer grasses send down their deep roots. The alkaline qualities of the sand attract chalk-loving plants. Seeds blown in on the wind settle and a precious and rare flora begins to form.

Some of the same flowers that grew well on the grassy slopes above the bay grew well here too; birds-foot trefoil, yellow with scarlet etching, settled in amongst the cropped areas of turf. Purple vetch climbed tall grasses, producing sculpted pea like seedpods, and buttercups grew in profusion, all shot through with tall moon-daisies that waved gently amongst the grasses. There were red and white clover in abundance, buzzing with bees, and delicate blue-headed carillons of harebells, bobbing and soundlessly ringing in the gentle breeze.

In this rare place there were incomers too, many alien to the Highlands; spiky leaved, yellow flowered lady's bedstraw and meadow rue; the tiny flowers of yellow rattle, whose spreading roots parasitise bullyboy grasses and help prevent them from swamping the other plants. White-flowered eyebright, plantain and yarrow joined in this orchestral, coloured carpet dancing to the tune of sea breezes. Màiri and Callum trod delicately amongst this vulnerable, rare little world between the sea and the land.

The harsh grating sound of corncrakes echoed around them, the ventriloquial cries of the shy birds shivered and croaked in the warm air. Cautious, dull and stripy, birds of the nettlebed and weedy plot, they prefer to challenge each other from their hiding places with 'krrrk, krrrk' calls, day and night, their voices rasping out from the cover of tall grasses or weeds. They could be heard around the croft too now, their harsh "craking" voices sounding well into the night, calling from overgrown vegetable patches and neglected stands of tall weeds; the sound of a Highland summer.

Hovering way above their heads in a rare, deep blue sky, calling sweetly down the summer air were more skylarks, their high, fluty notes rising and falling up and down the scale, lilting and seductive, heartachingly evocative. Secretive meadow pipits nervously dashed from grass stalk to grass stalk. Sneaking in amongst the tall grasses, a startlingly black and white oyster-catcher tried to look inconspicuous, despite its very obvious colouring and its long bright red bill and red legs; come to sit in secret on her hidden nest, her garish stripes cleverly folding in invisibly amongst the stark, grass stalk shadows. A plentiful supply of flying insects were providing ample food for swooping swallows; harvest mice and wood mice and tiny voles bustled and rustled amongst the tall grasses.

It was all glorious and heady and Màiri and Callum were forced to linger for a while, drugged by the beguiling beauty and warm scents. They sat lounging on the sandy grass in intimate companionable solitude; still and quiet, listening and dreaming, and watching the soft rolling waves shushing gently onto the starkly white beach.

They leaned comfortably against each other, Màiri's arm around Callum. She felt as happy as she had ever been; as happy as when she had last been here with her mother; older than Callum was now but just as content as he appeared to be. The sun drifted overhead, it was the kind of late spring day that comes with a settled spell of weather, rare in the Highlands for the rest of the year when the weather is ever changeable, but common enough in late May or early June. They began to doze in the warmth, soothed by the low buzz of insects and birdsong and the sweet, soporific smells drifting on a fading sea breeze; and after a while even the birds frantic efforts stilled as an infectious mid-day hush settled over the bay.

The sun was at its highest and they had the whole afternoon to themselves before having to head back and tend to their responsibilities; Màiri to Hamish's tea and to collect Dougall from Isla's croft, where Flora was no doubt dressing him up, using him as a tailor's dummy as she was wont to do, and Callum to feed the chickens and attend to his other chores, and of course to cheer Jess up; she too was having to suffer Flora's tender mercies.

The heavy-lidded hush stilled them and they both drifted in a dazy reverie for an hour or so; lulled by the warm sea breezes and the hazy sounds of nature amongst the soft waving machair and the hush of the rolling surf. After finally and reluctantly raising themselves they wandered out to the calm, rolling sea, across the broad sands, warm and gritty to the touch of their feet and they paddled in the cool water. They felt the chuckling eddies running coolly between their toes and around their ankles and shins, and every now and then Callum dipped a hand into the water to collect a shell or a drifting feather. He handed them to his mother to keep in her pockets; trusted keeper of his treasures. Small fishes darted about their feet and tiny crabs fled, scrabbling sideways from their whitened toes.

They walked almost to the end of the beach where a small, becalmed flotilla of stranded 'selkies' were hauled out, snorting and puffing softly to each other. They were large and blubbery with long Roman noses, looking a little haughty and rather dignified, with huge worried looking, round eyes. Màiri and Callum stood at a distance and admired their bulk; their grey and fawn coats were covered with a sheen of white sand where it had stuck to their wet bodies.

Màiri recounted the songs and tales of the 'selkies', telling Callum how they were supposed to have lured fishermen onto the rocks by singing lovely, haunting songs to them, disguised as beautiful maidens, and then how they carried the men off beneath the waves to become their watery husbands. The confusion with mermaids seemed unlikely seeing their bulky bodies flopped giantly up on the beach but they were fascinated by them all the same. The seals seemed to find these two humans equally fascinating. Callum crept closer and talked quietly to them; they puffed and huffed at him for a bit but were obviously feeling much too lazy and unafraid to threaten, let alone to flee, so after a while he said goodbye and they left. Màiri and Callum wandered back up the beach and onto the dunes to flop down again in the warm sun.

Màiri lay on her back and shaded her eyes from the glare, her black linen dress was sprayed with the pure, white sand which trickled over the folds of material and fell in grainy waterfalls back onto the sandy sward. Her long, bare, legs felt the warm breeze brushing the tiny hairs on the skin. She remembered the words of a poem, learnt by heart when she had been at school;

'To see a world in a grain of sand
And heaven in a wild flower
Hold infinity in the palm of your hand
And eternity in an hour'

She couldn't remember who the poem was by but it seemed so apposite just now.

Callum sat pouring handfuls of the fine sand through his fingers and watching tiny creatures climb over his legs, intent on their foraging paths, unaware of his living, observing presence.

-"Ma, why isn't Pa happy like we are?" Callum asked, slowly and thoughtfully.

Màiri was brought up unawares, an emotion caught in her throat, and she flushed hot and then shivered. The unexpected question had shocked her deeply and suddenly brought the whole business of Hamish's unhappiness and turmoil and her fears of it to the surface; somehow they seemed much more stark in the solace of this calm and peaceful place.

Callum's question had brought dark emotional clouds rolling in to shade the bright, spring sunshine. She thought carefully before she spoke. How to describe something she didn't understand herself, which troubled her every day of her life? She had known that one day she would have to try and explain it to Callum and had never known what she would say. And now, suddenly she had to find answers for him. But he was still so young, how could he understand something so dark, so complex? Should she burden him with such a terrible secret? On the other hand he was clearly desperate to understand; the fear of the unknown might be greater than the pain caused by knowing. Whatever she did he would be hurt; hurt by the secrets kept from him or by the knowledge of the suffering his father had experienced and was still living out. She felt the awful burden of truth.

Màiri began by trying to reassure him;

-"He's no always unhappy Cal. Some people find it really hard tae be happy" she said, avoiding for the moment dealing with the biggest question.

-"But why?" Callum asked simply.

Now she had either to cheat him or try to explain, an agony of dilemmas.

-"Oh, because of things that happened to them in the past, that affected them very much." She bought time with her words, avoiding the awful truth for a moment longer.

-"You mean like when your athair and màthair died, you must have been really sad then?"

Màiri paused, feeling the pain of loss squeeze her insides for a moment.

-"Yes Cal, very sad indeed!" Màiri looked away and smiled wistfully, trying to recapture the feeling of being with her màthair, in the happy times before she had become ill, but that time was still inaccessible, swamped behind the cloak of pain, and anguish of her loss. Would she ever stop grieving for her and for her Pa?

She had sat up and had folded her arms around her knees, hugging herself close, watching the gentle waves rolling in one by one onto the dazzling, wet, white sand.

She rested her chin on her arms, her long, black hair blowing softly in the breeze.

-"When my màthair died I came here, afterwards, after a few weeks -- I was quite a lot older then than ye are now -- I was all alone and -- when I came here I cried and cried all day. And then, when yer Auntie Nellie and Auntie Isla and the others looked after me and were kind tae me -- I gradually learnt how tae be happy again, even though I was still really sad about losing both athair and màthair. I could be happy again fer most of the time anyway. Then I met Hamish, yer athair, and then we had ye -- and both of those things made me properly happy again." She smiled at Callum and caressed the back of his neck. His dark eyes looked so serious and troubled she wondered again if she was doing the right thing.

-"But why didn't Pa get happier again?" Callum asked in a slightly puzzled and exasperated tone, beginning to show his frustration.

Màiri understood, it was a frustration she knew only too well, a frustration borne out of her despair. Callum continued;

-"Dae ye think something really bad happened tae him -- and he couldn't make himself properly happy again?"

-"Oh Callum my love!" Màiri said sadly. "Sometimes I think ye are tae wise fer yer ane guid. I fear it means ye will be badly hurt -- I worry – " she tailed off.

There was a pause while they both struggled with their thoughts.

Màiri looked again at this small boy of hers, so young, raw and sensitive to emotional truth, but she had made her mind up, she couldn't deny him. She gently grasped his shoulder and turned him towards her, so that he would look at her. She looked directly into his dark, brown, shining eyes, half-hooded by their long, black lashes, dark against his pale tan face. She loved him so deeply at that moment and felt him so beautiful and so vulnerable that she could hardly bear to go on. All of a sudden she was terrified that she was somehow about to hurt him irreparably by what she said, to cut him deeply with her words. She tried to swallow her fears and began to talk slowly and in a grown-up manner to him.

-"What I'm going tae tell ye Callum must be just between ye and me; ye mustn't ever let yer father or anyone else ken that ye ken. That will be difficult I ken - dae ye promise?" She didn't wait for his reply but plunged on "Because it would hurt him very much if he thought ye knew and that it had hurt ye in some way, which -" she paused again, still hesitating out of her fears for him "which I fear it will because ye love yer father and ye ken he loves ye. Dae ye promise not tae tell, ever?"

Callum looked serious and studied his mother's dark eyes, it was like looking back into his own.

-"I understand -- I think, and I wont tell anyone, I promise!" said Callum slowly.

Màiri didn't like having to make him promise like this, burdening him with something so awful that he would be unable ever to mention to his father. But how could Hamish ever deal with it if he knew that Callum knew? She couldn't not tell him, it wasn't fair to leave him with his doubts and fears any more, seeing his father suffer with no understanding – only fear. She knew it frightened him, when his father was in one of his deep dark slumps of emotional collapse and despair. It frightened *her*, it frightened her that one day he might slip away from them and not come back, stay there in that godforsaken, dark hole that he collapsed into, or even that he might not one day be able to stand it any more.....

Màiri began by telling Callum that, sadly, when Hamish had been born his mother had died at the same time. Callum didn't say anything so she continued,

-"So he never had a màthair tae look after him and be kind tae him and -- his father treated him very badly." She stopped and waited to see Callum's reaction. Callum looked shocked and then a little sad when this sunk in.

-"Ye mean his Pa didn't like him?" he asked incredulously.

-"I'm afraid not. No Callum he didn't seem tae like him at all! There must have been something – but fer some reason his father never loved him. He was cruel to him and never gave him any attention or praise, and -" she paused again, knowing she could never tell Callum about the beatings and the other, darker cruelties she suspected, "and in the end that sort of thing makes people dislike themselves, and that can make them very sad and sometimes it seems tae make them poorly. When yer Pa gets sad, a lot of his old fears come back, his fears frae when he was a child. He seems tae - withdraw into himself, curl up inside and try to shut it all out." She finished, she felt strange and guilty, explaining this to someone else, even Callum. It felt to her like a terrible betrayal of Hamish.

-"It's very hard fer him sometimes Cal but he keeps trying tae overcome it fer me and fer ye and Dougal; fer his family."

Màiri looked out towards the sea, feeling a constriction in her chest, a pain of sadness and frustration, and guilt, always guilt!

She carried on;

-"Yer athair is a very wonderful man Callum and we are all he has got sae we hae tae love him and be kind to him sae that he can feel better – dae ye understand that my love?" she asked quietly. Callum silently nodded, tears in his eyes. Again Màiri doubted herself for doing this to him.

-"Sae it's no because he does nae like us or because he wants tae gae away?" Callum asked, not sounding entirely convinced.

-"No! Of course not Callum! Nae son, he really does love us and he wants tae be with us mair than anything; he loves ye very much!"

She reassured him as convincingly as she could, but she remembered, that that was how she had felt in the beginning. She had felt that it was all somehow her fault that he couldn't be happy; she was a cause of his unhappiness. She had felt that if only she had been different, done something differently it may not have happened. She had tormented herself with it until she had become emotionally exhausted. But over time, as the years passed and Hamish's struggle to cope with his demons had become more pronounced, she had come to realise that there was nothing she could do or be in order to drive away his fears, his terrible pain. They came from somewhere deep inside him: and that realisation, in its own way, was far worse. So she hung on and gave him the kindness and love that she could because she didn't have anything else to give him, except some soothing balms and infusions to help calm him and to help him sleep. That's when she started to feel so terribly guilty a lot of the time, because she couldn't help enough.

She took Callum by the shoulders and sighed;

-"Callum, I cannae give ye all the answers. There are things none of us really understands; like yer Pa, he does nae ken why he behaves like he does, he tries sae hard not tae fall back into those dark moods." She sighed sadly "I wish I could make everything right but I cannae and nor can ye. It's all right tae be frightened of things we dinna ken Cal; the world is a complicated place and sometimes questions dinnae hae answers."

Màiri paused as she gathered her thoughts. Callum watched her, gazing straight into her dark eyes with his identical dark eyes, his brow furrowed, trying to take in what she was saying, hanging onto her answers. Màiri talked on, trying to weave a protective spell with her words.

-"I can show ye the ways o' the waves and the songs of the selkies and the colours of the loch and the beauty of the glen that is our hame; I can show ye the magic and the wonder in all of this!" she opened her arms and eyes wide and gazed around her at the incredible beauty and felt the life force moving all around them, the incredible power of nature. She continued;

-"but I cannae answer all yer questions, naebody can. Life is wonderful: we come into it alone and we leave alone but in between we have each other and all of this" she swept her arms along the length of the whole bay as if to encompass it all and to capture its wonder and present it to him as a gift.

-"But we also have darkness and pain Cal, and I cannae promise tae always be able tae make the pain gae away. I can only promise tae love ye and tae open yer eyes to the reality of it all. Alongside all the suffering and pain there is also joy, even for yer Pa." She paused to give Callum time for the words to have meaning.

-"Ye bring him joy. I can see it sometimes, the way his eyes take on a soft look when he watches you. So dinnae despair my son; the pain of being alive is worth it even for yer Pa!" and she hoped desperately that it was true.

She knew he wouldn't understand everything she had said, more importantly she knew he wouldn't believe all of it, he was too young still; but she satisfied herself that he had heard her words, they would remain with him till he needed them when he would understand them. She smiled sadly at him and briefly took his hand. A spark of understanding passed between them and Callum looked away, towards the sea.

Màiri gave Callum a consoling hug and held on to him for a moment and then he rose and walked away alone towards the water, his head down, pensive and distracted. Màiri desperately wanted to go after him, to try and ease his pain, but she held back, allowing him the time to assimilate what she had told him. At first she cursed herself for telling him and then realised she had been right to and then questioned herself again for telling him so badly. And in this state of indecision and self-recrimination she watched him wander distractedly towards the sea with the hot tears rolling down her pale cheeks.

Callum wandered along the waves edge, the water brushing his toes. He stopped from time to time to pick up a shell or two distractedly and let them fall back into the water; tears stung his eyes. He hated the idea of his father being treated badly by his own father, "cruel", his mother had said. What did that mean? Billy had told him that his father used to beat him hard and call him horrible names and make him work all day and laugh at him when he fell over or hurt himself. Was it like that? Billy said he had hated his father, but then his father had drowned and the beating had stopped. Billy had said that his mother still hit him sometimes and called him names but he said it was different, she also gave him things, just little things that she made or found, and sometimes she was kind to him. Billy had told him, in the strictest confidence, and he had said he would "bang his heid in" if he told anyone else, but that his mother still used to tuck him in at bedtime and tell him stories, but that Callum must never ever tell anyone, or they might think that he, Billy, was a sissy and he "surtainly wuz nae!"

But then of course Callum's Pa hadn't had a mother. Did Pa hate his father; he wondered, the way Billy had seemed to hate his; he supposed he must. Callum couldn't conceive of ever hating his athair. His Pa meant a warm smell of sweat and muck and soil and sweet hay and rough hands on his and a sad smile as they worked together. He thought of the times when he and his Pa shared the warm intimacy of the steaming cow byre on a winter's morning or marched together up the hill to inspect the sheep, two of Callum's steps to one of his Pa's, trying to keep up and to look grown up like his big Pa. Pa meant rough chafing of stubbled cheeks as he lifted him high in his arms as he carried him to bed when he was tired. Callum couldn't imagine his not being there and feared him drowning like Billy's Pa had.

All these thoughts found their way into his consciousness as he paddled along in the cool water. Then his thoughts turned to his màthair. It had been a wonderful day, a really happy day and he had spoiled it by asking awkward questions and upsetting her. He felt angry with himself, why had he done it?

Màiri sat and waited patiently, drying her tears and watching Callum struggling with his thoughts. She sighed; some of the magic of his life had been picked off today, had fragmented and left him a little more hardened to existence. The thought saddened her, a mother wants to keep her child protected from the unhappiness of the world; if not forever then as long as possible. But if she did how could he grow? How would he discover his own way of living and of being? How could he gain wisdom without pain? None of that made it any easier for her though. Was it really in his best interests for her to tell him why his father suffered so much, or was she just trying to make it easier for herself, by sharing the suffering with someone else, her son? She didn't know whether she had been right or not but she would not lie to him, of that she was sure. She had done her best and that would have to be enough, for what else could she do?

Callum came back after a while and placed a pretty, pink pebble in her hand;

-"Fer ye!" he said smiling, carefully placing the cool, hard pebble in her uplifted palm. "It's alright Ma, really!" he added.

Màiri smiled back sadly;

-"I hae another surprise fer ye" she said, "but ye will have tae wait, tae be patient. Is that all right?"

He pestered her to know what it was but she would not give in, she just led him back to the other end of the beach, where they had first begun. They linked arms as they walked back along the white sand, Callum now chatting happily, his worries about his father forgotten for now, pulled out, talked about, turned over and packed away, a little sadder and a little more damaged but his memories and understanding now rounder if less innocent.

Màiri selected a suitable place just a little way up the grassy slope from where they had sat tending to the buzzard. The breeze blew along the beach between them and the sea and they were half hidden in tall grasses amongst the sappy sward, surrounded by wild marjoram and red campion. Butterflies danced on silken wings as they brushed past them and bees buzzed lazily in the flowers. Their profiles were masked by the tall, shadow-striped grasses on the slope, shaded by bushes of yellow broom; its coconut scented, bright yellow flowers just beginning to appear.

They waited comfortably in silence, Callum as still and relaxed as Màiri. Time drifted slowly and mistily in a quiet, dreamy, stream around them as nature quietly went about its business. Everything seemed to breathe in and out in time with the low, liquid murmur of the green, salty waves on shifting sands, hushing up and over tiny pebbles in silvery ripples and rhythmically rolling sand grains up and down the shining beach.

After a while Màiri murmured quietly to Callum,
   -"He's coming, I see him, be still!"

She carefully pointed to a spot a few yards out in the green, sparkling sea. Màiri leaned over towards Callum so that he could line his eyes up on her finger. At first he couldn't see anything, and then he spotted a small, watery wake fanning out across the still, shallow loch. A little tilted crest of a wave was being pushed forwards by a small black, shiny nose, attached to a smooth, dark, flat, brown head.

The silvery wake fanned out behind the creature is it propelled itself by its tail and twisted its body gently this way and that, following its nose. Occasionally a sleek, bubble-silvered brown rump undulated up and down, smoothly breaking the surface. All of a sudden there was a loud 'plop' and a 'shlump!' and a long, thick, brown tail slid up and out of the water and then followed the whole animal straight down to the sandy bottom under the waves.

From where they were the sea's margin was as clear as green, liquid gauze. They could see the animal's sleek, graceful shape waving from side to side beneath the water to power its progress, the long tail steering it in a smooth elegant motion. A stream of bubbles floated up from the wedge shaped head, popping out from between its lips in a little, dancing, mercury stream. The creature snatched a flailing, brown shore crab with its paws and transferred it to its mouth, snapping on it with a row of sharp little teeth, its long whiskers bristling.

The sleek, dark, creature slid out of the water, looking a little nervous and wary on land in contrast to its uninhibited beauty and grace in the water. It padded quickly along the rocks, slinking on its belly; its long, sleek body undulating in a graceful motion as it moved. It twitched its long whiskers and darted wary looks around with its large, shining, eyes deep black and impenetrable. He was still clutching the crab, firmly in his mouth, its claws still vaguely waving grotesquely in its death throes.

The wet, sleek-coated animal settled down on a suitable, dry rock which allowed him a good view of what was coming from his landward side and also gave him cover, his shape blended in well with the wave rounded boulders on which he rested. He was curled up, concentrating on dismembering and eating his juicy crab but still watching between bites to make sure he was safe. He had good reason to be wary; mainly of humans, who persecuted his kind because, like the selkies, he fished and fishermen saw them as competition rather than us as fellow creatures trying to make a living on these wild shores.

-"He's a dòbhran!" whispered Màiri "He's bòideach isn't he?"

He was indeed beautiful, sleek, fit and in the prime of life; a creature of the wild coast, alive and vital and completely at home in this special place. His deep, shiny coat glowed chocolate and gold as it dried in the afternoon sunshine.

"We need tae be really quiet, we dinnae want tae scare him Cal, he's very shy" she hushed.

-"Is that why we say dòbhranach?" whispered Callum with sudden insight.

-"Yes" agreed Màiri "isn't he fine though?"

When the dòbhran had finished devouring his snack and had had a post-prandial groom he scampered across the rocks and over towards them across the grass. As he reached where they were sitting he stopped, right next to them, squatting at their feet while they held their breath, not daring to move. Màiri was sure he could see them for what they were, but he couldn't smell them because the breeze still blew their scent away from him and they were so still. His great long whiskers quivered as he eyed them, trying to decide whether to flee or not. They continued to hold their breath and watched him spellbound, admiring his large flat head and smooth, shiny fur and looking into those black, shiny eyes. He was so close they could smell his fishy breath.

After what seemed an age of suspense he finally decided they were of no account and scampered on, sliding on his belly into the nearest fresh water pool, twisting his body round and round in indulgent pleasure as he massaged fresh water through his fur with his great webbed paws. He chattered and chittered to himself, scrabbling with his claws right down to his guard hairs which protected him from cold.

-"He's washing the salt out of his fur" whispered Màiri to a bewitched Callum.

And then, after a while, they tore themselves away and snook off leaving the shy dòbhran and the selkies and all the other creatures of this secret bay to fall back into the calm seclusion that the outsiders had found when they had first arrived.

They wearily trekked the full two hours home, silently for the most part, dwelling on the events of the day, the beauty and peace of the bay and relishing the memories of the time spent together. They were buoyed up by the day and by the beauty and wildness of it all and the privilege of being able to share time with some very special creatures. They were both thoughtful about their conversation, fears explored, polished and put away for now.

By the time they reached Isla and Ian MacDonald's croft they were bone weary. Jess was overjoyed to see them and dashed out onto the path, excitedly chasing her fluffy tail round and round in circles to let off pent-up energy after being cooped up indoors most of the day and being poked and prodded by Flora. Flora had dressed her in a large, pink bow, which looked ridiculous as she spun round and round on her haunches. Dougall was tired and grizzly and Màiri whipped him up in her arms and soothed him. Isla asked them in and offered them a cup of tea and a bite but Màiri said if they didn't get home and get their chores done straight away they would fall asleep on their feet and neither Hamish nor the chickens would get their tea.

But before they could leave Flora was determined to take Callum to task over what she believed to be his neglect of her. She berated him for not coming round to play all week and, in his defence, he said:
  -"We maun work hard tae keep a croft goin' Flora, it's no all ale and ceilidhs bein' a crofter ye ken!"
  Màiri and Isla were hard put not to explode with laughter at Callum's sudden grown up seriousness. Flora however, was not to be put off so easily;

-"Callum McDonald I'll nae bear yer excuses ony mair: ye'll get yerself round here tomorrow an we'll gae doon tae the cove like ye promised or there'll be trouble!" and she wagged her finger sternly at him for emphasis.

Callum sighed and promised he would, so long as he could bring Jess. A much amused Màiri and Isla said goodbye and the little band took their leave and set off wearily up the steep path back to their croft.

The next morning, true to his word, Callum, with Jess following enthusiastically close behind collected young Flora from her croft house and they headed off together. Isla waved them off and told them to behave themselves while they were out and Callum and Flora made their way along the hard-baked, earthen track on the way to the cove. Flora tried to hold Callum's hand but there was a possibility of people about and he wasn't about to be seen, as a boy, holding on to a girl's hand in public, not even for Flora.

Now, at nearly eight years old, Flora had grown into a stocky young girl. She was short and wide, almost square in shape, with an untidy shock of white-blonde hair, the colour of her mother's and had her mother's green eyes that shone with intelligence and mischief. She had chunky arms and legs and nearly always wore patched dungarees; unless her mother made her wear a frock; in which case she sulked, and Flora was very good at sulking.

Callum was very fond of her but sometimes pretended he wasn't that bothered because she already had an overwhelming confidence in both herself and in his loyalty to her and it irritated him. But his nonchalant stance didn't fool anyone, least of all Flora.

-"Where'r we goin' Cal?" Flora asked in her high-pitched, demanding voice.

Callum very nearly made the mistake of pointing out that it was obvious, they were going to the steep, rocky path down to the cove, where they said they were going, but he knew that Flora enjoyed playing these little verbal games. What she meant of course was what did he have in mind for today's entertainment of Flora. It was Callum's place to come up with the ideas, it was Flora's part to say whether she was sufficiently impressed to allow them or not. Any system other than this gave Callum so much grief that he had learnt to let Flora have her way. So he said;

-"I thoc't we'd skim stanes, it's a guid day fer it!"

The air was still and warm, the loch calm, perfect for skimming small, flat stones across the surface of the water.

-"Boring! We did that last tame!" Flora said petulantly.

What she meant of course was that Callum had won last time.

-"How 'bout chasin' crabs?" he said, trying to inject a little enthusiasm into his voice.

Callum enjoyed stalking the little crabs in the shallows and then whipping them out of the water without getting nipped. So did Jess, she loved to jump about in the water and chase around them, splashing and barking furiously.

-"I want tae play Point chasin'!" Flora said airily.

Flora's suggestion was against the rules on two counts: firstly Callum was supposed to make the suggestions, but seeing as Flora made up the rules anyway he supposed that that didn't really matter; what did matter was that the game, invented by Flora, was scary, children were not supposed to go to the Point, where the game took place because it was dangerous, which was why it appealed so much to Flora. He knew though that Flora would go without him if he didn't go along with her and he couldn't allow that. He was the oldest, if only by a few months, and he always felt that he was somehow responsible for her, despite her bossiness. So he reluctantly agreed, quietly sighing and shaking his head to himself at Flora's folly.

As they headed down the precipitous track to the cove Flora skimmed on her hobnailed boots across the large flat stones that lined the path. She liked striking sparks and slipsliding her way dangerously down to the little stony beach. Jess barked at her to stop because she was frightening off all the little creatures which Jess liked to sniff out in her snuffling, doggy way and to lick and peer in at as they cowered amongst the pathside vegetation. Callum was no longer impressed by this risky behaviour of Flora's as he had experienced it so often, so he just sighed again and followed on at his own pace. Callum seemed to do a lot of sighing when he was with Flora.

Tendrils of bindweed and long grasses hung across their path to trip the unwary so Callum had to watch where he himself was going in any case. The path needed clearing but as fishing this year had not really got underway yet the adults had hardly used the path and nor was anyone seeking out seaweed or flotsam, they were too busy on their crofts, so the beach was deserted.

-"Are ye goin tae marry me Cal?" Flora suddenly asked, as she deliberately slid on yet another stone.

-"What?" Callum was flabbergasted. Why had she asked him that? What the Dickens was he supposed to say he asked himself? Was she trying to catch him out or what? What did she mean, marry her, he was an eight year old kid, was this a pretend game or what?

-"Can't I'm a kid!" He said, hoping that would end it.

-"We could have a long 'gagement!" she said emphatically as if he hadn't spoken.

A what? He thought, Oh hell! Why couldn't she just play ordinary games like other kids.

-"Anyway we're cousins," he said hopefully, wishing she would change the subject.

-"We're nae close cousins; Ma says yer lot are frae Keppoch and oors are McDonald's frae Skye, or t'other way roond, I'm no so sure now!" she said.

Just at that point Jess put up a rabbit and chased off up the hill after it and Callum used the excuse to break off the conversation and chase up the hill after her. He welcomed the distraction which had saved him from the tricky conversation in which he had found himself, having been, not for the first time with Flora, way out of his depth.

By the time he had rejoined Flora with Jess, who as always had been unsuccessful in catching the rabbit,

Flora had changed her mind about marrying him anyway.

-"Pr'aps I'll marry Ali instead" Flora announced airily.

Callum thought, 'Alistair?' 'Why should she want to marry Alastair rather than me?' Instead of being relieved that she had moved on to someone else the thought that she had cast him off so easily rankled somehow. She was infuriating.

When they arrived at the stony beach Flora set off towards the Point, regardless of Callum's entreaties.

-"Flora, the tide's on the turn, I dinnae think this is a guid idea! C'mon let's play crabbin instead!" He may as well have saved his breath to cool his brose.

When Flora determined on something she was not to be deflected.

He followed her dejectedly out towards the dark, slimy rocks at the end of the beach, where the loose stones fell away to reveal a smooth, barnacle covered, wave-cut platform. Here the crescent of the beach narrowed to meet the headland at the Point, eventually running out completely as beach met sea and where the sea was thrust aside by the vertical towering cliffs. Here the waters of the loch fell steeply away into the deeps.

The game Flora had invented involved going out as far as they could towards the Point, while avoiding having their boots wetted by a wave, and then being chased back by the advancing sea. Normally they would arrive in plenty of time to wait for the tide and they would then keep moving back towards the main beach as the waves rolled progressively closer and closer. The problem was that at the Point the tides were unpredictable, they could advance fast and sudden when you weren't expecting them to. The narrow shelf that they were now on fell away quickly into the swirling currents and, with the sheer cliffs to one side, there wasn't any room for error. This was the reason the children had been banned from this part of the beach, which is why of course Flora found it so irresistible.

When they had advanced as far as they could along the cliff face they both stood and waited while the tide rolled ever closer. Callum had left Jess on the main beach and told her to stay there, no sense in her being put at risk for Flora's whims. She was happily poking her nose into nooks and crannies amongst the pebbles, searching out fascinating smells and little crawling creatures.

The black-brown, wet, folded cliffs soared above them for around a hundred feet or more, cutting out the light and throwing their surroundings into perpetual gloom; everything dripped and shone dully with seawater and the green slime of algae; the air smelt wet, heavy and seaweedy. Myriad dull, white, ridged barnacles clung onto every surface alongside tiny pale, snakelike swirls of carbonated fish faeces stuck to the rocks. The sound of dripping water echoed against the cliffs, filling the soggy silence. To their right the dark, curdled waters of the loch sucked at the rocks and boiled malevolently: Callum shivered in the dank, clammy climate of the place.

The waves started breaking at their feet as they started to run backwards, Flora shrieking in excitement, Callum grimly determined not to leave Flora, knowing it was useless to try and talk her out of the game in her current mood of recklessness. They leapt from rock to rock for five minutes or more just ahead of the waves. Then a particularly strong and vicious wave swept across their feet, up to their knees, soaking them in cold, foaming seawater. Callum grabbed Flora to keep her from being swept off the rocks.

-"Come *on* Flora!" he shouted impatiently "we've got tae get back noo, before it's tae late"!

The waters were slapping and booming into the headland; the noise was becoming deafening. Callum and Flora were perched on a shallow pinnacle of rock, Callum steadied himself, then sprang across a pouring, bubbling stream a couple of feet wide that had now separated them from the shore. He landed uncertainly and waited for Flora to follow him, waving his arms wildly as he tried to remain upright on the precarious boulder. He turned towards her and she looked right back at him, smiled smugly and then folded her arms. He was flabbergasted; he was used to Flora's bravado but this was ridiculous and dangerous too.

-"Come on Flora!" he repeated impatiently "or it'll be tae late tae get back!"

She turned her back on him, meaning to mock him but instead slipped on the smooth, algae covered rock on which she had been so uncertainly balanced. She slid off the wave slicked rock while trying desperately to scramble back but then fell back again, up to her shoulders in the swirling, clammy seawater. She screamed and scrabbled helplessly at the slippery rocks, the sucking waves, malign and angry threatening to pluck her off. Callum was horrified. All he could think of were the swirling, pounding black waters all around her, waiting to suck her down into the, threatening loch. All he wanted to do was run, as fast as he could for the beach. All his senses were screaming at him to flee the terrifying, noisy waters and the looming, cliffs. He yearned for the sunlit beach behind him and the comfort of Jess's soft enveloping fur.

He could hear Jess barking frantically at them, calling them back. Flora, now realised just how serious her situation was. She was too late to save herself and was now shaking with fear; her small legs were just not long enough or strong enough to stretch across to the perch of a rock Callum was now desperately teetering on. He too was now surrounded by swirling, cold water and the tide was coming in horrifyingly fast.

Flora scrambled at the rocks on all fours, she couldn't keep her footing and her whole lower half was now under water; one more wave would see her pulled off and swept helplessly out as it retreated back out into the deep, open water. Without thinking what he was doing Callum leapt towards Flora; every nerve ending shouting for him not to do it, to go back. He plunged into the swirling water next to her and grabbed the strap of her dungarees. He flung himself backwards into the stream of boiling, black waves behind him lunging backwards with his spare arm towards safety, pulling at the water with all his might, pulling towards the shore. He was numb with fear and biting cold, the adrenaline was surging through him, overwhelming his wits.

Callum, mind blank, was lying face down on the hard stones of the beach, a large stone biting painfully into his cheek. He felt chilled and wet but couldn't move, Jess was licking his cheek, barking.

-'It's all my fault!' he told himself! 'I should've stopped her. I'm the oldest. I should've stopped her; what will I tell Ma? What will I tell Auntie Isla?'

After a cold, miserable age he raised his head. He was back on the main beach, bright with sunlight reflecting blindingly off the large white, round stones that made up the main part of the beach. He felt the welcome heat of the sun on his back, his shirt clinging wetly and uncomfortably to it. He heard snuffling. Thinking it was Jess he called to her and she poked her cold nose in his face. He pushed her away and located the source of this snuffling. It was Flora, sitting in a soggy heap on the stones, sobbing quietly to herself, her white blonde, normally spiky hair now flat to her head, plastered across her forehead. He had never seen her look so miserable. He was overjoyed! They were alive, he hadn't lost her after all, she hadn't been drawn down into the dark currents of the loch, drifting, submerged and carried along forever into the watery dark he so feared. He shuddered with cold and scrambled across the clicking, crunching stones on all fours, his knees failing him.

Flora looked up at him, lips trembling, waiting for him to shout at her. He just shook his head as he looked down at her face, miserable and snotty with crying and expelled seawater.

-"I thoc'd ye woz drowned!" she snuffled to him dejectedly.

He smiled wryly;

-"It's alright Flora, jest another of yer daft ideas that ended up goin' wrong. We'd best get hame and get dry or ye'll catch a cauld, Ma says ye should never sit aboot in cauld wet things or ye'll end up poorly."

The back of his throat felt raw, salty and snotty and his mouth and nostrils felt full of seawater still. He shivered in the sunshine, a breeze had got up and they were both soaked to the skin.

-"We're goin' tae be in sae much trouble Cal!" Flora wailed miserably "and it's all ma fault!"

Callum certainly wasn't going to argue with that anyway.

They plodded their laboured way back up the track, shivering and despondent; even Jess was subdued, having caught the mood of foolish repentance from Flora and Callum's mood of resigned forbearance. They went to Callum's house since it was closest and were greeted open-mouthed by an astonished Màiri.

The two of them stood on the doorstep, heads bowed, dripping and repentant, expecting a scolding. They both raised their heads and looked up at Màiri in silent pleading, wordlessly begging her not to be too hard on them. They had suffered enough discomfort and indignity already. Even Jess looked submissive; tail hanging, head down, shifting from one foot to the other, wide eyes gazing up pleadingly. Jess wasn't sure why but she too knew they were in trouble.

-"All right, what happened?" Màiri asked with an exasperated sigh.

-"We fell in the water Ma!" Callum said simply in a resigned tone.

Màiri clicked her tongue in an irritated, impatient manner and was about to tell them that that was obvious; what she had meant was how was it that they came to fall in the water in the first place and how did they become so submerged that they had managed to become soaked from head to toe. But she realised it probably didn't matter too much now, they had clearly learnt some sort of lesson, whatever the lesson was and were now in need of a bit of comfort and drying off. Màiri could sometimes be daunting when Callum had transgressed but right now she felt it appropriate to forgive them both and get them out of their cold, wet clothes.

When they had dried off and Màiri had given them both a mug of hot milk, sweetened with honey and some freshly baked, honeyed oatcakes, she took Flora home. Flora was dressed in one of Hamish's long shirts and a pair of Callum's thick socks and she carried her boots in her hand because they were still soggy, even though they had been sitting in front of the fire for over an hour. When they arrived at Isla's croft she opened the door to them and gazed down at the dejected Flora with a resigned and despairing expression. Isla glanced at Màiri and then back at Flora, Màiri looked back and smiled wryly, handing over a pile of Flora's still damp clothes. Isla sighed and slowly shook her head; the universal language of mothers passed between the two women. Then Isla escorted a repentant, forlorn Flora indoors in silence, not a word had been spoken throughout, nor was any needed.

In the important matter of reading Callum had turned out to be a late developer. It had taken him until the age of seven before he had, belatedly, grasped the basics. Miss Pargeter had told Màiri he was more than bright enough to have begun earlier, in fact he was easily the brightest of her pupils she had said, but for some reason he didn't quite get the point of reading for quite some time. Once he had finally learnt though he had never looked back.

He had started with the few children's books that Màiri had saved from her own childhood and he pored over Hamish's old bible for want of anything more suitable and the old, neglected religious tracts that had gathered dust on a shelf in the main room, and he had begun avidly to study an old, incomplete set of encyclopaedias of Màiri's, reading them over and over, dipping into them whenever he had a spare moment. Her mother had bought them for her many years ago when she had been not much older than Callum was now, from a little curiosity shop in Dingwall. They had originally been printed in 1848, 'The Empire and Geographical Encyclopaedia' with the L to Q volume missing.

Màiri still browsed through them herself from time to time on dark winter nights when her eyes had become tired with sewing by lamplight, or when she wished to be taken out of herself; to cast off her responsibilities of motherhood and of a wife for a short while. She was especially interested to learn about exotic creatures and countries from faraway. Callum seemed to be interested in everything in them, especially science and the natural world. Nonetheless what he craved most were stories, especially adventure stories, for what was a story without an adventure to it?

Though he would still question Màiri about tales related to the natural world, like those that featured the selkies, he wanted tales of action and danger and intriguing tales of heroes and mysterious peoples. By the time he was eight he had gone beyond Màiri's Gaelic myths and legends and her fairy tales, which had been told to her in her turn by her mother, and even the tales Miss Pargeter read out in class; like Robin Hood and Treasure Island and of course Sir Walter Scott's Highland tales. These no longer really satisfied him; he wanted storybooks of his own to read and to lose himself in.

So, one bright but chill Saturday morning in Summer, Màiri and Callum, and Flora of course, since Callum couldn't do anything without Flora wanting to share, were preparing to set off to join the public branch library at Kyle of Lochalsh. It was only a small library but they could order books from further afield if need be. It would be Callum's first ever visit to the town, or indeed to any town.

Màiri was now pregnant for a third time and found journeys into town in the old hay wagon with the two big Clydesdale's pulling up front an uncomfortable trial to say the least. She fervently hoped this would be the last of her pregnancies, she found them "vexatious" at the best of times and this one had been particularly tough on her so far.

She knew though that some women could have ten or even as many as fourteen babies, and often ended up physically used up; worn out, empty husks. It was very rare if all the babies survived, often dying at birth, sometimes not long after. This would be Màiri's fourth baby of course. She was secretly hoping for a daughter, not that it would in any way make up the daughter she had lost, but it would be some sort of consolation.

Callum however, was beside himself with excitement, a great adventure ahead and better still, they were being taken on the adventure by the big Clydesdales, Hector and Hecuba, whom he adored. They were huge beasts that towered over him; the stallion, Hector, was a uniform, glossy black all over except for his white socks and Hecuba was a glorious, shiny chestnut with a coal black mane and luxurious black tail. The horses didn't officially belong to the community: the Clydesdale, the work horse of Scotland, although beginning to go out of use, and within thirty years would become rare, were still sufficiently in demand to be an expense way beyond the means of a small crofting community, both to purchase and to keep. They still belonged to an estate to the south where, as young horses they had been trained to the plough and to pull a wagon, but when that estate had bought in tractors as a replacement to do most of the work, they no longer needed so many horses. The great equine behemoths, used for hundreds of years as an essential adjunct to a farm of any size, were beginning to be replaced by the even more powerful machines; the ploughman, no longer dependent on these fellow creatures, was instead becoming master of a dumb, if noisy machine.

So these two huge, beautiful creatures had first been loaned to the local estate and then, when they in turn began to mechanise, loaned on again to the crofters for the cost of the horses keep. The community had gained hugely by their coming and lavished praise and care on these magnificent creatures. They had allowed a great expansion of arable land, as at Hamish and Màiri's croft, where they had more than earned their keep in extra oats, barley and hay grown. The community had had to dig deep into their pockets and their savings to buy a plough and other second-hand gear, cannily bargained for by John Fraser at Dingwall market, but these great powerhouses had helped so much with cultivation, harvesting and transport that the community now had a surplus of oats and barley most years, a regular form of income little dreamed of a few years before. What is more they had the means to get it to market, or at least to the railhead at Kyle. It had released them from the sometimes crippling demands of carters rates to carry their produce and saved their feet from the exhausting trek into town on foot. Now they had regular transport of their own and a means to collect supplies as well as it making sending their own goods to market more profitable.

On this particular Friday Màiri was taking eggs, butter and cheese to market, kept cool under an old, wet blanket. Ian McDonald, who was driving, was going to collect fence posts and wire with which to enlarge and strengthen the enclosure for the old Aberdeen Angus bull who had escaped twice in the last three months.

Callum had risen early, completed his chores and quickly, after a fashion, put on his best clothes before preparing his breakfast of brose. He said goodbye to his Pa, who had smiled softly and wished him well on his visit and then he had rushed to the other end of the village to the paddock where Hector and Hecuba were kept. He waited in a fever of impatience for his Uncle Ian to arrive with the harness and grooming equipment and to prepare the horses for their visit to town.

He climbed up onto the gate of the paddock and watched the great beasts quietly grazing, wraithed in a fine, early-morning mist that hung over the fields. The little Shetland pony in the same paddock looked tiny in comparison, his great hairy mane hanging wetly down his neck and over his eyes. He also was a chestnut colour, like Hecuba, but he had white hocks and a luxurious creamy tail. The long ferny tails of the Clydesdale's were to be plaited into a short bob as part of the preparation for the journey, they had to look their best for such a special occasion.

Nonetheless Hero the 'Sheppie' would not allow the morning to pass without his share of attention even though he was not going to town like the others. Despite the Shetland's size there was no doubt that he was boss in this paddock. He would monopolise the sweetest patches of grass and nettles and the other two gave him precedence when it came to stabling. He always had to be first to his stall on a cold night, otherwise he kicked up so much fuss that the others would refuse to go in. Having said that, all three were the best of friends and kept each other company through hot summer days and kept guard for each other on dark wolf-roaming nights; their ancestral memories requiring the herd to stick together.

Ian McDonald arrived shortly after Callum, carrying a box of tools and a step-ladder. As the glory of the village the horses were to look their best on the journey into town. Flora trailed disconsolately and reluctantly after her father, bleary-eyed and sulky from sleep. She greeted Callum perfunctorily.

Once in the field Callum and Ian set to with a will, first Hector and then Hecuba were groomed. Flora was wary of the big beasts but Callum was overjoyed to be so close to them. The giant horses stood patiently, thoroughly enjoying the attention and the pleasurable feel of the stiff brushes combing out their manes and removing the dust and mud from their coats. They were both nearly seven feet tall at the shoulder, their heads and long necks towered over even Ian's huge frame; the large powerful, muscles rippled and flexed under their glossy hides, showing off their enormous power. Their broad shoulders were made for pulling against a heavy shoulder collar. They were gentle, powerful giants, war horses turned to more peaceful roles.

Ian held the stepladder while Callum climbed up to Hecuba's head, the great dark eyes looked kindly on him and her soft muzzle nuzzled him gently in friendly greeting. The giant chestnut head dwarfed him and her upright ears flicked sensitively as he touched her and talked softly to her. He could hear and smell her grassy breath and feel it on his face. She shivered in pleasure as he brushed out her long, black mane and softly brushed her neck and face. The second brushing and oiling brought a wonderful soft, silky sheen to her impressive, dark coat as she snickered and issued a deep, ecstatic rumbling. Lastly, Callum and Flora combed out her "feathers", the long hairs on her fetlocks which brushed the ground as she moved and which became muddy and tangled in the wet field.

By the time they had finished Hector and Hecuba looked magnificent, glowing in the morning sunshine. Of course after finishing the two great beasts they had to give the little Shetland pony Hero his due. He had waited impatiently and jealously for his turn, bickering and nudging them and curling back his lips to show his teeth in aggressive displeasure in order to grab his fair share of attention even though he wasn't going anywhere.

Ian led the powerful horses by their halters over to the stable which the villagers had constructed alongside Ian's main barn, site of many a ceilidh. While Callum and Flora held their halters Ian proceeded to complete their harness in order to make them ready for pulling the handsomely painted, green and red hay wagon. Some of the tack and harness had been left when the horses had been delivered by the estate grooms but they had also had to make or replace much of it themselves. The two great shoulder collars, the massive, padded leather collars, braced with curved metal rods were essential to all activities carried out by working horses and had been "borrowed" from the estate stables. The massive collars were shaped to fit over the horses bulky shoulders comfortably. Attachments were made to the collars using various fittings and harnesses in order to transfer their massive motive power through their hefty legs and their heaving, muscled shoulders to the shaft of a wagon or cart or the shaft of the heavy, forged plough.

Callum would have been much happier had he been allowed to ride into town on the back of one of these patient giants rather than in the wagon, but his uncle thought it too dangerous and instead he had been allowed to sit on Hecuba, holding on to her collar while the wagon was being attached and while they waited for their passengers to arrive. Callum softly crooned to Hecuba and stroked her huge chestnut head while Ian finished harnessing up the two great beasts to the hay-wagon and added the finishing touches to their appearance; highly polished horse brasses and feather head-dresses: they were going to town in high style.

Finally, the passengers arrived and were embarked on wooden benches on the long, four-wheeled wagon. Flora and Callum sat on the high box seat at the front next to Ian who acted as driver, holding the long traces to control the horses. Màiri and Isla were seated on the front bench in their best Sunday hats, held on by long strips of black gauze, both excited and loaded up with baskets and boxes which were stored all around them. Both had produce to sell; late vegetables, eggs, cheese and butter and Isla had brought along a few young hens in a wicker basket for her aunt who lived in a little seaside cottage in Kyle. Nellie Fraser was coming to do her shopping with her daughter-in-law, carrying a young toddler and babe-in-arms and the widow Molly McClelland dashed up at the last minute to take a seat, still straightening her hat. She was coming just for the ride and possibly for free tea and a cake in the little hotel restaurant if anyone was going to treat her, which of course they would. Lastly, dressed in classic Pilgrims gear, was John Fraser, wearing a long, black, nineteenth century coat and black, broad brimmed hat, with his neatly clipped and pointed long grey beard and a grim expression. He was riding, arms folded in splendid isolation at the back of the wagon in order not "tae be associated wi' a gaggle of cacklin' wimmin".

The party set off amid waves and cries of good luck from the few assembled villagers who were left behind and, in all the commotion no-one even noticed that Jess had sneaked quietly onto the wagon and hidden herself under one of the benches. She was, at this moment, greedily eying Isla's terrified hens, strapped into their flimsy basket. The party rattled and bounced their way along the compacted dirt track and on to the main road, harnesses clinking and ringing and glinting in the sun, red feather head-dresses waving in the breeze, the horses dark, polished flanks shining. They looked a magnificent sight these great beasts, proudly pulling their colourful wagon in the fast fading days of horsepower. The end of thousands of years of history, of man and horse linked in effort, slowly ebbing, ghosts fading into history like an image in an overexposed black-and-white photograph.

The road swung round towards the bottom of the Loch before heading off towards Kyle of Lochalsh. On their way the little party had arranged to stop to pick up boxes of fish from the little community at the end of the loch. It had taken a long time but Màiri and Isla between them, with help from Màiri's former school friend Moira McGregor, had gradually broken down the resistance of the little community and established, step-by-step, a degree of cooperation. With the provision of the wagon and horses the co-operation had increased in leaps and bounds. Now the fishermen of the hamlet had a means of getting their fish to market in Inverness and to Dingwall to be sold the same day they caught them. They had a regular income now without having to pay carter' fees. The wagon would take their fish once a fortnight to Kyle and then via train to Inverness. They had also a means of getting other goods to market; the women of the hamlet had started knitting jerseys from their own sheeps fleeces which they could also now transport to market more easily and cheaply.

By explaining that the horses were on loan from the estate Màiri had convinced them that they need not feel beholden to anyone for their use. Their pride intact, Morag and Moira and the rest of their community made use of the offer of transport and improved their outlook significantly by doing so. Did they but know it the Great Depression was about to hit the country and they would soon need all the help they could give each other just to get by.

When they reached the little hamlet all the children ran out to greet them. They had already passed a couple of men from the little community out fishing on the loch: they had waved in greeting. Normally not much happened in the little community and to see these fine, great horses pulling a large, colourful wagon and everyone on board dressed in their Sunday best and on the way to town was an experience the residents couldn't miss. Their dogs were barking, the children ran round and round the wagon and the adults came out to greet them, even Morag came out to see, looking as sour as ever. Moira and the other women of the village greeted them warmly and Moira invited them in for a cup of tea and 'a bite'. Jess, having heard all the barking and commotion joined in and gave herself away. It took serious pleading and persuading from Callum for her not to be sent back home in disgrace.

Màiri was desperate to avoid taking any food from these people, it was plain how much they needed it for themselves. The poverty in this little community was unmistakable despite recent improvements. The children, half a dozen of them, looked clean and scrubbed and Màiri could imagine the women desperately trying to keep them clean until the wagon had arrived. She knew how hard it was with Callum, even now she expected him to be sitting up in front of the wagon accumulating grubbiness. But she knew these women would have done everything to ensure that neither they nor their children could stand accused of being either dirty or neglected; the universal fear of the poor. Ragged they certainly were; clothes worn through and patched together until virtually unrecognisable from the original, the women's clothes were covered with a woollen shawl to hide their shabbiness but the children at least looked fairly well fed now and with healthy complexions. But the poverty showed, as it always does, in the women's faces; pale, pinched, with dark rings around the eyes, a look of quiet desperation and tiredness in their pale, normally unsmiling faces.

It's a real effort to smile when you're hungry all the time, smiling takes energy and an ounce of hope, poverty kills all hope. The women would always be the last to eat and the first to go without; the men, the breadwinners, would be fed first and most, then the children and lastly the women would eat whatever was left, if anything, even when, as was the case with at least half the families here, the woman was also the breadwinner.

Màiri, Isla and the widow McClelland joined Moira and Morag in Moira's little cottage. They thanked her for her offer of tea but pleaded lack of time as an excuse not to have anything to eat. Nellie and her daughter-in-law elected to stay on the wagon with the baby and toddler. Flora and Callum jumped down from the wagon to greet their classmates, having been given strict instructions from their mothers not to move away from the wagon lest they get lost or ruin their best clothes. John Fraser continued to stand on his dignity while remaining sitting on the wagon, a contradiction which wasn't lost on Màiri who understood all too well the man's complexities. He clearly felt outnumbered by Catholics in this community, and did not want to be seen to be openly fraternising; old prejudices died hard.

Ian MacDonald remained with the horses and answered questions about them from the goggle-eyed children who were amazed at their size. Young Fiona had admired Flora's pretty, flowery new dress and Flora told her that if she could have got away with it she would "gi'the awfu' frock" to her. She said disparagingly that she "could nae abide flowers" on her clothes and "could nae be dain' with wearin' frocks anyhow"! Callum and the two boys, Ali and Billy engaged in play boxing and spat on the floor when no adult was watching, just because they were boys and that's what boys were supposed to do, except that Callum couldn't spit properly and managed to dribble down his chin instead.

As she entered under the low, turf roof Màiri was shocked at how bare Moira's home seemed but was impressed with its scrubbed cleanliness. There were six, cheap, unmatched, bentwood chairs and a bare table in the middle of the floor with a simple wooden bench along one wall and a couple of lamps and candles. That was all. The little fire was lit with glowing turfs and the room was warm enough. A black kettle was hanging over the fire gently steaming. What distinguished the room was what it lacked, not what it contained; no ornament, no knick-knacks, no pictures or photographs, just a few seashells on a windowsill and a wooden candleholder, that was everything. Moira had retrieved a set of six cups and saucers from somewhere, obviously kept for best and probably a wedding present, and despite Màiri's pleas, she had placed a plain looking plate with six oatcakes on it in the middle of the table. They would all have to have one each so as not to offend, which made both Màiri and Isla feel terribly guilty because they knew it meant Moira going without later to make up for this simple hospitality. They chatted inconsequentially over tea and the oatcakes. Each bite brought a sick, dry taste to Màiri's mouth as she thought of how desperately little her friend Moira could afford to give even this small amount away.

Afterwards, as they went out of the door to return to the wagon Morag called out

-"Mrs McDonald!"

Both Isla and Màiri turned in response.

-"Màiri" Morag clarified.

It sounded strange, the use of Màiri's first name coming from Morag, she always treated them in such a stiffly, formal manner.

-"A word please" Morag added

Isla looked back a little apprehensively at Màiri but continued walking with the widow McClelland, escorted by Moira. Màiri turned to face Morag, slightly nervous, expecting some rebuke as normal.

-"Morag?" she queried.

Morag took her gently by the arm and paused a moment, seeming to try and find the right words. Màiri wondered whatever it could be that was causing her such hesitation, she normally had no problem in being forthcoming.

-"I want tae thank ye!" Morag said simply after a moment "Fer what ye have done fer the village", her face momentarily crumpled, the harsh lines of her face from years of weariness and hard weather collapsing into a half sob, immediately cut short as she recovered. It was always kindness that touched the rawest nerves observed Màiri. She had momentarily been privy to a side of the woman that Morag kept well hidden, her humanity, and she felt closer to the woman for it. She took Morag lightly by the arm.

-"If what I hear frae the south is right Morag we're all of us in fae a hard enough tame of it soon, so it's best that we stick together, don't ye think?" She asked smiling warmly.

The little party reassembled on the high wagon and waved goodbye to the small, excited crowd before leaving the grinning children and barking dogs far behind on their bumpy road to Kyle. The road twisted this way and that as it rose and fell over and between the high, dark hills, sometimes skirting steep rock faces on one side with just enough room for the wagon and a sheer drop on the other side of hundreds of feet below to rocky, wooded glens, down steep heather and gorse lined slopes. Callum had never seen so many trees; broadleaf oaks, willows and hazels and scots pine greening steep gullies and hillsides. The stunning backdrop of soaring, misty peaks took the breath away, even from those who had made this journey countless times; some of the peaks towered to over two-thousand feet, surrounded by more ancient rounded hills worn down by countless centuries; Sgurr Dubh to the north-east, Beinn Liath Mor, Sgurr Ruadh and Maol Cheann-derg; Gaelic legends in the form of mountains. They traversed broad glens, overshaded by the brooding hills on either side. The roadsides were strewn with wild summer flowers; buttercups and bog loving, yellow flag irises and ragged robin in damp ditches. They paused mid-morning to take in the view and stretch their legs on the south shore of sparkling Loch Carron which swept out regally towards the sea. The shining, transparent loch was framed by drifts of rosebay willow herb like giant pink candles. They passed little hamlets with squat cottages and at Duirnish Callum saw his first two-story buildings, covered by blue grey slate and rust-red corrugated iron roofs.

After an hour-and-a-half of bumping, bone-rattling progress they came into town and Callum and Flora dumbly gazed at everything with wide-eyed astonishment. A motorcar tore past them, honking and clanking like some bright, shiny monster of metal, chrome and glass; the children were agoggle and astonished by the noise and the power of it. The horses were also startled by the noise and Ian McDonald had to grapple with the traces and used bellowed orders to calm the skittish animals. It was the first time the children had seen a motor vehicle of any kind and they were numbed by the deafening racket and speed. They didn't know where to look first. The roads into town were mostly paved with asphalt and carts and cars and lorries seemed to be everywhere. So many people all in one place. Ian took them down Main Street and on to Station Road, to the railway station so they could watch out for a train from a safe distance. The road had skirted the railway for much of the last part of their journey but, as yet, the children had not managed to see one of the fiery, steaming monsters that travelled the rails. Callum had once thought, when he was high on the hill behind their house that he had spotted a feint cloud of steam in a far-off glen but now they were about to see one for real, close up.

After half an hour and still no trains Ian pulled the wagon over into Fishery Pier to hitch up the horses and watch the boats coming in. The women went off to agree prices for their goods with shopkeepers and hotels and to find out the time of the train to Dingwall. Callum and Flora helped Flora's father unload the fish boxes onto a railway trolley. John Frazer went in search of religious sustenance at the local kirk where he hoped to meet members of the Parochial Council.

The women shortly returned to assure Ian that they could now deliver the goods to the general store when they were ready and to a local hotel once the fish had been safely loaded onto the train. Màiri and Isla, accompanied by Mollie McClelland sat and waited on the wagon while Ian and the children took the fish boxes onto the platform and waited for the train. They didn't have long to wait; the 10:45 was due any minute. They spent the time studying the dark coastline and misty peaks of Skye, Isle of Mists, Eilean a' Cheò, which in the clear summer air seemed almost close enough to touch on the other side of the rushing waters of the Sound.

Callum could see a small white cloud puffing up between the low hills on the approach to the station and he pointed and squealed with excitement. Flora pretended she didn't really care for a 'smelly old train' although she too had never seen one. The railway followed the coast for much of its route from Duirnish to Kyle and as it rounded the last bluff they could see clouds of steam floating out over the water. Callum heard the howling whistle echoing across the waves. His heart thudded at the great gush of steam and the 'pump! pump! puff! puff! whoof! whoof! of escaping hot clouds and metal clanked and clanged as con rods pumped, couplings rattled and the wheels eased their oily motions. The heavy giant clattered and squealed on iron and the carriages rattled and sung on the silver rails.

Despite herself Flora jumped up and down and waved in excitement, she clapped her hands, her nonchalence forgotten in the noise and drama. The screeching of brakes as metal wheels slid on the gleaming rails and the 'peesht! peesht!' of escaping gases near deafened the onlookers as pressure was released and the train slowed. As if at a signal the railway station burst into frantic activity; the stationmaster shouting and bustling passengers pouring from first and second class waiting rooms and porters with trolleys scampering onto the platform. The washroom smell of steam and the acrid, nutty, coal smoke filled the air with a thick smothering fog.

Gentlemen and their ladies bustled from their first-class lounge; high-class tourists from a visit to Skye on their way to a hunting party, the endless social round of the leisured classes. The men wore deer-stalkers or fedoras and long, hand-stitched coats or thick cut tweeds. The fragrant women swept along in ankle-length, expensive frocks, costly material swaying elegantly, their three-quarter length jackets tight buttoned as corsets. Long-pinned hats sat askance carefully coiffed hair, held up in bobbed bundles, fine mesh hairnets placed just so by maidservants. Their delicate feet were confined in high-buttoned boots which had been shined to mirrors by hotel boot-boys or country estate skivvies. They paraded their polish and class as consciously as birds of paradise in front of dun-coloured sparrows.

The ordinary folk wore well-shined breeches, flat caps and boaters with bright coloured ribbons and large, floppy tam-o-shanters. They carried malacca canes and newspapers and puffed on pipes while the women wore plain black skirts with short jackets and knitted shawls over frilly blouses pinned at the neck.

Umbrellas and cases and boxes and bags of leather, fish boxes and cheeses and bundles of fleeces were all piled onto the platform waiting to be loaded by harassed porters in waistcoats, peaked caps and watch chains. The station-master grandly surveyed the scene and gave orders and directions. Chaos turned to order as carriage doors slammed and van ramps were withdrawn; all goods to be stowed away tidy and shipshape. Voices were raised in greetings and sad farewell. Smoke drifted up and away as the fireman got up steam. Callum and Flora stood transfixed and bewitched as they tried to take in the chaotic and wonderful scene; confused, excited and overwhelmed by it all.

The guard blew his whistle, green flags waved and the oily, monster hissed and wheezed into life; metal shunted into metal as con-rods engaged with wheels and steam belched as the leviathan began slowly to breathe. The locomotive set off in bursts of white vapour and acrid, brown smoke. The whistle blew and blasted like a howling banshee or a monstrous shrieking owl. The ear shattering noise enveloped the platform as the train departed in foggy drifts of white thunder. Heads hung out of windows amongst waving hats and handkerchiefs fluttering crazily in the steamy breeze. The wheezing beast was on its iron-clad, clanking way again around by the seashore and back over the hills.

Ian stood beaming broadly, his huge frame shaking with mirth at the soot-blackened faces of Callum and Flora, still open-mouthed, struck dumb at the fading spectacle. Neither had ever seen or heard anything so overwhelming and impressive and so wonderfully noisy in the whole of their short, childish lives.

The two of them spent the next half an hour in a daze being led, to the public library in the middle of town by Màiri and Isla who stopped at a public drinking fountain to wash the sooty smuts from the children's faces. Ian had taken the wagon back up Main Street to drop off their goods at the various purchasers, to collect the money and to go to the ironmongers to buy the posts and wire with which to contain the old bull.

Before they entered the grand looking, brick-built library Flora warned Callum that they needed to be very quiet because talking wasn't allowed in a library. Callum wasn't sure how they could make clear to the librarian that they wanted to join the library if they weren't allowed to talk, but mutely nodded and followed his mother up the steps. The children were still subdued from the astonishing spectacle they had witnessed at the station.

The library was a large, cavernous Victorian building with high gothic windows, churchlike and overpowering in its solidity: it was designed to subdue and impress. The librarian was a tall, thin lady with greying brown hair tied up in a large loop at the back of the head. She wore pince-nez glasses on the end of her long, thin nose through which she looked down in a severe fashion at these two little children as if to question their sticky presence amongst her precious books, in her hallowed fortress.

The library had an enclosed, sepulchral air; a chapel or crypt for the worship and contemplation of literature. The librarian carried out the business of registering each parent and child in whispered voices and handed each a card stamped so abruptly and noisily that the sound echoed around the hushed walls, almost shocking in its brutality. She pointed out the fiction section and the non-fiction section and explained that they could have only three books each which they must bring to the counter for stamping and return within the month or, and at this point she looked particularly severe as she declared that late books incurred a fine.

-"Ask me if you cannot find what you are seeking!" she said in a manner and a tone that clearly suggested that they should do no such thing.

Callum gazed up at the shelves and shelves of books with their multi-coloured spines, their varying sizes and bindings and couldn't believe his eyes. There couldn't possibly be this many books in the whole world he thought. Where did he start? Màiri took him to the children's section and left him and Flora to contemplate, in astonished silence as she and Isla browsed the novels and non-fiction shelves. Flora was gazing starstruck at the glowing lights;

-"Their 'lectric!" she said after a while in a hushed voice to Callum, in a tone of amazement.

Nearby a grim looking woman in black with grey, wiry hair pulled tightly back in a severe bun placed her finger on her lips and shushed Flora. Flora looked suitably chastened and turned her attention to the books, running her finger along the spines in a distracted manner.

Callum looked at book after book, at first being too intimidated to take any out of their neat rows and then, timidly sliding one out before looking around furtively for a disapproving adult. When no one told him off, he relaxed a little and started studying the books earnestly. After half an hour or more he had chosen Kipling's 'Riki Tiki Tavi' and a story about a knight called Sir Gawain and lastly, what he thought was a nature book called 'Wind in the Willows'. Flora had chosen 'Little Women' and a cowboy story and a book about butterflies.

Callum, accompanied by Flora who was trying hard to carry all three of her books without dropping them, looked for his mother. He didn't dare approach the librarian behind her high, wooden rampart without his Ma's support. When he found Màiri and Isla in the grown-ups section they were sniggering together about something but, on seeing the two children Isla quickly put the book that they were looking at back on the shelf before she turned to them and asked how they had got on. Flora whispered to her, in an exaggerated fashion that they were finished and asked if they could go now please; she was beginning to find the restriction on talking a little overbearing, she couldn't remember ever being so quiet for so long.

Callum left the building in a state of near euphoria. He couldn't believe that his little buff-coloured, cardboard ticket had given him entry to what seemed like an infinite world of ideas and stories and facts and pictures and photographs. It had opened up a whole new, magical panorama for him and he clutched his books really tightly to make sure he didn't lose them or that they didn't somehow disappear in a puff of smoke.

By the time Callum was ten he was an avid reader of novels and non-fiction and had read all of Walter Scott's adventure novels which, he much enjoyed but found a little odd, not really reflecting what he knew of Scottish life. They were grand adventures all the same. He read Robert Louis Stephenson's novels with baited breath, especially 'Kidnapped'. He had imagined himself as the young Davy Balfour . He had read popular history books on the Romans, the Saxons and Vikings and the History of Scotland, albeit somewhat contradicted by his own knowledge and experiences as a Highlander. He was fascinated by accounts of Bronze and Iron-Age archeological digs; but his favourite non-fiction reading was science, especially natural history.

Miss Pargeter, while commenting in his school report on his naughtiness and his propensity to question everything, including her authority, roundly commended his thirst for learning, his imagination and his marks for all subjects except mathematics with which he struggled mightily but largely in vain. He also had some talent at drawing and tried to emulate the pictures of birds, flowers and animals in his library books and from memory of his observations around the glen. He admired the beautiful, and closely observed drawings and watercolours that Miss Pargeter did and which she sometimes pinned up on the wall in the classroom. He wished he could paint like her.

As he got older he also found himself engaged with more and more of the work of the croft, helping his mother and father in the ever pressing round of seasonal tasks. The one thing he never helped with though was the fishing. His father still went fishing from time to time, although less so now that there was more arable land and more stock to care for, but the fish still helped them to eke out a living through the bare months of winter and early spring. There were some very bare winters in the years following the Great Depression. Nevertheless, Callum still couldn't be persuaded to accompany his father out onto the dark waters in the middle of the loch where the fish ran.

The small community was hit severely by the Depression; the prices for their surplus goods fell and they barely afforded the essentials. Poverty throughout Scotland, especially in the cities was terrible. Malnutrition and the death of children, weakened by lack of sustenance was higher than ever. Poverty stalked the glens again like a scavenging ghost, sucking the lifeblood out of communities. The only way communities could survive was by sharing and working together, which is what many of them always did in the Highlands. Many landlords were less than sympathetic, for those tenants without the protection of controlled leases on their croft times became impossible. Some fled to the cities as a last, desperate hope. In the glen the community held together and supported their neighbours at the end of the loch. Somehow, as the poor mostly do, they scraped and struggled and muddled through and there was still an occasional feast, such as at "Hairst Hame" and the like.

Màiri and Isla between them in those grim early nineteen-thirties became the mainstasy of their community. With the willing help of Nellie and John Fraser and young Maggie and Ian McDonald they seemed to be everywhere; organising collective planting in spring, getting together at the shearing in summer, collectively selling produce at the markets, starting a knitting club and clothes-making clubs, sharing their talents and energies and those of others by bringing people together and helping individuals and families when illness or hard times struck. Somehow they bound the two small communities together, regardless of religion; a tough task in Calvinist Scotland. Together with the leadership of Moira and Morag in their own community they found the energy to keep everything going. The children of the two communities were somehow always well fed, even if their clothes were so darned and patched as to be virtually re-made and their shoes often had holes in the soles. The close bonds already formed between the women of the two communities really counted when it came to the seemingly mundane business of the children's school dinners. Isla had one day expressed the concern to Màiri that the children coming from the other end of the loch might be having to go without now that times were so hard. Flora had reported to her that often these children seemed to have little in their packed school lunches other than dry oatcakes to eat. Isla didn't know how to address the problem without raising the acute sensitivities of some of the parents and suggested that Màiri talk discreetly to her friend Moira, as she usually did when she wanted to introduce an idea to their little sister community. Somehow by some clever sleight of hand and the tactful involvement of Morag she made it appear to be a joint idea, a shared enterprise between the two communities of providing cooked meals at lunchtime for all the schoolchildren. The women of the little hamlet took it in turns to help Màiri and Isla cook meals in Isla's well equipped kitchen and all contributed whatever produce they could spare at the time and in such a way that the honour of the poorer community was never compromised.

From then on Màiri and Isla, with many contributions from the Fraser's and others, always managed to ensure that the children of the two communities each had a hot, nourishing meal at least once every weekday. The shared business of cooking brought the women together as never before, even Morag loosened up somewhat and joined in with a will and even the occasional smile. It was an opportunity for Màiri and Isla to see that all the women got a good meal. When all the children had been served in their classroom, the women would return to Isla's kitchen for their own meal and they would talk and laugh and exchange worries. They shared personal stories because that's what stories are for, binding people together and creating a common history and culture. The women somehow kept their communities going even through the worst of times through a collaborative effort and with Màiri and Isla and Moira and Morag leading the way, often without appearing to do so.

The harvest was the most imortant time of the year when everyone from the two villages traditionally came together. The harvest of late September and early October in 1931 was for the villagers a very fruitful one in terms both of crops and relationships, although it didn't seem as if it was going to be until very late in the season. Dark, depressing, rain had continued throughout most of September and the crofters of both communities were desperately fearful for their crops and their hay. They risked being ruined. Starvation of beasts and humans and even the slaughter of breeding ewes and cows looked as though it would be a real and awful possibility.Disaster loomed darkly in everyone's mind. If the rain didn't let up fishing alone couldn't sustain the two communities through the winter, stomachs would shrink. The crofters, always on a knife-edge of feast or famine, were expecting the worst. If the weather failed them they were on their own, no one would come with help from elsewhere A dark, starving winter beckoned. Some might not make it through, especially the oldest and youngest.

Then, at the end of September, when desperation was turning to near despair, almost too late came an Indian summer, only broken by the odd short, refreshing shower. At last the ground dried out, the crops turned golden dry and the hay waved tantalisingly in the breeze, studded with late, glorious wild flowers. The horses were harnessed, scythes were sharpened and everyone prepared for a full two weeks harvesting; school was closed and the children were delighted. The harvest was ready, the opportunity of feast rather than famine opened like dark waves parting to beckon safe passage.

They started at Màiri's and Hamish's Croft, it being the highest at the top of the glen and the furthest to the west before the wild coast and moors took over. It was a glorious day, a light, early shower was enough to freshen the air but not sufficient to dampen either the crops or their spirits. The sun came out and huge, bubbling, white clouds slowly tracked across a brilliant blue sky. The loch shone silver and green and the air was filled with the smell of heather drifting down from the upper slopes. The last swallows swooped over the fields, fattening up for the long journey to Africa and the golden, yellow barley, waved lazily in the breeze across the surface of the crop.

The harvesters worked their way in a line across the field. Every now and then one would stop to use a whetstone on their 'huik' or scythe. The rhythmic scraping 'huick, huick!' echoed onomatapoeically. The line consisted of Hamish, Ian McDonald, John Fraser, two men from the neighbouring village and lastly Màiri, who could scythe crops with the best of men. The technique consisted of a rhythmic body movement; swinging the whole trunk pivoted from the waist to take the scythe a couple of inches clear of the ground at a slightly upturned angle. The slight dampness from the early shower had given just enough friction to the cut to give a good bite to the blade. If the technique were right the harvester could keep going all day; for those who, like Hamish, lacked the correct technique and tried to use the strength of their arms rather than their whole body, tiredness set in quickly and frequent rests were necessary.

The line of harvesters continued to move steadily across the field in a ragged line, like waders ploughing through a waist-high golden, pool, sweeping all before, ensuring that the barley fell tidily in a heap to the left of them, lying in alignment so it could be easily picked up by those following behind who would bind armfuls into sheaves.

Those following behind included Isla, young Maggie, Morag, Moira and the older children like Callum and his schoolfriends. None of the children were quite tall enough to wield a scythe yet but were nonetheless quick and nimble at tying and stacking the barley sheaves into stooks where they stood like sentinel pyramids, casting shadows across the field. The smaller children followed behind, gleaners collecting stalks missed by their older siblings and forming them into extra sheaves; nothing was to be missed. The stooks would be left in the field for the day, safe enough from showers now that they were piled up in pyramids, so long as heavy rain held off. It was always a frenetic, nervous time; the crops when cut were still hostage to the fortunes of the weather. Starvation hadn't been avoided yet and there were still plenty of crops on other crofts to be cut, dried and brought safely home.

When the harvesting team stopped for their midday meal, Màiri, as the woman of the croft whose crops were being harvested, was expected to feed the whole team, children as well; she didn't disappoint. There were great mounds of fresh-cooked mutton pies, bread, butter and home-made cheese, and mouth-watering summer puddings, bright pink and running with juice, made with her first crop of jewel-like red and black currants. There was also thick cream from her own cows, fed on rich summer grass. To slake their mighty thirsts there were flagons of heather ale and gallons of tea made over a small fire, carefully watched, a field fire now would be a disaster.

They ate and talked and joked and laughed in friendly fashion at each other's expense and the children played in the field, still with excess energy, chasing each other, leapfrogging and racing and playing tag. They ate with gusto like the adults and drank home-made ginger beer until they were fit to burst.

For today they were all as one and all was well, good food, sunshine and the company of your neighbours; it was enough, more than enough for now. Màiri started up a Gaelic work song as they returned to the field on that first day and everyone joined in, satisfied, full and refreshed and a little lazy in the warm afternoon sunshine. Three acres of barley to cut and then on to the weeping, long-eared oats, and tomorrow it would be the turn of Màiri's and Hamish's second field of barley and then Ian's and Isla's crops and so on for the next ten days to two weeks, if only the weather were to hold off.

Hamish was, for once quietly enjoying himself in the company of others, proud of Màiri who seemed at the heart of everything. Right now as her pure, melodious voice swelled out over the field to the accompaniment of the others he loved her more painfully and more complicatedly than ever. He worked hard next to the rest of the men and with Màiri at the opposite end of the line; backbreakingly hard, blistering work, cutting the barley and then the oats. When the crops were in it would be time for the hay. He didn't pray often now but he prayed then; for good weather, for his half-content mood to hold. His thoughts drifted as he swung the scythe, rhythmically, painfully but mentally removed.

He thought of good days, of the birth of his children including the last, Jean, or Jeannie as she had become universally known, and he thought of the night-times of frantic urgency with Màiri, when her close-bodied warmth made an intimate, secret encounter between them possible for a few moments. Jeannie was even now playing in a makeshift cradle on a blanket of straw, nearly eighteen months old, with young Flora doting over her. Jeannie was a happy young infant, engaging and undemanding, unlike Dougal who had been a handful as a toddler but who was now, at nearly six, doing his best to help, following the other children, collecting felled and missed stalks of oats.

Hamish thought about the time when he had first come to the glen as a young minister still in thrall and in fear of his father, fired up by his mission, inculcated into the ministry at his strict protestant college. When he had first met Màiri he had been beguiled, overawed by her beauty, her vital feelings and her enthusiasm. It had carried him along, secretly excited him but he had found his faith slipping away. He had begun to blame her for his own perceived wickedness. Had he lost his faith because of her or despite her? He didn't know but, away from the influence of his father and of the kirk, he had felt himself at sea, out of his depth, unable to resist Màiri and feeling less and less conviction and more and more self-loathing. He had at first been mesmerised and enveloped by the glen and its beauty and he had seen a chance of rescue; Màiri had made it clear she wanted to be with him, hard as he found it to believe. No, if he had lost his faith it was because he had found it wanting, it gave him no reason to carry on for its own sake. Once he had broken the spell his father and his father's Church had over him he could see no future for himself as a minister.

He didn't have a problem with God, just with the kirk's interpretation of God and with their punitive ways. He hoped he might find Him anew amongst these hills, amongst these people, with Màiri, but God had proved as elusive as happiness.

As a child Hamish had been unable ever to sort out what his real feelings or thoughts were. In the end he had become subsumed into his father's personality; always fearful, never sure about anything and never having any autonomy, always driven by demons, real and imagined. Coming to the glen and meeting Màiri had given him the chance of a second life but his emotional machinery had been forever damaged. He felt he could never really relax. He always had to be on guard against weakness lest the demons get the upper hand; the demons that lurked on the edges of his mind, always promising to creep into his brain; the fear that his nightmares would return, always the same in essence but different in form; slow footsteps in the passageway, the sound of a doorknob turning, the sound of breathing behind him, his bare knees pressing on the floorboards or stone flags, a cry in the darkness.

He swung his arms and his body to the rhythm of the scythe, stopping every now and then to retouch the edge of his blade, the smooth sweep of the whetstone resounding like a grating corncrake. He absorbed the sights and smells around him as he worked his way down the field. The crunching sounds of his swishing steel through barley stalks; the damp smell of the black earth under his feet filling his nostrils, the warm air full of the sound of birds and buzzing insects, the joyful chatter and tunes of those around him, the shrieks of the children fading behind him, all drifting into his thoughts as he swam in the flow of harvesting, carried along on the currents of the community, purposefully bound together. It was, for a moment as if he were on the sidelines watching himself, a part of the community and apart from them, slowly working his way across the field in the company of the others. He had never known such happiness, such contentment as he did during that late indian summer, that special harvest.

He looked over at Màiri, his wife; how it thrilled him still to call her that; he had watched her at the mid-day meal, confident and so at ease, beautiful and robust, a woman of substance and flesh, a woman of great physical and emotional strength and tenderness. He wasn't worthy of her of course but he was grateful that she was his all the same. He watched Callum, who so readily accepted him for who he was, his father. Being a father was a complicated role for him, as complicated as being a husband or crofter. There was so much anger and betrayal that had gone with his own father's role in his life. Callum was growing so quickly; he wished he could hold all of this; Màiri, Callum, Dougal and little Jeannie, this feeling, in the present, like a photograph, forever, for tomorrow to never come, for it always to be today, this Indian Summer, this harvest. Callum had caught his eye as he had looked back over his shoulder and his son had smiled at him with such pleasure and openness that it had almost made him feel he could weep.

He knew he had failed this family of his, he was never a good enough father, never a good enough husband or crofter, no good as a fisherman; then there were the times when he seemed unable to do anything at all, sometimes for weeks. He tried and tried, he was more practical now than he used to be, but still clumsy and awkward, lacking dexterity. He didn't have a feel for it the way Màiri did, however long he did it for. He knew that Màiri didn't blame him, she told him over and over that he was doing fine, she was proud of him but he knew deep down. He didn't feel sorry for himself, he accepted all of this with stoicism and resignation and was thankful for his lot and for Màiri and his family, despite knowing that he didn't deserve them.

Màiri looked over at Hamish. She wondered what he was thinking as he worked away quietly, uncomplaining, however hard things were. She really admired him, not many men with no practical experience could have, or would have taken up such a life as this. She knew it didn't come easy to him but he worked so hard. She told him as often as she could how much she admired him but she knew he didn't believe her, couldn't seem to believe her. Today he seemed more content than he had for a long time, -"Please God make it last, make it all last!"

Hamish reflected on how much he was enjoying what he was doing today; this hard, physical, repetitive task. He didn't need to concentrate too much, he let his body and eyes do the work while his mind drifted. The thing he loved most about his life was being out in the open; amongst nature, in the fields, feeling the breeze, the Sun, the rain, hearing the birds, seeing creatures going about their lives around him, uncaring and unregarding of his presence. At first it was so alien to him but then after his first year or so he had become subsumed into the natural world, part of the natural landscape, part of the seasons, his life followed the pattern of the weather and the natural rhythm of this world he had become so much a part of.

Màiri took another bite out of the crop with her huik, seeing the oat stalks fall satisfyingly in alignment to her left as she stepped forward to take another swing. She had a natural, graceful rhythm as she swung into the stroke, seeing the crop fall, another day's oats to see them through winter.

Hamish glanced over admiringly at Màiri. She had a natural elegance as she moved, so unlike his own striving and awkwardness, even when engaged in such a hard physical task. Her long black hair swayed in the breeze with each movement; he noticed the roundness of her breasts pressing against her dress and the curve and swell of her bottom and her strong, straight back, her strong shapely legs, planted firmly as she rhythmically swung her scythe with ease, her grace and dedication were a moving supplication to the gods of the harvest.

Màiri glanced across at Hamish again, she had seen him look, she smiled; she had never felt so attached to him as she did now, one on either end of the line, spread out across their field, Màiri making sure she didn't get too far in front of Hamish. He was doing well, despite his lack of technique, she hoped he could keep it up for the next two weeks, it was going to be really hard for him. She must do what she can to take the strain off him. She sighed, she wished she could have a proper conversation with him about all this but whenever she broached anything remotely sensitive he seemed to pull away and shut down, unable to deal with his emotions, with intimacies, he tended to pack them away.

He was a fine looking man still she thought, stooped and somewhat downcast but all the hard work had made his muscles lean and hard and he moved differently from when she had first known him, with a more physical stride, still awkward but more relaxed. If only he could relax his mind too, let go of his worries. He always seemed to be holding something in, not letting go lest something terrible happened, always on edge, always distracted. She studied his face, more relaxed than she had seen it in a long time, no longer frowning, the lines less pronounced, she could almost believe he was enjoying himself for once.

Hamish looked across and caught Màiri's eye, they stood still for a moment and gazed at each other across the width of the small field.

By the end of the long day, working almost until last light, everybody was sore and dog tired, the little group from the hamlet still had to make their weary two-mile trek in the darkening evening to the end of the loch. Those from the glen took their leave of Hamish and Màiri and went back to complete what chores could not be left until tomorrow. Tired small children grizzled and were finally laid to bed, tired out from so much fresh air and a surfeit of exercise and excitement. Callum had fed his chickens and then fed Jeannie from a bottle and put her to bed in her cot near her parent's bed while Màiri got their supper and Hamish belatedly milked the desperately lowing cows. They ate in silence, eyes drooping, desperately sleepy; Callum and Dougal could hardly hold their heads up for weariness and Màiri had to help them to bed in their own room.

Hamish was exhausted but content and, as Màiri treated the blisters on his hands with balm she looked him in the eyes and kissed him tenderly; he was too tired to resist. As they lay in bed afterwards they made love, slowly and tenderly for once, feeling each other's bodies with lazy passion and affection, slowly exploring each other in the dark; Màiri's soft, round breasts and

Hamish's firm hard buttocks, their thighs entwined, his rough skin and her soft, pale belly, each making the other's skin tingle and shiver with pleasure and joining at last as one in deep, shuddering delight, simple and unselfconscious.

CHAPTER 6

HIGHLAND HARVEST

The harvest continued for nearly three weeks. They took it in turns every three or four days for the first two weeks to go down to the end of the loch to the small hamlet and help to cut crops and mow the hay. They were well fed there on tasty, fresh fish grilled over a fire and oatcakes with jam made from wild berries and tattie-scones fried in hot dripping, all washed down with home-made heather ale; everyone had their own recipe and had made their own the previous autumn. There were gallons of strong tea for those who preferred, or who, like John Fraser were tee-totallers.

The banter and the chatter and singing went on all day, for the children it was one glorious late summer holiday. The fields glowed with golden stubble, peppered with birds; hoodie crows bullying, martins chittering and swooping overhead, diving, graceful swallows scooping up the clouds of insects disturbed by the harvesters and hundreds of chattering sparrows, pink-breasted linnets, thick-billed finches and brown and friendly field mice. Harvest mice dashed out of cover, stocking up grain for their winter larders. All had their fill of the fat, fallen kernels of barley and oats. It would help all these creatures through the autumn with a few pickings left over for the winter birds.

Every few days Ian McDonald would harness up the thick-muscled horses to the hay-wagon and go out with a team to collect the dried crops, stooks of oats and barley and pale-green juicy hay, clustered with dried flowers, clover and herbs, nutritious and tasty to feed the penned-up stock over winter. As the barns piled up roofwards the prospect of winter hunger faded. The golden crops safely brought in scattered dark clouds of worry.

Callum was in child heaven; no school, all day with his friends and with Flora, the adults cheerful and singing and generous, lazy mid-day meals and plenty of time to play, not getting home until near dark and working with his Ma and Pa and the rest of the community in the fields all day. The late autumn sunshine and chattering, abundant wildlife and the beauty of the scene against a panorama of heather-covered, soaring peaks were a glorious backdrop to that memorable harvest. They walked home as a family group, with his father's arm on his shoulder and his Ma beside him, carrying Jeannie and holding Dougal by the hand, in the light of richly glowing sunsets which set the loch on fire and burned the flaming sky purple and orange, scorching the days on his memory forever. It was a never to be forgotten hymn to his home and his boyhood, to his community and to that golden, autumn harvest when he was nearly ten.

Although they had two nerve-racking days of heavy rain the sun soon returned and the hiatus gave them all a breathing space to tend to blisters and aching backs. They also took the opportunity to catch up on necessary chores and organise more space in barns and sheds in hopeful anticipation of the rest of the bountiful harvest.

There was so much barley and oats in the end that threshing took nearly two weeks at the larger village and nearly a week at the hamlet. The machines were the same design as those used by their grandfathers and, at the hamlet, it was indeed the same machine that their grandfathers had used. The machines were operated by two large wheels, either driven by hand or by belts attached to a motor which in turn operated the rollers and the mesh belt that carried the straw away and through which the kernels and chaff and dust fell, only to be blasted by two great bellows-driven blowers that separated the chaff and the dust from the grain. The thresher in the glen was larger and driven by an unreliable diesel motor. The sheaves of barley or oats were untied and fed into the large hopper at the top of the machine which produced straw at one end and barley or oats at the other. The seed was collected in a hopper and tipped into hessian sacks ready to be stored while the chaff was discarded or spread on the fields.

Callum loved watching the big threshing machine; it rattled and shook furiously, puffing blue smoke and belching loudly. It ran on low-grade diesel which smelt sour and acrid. The noise of the vibrating engine made speech impossible and hand signals a necessity. Ian McDonald, in whose barn the threshing took place, supervised Callum while he fed the unbound sheaves into the great maw of the machine, a shadowed, pulsating throat of wooden casing through which the stalks tumbled onto a vicious metal spiked drum. The straw provided animal bedding through the winter for spring lambing and for Callum's chickens, while the oats and barley fed people and livestock and this year provided a fair few sacks left over for sale at Dingwall agricultural market.

Callum loved to walk around the croft and see the fat, bulging hessian sacks stacked to the roof beams in the little barn and in the shed. He was amazed at the hay lofts full to the brim. Outside he would stand and gaze at the hay and straw stacks towering above him, held down with old fishing nets tied to heavy rocks, safe against the powerful autumn gales. All that bounty was to Callum a wonder and a material reminder of that glorious Indian summer. Even at his age he understood the precarious nature of farming this far north, in such a difficult land and with such harsh weather. So the success was extra sweet for everyone.

Three days after the last crops were in it started to rain, torrentially, as it can only rain in the north-west of Scotland in October. The winds picked up and the rain came in from the sea in horizontal sheets, stinging, cold, drenching rain. The water flooded off the hills in white torrents, every gully and burn swelled and boiled and burst its banks and flooded the surrounding countryside. The burn that ran over the cliffs in a waterfall turned into a bulging, angry crashing niagara. The path down to the cove was impassable, it had become a seething torrent, clogged with torn vegetation and uprooted rocks. A biblical flood of rain washed away the last shreds of the Indian summer. The glen became a dark, underwater chasm, water flowed, oozed and sucked over and under the ground; a dark, miserable fury of black rain washed over the land.

To go outside was to be drenched in an instant to the skin, even oilskins were not impermeable, rain squeezed and soaked into every gap and cranny, every bodily crease became sodden and oozing; cold, slippery water got in everywhere, under doors, through window joints and cracks. The sodden turf roofs heaved and swelled with rain and dripped miserably onto floors. Everywhere was water, the glen had become a grey, oozing liquid, no longer solid but a watery, floating land.

The deluge continued almost without a break for a month until November brought relief of a kind; it began to snow. A North Atlantic anticyclone brought cold, arctic weather and the glen shivered in white. The family had been cooped up in the house for much of the time during October, getting on each other's nerves, huddling around the one fire trying to dry out or keep warm. Damp clothes steamed on every available surface; Màiri couldn't keep up with the wet clothes. The house felt and smelt of damp, boots were always damp and the leather became stiff and chafed where it had dried out in front of the fire; discomfort was constant: the harvest seemed no more than a distant dream. And when the snow came it was a blessed release, winter came early but at least everywhere wasn't streaming rain. Summer had run straight into winter, autumn had been skipped that year, just a miserable wet comma in the year's sentence.

Callum hadn't at first realised it but, since his mother had talked to him about his father's moods and why he was as he was, he had become more sensitive, more alert to his father's moods and feelings. He had become more protective of him and made sure he paid him more attention, spent more time with him. That's how he had come to notice the first signs of his father's black moods returning. Hamish had become quieter than usual and moved about at a slower pace, had less good humour and there was no sign of lightness about him anymore; he appeared to be imbued with heaviness and melancholy.

As the weather had closed in around them, the days becoming shorter and darker, the long dreary dampness of October oozing into their very bones, Hamish had begun to lose his struggle with the demons who began to worry and gnaw at his thoughts and cast a cloak of deep pessimism over his very soul. Gradually, the inner core of his being became saturated with despair and loathing. As his strength and vitality ebbed away, his will sapped by thoughts of worthlessness and pointlessness, he sank into a deep well of self-contempt and hopelessness.

Màiri also noticed it, with a heavy feeling of inevitability, a stomachleadening helplessness and sadness. Callum spent as much time as he could working with his father, his athair. As early as he could he would raise his small, sleepy body and wash briefly before heading out to find him after he had had his brose and a quick mug of tea for his breakfast.

He usually caught up with him in the cow-byre, cleaning out the stalls and filling them with fresh straw, stuffing the mangers with hay and tethering the cows ready for milking. Callum did what he could to help, sweeping the stalls out and fetching water and soap for his father. Màiri and Hamish were scrupulous about cleanliness when it came to milking. They would wash their hands thoroughly and the same with the cows udders, soap and water and then thoroughly rinsed. The cows objected but it had to be done. Callum would help and be careful to keep out of the way of the cows kicking back legs when he did so for they could be tetchy sometimes. The buckets for the milk also had to be properly sterilised and then milking could proceed. Callum had been shown how to milk by Hamish; the rhythmic action of squeezing and drawing down with the fingers in order to gain a steady stream of frothy, creamy milk.

The bodies of the cows warmed the little byre, their breath steaming in the air. It was an intimate little space, the closeness to these animals, their warm breath on the neck of the milker as he or she sat on the three-legged stool, the cow looking round to see what was happening. There was the constant, tinny ring of the milk as the stream of warm liquid hit the sides of the buckets accompanied by the soft crunching and slurping sound of the munching cows filling the byre.

The cows were content to eat their hay, juicy and still pale green with scented herbs and dried flowers, nourishing and familiar. Cows dislike the unfamiliar, the milker has to have a relationship with the cow while squatting on the stool, close in against its flank; resting the head into the cows body gives reassurance, talking to her softly helps. Cows can be very awkward and uncooperative if they've a mind. Hamish had taken time to learn that, he had had to watch Màiri to realise what was needed.

She knew each cow intimately, knew her temperament, knew her likes. She would sing softly to them in Gaelic, she said the cows were Gaelic and they understood their own language. Hamish couldn't sing to the cows, he was too self-conscious and he didn't have the Gaelic, but he would talk to them softly, he had learnt to trust them now and they he, he could talk to them now even when he felt unable to communicate with anyone else. He usually just murmured some nonsense to them, asked them how they were, reassured them softly. Occasionally they would grunt back or gently murmur in their throats.

When he first brought them into the byre for milking, or joined them if it were deep winter and they still needed milking when they had been brought in to stay, they would moo and bellow loudly, earsplitting in the confined space but with an energy and unself-consciousness that felt cheering somehow. It was just a greeting and an expression of their simple needs, for fresh hay, water, to relieve the pressure on their udders and for a little extra company. Since they had acquired two milking cows he had noticed that they were much more relaxed, they watched out for each other.

On one bleak November morning, squatting in the close warmth of the cow byre Callum was watching his father leaning into the cow, Ella, talking softly to her, the curve of his back wrapped in an old thick, black coat against the icy cold of the early morning air, tied at the waist with twine. What would farmers do without binder twine? Callum had been up half an hour, he had had a quick breakfast and a slurp of tea, both made from the big black kettle that hung on a hook over the fire, always filled, always hot. He had wrapped up warm; a thick knitted jumper and his old jacket, a cut-down, cast off. But he was used to the cold and it didn't bother him, except for the blistering, red, bunion-like chilblains that you didn't notice until you warmed your feet and then moaned with the agony of the sharp pain and unbearable itching.

Callum didn't chatter idly as some children of his age would, he would comment on the cold, check before he did something, ask his Pa what to do next. He was there helping and keeping him company while desperately trying to hold on to him by a silent act of will, to keep him from plunging into black despair again where he couldn't reach him.

This particular morning he could feel him slipping away. Hamish had almost stopped talking again, not that he did much normally but in the last couple of days, he had stopped talking to Callum at all unless Callum prompted him to do so. Normally he would mention what was happening on the croft, how the animals were doing, whether he thought any of them were poorly. He never patronised Callum, never spoke to him as if talking to a child, he spoke in a similar tone to that he used with Màiri. Callum liked his father's voice, it was soft and deep, he sounded his words clearly and with a roundness of tone and a fineness of speech, a bit like Miss Pargeter who had also been educated in Edinburgh. His father would use words that Callum only otherwise read in books, words he didn't hear other people, even his mother, using. When his father was becoming 'poorly' again, the term Callum used to explain it to Flora, his voice became flat in tone, listless and very quiet, almost inaudible, even in the intimate space of the cow byre. He was doing it now, asking Callum to pass another clean bucket, so low spoken that Callum had to lean towards him to hear. As Callum took the already filled bucket from him he managed to slop some of the milk on the dark, rough cobbles of the byre.

-"Careful boy!" Hamish shouted loudly, the words ringing off the stone walls, echoing in the small space. Callum stopped, wide-eyed, frightened at the sudden, harsh, unfamiliar tone, Pa hardly ever shouted at him and then only when he had been really naughty.

Hamish jumped up and grasped Callum. He meant to apologise, to comfort him after his involuntary outburst. Callum stood stock still, wide-eyed, looking up at his father fearfully.He dropped the bucket on the floor and more pure white, creamy milk slopped out over the rim onto the dark cobbled floor, slowly seeping away between the cracks. Hamish was horrified; he was looking down at his own face when he was a small boy, looking up at his father in fear, tears in his wide eyes.

-"No!, No Callum! -- I'm so sorry, so sorry!" He desperately grasped Callum to him and hugged him; something he had never done before.

-"I'm so sorry. I didn't mean to shout and startle you, really, I'm sorry!" He clung on to his son and rocked from side to side.

-"Shhh son, shh! I didn't mean it, it just -- it just came out wrong! I'm sorry, sorry, sorry ....." Hamish couldn't speak any more, his face was ashen, frozen in a look of horror as he recoiled from this small, harsh act. The thing he feared most was behaving towards his own son as his father had done to him; he was horrified that he had frightened Callum, stricken by having brought on that look of fear.

Callum held on to his father feeling the strength of his father's emotion and pain.

-"It's alright Pa. It's alright really! It doesnae matter, I'm fine!" He hugged his Pa, pushed himself back and looked him in the face and smiled. His father gave him another long hug. He was still ashen-faced, shocked and ashamed and wiped Callum's tears away with his rough thumb. Hamish said, in a more controlled, softer voice

-"I'm sorry Callum, I shouldn't have shouted. It just came out -- but there's no excuse. I was wrong." He looked at Callum and Callum smiled again and nodded.

Hamish picked up the stool again and sat down, stooping, leaning into the side of the cow, head down and carried on milking. Callum stood behind his father and rested his hand on his shoulder. Hamish was quietly shaking, the tears flowing silently.

When the milking was finished and the churn filled near to the brim with bucketfuls of creamy, foaming milk, Hamish placed the lid on and said with a strained half grin,

-"Let's get this over to your Ma eh!" He had recovered a little, he was almost himself again.

He rolled the large, silver steel churn, fat at the bottom, its shining belly tapering inwards towards the top, out of the byre and over towards the croft house. The metallic crunching of the heavy churn on gravel rang out loudly across the yard in the cold, still air. Màiri came out to meet them,

-"I've just fed the weeuns. Have ye had yer breakfast yet ye two?" she asked

-"Aye Ma" replied Callum. She looked at Hamish, seeing his white face and subdued manner and asked if he was all right.

-"Aye! I'm just going with Callum to check on the rooster. He said he's not looking too well." Hamish said, a little cowed and subdued.

He would tell her later what happened and how ashamed he was; she would tell him not to worry, Callum would be fine, it wasn't such a big thing and he was resilient. She would hold him and comfort him and for once he would let her, his resistance weakened.

Màiri knew the scars her husband bore, vicious scars on his body, she had felt them, seen them, even though he had tried to hide them from her, but she also knew there were even worse scars on his mind. It saddened her deeply and angered her that anyone could so damage a child that he should grow up so defeated and defenceless, so open to hurt. Hamish was made of raw flesh, if he were prodded it went deep, he shrank from emotion because he had no skills to deal with it. He had been crushed and he would be forever crippled by it, just as surely as if his father had smashed his legs or arms.

So Callum showed his Pa the rooster, or 'coileach', which was of course a word his father didn't know. The two of them sat on their haunches and watched the old rooster, who cowered in the cold dirt and hardly stirred, all his bold strutting and bullying, his ample confidence gone. Hamish picked up the big brown rooster very tenderly and looked at it carefully, smoothing his feathers and cooing softly to him. He looked the bird over, looking in its eyes, at his floppy red comb,

-"I think he's just a bit off-colour Cal. I don't think it's too serious, he needs wee bit of cossettin". Hamish said thoughtfully,

-"He may have a touch of cold. I'm not sure if chickens can catch colds but his eyes are a bit weepy. How about we take him indoors, warm him up and give him some special food, maybe some bread and milk and a bit of powdered kelp?"

-"What's cossettin Pa?" Callum asked

-"It's when you take special care of someone Callum".

So Hamish further bent his will to being well, for Callum as well as for Màiri and Dougal and little Jeannie of course. He kept as busy as he could; he tried to shut out all thoughts of his demons and pushed himself to keep busy, keep busy. If he stopped he feared he would be unable to start again. As soon as he woke in the morning, after sleeping fitfully, he got up, got dressed, and breakfasted quickly, went to the cow byre and then mucked out, milked the cows and fed the sheep on the in-bye land and fed the grazing cows. He took his oars and his nets down to the cove and rowed furiously out to the middle of the loch and flung his nets out equally furiously and then rowed back with whatever fish he had caught.

He would haul the heavy boat, ten feet of deadweight wood, sitting on its keel out of the water and on to the pebble beach. The boat was an open rowing boat, a two-man birney. It was clinker built, the wooden planks making up the hull being laid in an overlapping fashion. It had a high, straight stem which protruded for a good five inches above the boatrail of the little craft. The stem post was fitted with a heavy iron ring to help haul the boat on a stout rope, stem first out of the water and up the shingle bank to safety. It had two seats and was remarkably stable even in choppy water, but being open, it flooded fairly easily in a high sea. These birnies were designed to use on the sea loch but similar, longer craft would be taken out on the sea. In 1848 forty open boats and thirty seven of their crew were lost trying to get back into harbour at Wick during a sudden storm. Hamish was always aware of the danger, especially as a lone fisherman.

Callum accompanied his father around the croft whenever he could, when he wasn't at school, when he wasn't doing his own chores he was with him, quietly helping alongside. Neither needed to speak, they both knew their tasks by now. Callum knew his role, the things his proud father preferred him to do, the things he didn't or which were too awkward for him or too physically demanding. Working alongside his father made him feel better, feel as if he was helping him to keep going and reassured him that his father was still alright; he didn't worry so much about him when he was nearby. Callum could sense his father's moods when he was close to him. He knew his father's touch, his shape, his feel, his little sounds. When his father took his hand or when he lifted him up he smelt his man smell, sweat and soap and felt his roughness and his bigness, his unique presence. All this he was aware of and not aware of at the same time. Its familiarity made Callum feel safe, made him feel everything was under control.

But it wasn't; Hamish couldn't keep working furiously forever, the sun wouldn't hold back the tide of northern darkness that was gradually enveloping them. Just as the day length ebbed so did Hamish's spirit and resistance; he couldn't hold on, he was being torn away from his family, from Màiri and from Callum who was trying so hard to hold on to him. Hamish was desperate; he was gradually sliding down a wide, dark hole and scrambling for handholds as the darkness dragged him in and the demons cackled and mocked him for his weakness.

Callum felt his father slipping away from him, day by day. It was as if he were trying to hold on against a terrible cruel sea, a great force was dragging them apart. He didn't understand, couldn't comprehend the power of Hamish's disturbed mind or the demons and memories that lurked there, rotting his spirit. Hamish was drowning in sorrow and Callum was unbearably distraught.

Màiri held Callum as he wept and shouted and told her of his anger, not at his father but at the possession that had taken him. He begged her to stop it happening, to help him hold on to his Pa. Màiri tried to reassure him but she couldn't tell him it was going to be alright, she was in despair herself. She had watched with emotion-wrenching sadness as Callum had tried to save his Pa from whatever in God's name was happening to him again. She had tried every bit as desperately as Callum to cling on to some vestige of the man she couldn't bear to be without. She feared terribly what was coming.

And slip away Hamish did, for nearly four months this time, into a wide, deep pit of hopelessness, loneliness and fear. Just dragging himself out of bed each day cost him an enormous effort of will. He was taking part in a living, exhausted waking nightmare, all his resistance broken. He now saw himself as if from a distance, from outside himself, with no power over what was happening. He no longer belonged to his body and mind, they were somewhere outside him and all he had were echoes. The voices in his head tormented his disturbed mind and he felt rather than heard the demons mocking. For four long, dreadful months he was lost to his family and lost to himself, a palimpsest, his old self overwritten and smothered by a powerful doppelganger, a dispairing spirit, barely able to function, until, in the end, he took to his bed, turned his face to the wall and gave up his mind to the ghosts in his head.

Màiri and Callum eventually gave up too, in anger and pain and with a terrible feeling of defeat, failure and resentment. Màiri had experienced it many times, each becoming worse, more profound in its nature but every time the inevitable regression of Hamish's decline slid inexorably into a total slump she felt all hope leave her, to be replaced with a dull emptiness.

Callum was too young, experience hadn't yet provided him with any defences nor explanations that made any sense; surely, if his father really wanted to he could get up, go to work on the croft again, speak, hear and see, move his body. He knew his father was terribly sorrowful but he didn't, couldn't, understand why he couldn't make his mind do as it was told. He couldn't understand the difference between his father's brain and his father's mind, nor had he had the sort of experiences which would have allowed him to understand what can happen to someone's mind when they are treated intolerably over a long time. Callum just wanted his athair back again and try as he might, despite his best efforts not to think badly of his father, he couldn't help thinking that his father had somehow betrayed him.

Dougal and young Jeannie were also affected, each in their own way. The lack of sophistication in children seems to make them extraordinarily receptive; they don't have layers of experience, the extra baggage, haven't done sufficient living, to blunt their emotional senses. These young children, Dougal at six, a bouncing, fair-haired, chirpy young boy and Jeannie, a dark haired, three-year-old toddler, getting into everything, having to be watched all the time, these two children didn't really know and weren't really aware of how extraordinary their father's behaviour was. But what they picked up was the emotional atmosphere, soaked it up like sponges and became morose and irritable, adding to Màiri's already heavy burden.

The whole family were constantly aware of Hamish's presence and his current state. In the dark corner of the main room, he lay on his and Màiri's bed, his back to them, covered in heavy blankets, not moving but sleeping fitfully or laying awake, frozen, eyes wide open, fearful and staring at his imagined horrors happening beyond the blank wall. He was a lifeless, miserable hump of bedclothes. Family life went on around him in hushed tones, all of which he was completely oblivious to. Màiri fed him, patiently, twice a day, spoonful by spoonful, excruciatingly slowly as she managed to get him to swallow some warm porridge or broth or to get some lukewarm, herbal tea into him to calm his nerves. She would help support him to the outside toilet three or four times a day; an earth closet with a board with a hole cut in it for a seat. When he needed it she would wipe and clean him and wash him and shave him and change his nightclothes, carefully and lovingly, soothing and quietly talking to him as she would have done for a sick ewe or cow and as she had with each of her babies. He was as helpless and as dependent as an infant. This time his mental and physical collapse had been total.

After a while and after a fashion the family re-established a pattern of existence around Hamish's recumbent form.

Callum had taken to getting the two 'bairns' up; Dougal from their shared bed in the boys room, a little bedroom off the main room and Jeannie from her cot in the main room by the banked-up, peat fire. She could keep warm there and Màiri could keep an eye on her and comfort her if she might wake in the night, gently hushing her to save her from waking Hamish, even though she knew he wouldn't even notice.

Callum would rise very early, before first light and get himself washed and dressed and carry out his usual chores. He would supervise Dougal's morning wash, which was otherwise less than thorough to say the least and make sure Dougal dressed himself properly and help him do up his buttons and the laces on his boots.

He would release Jeannie from her high-sided cot from where she would plead to be let out, leaping up and down on her mattress with frustration, and in a paddy she would throw her constant companion, a rag doll, which had been cleverly made by Isla, onto the bare, cold floor and then plead tearfully with Callum to retrieve it for her. He would cook their brose made from milled oats with water from the black, iron kettle and make himself tea and Dougal and Jeannie a drink of warm milk. While he did all this Màiri tended to Hamish and fed him; it took a long time because Hamish resisted pathetically though weakly, making it many times slower and more difficult.

After breakfast Callum and Dougal would walk to school after saying goodbye to their Ma who, having done what she could for Hamish, would start her round of crofting work for the day. Luckily in winter this was greatly reduced and also fortunately the good harvest had allowed them to survive without Hamish having to provide fish as well, although they would have made a welcome change. She would have to take Jeannie with her wherever she went and at three years old she was in need of constant attention, making work slow and difficult.

At least at school Callum could forget about his father and his responsibilities for a while and he could be free to join his young friends away from the daunting atmosphere of home. Callum really began to enjoy his books and his lessons, both as a refuge from the difficult emotions of home life and for the fascination of the learning itself. When he was at home and everything became too much for him he would disappear outside with Jess, find a corner, in a grassy hollow or the remains of a haystack and curl up with a book; a world of wonder, a story. He would become a courtly knight on a white horse, chasing down dragons, or a cowboy on the range herding long-horns, chasing rustlers and "chowing down" on beans and black coffee on a dark night in the badlands, listening to the howl of a coyote. Or he would be a Cherokee Indian stalking buffalo across wide-open, grassy plains or the last of the Mohicans paddling lonely creeks in a birch bark canoe. He could be a pirate on a stormy sea, an airman in a biplane or a soldier of fortune in a land far away, hot and mysterious.

At school he learnt about history, well English history anyway and the history of the Empire; there never seemed to be much about Scotland. He enjoyed geography and Miss Pargeter even introduced them to a little science and of course he liked English which he was good at; he loved writing his own stories. He still struggled with maths though, the numbers never seeming to do what he wanted or even what he expected them to do. But most of all he liked Miss Pargeter, she was pretty and smelled of perfumed soap and she had a way of making everything she taught, except maths of course, sound so interesting and somehow important, so that he really wanted to learn it and lastly she praised him whenever he did something she thought was good, which was fairly often. Of course she was also very strict, especially with him and Billy, the two of whom she called "my wee rascals" and with Flora who she sometimes used to call "a little madam" although he wasn't quite sure what she meant by that. He could completely relax at school and lose himself in the world of the classroom where he lived out his weekdays with his school friends and Miss Pargeter and of course Maggie.

Maggie Fraser, now twenty-six and courting a young man who was a ghillie, or gamekeeper, on the estate, had been taken on as an assistant teacher. Maggie was bright and a wonderfully patient teacher of the smaller children who particularly loved her. She treated all of the schoolchildren as if she was their grown-up sister and it was to her they all went if they scraped a knee or cut a finger or had been bitten or smacked by one of the other children. It was Maggie who kept an eye on all the children, now twelve of them, from five years old up to eleven, at playtimes and was there if needed at dinnertime when the children went out to play.

She comforted them when they were sad or frightened and were finding school a little overwhelming and she made them laugh and she told them stories. She had long hair, pulled up in a loop and, although a bit awkward was quite good-looking in an unusual sort of way. She was generous and open and never harsh with them and she taught the little ones their letters and numbers and listened to them read and supervised all the children when Miss Pargeter was busy. School for all of them was a safe and friendly world where the two women looked after them well and where they learnt and played with their pals and were told off, but never smacked because Miss Pargeter didn't believe in it and where their mothers took it in turns to cook for them and bring them in their midday meal and where the hardships and the upsets and the harshness of their home lives didn't impinge on them for a while.

Somehow, the struggling McDonald family got through that winter of 1931 and as spring returned Hamish began to stir, like a soulful, hibernating bear. Slowly he began to recover his wits and regain some strength. A spark of life returned to his dead eyes; the haunted, grey look of his face began to fade and he gained a little natural colour.

Màiri was exhausted, ground down with a bitter cold winter of hard work and worry. She was now thirty-three and right now looked at least ten years older. Somehow she had managed to keep the croft going, though she had lost three ewes in a snowstorm, a bitter blow and no reward for her desperate hard work to keep them all fed and safe. Fortunately the four remaining grazing cows was safe and well; she had had to send one to market when she had run short of food for her family and feed for the animals but the croft work had been kept up somehow and they were safe through for now.

She rose one glorious morning in April to find the sun returned; its wintry, watery, pale imitation had been replaced by a burning yellow orb with real heat in its rays. After Callum and Dougal had gone to school and she had raised Hamish and dressed him, she left him sitting in the old rocker by the fire, hollow-eyed and hollow-cheeked, his gaze blank, but at least he was up and dressed. With Jeannie in her arms and Jess circling around her feet, hoping for a walk, she fled the house; her morning chores could wait, the cows had been mucked out and milked, the animals fed. The morning was still and fresh, the sun warm on her face. The air had a yellow glow to it and an overnight rain shower had washed everything fresh and clean. Everywhere she looked she could see green shoots pushing up out of the warming soil, she breathed in great lungfuls of the bright, clear air which held just a taste of salt and seaweed. A couple of squabbling, white gulls piped to each other as they chivvied for position in the air over the cove, their strident voices echoing round the glen. It was so still she could hear the gentle shush and lap of wavelets as they capered and rippled along the shoreline onto the stony beach way below her.

She turned up towards the hill, encouraging Jess to follow; she had decided to take a walk up the beinn over the lower slopes. She felt she needed to rise up over it all and look down on her life from way up there; to take stock, to breathe freely, to feel herself alive again. Jeannie rested quietly in her arms, she too seemed to have picked up the newness of the day; the soft lullaby of the gentle morning air created a contemplative mood. Jeannie was old enough now to have begun to develop a character of her own, she was quiet and sensitive and loving, quick to rise to anger and emotion which subsided just as quickly. She was happy and easygoing and liked to sit and watch her brothers as they went about their day or played with each other. She would tell Dougal or Callum off if they were squabbling or being naughty or loud or if they didn't listen to her. They had both learnt to be attentive towards her and allowed her to reprimand them without a protest. Most of all though Jeannie looked after her mother. When Màiri was tired or upset or felt defeated Jeannie would appear quietly and stand or sit next to her, without speaking, perhaps putting a hand on her knee or gently touching her face. Once or twice the delicacy of it had touched Màiri so deeply that she had had to pick Jeannie up and smother her face in Jeannie's small body so as to hide the tears which sprang to her eyes.

Màiri took great strides up the hill, her strong, long legs carrying her swiftly up the steep slope. She had been born here on this steep hill and had always been used to having to climb up or down wherever she went. Jess followed behind, glad to be out walking with some of her pack, sniffing fox paths and hare trails and putting up the occasional red grouse; her black and white form weaving between the bare, black stalks of heather.

Màiri reached the final approach to the summit, an area made up of a long series of steep interlinking slopes. Then she rested: she was about five-hundred feet above the loch; it had taken her an hour to reach this spot since leaving the croft but it was well worth it. There was a good sitting rock, worn smooth by ageless time and weather, a large boulder with a handy depression just the right height for a seat. She put Jeannie down; she had felt increasingly heavy on the last hundred feet or so. Jeannie immediately started tussling with Jess, rolling over each other in a furious game like puppies and then both settling down to sit and study the ground closely. Jeannie picked up twigs and pieces of stone and Jess snuffled around like a truffle hound making little "huff! huff!" sounds as she breathed out.

She looked out over the loch and the Inner Sound to Skye, Eielean à Cheo, the Island of Mists, the smooth rounded beinns of the Red Cuillins protruded like the bodies of great fallen giants or Norse heroes and the younger, spiky, black Cuillins off to the south shimmered in a blue haze; only 50 million years old, dark and mysterious, a snow-topped fairyland of a mountain range. She knew that way up in their dark, craggy recesses beautiful golden eagles still lived, away from the persecution of men, secure in their high, snowy eyries.

She breathed a great sigh of relief and relaxed back against the stone; from way up here her troubles seemed a long way away. Hamish, sitting in front of the fire at the croft, now a tiny dark oblong against the green of the in-bye land, seemed less of a problem. She had come through the toughest winter of her life so far. But it was over; she prayed that Hamish would be fit enough to help with the lambing in a month's time; Callum wasn't big enough to help with that very much yet but she knew now that they were going to manage and she couldn't have been sure of that even a week ago.

She felt the tiredness easing its way out of her bones and she wondered about this hard life of hers; was it worth it she questioned? So very much effort for so little reward; but she couldn't imagine leaving this place, this croft where her parents and grandparents had farmed. She was so much a part of it all, it seemed to give her her life's blood and gave her the rich air to breathe; its beauty still astonished her however often she saw it. If she wasn't content than it was because of Hamish's suffering, or perhaps because there were things her children didn't have, although she was aware that what they had in this place was priceless: for her part she wished for no more. And so she sat and dozed high up on the hill as the gentle sun warmed her face and her world was spread out in glory at her feet. She was a Highland Queen and these were her tribal lands. This place was in her bones, her soul breathed to its rhythms, she belonged only here.

That year's lambing in late April was tough, they lost six lambs and a ewe and Hamish was not really up to the job. He was still recovering; listless and morose, he struggled to focus on what was going on. Callum helped as much as he could and was as upset as Màiri when they lost lambs but they got through it to the summer somehow and she hoped Hamish would be capable of taking a full part in the harvest.

One day in early summer Callum came home from school and told Màiri, somewhat apprehensively, that,

-"Teacher wants tae see ye aboot me".

He didn't know why and his manner suggested it might not be positive. Màiri was aware that he would be coming up to eleventh birthday soon and would have to go up to senior school so she didn't want him to leave with a poor report.

-"Hae ye done something Callum?" She asked suspiciously

He shrugged and looked a bit shifty.

-"Thank you for coming Mrs McDonald. I'm glad Callum passed on my message, I've been wanting to talk to you about him for a while".

Miss Pargeter wore her usual high-necked, lace-trimmed cotton blouse, pinned at the neck with a little cameo brooch. Her dark hair contrasted starkly with her pale, white skin, so translucent on her neck that Màiri could see individual veins. Her hair was pinned up in a large, loose bun and she wore a long dark, grey skirt, emphasising her tall, slim elegance. Màiri noticed that she had a slightly beaky nose but that her large dark eyes distracted from it and gave an overall pleasing effect to her pale face and starkly pink lips against the plaster-white skin.

"I hope nothing's wrong Miss Pargeter?" Màiri asked a little anxiously

-"No, no, not at all! I wanted to talk to you about Callum's future. He's a very bright boy Mrs McDonald and he's a good scholar, despite his high spirits"

Màiri guessed that "high spirits" was a euphemism for being naughty rather a lot.

"Aye, he can be a handful but he means well" said Màiri a little defensively.

-"I shall really miss him when he goes to the senior school" Miss Pargeter said a little wistfully, -"He's so interested in everything and he is as bright as a button. I'm worried that it will all be wasted unless we can get him some extra tuition somehow". said Miss Pargeter and then, realising she was being indiscreet, qualified her statement somewhat.

-"Not that I'm not sure the senior school will give him a good enough education' she said diplomatically 'but they're not really going to expand his horizons sufficiently I think; not for a boy as clever as Callum".

It was something that had worried Màiri. She knew the senior school well and knew that they saw their role as turning out compliant farmboys, fishermen and workers for the local estates; no more and no less.

They were sitting in Miss Pargeter's little "office", the store-room next to the "big childrens" classroom in which there was a little desk and chair and books and stationery, piled up on the shelves. There was a large cupboard and one spare curved back, bentwood chair. Miss Pargeter had added some flowery curtains at the little store-room window and a bright coloured cushion for her chair; the overall effect was intimate and quietly feminine.

-"Oh excuse me Mrs McDonald what am I thinking of! Please take a seat" Miss Pargeter pulled out the spare chair and placed it in front of the desk and then went round behind her desk and sat down.

Màiri had noticed that Miss Pargeter had looked a little nervous at first and not quite so confident as she usually did. The intimacy of the tight space and her younger age seemed to have made her a little awkward in dealing with the confident seeming older woman. Màiri sat down, noticing that Miss Pargeter looked a little more at ease when she had seated herself behind her little desk; it was a more formal arrangement which gave her back her role as schoolmistress.

-"It's kind of you to take an interest Miss Pargeter but I'm no sure what I can do. The school gave me a reasonable education to age thirteen and I expect it will dae sae fae Callum. Although I would wish him to learn more than I did. The fact is we cannae afford anything extra, we're only a crofting family after all." Màiri felt defensive in the presence of the more well-to-do teacher and irritated at her apparent lack of realisation of the situation. How could they dream of paying for a tutor; most years they made little more than enough to pay the rent on the croft and essentials along with extra animal feed and repairs to the buildings? Miss Pargeter however, knew she was getting into difficult territory and despite Màiri's defensiveness she knew well enough the financial situation of the local people and she knew also that they were proud of their self-sufficiency.

-"Please don't think I'm unsympathetic Mrs McDonald, nor that I am trying to interfere but I would like you to think about a suggestion if I may." She paused, nervous, not sure how to carry on. -"I've been thinking of asking the estate owners if they could provide scholarships for brighter pupils at the school, to study beyond the normal level and perhaps to go to the

Academy at Dingwall if they can pass the entrance test. I think Callum would be an ideal candidate. What do you think?"

-"No Miss Pargeter! I'll no except anything from those people." Màiri retorted shortly and then, realising how ungracious she was being, modified her tone; - "I'm sorry I didnae mean tae sound ungrateful. I really appreciate yer interest in Callum and I tae have been wondering how I could try tae ensure him a better education when he's older but I will not be beholden to those people who stole oor land and drove oor ancestors frae their pastures and the rich farming land that was rightfully theirs. It may sound strange tae ye when it was sae long ago, but oor land is important tae us and the injustices of the Clearances are still strong in oor minds!" Màiri was polite in tone but emphatic.

Miss Pargeter looked crestfallen and a little embarrassed, she shifted uncomfortably in her seat. Màiri had a sudden insight; she saw Miss Pargeter's life as a lonely one amongst the crofting people; living in a small cottage on the estate with nothing in common with the estate workers, separated by her class from all those she lived amongst. She was constrained by her position as schoolmistress, having no one to confide in and dedicated to doing her best for the children. It couldn't be easy for a young, educated, single woman, limited by the expectations of her class, living in such a remote place with only the children and only young Maggie for company.

-"I'm sorry Miss Pargeter, I've been ruid and ungrateful" Màiri said in a conciliatory tone -"I ken ye're trying tae help and I just threw it back at ye. I am really very grateful that ye're thinking of Callum and I wish there was some other way we could give him the education he deserves" after a short pause she continued, -"I realise it must be hard fae ye here, the only teacher, even if ye have help frae young Maggi." she sighed "Ach! We've had a lang, hard winter and a tough spring, I'm jest a bit frazzled but it's nae excuse. I really am sorry I spoke harshly."

Miss Pargeter looked a little less uncomfortable.

-"No it's a fine really. I should have realised that the villagers would resent the estate owners, I ken the history well enough. I do think though that we need to find a way of getting extra tuition for Callum if at all possible; maybe, when he's a little older and I will help all I can. Perhaps the church might help if that is acceptable?" she suggested tentatively.

"I'm very grateful" Màiri said. "If we can get a better education fae Callum then I'll do almost anything. He's sae interested in everything and he reads sae much. It would be a shame not tae give him mair of a chance."

The two women talked a little about other things and promised to meet again to discuss Callum, when Miss Pargeter had made more inquiries. Màiri found that she really liked the young woman whom she suspected was very idealistic and she suspected saw her work here in the glen as a vocation to help improve the lot of the children of the Highlanders.

-"Mebbe ye will come up tae the hoose one evening fae a bite sometime soon?" asked Màiri -"It must be a bit of a trial having tae get yerself a meal after a day's work with the bairns. I expect they are a right handful sometimes, it's hard enough just having three tae cope with!"

-"That's very kind, thank you Mrs McDonald, I would love to!" she looked really pleased to be asked.

-"Guid, mebbe in a couple of weeks when we hae a few young hog's tae gae tae market".

Miss Pargeter, not having experience of crofting life or of going short didn't see the connection between the two events but Màiri knew that when her hog's, young male sheep, went to market, she would send one of her old barren ewes and have it butchered for her and so have meat for dinner, as well as money to buy flour and other ingredients to make a meal worthy of inviting someone like Miss Pargeter to.

Early summer could be the leanest time of the year, stores put by in autumn had run out and this year's crop had yet to bear fruit. This was the time of year when, if there hadn't been a surplus the year before to provide money to buy in food in the lean times, then times could get very hard indeed. But the cows produced milk from new grass from spring onwards and, provided Màiri could find the oats or barley for them the hens produced eggs. So they at least had eggs, cheese, butter and milk and Màiri could afford to buy in a little flour to make bread and she foraged on the green banks and hillsides for greens and at last, by mid-summer, Hamish was well enough to fish again.

Herring were becoming more scarce and they had to eat everything he caught, there was little for salting down for later on. Màiri spent a large part of her life worrying about food; about where it was going to come from, how to make it last when they had a surplus. With three growing children to feed as well as herself and Hamish food was her biggest worry. Their clothing always came second and as all the children in the glen and the surrounding area were in the same situation going ragged was accepted as a matter of course. Màiri also knew that in the cities there was real hunger, real starvation and disease, just as there was in the countryside for those who didn't have a patch of land to grow food on. Itinerant labourers would occasionally wash up in the glen, literally and metaphorically at the end of the road.

-"I'll dae anythin' missus if ye could jest manage somethin' tae eat!"

Màiri would usually find a job for them and give them bread and cheese and a mug of tea and a few pennies if she had them, even if they were her last. She knew there were many men during those years tramping the roads looking for work, starving; ragged beyond belief many of them, holes in their shoes if they had shoes and not having eaten for days.

One day in early summer one such young man; tall, thin and stooped, came tramping and wheezing up her steep path in a tattered coat and a battered black, pork-pie hat. He had bound rags to his feet in place of shoes. He had afterwards told her that he had had his shoes stolen while he slept in a hedgerow down south. She could believe it, she could believe that people would sink to any level in these desperate times. He said his name was Earnest and that he had been a clerk in a shipping company in Glasgow and lost his job when the company went bankrupt, as so many companies had after the crash of 1929. Although the financial crash had been brought on by reckless bankers and financiers overreaching themselves, it was now the poor who were paying the heaviest price; as ever thought Màiri.

Earnest said he had been walking the roads for the best part of a year after being evicted by his landlord for being unable to pay the rent. He had walked the length and breadth of Scotland looking for work. He told her that Glasgow was terrible now, with widespread hunger and disease: unemployment affected whole areas of the city where virtually no one worked. Màiri had once been to Glasgow as a child and it had seemed to her to be rich beyond belief, with its great buildings and large shops filled with luxuries. But then, as Earnest had tactfully pointed out to her, she had not seen the rows of blackened, smoky tenements in the backstreets where the poor lived.

Earnest said he was afraid he wasn't much good at any sort of manual work so Màiri had hit on the idea of getting him to teach Callum to do his sums in return for a meal, much to Callum's horror. First, Màiri fed the downtrodden young man with a thick broth, a couple of fried eggs on oatcakes and a hunk of cheese. He was very politely grateful; he hadn't eaten so well for over a year he said. Màiri finished it off by providing him with two cups of tea. He drank his tea delicately with quiet relish, holding the cup between finger and thumb and sipping in a genteel fashion. The children were fascinated by this raggedy, skinny, quite tall young man. He seemed to be made up of a bundle of rags tied up with string, he was clean-shaven and well scrubbed but hadn't a single item of clothing which wasn't badly worn or threadbare. He had a tattered blue and white spotted kerchief tied round his throat and, when outside, always.wore his battered hat at a slightly jaunty angle, which gave him a rather jolly air, at variance with his otherwise sorry state. Màiri gave him a pair of Hamish's old boots to wear. They fitted well enough when packed with old newspaper and he was pitifully grateful.

Callum was in awe of this tattered young man with his elegant manners as he escorted him around the croft at Màiri's insistence, in order to get both of them out from under her feet while she got on with her chores. The young man chatted inconsequentially in a cultivated accent about his work in Glasgow. He had worked in a dock warehouse and seen the great ships come and go, loading and unloading goods from across the British Empire; tea, cotton and spices from India, crockery from China, mutton and fleeces from Australia and New Zealand and manufactured goods from the United States and from Europe and sugar and coffee from the colonies in the West Indies. Callum was fascinated, it all sounded so exotic.

The young man also told him about the towns and villages he had visited across Scotland and the dogs which had chased him and the strange places he had slept. Apart from barns and hedges he had also slept in park shelters and under rowing boats on the beach to keep the rain off and in the woods to avoid the police, who would move him on if they spotted him and even under an old broken-down cart in a farmyard and in stables with the horses and in byres with the cows to keep him warm. Callum thought it would be cosy to sleep in the straw with the warm, friendly cows in the byre but supposed his mother wouldn't allow him to try it.

Earnest was true to his word to Màiri and taught Callum to do arithmetic. He did it in a way that Callum found relatively easy. He showed him, on a scrap of paper with a pencil he pulled out of his pocket, all sorts of shortcuts to adding up columns of figures or dividing up numbers and for doing long division and long multiplication. The way he showed him just seemed to make sense and he made it interesting by telling him little stories about his time in the shipping office when he had to account for all the wonderful goods that came off the boats. Such a good teacher was he that Callum thought that maybe arithmetic wasn't quite so bad after all.

Màiri was quite taken with this bright, cheerful young man who had fallen on hard times so she suggested he stay on for the harvest. They couldn't pay him but she would feed him and he could sleep in the hay barn if he liked and continue to teach Callum and then help with the harvest. However unskilled he was at the work every hand was needed at harvest time, which was probably only a couple of weeks away now. He happily agreed to stay until after the harvest and thanked her effusively for her kindness.

Early one Saturday morning, at the beginning of September, when Earnest had been with them for nearly a week, Callum was sitting in the small barn where they kept the hay, which was almost empty because it was the end of summer and this year's hay hadn't been mown yet. There was just enough for Earnest to make a bed on and Màiri had given him a blanket to cover himself with. Callum had just brought him a steaming mug of tea. Callum was sitting on an empty herring barrel watching Earnest drink his tea. A hen wandered in, picked at the ground and then, on seeing them, scuttled out again squawking loudly in alarm. Jess was sitting at Callum's feet, also watching Earnest who seemed completely unconcerned with having an audience while he drank his tea in bed, in silence. He had hung his old coat on a nail in the wall and draped his tattered trousers over a wooden beam above his head; his boots were carefully aligned on the floor beside him where he could keep an eye on them; he wasn't about to lose another pair. He sipped his tea in his usual delicate manner and, when he had finished it, asked Callum if he

-"Would be sae kind as tae ask yer Ma to furnish me with a bowl of warm water sae that I can complete ma morning ablutions?"

Callum ran across the yard and indoors followed by Jess; he hadn't understood exactly what Earnest had asked for except for the part about a bowl of warm water and so assumed that he wanted a wash.

-"Earnest is after a bowl of water Ma!" shouted Callum breathlessly as he dashed into the main room of the house. Màiri smiled and filled an old tin bowl from the newly warmed copper in the stone-floored scullery. Callum concentrated hard as he carefully carried the bowl of steaming water with an old towel draped over his shoulder across the yard and over to the barn. He had to carry it all the way along the rough winding path that ran across the garden and then across the half cobbled, half packed-earth yard to the ramshackle stone building where he placed it on an upturned herring barrel just as Ernest had indicated. Earnest was standing waiting in a pair of well-worn, grubby long-johns and his tattered grey-white shirt tails. Màiri had placed a lump of coal tar soap in the bowl, cut from a ten-inch length she had recently purchased from the local hardware store on her last trip.

Earnest stood, poised and concentrating, in front of the still steaming bowl ready to begin the serious business of his 'ablutions', oblivious to his audience who looked on eagerly. He first rolled up his sleeves carefully and then proceeded to vigorously soap his arms, hands, face and neck. Callum and Jess avidly followed his every move. He gave his ears a vigorous rubbing with soap suds and then sluiced handfuls of water liberally over his arms and face before plunging his face in the bowl and making a sloshing, bubbling sound by blowing energetically. Callum and Jess were spellbound at this enthusiastic and vigorous washing activity. Having rubbed himself roughly all over with the towel Earnest strode purposefully to where his old ragged coat hung limply from its rusty nail on the wall and plunged a hand into one of its deep pockets from where he produced a cutthroat razor and a piece of broken mirror. He then looked around, brow furrowed deeply, obviously dissatisfied with the position of the bowl and placed it on the floor, after which he carefully and deliberately moved the barrel and set it up next to the only window, a little cobwebby square pane of cracked glass. He place the sliver of broken mirror on the recessed windowsill and then bent his knees until he could see his reflection and made his approval known with a brief "Ha"!"

Having set the bowl down on the barrel by the window he proceeded to lather his chin generously with soap suds and then began to scrape away with his now opened cutthroat razor whilst bending down to see his reflecion in the sliver of mirror. He did all this with the flourish and skill of a professional barber, wiping the blade from time to time on his sleeve to get rid of the soap suds. He took his time, carefully shaving each area of skin, pinching his nose with one hand and seeming to hold it up out of the way as he carefully scraped beneath it. Then he tipped his chin up and looked down his nose at the mirror while he scraped upwards under his jawline. He finished with a little flourish and wiped his face with the towel before again going to his coat, plunging his hand in and coming out with a small glass bottle and carefully unscrewed the lid. He tipped the bottle up on his palm and rubbed the contents all over his chin. A strong pungent odour of perfume filled the barn. Jess wrinkled her nose, then recoiled in appalled distaste; it was too much for her, she padded out of the barn in disgust.

Callum continued to watch, mesmerised, he had watched his Pa while he shaved but he had never seen a performance like this. He wondered what was going to be next out of the coat pockets. Earnest didn't disappoint; replacing the razor, bottle and mirror after a last careful examination of the chin, he dipped deep into an inside pocket and came out with a toothbrush and a little round tin of tooth-powder. He then cleaned his teeth with the same diligence shown to all the other aspects of his morning wash. Lastly he rinsed his mouth with soapy water and spat it out into the bowl with a flourish in a long, thin stream.

He did all this while completely ignoring his audience. Next he painstakingly dressed in the rest of his rags and pulled on his new boots with a sigh of satisfaction. With a deliberate finale he took a wooden hairbrush from a coat pocket, carefully brushed his hair and then, equally carefully, placed his battered hat on his head at just the right angle. Finally he again took the sliver of mirror out of his pocket, held it up to check how he looked and, apparently satisfied, turned and addressed Callum, as if only just noticing his presence.

-"Now what's next on today's itinerary young Callum?"

"We've tae feed the chickens and then Ma says we've tae hae some breakfast."

-"Good-oh! Breakfast! What a wonderful sound that word has. Come young man we must to our task, tarry not!" he announced theatrically, exaggerating the rolling of his Rs.

Callum enjoyed the way Earnest talked; he couldn't understand half of it but it sounded like some of the stories he read in books. And with a - "Lead on Macduff!" from Earnest they headed off to the chicken run to feed the hens.

The ungainly birds frantically appeared from around the croft and outbuildings, bouncing from side to side and cantering after the two of them as Callum called out and rattled the grain bucket noisily.

In the end Earnest stayed for nearly a month. Callum spent as much time with the fascinating young man as he could; everybody enjoyed his company, even Hamish with whom he had good-natured conversations about the relative merits of Edinburgh compared with Glasgow and they discovered that they had many places in common. Young Jeannie was enthralled by the young man who completely spoilt her, giving her piggybacks and carrying her round on his shoulders and showing her how to play 'cats cradles' with a long strand of wool. Dougall listened to his tales of the cities he had worked in and visited and of his travels on the road with open-mouthed wonder. It was as if he had opened up a world the children had no connection with, these faraway, fascinating, bustling cities with their spires and cathedrals and tall buildings, their castles and palaces.

Callum learnt about arithmetic and geometry and science and the geography of the British Empire that stretched around the world, but of which Earnest for some reason didn't approve. He said it was another form of slavery and that all people should be free to rule themselves. Màiri, having resented the rule of the English in the Highlands for so long, couldn't disagree.

In Earnest's capacious pockets he carried a tattered old book; a collection of Dickens tales, which he read to the children, acting out all the different parts as he did so. He was a consummate amateur dramatist and kept them enthralled. He said that he had read the book over and over, it had kept him company all the time he had been on the road.

At harvest time Earnest joined the rest of the little community in the fields, helping stack the sheaves of oats and barley and fork the hay onto the wagon when it was dry and ready to stack, and he was very good with the horses who seemed to take a liking to him. And when they sat down in the sunshine to eat their meal at mid-day on the first day of the harvest he produced a harmonica from out of one of his crowded pockets and played them all ragtime tunes from the 20s as well as a couple of Glasgow tunes to which he wouldn't tell them the words because he said they weren't suitable for mixed company.

Finally, when he left to take to the road again after their harvest supper, to seek work in Inverness or Aberdeen or anywhere else he could find a job, they gave him a great send-off and everyone in the village came to see him go. Before he set off, a good deal plumper and tanned from all the outdoor work, Màiri gave him a large parcel of food and slipped her last shilling into his pocket and then wished him - "All the luck he needed and a wee bit mair". Callum and Jess escorted him down the path as far as Signal Rock, where the glen ended and the rest of the world began. After he had said a hurried and slightly tearful goodbye and had disappeared into the distance Callum discovered Earnest's treasured harmonica had been slipped into his own pocket.

The glen seemed a much smaller and quieter place after Earnest had gone, the way a place often feels after exciting visitors from far away have been and gone again. They all settled into their old routines and prepared for winter, a little sadder for no longer having the cheerful young tramp in their midst. Earnest had brought a taste of the city and the outside world to the glen and some of the younger ones began to hanker after seeing some of the wider world, Callum not least among them.

CHAPTER 7

BIG SCHOOL

When Callum reached his 11th summer Màiri and Hamish had a difficult decision to face: they couldn't afford to send him to the Academy at Dingwall, to be educated; the costs of his travel and uniform and the fees were way out of their reach. If he went to a to the local school in Kyle of Lochalsh for 11 to 13 year olds he would learn little more than he already knew but at least he might pick up something extra. Màiri knew and Miss Pargeter had confirmed, he had a fine brain and was interested in learning but, outside the main cities, the children of the poor struggled to get a decent education once they reached the age of eleven.

Many didn't bother; the children from the little hamlet at the end of the Loch would not be welcome at the local school, Catholics had their own schools but there wasn't one anywhere nearby. So when those children reached eleven years old they simply left. The boys were expected to begin working for a living, as did many other children in out of the way places, given a place on a farm or an estate for a few pence a week or, as with

Alistair and Billy, they would simply work alongside their parents at fishing and crofting, something they had already begun to do anyway.

Poor girls would either take on more of the work at home alongside their mothers or go into service; Fiona, in a year or two would go into service in a hotel for rich tourists on the Isle of Skye and would end up marrying a local fisherman at age sixteen. Flora went to stay with an aunt in Plockton who would teach her to become a dressmaker and who would take her on as an apprentice when she reached thirteen. For most of them their childhoods were now over.

And so Callum MacDonald was the only child of that year amongst the people of the loch to go up to the big school for eleven to thirteen year-olds, all the way to Kyle. He had to get up even earlier now in order to get through his chores; to feed the chickens and collect the eggs, fetch water for the copper, get himself ready and then walk the five miles to school. After school, he would have to walk the five miles back and do his evening chores. In winter he walked to school in the dark and walked home in the dark. The path was often in deep, threatening shadow where it plunged into gullies or gorges and at times he found himself alone in a vast open glen with nothing but a bubbling stream or a distant, roaring stag for company and a million, million stars in a black velvet sky above his head to guide him homewards.

His two years at the senior school were to prove to be the worst of his young life so far, effectively marking the end of his childhood too. His schoolmaster for that grim two years was a man called George Robinson. George Robinson was a rotund, thickset man about five feet eight tall, an ex-naval chief petty officer. He had 'a full set', thick beard and impressive moustache, the moustache twirled at the end into points with slightly upward, waxed curl. He strode around the classroom as if marching on a parade ground. He had a voice like roaring thunder and a vivid purply-red complexion, with round bead-like, dark eyes set in folds of red flesh and his eyebrows curled up at the ends in sympathy with his moustache. His severity and reputation for brutality saved him from being the comic figure he otherwise might have proved to be.

There were forty-five boys and girls in the class, packed in on benches like herrings in a barrel, with a line of desks in front of them. They sat, ramrod straight with two aisles splitting the rows of desks into three sections. If a boy or girl were called out to the front they might have to climb over six or seven others to get out to one of the aisles. Mr Robinson demanded immediate and absolute obedience and absolute silence, unless of course when he asked a question when he required an immediate response. He carried a wooden yard rule around with him and he used it as both a pointer and to enforce his will, by lashing out at the children with it. At any moment he might swipe out at a child sitting trapped between their classmates, for any real or imagined infraction.

Possible infractions were many; using Gaelic was considered one of the worst. Mr Robinson, in concert with many outsiders at the time, knowing not a word of it themselves, considered Gaelic to be a backwards and barbaric language. Other infractions included talking without permission, not appearing to listen, being insolent or appearing to be, failing to respond to a command immediately, answering back and so on and so on. The rules were so many that Callum often wondered whether just being a pupil wasn't in itself something of an infringement of the rules.

Serious misdemeanours: which included fighting or perceived or real insolence required a thrashing with the tawse. The tawse was made by a saddler from thick but flexible leather and varied in thickness according to the age of the offender; it was used across Scotland on school pupils and young criminals. It consisted of a wide band of leather, rather like a thick, wide belt, split at the end into four or five tails. For schoolchildren the tawse was applied to the hand. The victim, for surely victim they were, was made to stand facing the teacher, hand held up at chest height opened out with palm uppermost and supported at the wrist with the other hand, which prevented the open hand being withdrawn when struck by the tawse. The teacher would use varying force according to the nature of the supposed infringement and the degree of sadism of the teacher. He or she would swing the tawse through the air, beating the palm of the hand the required number of times, in Mr Robinson's case anything up to an exceptional twelve times.

The girls were not exempt from being hit with the tawse though it was more unusual and they were never given more than three strikes. It seemed to Callum, from his, admittedly not entirely objective viewpoint, that Mr Robinson appeared to derive some particular pleasure from causing red weals to rise on the soft skin of a girl's hands and to evince tears from their eyes. The boys were allowed no such luxury, tears were simply not allowed, the other boys would punish mercilessly anybody who shed tears for any reason, even after a thorough thrashing with the tawse.

Lessons were a straightforward process of dictation; Mr Robinson spoke, his words were recorded, he set a problem, showed on the blackboard how to solve it, the children copied it and then at the end of the week there was a short test. Points were awarded, failure was rewarded with a beating; a smack on the head for a minor failure or a crack on the hand with the wooden rule if more serious: major failures were punished with the tawse. Questions were discouraged and the word 'why' was, as Callum soon discovered, rewarded with a brutal reply. One learned very quickly never to ask why about anything. Mr Robinson spoke and his word was law, he was a vengeful God of the classroom, to be obeyed and never questioned. It was no doubt of huge satisfaction to him, though it is rather doubtful whether his pupils gained a great deal from it. Mr Robinson saw his task as a simple one; to produce obedience and submission and a modicum of knowledge in the lower orders and he did so with great efficiency.

Mr Robinson always gave a thrashing with the tawse on the left-hand because writing, or doing anything much with the hand that had been beaten for the rest of the day was almost impossible. There were of course no left-handed writers in the school. Some teachers, as with many of their contemporaries in general, held some extraordinary prejudices, such as that against Gaelic. that rich language and culture which was dismissed as of no value. It was the same with left-handedness, it was a mediaeval prejudice which was blindly followed in most schools of the time. Alongside an iron-bound desire to instil conformity such prejudice was a powerful force for spreading ignorance.

Callum learnt a little geometry, English grammar, basic mathematics and English history dates, such as imperial conquests, never any Scottish history except as an adjunct to that of Britain as a whole. And he learned how best to avoid being beaten, something he was not entirely successful at putting into practice.

Being beaten by Mr Robinson was far from the only hazard involved in going to the senior school: the bear pit of the playground was a major battleground, full of dangers. Another George was king of the playground and ruled his domain with a large fist and there came a day when Callum was to feel the wrath of both Georges in the same day.

Georgie Donaldson was a big-built, red-haired boy nearly two years older than Callum. He had a fiery temper and a bullying disposition. He was the largest and the oldest and he demanded that everyone else in the playground do his bidding. Sooner or later it was bound to get round to Callum's turn to be bullied into submission. On his sixth-week at his new school

Georgie approached with a group of cronies: Callum, already knowing of his reputation, tried to ignore him but there was no escape. He was trapped in the corner of the small, asphalt playground, up against a wire fence.

-"Ye, McDonald, what dae ye hae fer yer bait taedae?" Georgie demanded.

Callum knew that George had a habit of stealing other people's mid-day meal and there was no way he was going to give him his.

-"Gis yer bait ye wee pillock or I'll bash ye!" George spat out at him when he saw Callum hesitating.

-"Gae boil yer heid!' said Callum tremulously, it was a curse he had heard Earnest utter in an unguarded moment.

-"Gis it or ye're deid!" spat Georgie again.

Callum was scared, faced with this large, aggressive boy, almost a head taller and much broader with his little gang of grinning mates, who were gaining a vicarious sense of power from watching Callum's imminent and certain humiliation. He heard himself say;

-"Gae feck yersel' Georgie Donaldson, ye're no havin' ma bait, sae there!" he heard himself say.

Callum, balled his fingers up and closed his hands up tight, his heart was pounding. He watched himself put his fists up and adopt a stance he hoped was that of a boxer – "What was he doing, was he insane?" he asked himself.

Georgie swung a great big fist at him and it caught Callum on the side of his head; it made his ears ring and his head spin. Not to be daunted, and despite feeling distinctly woozy, Callum lashed out and caught George

STUART EDGAR

on the chin, only lightly and ineffectually but it shocked him; he wasn't used to boys hitting back. By now they had the attention of the whole playground; many of the boys shouted loudly and excitedly "Fight! Fight! Fight!" Callum could taste the iron and salt of adrenaline in his saliva, his blood was up, his vision narrowed down to just a large, shadowy figure in front of him, dark against the bright sky, everything else was a blur. He was afraid of getting hurt, even more afraid of appearing cowardly though. He noticed girls watching and somehow it was important that they didn't see him humiliated. He lashed out again, aiming for the blur of Georgie's face above him, just a pale, slow moving blob. He registered Georgie hitting him time and time again but oddly he didn't feel it, he just kept wildly lashing out at the pale face above him, then he saw blood, he didn't know whose but by then everybody was dispersing rapidly. There was a hush over the playground, as if in the eye of a storm, the first assault passed and the next about to arrive.

Then Mr Robinson was standing over him, huge and threatening, purple in the face and bellowing. Callum had no idea what he was saying; he was swaying on his feet, incapable of rational thought. He just concentrated on staying upright. Mr Robinson grabbed him by the ear and marched him indoors in an undignified manner. By the time Callum had begun to recover his wits he had realised he was in deep trouble.

He was standing in front of the whole class, everyone was white faced, frightened by Mr Robinson's sulphuric fury. He was yelling almost hysterically at Callum but Callum was very calm now.

-"Who were ye fighting with laddie?" Yelled Mr Robinson "Point him out!"

One of the first things Callum had been told when he arrived at the school was that you didn't snitch on your mates, even if, like Georgie, they weren't really your mates. It was them and us, the teacher versus the pupils and the pupils stuck together regardless. It seemed Georgie Donaldson had melted back into the surrounding crowd when Mr Robinson had appeared, leaving Callum to carry the can on his own. Callum sighed to himself, he knew it was going to bring extra wrath down on his head but he had no choice. Dumb insolence was the only option open to him; so in a resigned manner and a flat voice he said;

-"Nae one Sir"

-"No one!" Mr Robinson was incandescent with rage.

Callum fully expected him to explode like a bursting balloon; he had never seen anybody go such a deep shade of purple before. Despite the fear he seemed to have an awful fascination with the man's reactions. Mr Robinson took a deep breath, gasping for air;

-"If ye tell me who it was ye will only get six strokes of the tawse, if you do not ye will get twelve!" He emphasised the 'twelve', "Do ye understand me laddie?" He hissed wickedly.

There was a sharp sucking in of breath from some of the other pupils in the class; they had never actually seen anyone get twelve strokes of the tawse before, although it was sometimes threatened. That only happened in Borstals; children's "correction" centres and adult prisons.

-"Yes sir!" answered Callum, ashen faced.

-"Well? Are ye going to tell me who it was?" Mr Robinson yelled impatiently.

Callum took a deep breath; he couldn't remember ever being so frightened, he just wanted to be back at home, on the croft with his Ma. He was shaking, he bit his lip;

-"Nae sir" he answered quietly.

-"Right laddie, stand over here!" Mr Robinson pushed him by his shoulders to a place near his desk where he had more room to swing the tawse;

-"Raise yer hand and stand still!" Mr Robinson ordered then strode across the room and collected the tawse from where it hung on a nail on the wall casting its dismal, dispiriting shadow over the whole class. There was absolute silence in the classroom.

Other than swaying slightly after each blow Callum stood stock still and expressionless as the tawse came down again and again. Mr Robinson was straining to put his full force into each strike, pausing each time to let the full effect sink in before striking again; vengeful, vicious and vindictive. Callum bit his lip harder, tasting blood, feeling the sharp pain of it – anything to distract him. Swishing through the air like a stooping hawk the tawse cracked destructively across the palm of his hand; biting pain, the fire leaping upwards until gradually it encompassed his whole arm. It became worse and worse, sharp electric shocks, a throbbing that seemed to take over his whole body, his whole head; each blow brought a terrible fire to his skull which seem to occupy his whole brain, scarlet and black, white hot needles piercing every fibre of his body. After the twelfth blow he stood a moment, rooted to the spot, gently swaying and unable to move his feet.

-"I said to sit down!," he heard Mr Robinson bellow, somewhere in the distance.Callum hadn't made a sound throughout, not a breath nor hint of a whimper had escaped his lips.

He saw himself, as if in a pantomime, walk back unsteadily to his bench. The other pupils silently stood up for him to allow him to squeeze past and take his seat on the bench. 'Guid man!' he heard someone whisper. He was light-headed and faraway; he somehow got through the rest of the day. He couldn't move his arm, every little knock brought shards of violent, hot pain shooting up to his brain. He was left alone; alone to somehow eat a little of his lunch while leaning painfully against a wall in the playground, alone and silent in the classroom, his nearest classmates giving him room on the bench in hushed awe and fear. He had been somewhere, experienced something the other pupils didn't want to imagine happening to them, so they kept a distance, lest they somehow become infected with the misery he was going through, or somehow become connected with his fate.

His left hand was a bloated, bleeding and swollen mess. He wasn't sure how he managed to walk the five miles home; it seemed to be a dream and to take him forever. When he arrived back at the croft Màiri looked at his ashen face and asked what was wrong. He tried to lift his left arm but the pain was too much, hot tears at last rolled down his face.

While he sat at the large, whitewood, dining table Màiri bathed his hand and gently rubbed a soothing balm into the livid cuts and weals. The hand was puffy and had swollen to twice its normal size; he winced at her every gentle touch.

-"How many?" Màiri demanded curtly.

-"Twelve" Callum mumbled and she blanched; her face white, cheeks pink.

She clamped her lips tight together and said nothing breathing out her strangled anger in short, staccato puffs.

The next day was Saturday, Callum had a fever and his mother made him stay in bed. She had bound his hand with clean rag bandages over a warm poultice and gave him a warming infusion of herbs to drink which had helped him sleep and eased the pain a little. He lay in bed and read Treasure Island by Robert Louis Stevenson and drifted in and out of a strange dream about the tropical island and pirates amongst whom he recognised the hazy face of Georgie Donaldson and a great bear of a creature he afterwards recognised as Mr Robinson. He thought he heard his mother and father talking quietly in the next room and it seemed to him, in his half awake state, that at one point he heard his father crying but thought he probably imagined it. He also thought his father had come in and kissed him on the forehead and stood silently by the side of the bed while he dozed but that couldn't be he told himself, his Pa didn't do that sort of thing.

On the Monday morning he and his mother went by wagon to Kyle, with the great dark horses Hecuba and

Hector pulling enthusiastically and an unusually restrained and dour Ian McDonald driving. He said nothing but his great shoulders were hunched and tense with restrained feeling. Callum felt every lump and bump in the track as sharp shards of pain electrified his hand and arm. Màiri had decided he needed more expert attention; they were making a rare trip to see the Doctor.

Dr. McKenzie was a kindly, elderly man with extravagant grey whiskers and a balding head who habitually wore a black three-piece suit, shiny at the elbows and knees. He was tall, bony and slightly stooped with large, rheumy eyes and an almost perpetual dewdrop on the end of his long, narrow nose.

-"How many did he receive Mrs McDonald?" the doctor asked gravely as soon as he saw the hand.

Callum noted that doctors, like shopkeepers, ministers and other important adults were wont to talk to parents about children as if they weren't there.

-"Twelve" said Màiri tight-lipped.

-"Good God!" Exclaimed Dr Mackenzie and muttered something under his breath about 'that bluidy man'.

-"Ye're not the first to bring in a boy in this state Mrs McDonald," the doctor said wearily.

Màiri said nothing but looked grim.

The doctor, after carefully unwrapping Callum's hand, gently rubbed in some antiseptic cream and carefully rebound the hand in gauze and a clean bandage. He complimented the manner in which Màiri had cleaned and bound the wound. Although his long, bony hands shook alarmingly with intention tremors he was remarkably dexterous. He bound Callum's arm in a sling, carefully folding over a large square of white bandage material and tying it behind Callum's neck.

-"There ye are young man, ye look like a wounded soldier now, ye'll be the envy of all the other boys, and the target of some solicitous attention frae the lassies I don't doubt." He smiled and placed his two closed fists in front of Callum,

-"Choose?" he demanded.

Callum indicated his choice a little shyly: Dr McKenzie turned his hand over and opened his palm to reveal a round, hard, sherbet lollipop, coloured in bands of pretty pale greens and pinks. Callum was hardly ever given sweets except at New Year and Easter and on his birthday. He looked to his Ma who smiled and nodded and he took it with an enthusiastic "Thanks!" and popped it straight into his mouth, before anyone suggested anything foolish like saving it until later.

Màiri paid the receptionist a shilling and another two pence for a round box of aspirins; a great deal from her limited funds, and then they headed back down Main Street to where Callum's uncle was waiting with the wagon. Màiri smiled sadly at Callum;

-"Well young man, it is evident that ye are tae live after all!" and kissed him on the forehead, in public!

Callum looked about nervously to make sure no one had seen. Màiri left Callum with his uncle Ian and the horses and strode off down the street, still grim-faced and determined, with a clear purpose in mind, a woman determined. She said nothing of where she was going. His Uncle Ian called him "A puir wee, wounded soldier!" and lifted him bodily high up on to the wagon's box seat where Callum sat surveying the view and sucking contentedly on his lolly, begining to rather enjoy the attention, now that the constant fire in his hand had eased.

Callum stayed at home for all the next week. After the first couple of days his hand was beginning to recover and he felt a lot better and began to enjoy the role of patient. Jess was allowed to sit on his bed and keep him company as he tried to look pale and wan. He had read all his library books by the fourth day and he had had enough of being a patient and got up and dressed with difficulty and helped his mother feed his chickens and collect the eggs. He and Màiri spent a lot of time talking that week about every subject under the sun as Màiri sat at the side of his bed and stroked his dark hair, which was fine because nobody else could see. They talked about the croft and about what being a crofter meant, about the glen and the wider world and what he might get to see of it and about his plans for the future which he was somewhat confused about what her hopes and fears for him were. One thing was certain though he said, he was determined to travel, to see some of the world beyond the glens and the mountains.

When he returned to school on the following Monday morning he found that his popularity had suddenly much increased. He had become something of a hero for standing up to Georgie Donaldson; and his capacity for taking twelve strokes of the tawse without crying out was hugely admired, even though he knew it was fear that had kept him silently rooted to the spot.

His hand had largely recovered but was still tender and the palm was still bandaged which, at least in his wilder moments made him feel a little like a wounded hero having survived a great battle. Of course it gained him a great deal of sympathy, especially from the girls which, curiously he found himself enjoying a great deal, especially as all the girls had pretty much ignored him before.

Georgie Donaldson's fortunes though had taken a decided turn for the worst. He had fallen precipitously from his position as king of the playground. His disgraceful behaviour in not admitting to Mr Robinson that he had been Callum's opponent in the fight and thereby leaving Callum to take the full punishment was generally agreed to be cowardly and dishonourable. In addition, it appeared that Callum had given a more creditable defence than he had realised and Georgie therefore no longer appeared quite as fearful to the other pupils as he had. He had made few real friends with his bullying ways and now that the other pupils had gained a more worthy champion he had lost much of his following. He still threw his considerable weight about from time to time but with little real effect or conviction and began to appear something of a much diminished, sorry figure, quietly leaving school not long after.

Even Mr Robinson seemed more subdued somehow; he had lost some of his wilder bullying ways too. Despite being in trouble from time to time Callum was never again struck with the tawse and Mr Robinson never again gave anyone more than three strokes with it.

Callum couldn't be sure but he suspected that his mother and the doctor had something to do with his more restrained behaviour.

Callum's dreary studies continued nonetheless. For the best part of the next two years he had to carry on putting up with the daily, tedious incantations of Mr Robinson. He was always top of the class but he considered it to be an easy victory since none of his lessons even began to stretch his abilities, and anyway he suspected that few of the brighter pupils could be bothered trying, their futures were mapped out, they were just marking time. He began to lose any real interest in learning and concentrated on his work on the croft and the study of nature in its abundance all around him.

So for the next two years he got on with working on the croft and went out on expeditions into the wild countryside around his home while he dutifully but rather pointlessly attended school.

In the early spring of 1934, when he was twelve he set off on a particular expedition up the beinn; he knew of a pair of golden eagles who nested there and he was determined to get as close as he could to see the chicks. The eagles often flew over the glen, calling harshly or gliding swiftly on broad wings, quartering the ground for sight of possible prey. He had never seen one close-up and had always yearned to do so.

He set off early one morning after breakfast along with Jess; he carried a canvas pack over his shoulder with his lunch and a flask of tea and, carried, rather awkwardly wound round his chest and half-secreted under his jacket, a coil of rope. He had surreptitiously borrowed the fifty feet of stout hemp rope from his father's store of fishing gear. The lower slopes were straightforward; he could have managed them in the thick dark of night he knew them so well. He followed sheep and fox trails between the newly green heather, Jess stopping from time to time to sniff the language of the wild beasts where they had left smelly indications of their passing. Callum too could smell the rank, acrid trail of a dog fox; he knew the old fox well. He played a game of cat and mouse with him in his constant battle to keep his chickens safe. The fox had already had two of his hens. Callum didn't resent him, he knew he was just doing what came naturally and had a mate or perhaps cubs to support but that didn't mean he would make it easy for him.

When he had mounted the lower slopes and reached heights of around five-hundred feet he stopped and rested as he surveyed the scene. It was a clear day and the Outer Hebrides glowed a dark, golden brown on the misty horizon. After a brief rest he continued upwards, the vegetation becoming sparser, outcrops of bare, grey rock becoming more pronounced. At around eight to nine hundred feet he stopped to get his bearings. The summit was only another eight hundred feet or so above him but he was looking for a particular outcrop of rock off to one side. The outcrop, a shattered tangle of broken rock shards and mini peaks was about a hundred and fifty feet above and to his left.

He told Jess to stay put and slipped his pack from his shoulder. He placed it on a high boulder held down with an additional rock, checking to make sure it was safe against Jess who might get hungry and decide to ferret out his lunch. He checked the rope, making sure that it lay securely across his body so it couldn't slip off or get in the way as he edged his way across to the rocky outcrop. He had climbed above the level that he thought was where the nest, or eyrie was. He was at about fifteen hundred feet and intended to observe the nest from above until the adults were nowhere to be seen and then climb down.

He had to be careful where he put his feet now because the dark rock was loose, coming away in flakes where winter ice had expanded cracks and weakened the surface. He was on a rounded shoulder with a hefty drop below him. He slowly traversed the slope, hand over hand, sometimes on all fours. He reached the outcrop without too much of a problem and, concealed now in a crazy tangle of broken rocks, he peered over the edge. There, on a secure ledge below him was the nest, pretty much where he expected it to be. It was a huge pile of sticks and branches and dead vegetation. He was excited and a little frightened, he knew that a pair of eagles tend to use the same eyrie year after year so expected this nest to still be in use although he couldn't see any chicks at the moment.

He lay still and scoured the sky. Before long a large adult flew into view, drifting lazily down the air currents towards the nest. At the last minute she tilted her wings upwards and spread them wide, spilling the air and letting her large feet down. He had never seen an eagle so close before, she was less than ten feet away as she stalled in the air, her huge glorious wings open for his inspection, ready to drop gently onto the nest. He could see her individual feathers, large yellow eye and the golden sheen of a reddish head and paler chest, a contrast to the dark chestnut feathers of her back. For just a moment the magnificent great bird hung in the air in full view, the wind caressing her feathers. He knew it was a sight that would live with him for the rest of his life.

She dropped lightly onto her nest below, her talons gripping the edge tight as two bundles of fluffy white, spiky feathers suddenly burst into life. He could see their long stringy necks and outsized beaks opening and stretching towards the mother bird but she had just been out stretching her wings, they would have to wait for the male bird to bring in food. The female began to preen herself and the chicks subsided again, dozing amongst the flies and remains of prey.

When the male eventually came in it was the with the same astonishing style and control as the female bird; again the stall in the air just in front of him, the male a little smaller than the female. As he flapped to adjust his position Callum imagined he felt the draft from the huge wings, over six feet across. The male bird clutched the lifeless form of an unlucky rabbit in his talons and, as he alighted awkwardly onto the nest below, one long-taloned foot trying to grip, the other awkwardly holding the rabbit carcass, the female snatched his prize. She cackled loudly at him and thrust her powerful beak aggressively towards him. He took the message and flew off, his great wings flapping and catching the air like feathered wardrobe doors. He spread out his wings, tipped forwards and effortlessly glided into the void below. Callum's stomach went with him as the soaring bird drifted out over the crofts and the loch and powered onwards towards the sea, banking to catch the thermals and soaring out over the ocean, ever higher before drifting back inland again.

Already the female was tearing pieces of meat from the carcass, delicately feeding first the larger chick and, when he or she had had enough, feeding the smaller one. Callum knew that if there were not enough prey or the male otherwise failed to bring in enough food, the smaller one would starve and probably be eaten by the other. But thought Callum, that's the way of it in nature, these great predators lived on the edge of everything and did what they had to to survive just as the crofters did.

Callum had to wait an uncomfortable hour or so, distracted by the heat and flies flying up out of the nest, until both the adult male and the female had flown off after prey before he started his climb down to the nest. He tied the rope to a solid boulder and threw the remainder over the edge of the bulging shoulder of rock. He looked down as the rope coiled out; it was a good forty feet or so to the nest: these huge birds had made it look like a mere hop. He almost changed his mind, his head was reeling, he imagined himself slipping, falling, bouncing off rockfaces as he fell hundreds of feet, to be smashed like a rag doll at the foot of the beinn.

He knew he didn't have much time before the female returned; he knew she rarely left the nest for long while the chicks were so small. He took a deep breath, grasped the rope with both hands and slid clumsily and painfully over the edge. The birds had chosen their site well, the rocky shoulder of coarse, sparkling schist bulged out below him for the first half of the climb and then the rock face dropped sheer to the ledge for another twenty feet; not a long way but if he fell he would probably break something and was well aware that nobody knew he was up here. No-one would look for him up here if he got into trouble. He had not told his Ma or Pa where he was going because they would have banned him from trying anything so dangerous.

He inched his way down the rope, his fingers painfully scraping on the hard, crystalline rock, the rope was pulled tight against the outward bulge of the cliff face by his weight, squeezing his knuckles. Once he was a clear of the shoulder he quickly shinned down the rest of the rope to the ledge where the end coiled into the nest itself. He carefully landed on the edge of the massive, untidy pile of sticks, branches and debris. He swayed dangerously on the edge. The smell was almost unbearable; there was white guano everywhere. The nest was liberally sprinkled with the remains of the chicks meals; bones, dried, rotting meat and rejected parts of now unrecognisable animals and birds. He thought he spotted a lamb's foot and hoped it wasn't one of theirs, perhaps born early up on the hill, away from the safety of its home croft, perhaps stillborn or dying of natural causes but perhaps predated. Living alongside these huge predators was a risk for the crofter's but as far as Callum was concerned they had as much right to be here as the crofters had, perhaps more;

they had inhabited this land long before humans came and settled.

They had been around before humans had existed as a species and anyway, an eagle couldn't be expected to differentiate between natural prey and a crofter's lambs, it was all a necessary means to feed themselves and to bring up the latest generation of offspring. It was the same with the fox and his chickens, the fox killed to eat, just as we did, and if we put all of its prey in one place to make it easy for him then he would take advantage. If he got carried away and slaughtered indiscriminately we would call him wicked names and chase him down and kill him, and we would miss the irony of the situation. It made Callum angry.

It was the flies that made the nest site so hard to tolerate, that and the smell; the flies were everywhere, the buzzing filled his ears, the bloated, black, shiny insects feasted on the remains of the chicks meals and the warm sunshine brought the full effect of rotting meat to his nostrils. He reached over and gently grasped a chick, a plump little grey bundle of fluff, a fat belly with gawky, lashing vestigial wings, still covered with baby down, the adult feathers not yet starting to come through, a scrawny neck and a huge beak, hook-pointed and sharp like its parents and huge, prehistoric feet. He smiled at this strange looking, awkward wee bird which was looking up at him with wide-open beak, expecting him to feed it and making an odd, frantic squawking, mewling sound. It's wide yellow eyes peered up at him. He laid it back down and decided it was time to get back up the rope, before that huge female bird returned. He had seen an eagle's nest close-up and held and inspected a chick; that was more than enough for one day.

He started pulling himself up the rope, hand over hand, his feet locked together, legs wound round the rope, gripping it tight. He had strong shoulders for a boy of his age as a result of all the heavy work he did on the croft. He felt, rather than saw the female eagle return; he felt the draught as she swooped down on him, her claws parting his hair; belatedly he heard the angry "raaark!" She banked away, somersaulting in the air, spreading those vast wings and then turned back towards him. He twisted his neck round to see, she was almost as big as him and those large outspread wings darkened the sky above him. She came at him again, her fearsome talons extended and raked the air close to his head again, she seemed to be trying to scare him off rather than attack him but he wasn't prepared to hang around and put it to the test.

Hand over hand he frantically dragged himself back up the rope as fast as he could manage. When he reached the shoulder of rock above him his hands were restricted by the tightness of the rope straining against the bulge of the rock-face and he had to force his hands underneath the rope. The surface of the rock was like sandpaper on his flesh, his fingers bloodied in his haste. He flattened himself against the rock each time she made a pass close to him. He watched her soar by; so close on one occasion that he felt the long flight feathers graze his cheek. He lay still as she came in again and again. He tried to become part of the rock-face. He studied the small patch of rock in front of his nose, seeing the blue-grey lichen, the tiny specks of shiny quartz glinting in the pale morning sunlight. He lay still, breathing hard, intently conscious of the long drop below him. His hands ached, his knuckles were scraped raw by the chafing rock, his compressed fingers became numb.

He hung like that for what seemed an age, his shoulders feeling as if they were being wrenched out of their sockets, his full weight hanging off them. Eventually the female eagle decided he was no longer a threat and settled back on the nest composing her wings carefully and leaning down to check on her chicks, now seeming perfectly content, glorious in her majesty, queen of the skies: even now he couldn't help but admire her fierce beauty.

Having finally reached safety he sat for a while gazing at the view while the adrenaline began to dissipate and he slowly stopped shaking. He looked down at the view of the croft, tiny from up here, the glen and the surrounding land spread out like a map, his home was like a little green symbol drawn on a green sheet of grass, the grassy roof springing to life with spring rain and sunshine. The paddocks were filled with ewes milling around, grazing on early spring grass, brought in off the lower slopes for lambing. The barns and sheds in the yard were slate grey oblongs against the pale ground of hard-baked earth.

The sandy ribbons of pathways lay silent in the mid-day heat contrasting with the ever-moving, glinting currents of the azure-green loch. It was an ageless scene and could have been any time in the last thousand or two-thousand years. He could hear Jess barking below, she was fretting about him, worried about the length of time he had been away: he'd better make his way down, before she tried to cross the dangerous scree-covered slope to reach him.

He sat and ate his bread and cheese and drank his tea, exhilirated, triumphant. Jess fossicked about amongst the rocks and poked her nose into crannies and cracks as he gradually calmed. When Jess became tired of exploring he tossed her the meaty bone he had brought for her in his pack and she settled to it with a will. All in all it had had been a spectacular morning. He felt especially privileged to get so close to the king and queen of the air and to have seen the chicks close-up; he wished them well and fervently hoped the estate gamekeepers didn't find the nest.

He felt the same about gamekeepers as his mother did; they were lackeys to the estate owners who cared little for wildlife. He knew there were good keepers as well as bad but as a group they viewed nature as if it were there at the convenience of their masters and if any creature got in their way they killed it without compunction or afterthought. They decided what lived and what died on their master's estate and they saw their role as being in constant battle with an antagonistic nature rather than in harmony with it. They had an odious practice of nailing up the dead bodies of slaughtered predators on barn doors, as if they were criminals or somehow malign rather than creatures doing what came naturally; stoats, hoody-crows, buzzards, beautiful hawks and mystical owls, ghosts of the night. He'd never seen a golden eagle pinned to a barn door but he expected it happened. They caught creatures in vicious gin traps and they called the predators wicked. Callum had come across such barn-door gibbets from time to time and it made him sad and furious to see such beautiful creatures so treated. They called them pests and vermin and once they had demonised them it became easier to justify killing them.

As the spring of 1934 turned into summer the weather turned foul; dreadful, leaden, heavy skies, and rains that carried on for weeks, turning the soil into a boggy mess. Crops rotted in the ground. By the time the weather improved a good third of their produce had been lost, the potatoes that Màiri had planted in her plot had turned mouldy and she had lost most of her summer cabbages; oats and barley were decimated and, after a while, it looked as though they wouldn't be able to cut the hay for the wet.

Not until September did the weather clear and give them a brief space to bring in what was left of the crops. The sky always threatened rain; monotonously grey weather that well-deserved the Scottish description of 'dreich'. Everyone set to, the adults from both hamlet and village; men and women, children, even Flora and Fiona were called back from exile to work to get the harvest in, every hand was needed if anything was to be rescued from the disastrous summer, before the god awful rains came again.

What a harvest that was! They worked from first light until the last rays of sun faded over the Hebridean horizon; and then, a few hours later, they were back in the fields. There was no joy in this harvest, just backbreaking, unrelenting toil, a race against the bad weather returning. Callum was now big enough and strong enough to join the men and Màiri in wielding a scythe. He took his place proudly in the line with his father on one side and his mother on the other. As they moved across the field there was little of the usual banter or singing, just a steady concentration. They all knew how close they were to starvation this coming winter, there was no time to lose; if the rains came back now they faced real disaster. As they lifted their heads from time to time to stretch acing backs they cast nervous glances at the sky.

After the first few days Hecuba and Hector were harnessed up; they spent the day tethered in the corner of the field browsing, waiting to be hitched up to the wagon the moment they were needed. The crops that had been cut a few days before were hauled in just as soon as they were dry enough. The urgency of securing as much of the crop as possible affected everyone.

There were no long, relaxing mid-day meals this year, no singing or children playing, a quick bite and a rest and the occasional song of sharpening stone on huik and then back into the field to steadily scythe their way through the rest of the crop in grim silence. In the end they just managed to clear most of the last field of hay on the Fraser's croft as the rains returned with a vengeance. But so much had been lost, heartbreakingly battered into the dark soil by the heavy, bitter summer rains. The rains continued on into autumn, grey and cold; a damp that soaked deep into the soul.

Callum was pleased that he had been able to renew his friendship with Billy and Alistair during the harvest. Both now had filled out and seemed to move in a more grown-up way, more confident and with an assuredness about themselves that Callum still lacked. Billy was to go for a cabin boy in the spring on a herring drifter out of Mallaig, the big west coast fishing port. He was looking forward to it, even though he knew it would be a hard life, but then he had grown up with bone-weary hardness. How much worse could it be? Alastair was staying on for now to help look after the croft and had started going out with the other men of the Hamlet to fish in the loch. Soon though he too would be away to Mallaig to the big boats.

Flora turned out to harvesting in a completely inappropriate, body hugging summer frock that she had made herself; quite the jeune fille, her young body beginning to bud into adulthood. Young Fiona was dressed more sensibly in an old black frock and calico apron. Callum now found that he felt awkward and clumsy around the two girls; he was tongue-tied and gauche. He felt a prickle of excitement run down his spine when Flora spoke to him and had an odd feeling in his groin when she bent over towards him, and spoke gently in his ear, revealing a confidence about nothing in particular, her perfume wafting over him, filling his nostrils with a female miasma. He didn't quite understand why he felt as he did, it was just Flora after all. But it wasn't the old Flora he had played with and had childish squabbles with just over a year or two ago. She was now having a very disturbing effect on him, plunging him into complete confusion. And there seemed to be some sort of game or conspiracy going on between Flora and Fiona; he didn't understand it but it seemed to involve him. He was out of his depth with not a clue as to what was going on but he was aware that he was having embarrassing and beguiling feelings about it all. His mother looked on and seemed to be amused by his confusion, which irritated him enormously.

Callum had grown in the last couple of years; he was now about five-foot-five, quite tall for his age and times and muscular and spare from his active, outdoor life. He was becoming an attractive young man albeit in a rather gawky, rangy and untidy sort of way. His dark looks and large, shining brown eyes and his unselfconsciousness seemed to be very appealing to these post-pubescent young women would he but know it.

Soon he would be thirteen, old enough to leave school and be free to work full-time on the croft. Màiri was distressed at his lack of opportunities; she had dreamed of so much more for him and fervently prayed that even now some opportunity would arise or that she herself could find a way of giving him some way out of the glen. Beautiful as it was there was little here that offered him any way out of near poverty and which would provide him with any sense of intellectual achievement. She didn't want a life for him where his constant and only daily concern was how to feed a family, although his going away would rip at her strong feelings for him.

Màiri also had her own, more immediate concern of how she was going to feed her own family through to next spring and how to feed the animals. She estimated they had brought in at best two thirds of the usual harvest. This year's lambs had already been sold at market to lowland farms for fattening-up as had this years calves. She had just enough money saved to buy in winter feed for the beasts that were left and a little more. She had to buy essentials for themselves; potatoes to replace those she had lost, flour, salt and tea, paraffin for the lamps and some extra vegetables. She had nursed through some winter cabbages and leeks in her little garden but that was all. It would be a very thin winter this year. She would need, against every instinct to the contrary, to send some of their breeding stock to market; always deeply depressing for a farmer: you built up a herd only to see it decimated by a bad harvest and have to sell your finest breeding beasts at rock bottom prices for lack of winter feed. This year she really did feel that they were living and farming on the edge, between survival and starvation, civilization and wilderness.

She was full of wonder and respect for her grandparents who had been shoved onto this marginal land in the last of the great Clearances. They had established the croft, built this house in the wilderness and managed to grow food and make a living on such poor land with nothing more than their bare hands and a few basic tools. She couldn't imagine the hardship of it all, nor how they had survived. They must have suffered terribly, especially in those first winters. They must have had enormous fortitude to carve out some sort of a life from such unrewarding and harsh circumstances. They had no security of tenure then and there was no knowing if they would be moved on again by a heartless, greedy landlord. She had tried hard to emulate them but sometimes, when things got really tough such as now she wondered if she should continue to follow their example, sometimes it just seemed too damn cruel.

Along this coast were many abandoned crofts and villages, communities driven out of their homelands who tried to make a go of it on the marginal lands they were left to settle. They were forced to try fishing with no knowledge or equipment, like the village she heard of in Caithness, and which she firmly believed to be real, who were apparently forced out by the Duke and then the Duchess of Sutherland. They were pushed out to the cliff tops of Cape Wrath. Their ancestral lands to which they had no deeds beyond their trust and history, had, they claimed, been stolen from them. Well named, the storms at Cape Wrath are and were terrible. The winds were so strong that when small children were outdoors they often had to be tied down with a rope for fear of being blown over the edge of the towering cliffs.

All that's left of most of the communities and individual crofts now are piles of stones, bracken and moss covered mounds, a few scraps of possessions buried in the turf, the whole now home to small creatures, their owners fled to the Americas or Australia, those of them who didn't starve to death or manage to eke out a life on the coastal margins.

Màiri couldn't bear to leave this place though, hard as it was, it was in her blood, the soil had soaked up the tears of her grandparents and parents. Their suffering would be wasted if she were to give it up now. So hard won was this scrap of land she felt that to let it go would be worse than defeat, it would be a terrible betrayal. Besides, she loved this place, harsh as it was.So deeply did she love it that sometimes it felt as if it had inhabited her, it was what she was.

But she had others to think of; Dougal and Jeannie were growing up. Jeannie was now four years old and would be beginning school next year and Dougal, now seven had already been at school for the last two years. He wasn't as interested as Callum in studying although he was bright enough. He was more interested in the work of the croft; following his Ma and Pa around, watching what they were doing, helping out by opening gates, fetching hay or straw and feeding the animals while one or the other of them watched. He wasn't a dreamer like Callum but practical and down to earth, with a clear sense of what he was and what he wanted to be in the future, even at his young age.

Time seemed to pass so quickly in the yearly round of crofting; Màiri felt a melancholy, a nostalgia for a time when everything seemed less complicated. Callum especially was growing up so fast. She worried about him, that he was beginning to fret with frustration. Much as he loved the croft she knew he had a thirst for knowledge and to see places outside the glen. The croft would never be enough for Callum, she had always somehow known that. He had seen Flora and a Fiona go away to begin new lives, Billy was going to sea, of his old school friends only Alistair had stayed on to look after Moira, his mother, but soon he too would be gone for most of the time too, off to sea like Billy, for a week or so at a time, in all weather on the herring drifters, out of Mallaig, the West Coast fishing port, down the coast to the south. So many young people left these glens; she knew it was the same out on the Islands too. There weren't the opportunities for them at home but it was always a wrench to tear their roots out of this beguiling soil.

Màiri worried about Hamish too, what with winter coming on, would he sink into a dark well of despair again?

Hamish worried too, he worried about the future. He could see that they didn't have enough oats and barley to feed them through to the spring. He thought the hay would probably last out but only if they sent a few of their breeding animals to market; the thought sickened him. He had got to know each of the animal's as individuals, they had served him and Màiri well, given calves or lambs and they in turn had treated the beasts well, cared for them when they were sick, encouraged them when they gave birth; they knew each of their names and their individual ways. And now they were going to have to sell some of them, to betray the animals trust in them.

If he were a better farmer they would not be in this situation he mused melancholically. His family would be better off without him. He saw it as his failure that they had such a poor harvest, to fail to adapt to the harsh weather. "It was his damn fault!" and he cursed himself. His anger and his frustration turned inwards again, and it began to gnaw away at his guts, like a persistent rat in a cage.

The day they collected the animals together to go to market was a dreadful one for both of them. Both Màiri and Hamish saw accusations in the eyes of each animal as it was separated from it's herd and then penned up. When it came to the two grazing cows that they were going to send off Màiri almost broke down. She knew these great, dark, gentle beasts so well, had helped them with calving and fed them each day in winter: they were part of the family. They had been with them six years, reliably producing a calf every year. Out of the original small herd of five breeding cows there were just two left now. They didn't know when or if they would be able to replace them. Maybe they should stick with sheep thought Màiri, you didn't get so attached to the ewes, they were up on the hill most of the time and they were independent beasts, but cows needed some attention and were dependent and that made them more vulnerable, more attached.

When the animals had gone Hamish went to the lean-to to tend to his nets and brood; Màiri went to get the midday meal and to see to young Jeannie. She squared her shoulders; they would manage; things had been worse before now. But she still saw those large, accusing eyes as her cows were chivvied out of the yard and off down the track to Kyle and the railhead and was heartily glad that Callum and Dougal were at school: she wouldn't have wanted them to see that.

Dougal and Callum had picked up on the gloomy atmosphere when they had returned that day from school. They had known the animals were going to market. They both knew the animals as well as their parents did; Callum had taken his turn in caring for them and felt their loss keenly. Dougal had got to know the animals while beginning to help Màiri with her tasks. He followed her around the way Callum used to, trying to be helpful and getting in the way and slowing Màiri down, though she still appreciated it. Dougal seemed to be comfortable with the everyday world of the croft; he enjoyed the daily round and liked nothing better than following Màiri, or occasionally his father, watching them at work and trying to copy what they did. Though still only just seven he accepted the need for selling the animals in a more matter-of-fact way. He had understood, in a practical and philosophical manner beyond his years, that there were ups and downs in the fortunes of a crofter's life and you just had to get used to it. He knew that animals were fed and watered, cared for as well as could be and were then sold when necessary. They would find new breeding animals, it was a blow but they would build up the herd again.

Callum however, couldn't help but build up emotional relationships with the animals on the farm, at least with those he got to know year in year out and he knew the joy of having them come to trust him. He felt keenly the betrayal of that trust in selling these animals on. He too felt the guilt of treachery towards these creatures who had served them so well in providing offspring for market and on which they had depended for their living.

September dragged on; the wet and windy weather continued with grey, flat clouds filling the sky from horizon to horizon. The unrelenting work of the croft went on. It would soon be time to bring the sheep down off the hill: there was enough grass remaining on the in-by land to keep them going for a while. That would ease the pressure on the hay over winter but it would be a close run thing come spring. Màiri sincerely hoped spring came early next year; if it were late there would be more breeding ewes going to market, most likely with new lambs in tow: that would be almost unendurable.

She was still worrying about Hamish. She could see the signs of his dark, brooding moods returning. He was becoming more morose, withdrawn. She knew he blamed himself for what was the fault of the weather, as if he personally were responsible for half-ruining their crops. When she looked into his eyes they were far away, focused on somewhere or something that she would never be able to see. His gaze fell on another world, a world of dark foreboding, a place where half-revealed fears and loss of sanity lurked. She could feel him being inexorably dragged away from her world into some god-forsaken realm of twilight existence where she would no longer be able to reach him and she knew she was powerless to prevent it.

With the first storms came a change of the direction of the weather. Northerlies brought freezing cold, Arctic air down from as far away as Svaalbad and Finland. Dark thunder-heads rolled in, one after another and pelted the little black house with vicious bursts of rain and hail. Burns swelled and broke their banks and indoor walls and roof beams dripped disheartening pools of cold, seeping rain onto the hard, earthen floor.

After ten days of terrible weather the sky cleared to an icy, steel, blue and the wind veered south-westerly bringing in high-pressure from the Atlantic. The pale and watery, autumn sun scattered spotlights of silver between ragged, blue-white clouds and lit the brittle, cold air with shards of northern light over the breathless loch,though it contained barely a candle's-worth of warmth.

Hamish rose early on one such bright, clear morning, as the first sunlight flickered across the bare floor, piercing its way through the small, deep-set windows. He had lain staring at the ceiling for the lonely hours before dawn, his head filled with dark thoughts. He washed and shaved, then paused by the bed to look down at his sleeping wife. He gave her a brief, uncharacteristic kiss to the forehead and then put on his heavy, black coat and scarf. He went out into the sharp, cold air of the morning. He collected his oars from where they hung on the iron hooks of the dark, lean-to. He took a look around him, how often had he sat here quietly mending nets in the light of a paraffin lamp in quiet contemplation? He swung the long, flat-bladed oars onto his shoulder. They were heavy and unwieldy but he had learned just how to balance them so that they didn't impede walking: just as he had eventually learnt so many things that were foreign to his nature since coming to this place.

He slowly and steadily made his way down the precipitous path to the calm, stony cove, not even noticing a fellow fisherman step aside for him and grunt in greeting. His boots, shifted and cracked the large stones. He noticed, as if for the first time, the salty, seaweedy smell of the clean, morning air and the preternatural hush at the top of the tide. A red legged oystercatcher dabbled along the shoreline, looking for mini-crustaceans, the water gently lapped as the loch slopped onto the stones; it soothed him and stilled the voices in his head for a moment. He startled a gull which rose and ripped the air with raucous-voiced nagging, tearing at his anxieties again.

He heaved his boat onto its keel-spine and it gave a stone-crunching lurch as it settled, upright and empty on the beach. He grasped the dew-laden rope haltering the boat and dragged it towards the water. His scuffed boots were immersed in the shallows as he gave a final, awkward push and the boat floated off; gentle waves slapped against the planks sides.

With contemplative calm Hamish swung his legs carefully over the boat's side and hauled himself in. It tilted alarmingly from side to side, the motion gradually decreasing to a shallow roll before settling at last on the pond-like surface. Gentle ripples fanned out across the loch. The table smooth water dully shone quicksilver and pewter as he began to languidly row towards the middle of the loch, barely disturbing the dark water. The oars splashed as they sliced through the cool surface like a well honed blade through tightly stretched skin. The rhythm of rowing soothed him and calmed the chaos inside his skull; his dulled sensibilities took in the calm beauty of the day. The gentle mist still clung in tattered rags here and there on the pool like surface; ephemeral will-o'-the-wisp's danced lazily in the barely warm air above the waves before dispersing skywards in the quietly moving breeze.

When he reached the middle of the loch where the dark, deep currents ran he shipped his oars and drifted in a barely discernible current. A soft, skin-stroking breeze stirred the damp air around him. He was superficially calm and serene, the only signs of the terror within were the incised creases around his world-weary eyes and the clenched, furrowed brow. The voices had stilled, taken pause.

He drifted in a dream state, a living, daytime, inner terror, a waking nightmare. He heard the dreadful, heavy footsteps again as they made their way down the stone floor of the passage in his mind. He shivered in only his child's nightshirt and he felt the cold, hard flags pressing on his knees through the flimsy, cotton material. The steps shuffled to a stop outside the door behind him. He heard with his mind's ear the feint squeak of an unoiled door handle. He sensed, with the upright hairs on the back of his neck, the harsh, hot breath of his would-be assailant and shivered with lonely fear in the darkness. Hamish breathed out, a long, anguished sigh of resignation. This time he would cheat his assailant, escape this last time from the cruel, crude banality of what was again to be inflicted on his boyhood self.

He rolled himself easily and gently over the boat's rail, the stilled, shining water parted and closed over him with hardly a ripple as he slipped under. As he was turned onto his back by the swirl of the current he could see the glinting light already drifting up and away from him; a trail of bubbles trickled upwards from his open mouth and his sea-soaked clothes His sodden coat and heavy boots were pulling him inexorably down into the numbing, cold darkness.

The bitingly cold water rushed and roared in his ears, blocking out the inner sounds of his terrors. He felt relief, release. Then his lungs began to scream and grasp for oxygen: a raw survival-panic clutched at his heart, even as he offered up a small desperate prayer, a plea for peace. His body and instincts spurred him to struggle and to reach for the pale splinter of light way, way above, as he drifted ever further away from the light the pressure in his skull seemed to implode into stars. He desperately pleaded for it to be over and gasped one huge mouthful of salty water, choking and breathing the loch down into his lungs. His hands clawed crablike and his raised arms begged in supplication towards the retreating light and he lunged desperately for the surface, his body struggling in a last survival spasm.

His burning, spasming lungs at last gave out as the chilling water rushed in through his silently screaming lips. The faces of Màiri and Callum came to him then with perfect clarity and more vaguely the two little ones. He heard again the sounds and breathed in the sweet smells of one wonderful, warm, Indian summer and a late golden harvest of long, long ago; and then his world ended. He drifted softly into dark water-filled oblivion. Hamish had finally found his peace, in the deep, dark fastnesses of the loch.

Time passed, the water stilled as the rocking boat gently settled, drifting slowly. The call of a curlew bubbled and fluted evocatively down off the moors and far out over the misted surface of the cool, running water. A pair of gulls lazily spiralled upwards on a rising pillow of air above the boat. All was dead calm before the tide at last began to turn again. Life was returning to the loch.

Màiri rose from her bed, pulled a coat over her shoulders and dragged the heavy, old black kettle over the fire. She idly wondered why Hamish had left so early this morning.

CHAPTER 8

GRIEVING

It was Nellie who came with the news. Hamish's boat had been found by John Fraser and one of his sons drifting far out in the loch. They had searched over and over, calling all the time but could find nothing. Nellie had sat Màiri down and told her plainly and matter-of-factly, no embroidering, no platitudes or pleas for calm. The boys were at school, Jeannie was playing on the floor with two home-made rag dolls.

When Màiri had first seen the look on Nellie's face as she stood in the doorway she had known, worry, concern, embarrassment: why are people embarrassed by others grief she wondered afterwards. She had known immediately, known that Hamish wouldn't be coming home, not today, not ever again. An icy hand had clutched her heart and squeezed until she could barely breathe. She had swayed on her feet as if she had received a physical blow. Nellie had half led, half carried her to a chair and had told her the bald facts. The Fraser's had towed the boat back and dragged it up onto the stony beach, dripping from the water of the loch, a silent witness, eloquent in its emptiness.

The horror of death, that terrible, ultimate, irretrievable divide; final, catastrophic never to be seen again; familiar human warmth made cold, unreachable. The shock of sudden death, separation and disbelief, unbelievable breathtaking agony, white faced emotion, stunning loss. Màiri was emotionally paralysed, a yawning chasm of unimagining froze her mind. The icy terror of being without someone so close, so familiar, animated her Hamish; now gone, so vital and real and now dreadful nothingness, emptiness; empty bed, empty home, empty croft yard, empty fields and hills, empty heart. She felt cold to her very core, hollow and deserted. She was confused by death, she couldn't understand it. She was haunted by death; her father, her mother, her tiny daughter and now her husband, cut away from her like an amputation, part of the self.

Her mind tried to shy away from the vision of a loved, familiar, once talking, living companion, now suspended in the chill darkness, the chasm of the deepest loch waters, the currents softly suspending him in the dark as fish nibbled at his flesh. The horrific vision crept in like a poisoned miasma to freeze her heart. Such a calm, still day; why? Why had he disappeared, gone over the side of his boat to be lost forever?

Nellie was saying something but it wasn't registering, the words didn't make sense. She couldn't function, she was far, far away. She tried to concentrate.

–"Shall I take wee Jeannie fer a while or would ye prefer I stay" Nellie repeated, insistent, slowly as if to a child.

–"Ah! Oh, aye, please, until the boys come hame, thank ye Nellie" she said distractedly.

–"Ye're sure ye dinnae want me tae stay, or perhaps tell Isla tae come up?"

–"No, no Nellie. I prefer tae be on ma ane, just now really, thank you!"

Jeannie could feel something was wrong, she knew, in that intuitive way that young children have of picking up invisible signals or atmospheres. Something terrible had happened but her mother and Auntie Nellie were speaking too softly for her to hear what it was, trying to keep it from her.

Màiri explained to her quietly that she should go with her Auntie Nellie while her Ma "sorted some things oot" and she would collect her later. She reassured her that everything would be all right, everything would be fine. But Màiri knew it wouldn't, nothing would be right ever again now. She tried to behave normally so as not to frighten Jeannie but her own world had just stopped. She was numb, frozen in that moment when she had opened the door to Nellie, it kept repeating in her head, as if trying to convince herself it was true.

How was she going to tell the boys? How would they react? What was the best way to do it? Màiri spent the rest of the day wandering around in a daze. She kept forgetting what she was supposed to be doing. Jess kept getting under her feet and she shouted at her and then felt sorry and made a fuss of her.

She went to tell the cows. She told the milking cows everything; when Hamish was poorly, when something big had happened and she told them of her worries. The milking cows were still in their byre eating hay when she entered. It was almost midday. Hamish used to leave them after milking and then she would let them out later on. They were late being let out but they didn't seem to mind. It was warm and familiar in the byre and they had food and water. She tried to tell them about the terrible thing that had happened but the words stuck in her throat. Leaning against Ellie she broke down, her tears flowed for what seemed like hours. She didn't know how long she stood there, her heart breaking, leaning against the warm flank of the cow, her head pressed against her. The cow carried on munching and looking round at her, mumbling now and again.

When she left the byre she wandered around the croft stopping at places where she remembered being together with Hamish, working together, talking, sharing experiences. She touched things he had touched as if trying to draw something of him into her. She went in to the lean-to where Hamish spent so much time mending his nets and sitting thinking. His nets were still there, where they always were when he wasn't out in the boat. His nets were still there! Màiri cried out in anguish;

–"Oh no Hamish my love not that, oh no!" She slumped down on the herring barrel he had used as a seat. Realisation sinking a barbed harpoon into her heart. The truth shook her to her very soul. She sat in utter misery, thinking nothing, spent, empty and drained of all hope.

She had no idea how she got through the next few days, she was so numb. She carried out her tasks mechanically, out of habit. She had told the two silent, pale faced and wide-eyed boys plainly, quietly, that their Pa had had an accident, he had fallen from the boat and drowned. They both knew boys or girls who had lost their Pa or an older brother or Uncle at sea, it was inevitable in a fishing community but of course they never expected it to happen to their family. Callum knew that Billy's father had drowned in the loch but not Pa! Màiri did her best to comfort them, to help numb the pain of loss to cushion them somehow. Dougal had cried and been grievously upset, shocked and not really able to understand but after a few days he had accepted, reluctantly, the absence of his father. He was still sad but got on with his life again.

It was Callum she worried about. He was angry, deeply wounded and then confused. Once the numbness of the initial shock and anger had begun to wear off he was silent and brooding, tight-lipped and unreachable. He spent a lot of time on his own or with Jess up on the hill of down at the cove. He had stopped going to school, what was the point? He was due to leave next month anyway and he hadn't learnt anything new for weeks. He did his chores, ate his meals silently and spent as much time as possible away from the house. He wouldn't go near the lean-to, Hamish's presence there was too strong. He was away up the hill, sitting brooding most days, just looking into space, drifting, looking down on the loch where he knew his father was, or at least his body, floating in the currents. Up here, on the moors the horror and the pain of it were diminished a little.

When Màiri tried to talk to him he shrugged her off. She thought he blamed her somehow and perhaps he did. He was confused and angry and he didn't know how to control his feelings, they were raw and unruly and swamped his reason. He couldn't accept his father was gone, the fact of his absence, the finding of the empty boat, these weren't enough; "he couldn't be gone!". It was too big a thing for him to comprehend.

After a while the pain became duller, blunter; its edge no longer wounding his mind. Gradually over the weeks he began to grieve, Màiri noticed the change in him, the anger dissipating little by little to be replaced by a deep, morose sadness. She made sure she stayed close without crowding him, she made it known by nods and smiles, a touch that she understood. But it was hard for her to watch him suffering and unable to comfort him though she knew if she tried he would only pull away. She had to give him the time he needed.

Màiri had thought he was beginning to assimilate the fact of his father's death and began to breathe a little sigh of relief though her own pain was still an open wound, raw and bleeding. Then, one morning as she was getting Jeannie up and helping her dress and Callum was busy boiling the black, cast-iron kettle and making brose for himself and Dougal, he reached up to the shelf beside the range for the tea caddy and something heavy fell off. He stopped and stooped to pick it up; it was Hamish's knife, with the diamond-cut Bakelite handle. He held the heavy knife in his palm, puzzled, frowning; how often had he seen his father use it? He always had it with him, when he rose in the morning he would attach it to the string on his belt by the metal ring at its base and slip it into his pocket. Suddenly, with a searing horror he knew, he knew. He turned, as if in a dream, turned to face his mother. He hated her then,

–"You lied!" he shouted angrily, accusing, harsh and dashed for the door, banging the heavy knife onto the table with a dull thud, leaving the solid evidence of betrayal, a silent accusation.

He swung the heavy door back with furious strengths, so hard that it crashed into the wall. Màiri looked up in shock and little Jeannie stood petrified, suddenly pale and wide-eyed with fear. Màiri sprung up from where she had been crouching, helping Jeannie. She saw the knife on the table and felt a lurch in her stomach as if she was falling.

She remembered now when she had put it there. She had forgotten, maybe deliberately. That day, when Nellie had come to the door and turned her life upside down, shattered her hopes for the future, plunged her into grief and regret, she had found Hamish's knife, laid carefully on the stool by the bed. After finding the nets in the lean-to it just confirmed what she already knew. In a daze she must have placed it away on the shelf and forgotten where she had put it. It had been Hamish's way of letting her know, returning the gift she had given him in life.

Dougal had stepped into the main room wondering what the noise was about.

–"Look after Jeannie, give her her breakfast!" said Màiri in as restrained a voice as she could manage and quickly followed Callum out of the door. Dougal looked confused, open-mouthed but she had gone out of the door with a look of tortured anguish on her face. She looked round frantically and couldn't see him, her heart racing, panic setting in. Where had he gone? What would he do? She had never seen him so angry with her. Should she have told him? But how could she? How could she tell any man's child that his father had deliberately killed himself because, he was, almost literally out of his mind with fear?.

Then she spotted him pounding wildly and recklessly down the steep path to the cove, arms and legs lashing the air, lurching over the smooth stones with no apparent thought for his own safety. She dashed after him, she had to catch up with him before he did anything foolish, before he came to harm. She knew how headstrong he was, how his fiery temper could suddenly flare. She feared that in his current state he was capable of anything. She was terribly afraid; she had a powerful sense of foreboding.

Callum crashed onto the beach and flew across the stones, his feet smashing and grinding the large flat cobbles together. Splintered shards of stone flew off as his stamping, crashing feet bashed them into each other. He ploughed headlong into the surf, the green, white waters flying up in brilliant silver splinters as he tore into the waves, forcing hard against the dragging, ice-cold sea. He pushed with all his strength against the deepening water as its weight pulled at his legs, slowing him down. Oblivious to the cold he threw himself hard into the waves, arms flailing. He stumbled forward, angrily smashing the water with his feet and, then, as he got deeper with his hands and fists.

He plunged his head under the water, feeling a tightening band of cold across his forehead. He pushed wildly on, his feet floating free of the stony seabed and still he lashed out at the water, the anger in his head bursting out in physical violence. He cursed and swore in English, Scots and Gaelic, the words spat out of his mouth in a staccato of phlegm as he swallowed water and gasped for air. He was like a banshee, he had no thought of what he was doing or why, he had been hijacked by raw emotion, all reason had fled.

He sank under the water, swallowed sea instead of air and choked and coughed, his arms lashing crazily against the water, he floundered, struggling to stay up. By now Màiri had reached the water's edge and was screaming with visceral fear and sheer desperation,

–"No Callum! Come back, for God's sake stop!"

She gasped, shivering with cold and terror. She had come out in only a black linen dress and the air was bitingly cold. Dark bubbling clouds banked up overhead and the wind was rising to strong. She plunged in: Callum surfaced and saw her

-"Get back, stay away!" he shouted angrily, spluttering through choking seawater and breathlessness.

He pushed further out and she drew back, she didn't want to drive him into even deeper water, he was already out of his depth, struggling and gasping for air.

The bruised clouds rolled angrily over the loch spitting drizzle, striking Màiri in the face like buckshot. Callum lashed out at the water again, his head numb, barely feeling his arms or his feet now, the penetrating cold beginning to slow his movements. Gasping for air, his breath coming in shallow, panting jerks, his muscles no longer under his control. Try as he might he couldn't slow his breathing, his heart was thumping, his lungs desperate for a breath. Time and time again the water gushed up his nose and into his throat as he struggled to stay on the surface. Waves broke cruelly against his face. He was beginning to drown, careless of the danger. The raw, harsh taste of seawater and snot filled his nostrils and the back of his throat in a thick stifling mucous.

Màiri fell to her knees, screeching and moaning; the bitingly cold water washing around her thighs as she begged Callum to come back, invoking God, anyone, anything to bring him back. If he died too she didn't think she could go on. She begged God to take her life instead of Callum's if He would only bring him back from that cruel, dark sea.

Callum was beginning to slow now, he could barely feel his limbs, his head was numb, he could barely think, he didn't know what he was doing in this ice-cold water. Panic set in and fear surged up from inside him. He thrashed his blunt, cold limbs, trying to drag himself through the water. Gasping and retching he threw himself towards the shore in a last, desperate realisation of his plight; a forlorn bid to save himself. He didn't want to die, not here, not now, not any more. He struggled and struggled, his legs seeming to no longer work, he was becoming weaker, a dark, star-filled vision darkening, clouding his eyes.

But the tide had had turned while he had been thrashuing in the water. A wave gave him a weak push away from a watery end. The loch had had one watery sacrifice from this family: it didn't need another. He fell to his knees and struggled to keep his head above the water. He floated, crawled and dragged himself shorewards. Màiri thrashed herself forward, rising to grasp him, forcing herself against the flow of the waves. She grappled with his wet shirt and got a hold. Terrified of the water but desperate not to lose hold. Pushing herself on leaden legs she dragged him with a frantic strength towards safety. With a last rush they both crashed heavily on to the hard, wet stones, exhausted, spent.

The heavy, blackened clouds poured down their burden of torrential rain. It bounced off them in a fierce downpour. Màiri and Callum were oblivious to it all, holding on to each other in desperation, shaking with cold, blinded by tears, both shivered and trembled with overwhelming emotion. It seemed as if an age passed.

Someone was speaking but Mairi was too numb to notice, or appreciate its significance
    –"Màiri, let me help ye up! Fer God's sake Callum ye'll catch yer death laddie!" It was Isla, insistent and anxious, kneeling over them.
    –"What's been going on Mairi? I saw ye go flying doon the path. I followed and was fair oot o' my wits when I saw young Callum in the sea. Here, come on woman, ye maun get up and oot the cold, ye'll freeze tae death. Ye tae Callum."
    Màiri tried to struggle to her feet but was barely able to kneel. They looked up at her uncomprehending. Isla rose, grabbed Màiri by the arm and hauled her up.

Callum rose unsteadily, seawater and cold rain streaming off him, shivering uncontrollably.

Isla clung to them both, shushing and clucking like a mother hen. Somehow she got them both up the precipitous path to the croft. Callum and Màiri said nothing, drained of all feelings and exhausted.

The two smaller children looked on in wide-eyed silence, pale with fear and bewilderment as they crashed in through the front door. Màiri tried to reassure and comfort them, still shivering from the cold and fear, her grief still threatening to overwhelm her. She and Callum huddled around the heat of the range before Isla chivvied them off to change into dry clothes.

Callum, shamefaced and subdued said sorry to Màiri and she hugged him and said it was all right, she understood, it was hard for all of them. She resolved as soon as he would allow her to take him aside so they could really talk, so they could try to understand. The little family, numbed and fragile, were desperately clinging together, each trying to sort out a space to grieve alone in their own ways while being aware of the bewilderment and pain of the others.

The next few days and weeks dragged on; the weather seeming to complement their mood, dismal, miserable and dreich, interspersed with shattering storms and mountain-shucking, earth-pounding rain. The mist and drizzle screened the loch as if to draw a grey shroud over Hamish's watery resting place or to give the family a pause from the fact of his death. But nothing could take away the pain, made more poignant by his suffering in life, so much of it a living torment.

Màiri spent time talking to Callum when he was willing to hear. He still struggled to accept the fact of his Pa's death and the manner of his going. It would strike him when he least expected, a terrible veil would descend on his mind and he would try and deny the evidence of fact, the absence of someone once ever present and so familiar. He struggled with disbelief; to Callum, death was still an impenetrable impossibility. He didn't yet understand the nature of mortality. The death of someone so close for someone so young, the disappearance of a parent, the father of the son, strained credulity and rocked his universe. Forever, infinite loss, impossible to grasp, a betrayal to try and to believe.

To Dougal and Jeannie, so much younger, the assimilation of the loss of their father, who found it so difficult to express warmth was less difficult. Màiri gave them the extra security they craved as a result of his loss. But Callum, who had grown close to his father in the last few years, who had seen his struggle to stay well for his family, who knew something of his pain and of his childhood, it was grievously hard.

As for Màiri she had to keep going, but all the subtle hues and joy of life in the glen had drained away. The unsayable, invisible presence in the loch plagued her; the loss of her life's love wounded so deep it seemed it would never stop bleeding, never heal over, she would never feel completely whole or carefree again. And then there was the guilt; if only; if only she had done this or that, why didn't she foresee, perhaps she wasn't attentive enough, and she would rebuke herself.

At the prompting of Isla Màiri agreed to a memorial service for Hamish. With his body deep beneath the loch, borne on dark currents, with seaweed for a bier and fishes for his mourners there would be no earthly funeral. So, weeks after Hamish had so quietly and uncomplainingly slid beneath the silver blue mirror of Loch Gorm, now carried along lifeless in its deeps, his family, in sombre attire and white faces, huddled together for comfort in the tiny stone kirk beside the loch to celebrate his life and mourn his passing. Callum stood beside his Ma, grim-faced and bolt upright. He had secretly put gravel in his boots to cause him discomfort and distract him from the grief, and perhaps to pay a penance for any kindnesses to his Pa he had omitted when he was alive. To weep now, in front of the boys and men of the community of the loch would be to lose his dignity and with it his newly gained, fragile manhood but nonetheless he felt his heart fit to bursting.

The little kirk was packed, all the adults and older children of the village and a few from the little hamlet down the loch, including Moira and surprisingly Morag, although perhaps not so surprisingly after all, she too had lost her man to the sea. Catholics and Protestants alike were squeezed together onto the pews. Màiri and Isla, despite John Fraser's harrumphing, had decorated the window ledges and the table where communion was taken, with what wildflowers were still to be found in late October. Boughs of wild berries and haws, holly leaves and delicate ferns and ivy enriched and enlivened the little kirk. They added a touch of lightness and joy to the sombre gathering, symbols of the living and a bouquet for the dead.

The service was brief, the minister curt but sympathetic, a no-nonsense approach. He was an older man, greybearded and all in black, dignified, a Wee Free but not without wisdom and compassion, a little too grim-faced for Màiri though.

–"A grievous loss of a minister of the kirk to be sure but to take up another sacred duty as head of the family" as he had put it, which was not particularly appreciated by Màiri who saw her and Hamish's roles as being more of a partnership.

Nevertheless he referred to Hamish's suffering as, "a great burden and torment which our brother Hamish bore with dignity and of which he is now free and at peace with our Lord."

Màiri dearly prayed that his soul was now at rest. She was never sure about God, she didn't believe he controlled the affairs of mankind; that would make him too cruel. Her's was a simple faith, if strained by recent events. She believed there was good in most people and hoped that there was a purpose to life. She felt the deep ache for Hamish that she always felt when she thought of him now. She still desperately wished she had known what he was intending when he had left their bed that day; if only she had done something differently. But she had come to realise that we can never know someone else's mind, we can never make their most fateful decisions for them.

They had the Twenty-third Psalm to end the service: 'Yea though I walk through the Valley of the Shadow of Death I shall fear no evil for Though art with me ...' Màiri thought that was as good a metaphor for the deep reaches of the loch as could be found in the Book of Common Prayer.

As the congregation shuffled silently out of the tiny kirk Callum heard more than one mourner whisper to another "Aye it's the Hebridean way."

After the service Màiri, accompanied by Isla and the children, climbed their way, in silence down to the cove. Moira and Morag quietly followed on behind, saying nothing. Hamish's boat was still drawn up on the beach alongside the other boats, the cold drizzling rain had given the scarred, wooden hull a silvery sheen. At the sight of it Màiri stumbled and nearly fell to her knees but lsla and Moira, who had taken an arm each as soon as they had reached the white, shingle beach, took her weight and helped her to the waterside.

The water was a lifeless, forbidding grey. The overcast sky, reflected and shattered in the loch's surface was pockmarked by myriad splashes of fine rain. The subdued waves slapped sullenly onto the shore, each wave sounding like a barely discernible breath. The loch was in brooding and melancholic mood, as if both jealous and guilty at what it had taken to itself. They stopped at the shoreline, each silent with their thoughts. Màiri scattered a handful of small green and white autumn flowers amongst the wavelets. They all watched silently in a kind of fascinated dream-state as the flowers gently swayed back and forth in the water, gradually dispersing and being pulled imperceptibly by the tide out towards the middle of the loch.

Callum stood impassive, immovable. Swaddled in his father's best, long dark coat. He fancied he could sense his father's presence; his slightly sweaty, soapy man-smell; he felt its warmth wrapped around him, the collar pulled up against the rain and cold. Jeannie reached out and clasped his hand, her small white face and confused dark eyes looked up at him and undid his resolve. He hoped no one noticed the tears on his rain-slicked cheeks. It was so often kindness that weakened the reserve. Dougal, white faced and cowed by the gravity of the situation quietly walked up to him and stood close. The three children of the drowned man silently looked out on the gently swelling sea. The sodden green and white flowers drifted further and further away and then were lost to sight.

CHAPTER 9

A STRANGER

Slowly, life returned to some kind of normality on the croft. Callum took on more of the work, seeking some sort of consolation in the land, just as Hamish had done in his misery. At thirteen years old he was now expected to work. If he was bright enough, which he was and also if he came from a well-off family, which of course he didn't, he would have gone to a better school and studied longer and taken his leaving certificate at sixteen. But he enjoyed the work, and without his father there there was now plenty of it for him to do. He was growing fast, strong and fit: he would soon be as tall as his mother and then overtake her. Physically he was fit and strong, even if spiritually and emotionally he was badly wounded.

Every month or so now, to keep up some sort of pretence of regular routine, Callum and Màiri would go to town in the wagon. Ian would sometimes let Callum drive the horses part of the way, on the easier stretches. Màiri would take a supply of eggs and butter and, at the end of the summer, honey as well, to sell to local shopkeepers. Previously before they had the Clydesdales, she would have had to send her produce via carter, which used to take at least half of the profit. Nowadays, she could sell to whomsoever she wished in order to get the best price and keep all the profit for herself.

Callum and Màiri would also go to the library to change their books. There was a new librarian who they had come to know who was friendly and made helpful suggestions about books they might like to try. Màiri most liked adventure and travel books, Nineteenth Century explorers like Richard Burton and David Livingstone and especially those which described the travels of Victorian women. She enjoyed the accounts of plant hunters most of all; Joseph Banks, John Rae and Douglas and the Scottish plant hunters. The idea of going to a foreign land far away and experiencing landscapes, plants and animals so different from those in the Highlands fascinated her, the pictures of exotic plants absorbed her. These books allowed her to escape for a while. For a short while it eased the pain of losing Hamish which otherwise was ever present.

The librarian was called Mrs Douglas; she was middle-aged, round and short with half-moon glasses perched on the end of her nose which were attached to a cord round her neck to save her losing them. She had a halo of thick, curly, indistinctly brown hair and a ruddy complexion. Her complexion owed much to rather generous amounts of a proprietary brand of fortified sherry wine, which was allowable for a lady of her standing, in a country where many frowned on the consumption of alcohol, since it contained health-giving vitamins and herbal essences and was not considered alcoholic at all really. She wore bright, floral print dresses with lacy collars and dangley bracelets with little silver charms attached. Her bracelets clinked and rattled as she signed books in and handed them out and checked the precious little buff library tickets.

Each ticket allowed one book to be borrowed by its owner for up to one calendar month; each borrower was allowed three tickets but, for avid readers whom she had a particular liking for, such as Callum, she might occasionally stretch a point and allow an additional book as a special treat.

Màiri liked Mrs Douglas. She was kind and interested in people and always wanted to know what was happening on the croft. She was very discreet though she sought to know all about other people's lives. Besides, Màiri suspected that knowing the intimate details of the lives of others gave her a secret, if guilty sense of power. Màiri didn't think it appropriate to tell about Hamish though, especially with Callum present, but when she asked about him, not that she had ever met him a course, Màiri simply said quietly that he was "no longer with us." And Mrs Douglas was sensitive enough to realise that she should probe no more; disappointing but understandable.

Instead she asked about the work of the croft and of the animals, she was very much an animal lover. Although Jess was not allowed into the library of course she was always brought on visits to the little town and tied up outside whichever shop or other establishment was being visited. When they called into the library, Mrs

Douglas would always slip out and say hello to Jess and make a fuss of her and give her one of her teatime biscuits. Not surprisingly Jess looked forward to visits to the library and would strain at the lead as they approached.

Mrs Douglas sometimes kept books on one side that she thought would be of interest to particular readers. She was unerring in matching books to people, even if at first the person wasn't sure. She felt she had a mission to raise the literary aspirations of her clientele and would often prompt her protégés of all ages towards something more challenging. On this occasion she offered a slim volume for Callum to consider

–"Now this book is very difficult young Callum, very challenging indeed for a young man of your age. It is a book of poetry but don't let that put you off. You will of course have read some of the Scottish bard's works at school I presume" she meant of course the wonderful Robert "Rabbie" Burns . Callum nodded gravely, he wasn't that keen on poetry, as weren't most boys of his age, he sought action adventure stories not contemplative odes., Even Burns he sometimes found, well a bit soft and soppy, although he quite enjoyed his nature poems.

–"Well this gentleman is sometimes known as the English Robert Burns. This poor man had a very hard life and ended up in a lunatic asylum. Just about all his poems are about the place where he grew up. He began his life poor and continued to be poor despite his success but he loved the creatures who lived in the countryside and the countryside itself. Although his language seems a little old-fashioned to us nowadays, he has" she paused over the choice of word for a moment "a particular phraseology. He truly evokes the intimate detail of nature in all her wonders great and small."

Her enthusiasm for the poet was evident in the excitement of her voice and in the glow of her cheeks which blushed even pinker than usual.

-"Thank you very much Mrs Douglas" said Callum, doubtfully taking the book.

He was rather hoping to be able to have three adventure stories and a book on wild animals in Africa which he had seen the last time he was here, but he didn't want to offend her.

When they had left the library and they were on the way back to find Ian McDonald, Màiri said,

-"She means well Callum; ye will read the book won't ye: she will want tae ken what ye thought of it next time?"

-"Aye, I'll hae a look at it, but *poetry* Ma!, He sighed and shook his head sadly. Màiri smiled. The thought occurred to her that it had been a long time since she had smiled, since either of them had smiled.

Màiri still had to collect her groceries from the store on Main Street so they headed off up the hill, Callum clutching his books close to him and holding Jess's lead in his spare hand.

If Jess wasn't kept on a lead she would go up to anybody they met, sniff them and then abruptly set herself down in front of them for a fuss, which, unless they were dog lovers was often irritating for them. More than once some poor soul had fallen over her as she squatted in front of them, Tongue lolling, tail sweeping the pavement in anticipation, she would also stop to carefully investigate every interesting smell if she got the chance and Callum would have to keep on coming back to collect her, so now she had to be on a lead and she whimpered and whined and sulked all the time in protest and made a terrible fuss. However, she enjoyed riding in the wagon so much, poking her head over the side, engulfed in new sights and smells and creatures that they didn't have the heart to leave her at home.

Callum tied Jess up to a cast-iron lamp-post outside to grocer's shop, where she busied herself inspecting the interesting messages left by the neighbourhood dogs before adding her own contribution. The grocer's shop, which also served as a greengrocers was large and double fronted with huge plate glass windows. The woodwork and facias were freshly painted in cream and green. They inspected the display outside the shop; vegetables and fruit beautifully set out, standing on a large shelf with folding wooden legs so that the display could be packed away at night.

There were purple turnips and creamy-white cauliflowers, pale celery and earthy, yellow potatoes, stacked in a giant pyramid. Leafy vegetables of every shade of green were neatly piled in their own shallow, wooden trays; cabbages and leeks and stick beans and runner beans and brussels sprouts and a few flaccid looking lettuces, sad and slug chewed. Tastefully arranged in contrasting bright coloured pyramids were late tomatoes and bunches of radishes, a few early red apples and bright orange carrots set out next to golden, shiny strings of onions and just one hand of six, exotic, yellow bananas, just beginning to brown at the edges. Callum had never tasted a banana, they would be much too expensive, out of reach of a poor crofting family. Màiri glanced dismissively of the large, flat, field mushrooms with chestnut brown gills which she thought expensive and not anywhere near as impressive as the plate-size mushrooms and large puffballs which she could gather for herself around the glen.

She selected two large cabbages from the display, reflecting sadly that they shouldn't be needed if it weren't for the weather having decimated her own crop. Even more regretfully she knew she would have to ask for a few pounds of potatoes to augment the few she had managed to save from her field before they rotted in the ground. All the vegetables were much more expensive than in previous years; the bad harvest had been widespread and there would be shortages. The two of them entered the shop and the bright, silver bell, set in a spring above the door, rattled tunefully in greeting.

The shop floor was around forty feet square, scrubbed boards, tidy and spotless with carefully arranged barrels and tubs of loose goods lined up in serried ranks. The effect was open and airy. Interesting, meaty smells pervaded the air. Callum's mouth watered; the evocative aromas of cheeses, hams and spices assailed his nostrils and suddenly he felt ravenously hungry; it seemed a long time since breakfast.

The full-length counter at the far end of the shop gleamed silver and white; the polished chrome fittings and white marble slabs gleamed from under a counter-top of scrubbed deal, much scored from slicing, cutting and scratching in the busy shop. Behind the counter, which ran the full width of the shop, was a fine merchants chest, bounded by beading along its top edge with contrasting, inlaid wood veneers. The waist-high chest of drawers was topped with a worktop, much cluttered with goods, weighing machines and grocer's paraphernalia. It was made of the same scrubbed deal as the countertop.

Atop the worktop, behind the gleaming counter was an equally polished, five-foot, tall mirror, acid-etched in Victorian curlicues and acanthus leaves, inscribed with 'Robertson and Son, Grocer and General Store - purveyors of fine food and comestibles' followed by a date of "1886". Though no longer in the hands of the original family the shop was still known locally as 'Robertsons' or 'Robertsons of Kyle'.

Callum, who had never before visited Robertsons was overawed by the space, the opulence and variety of goods. He admired the merchants chest with its myriad drawers which secreted herbs, spices, teas, string, rubber bands and boxes and in the larger drawers stacked sheets of greaseproof pape used as wrapping for goods such as cheeses and cooked meats.

Standing expectantly behind the counter were two smartly dressed, middle-aged gentleman: one was round, short and with a fat moustache and balding head; the other, tall, square-built and looking like the ex-military man he was. Contrary to expectations the military looking man was always smiling, generous and welcoming, whereas the plump, round man was stand-offish, formal and, Màiri knew from previous experience, something of a snob. He was barely polite unless dealing with a well-padded customer in which case he adopted a servile and obsequious manner. These men both wore formal, dark trousers, highly polished, black shoes and a white starched shirt covered by a green and white, vertically striped, full-length apron, straining over plump bellies and tied in a bow at the front. Màiri thought it perfectly appropriate that the owners of such a well-stocked shop should show evidence of enjoying their own produce, arrayed in such abundance all around them.

The round, glum looking man, Mr Fraser McCulloch, always wore a formal tie, usually black with silver tie-pin. The taller man with the military bearing, Mr Johnstone, always wore a bright coloured bow tie. He had bushy, greying side whiskers and a mop of salt-and-pepper hair on top; his neck was shaved all round, almost up to his ears, a habit of many years of military service. The general effect was mildly comical.

Both men wore straw boaters; once a sign of their trade but now perhaps becoming a little too formal. Mr George Johnstone Màiri knew had been an army band leader and he played the trumpet beautifully. He played with the town band who sometimes performed concerts in the little town hall and at theatrical events and on other special occasions.

Màiri disliked Mr Johnstone-McCulloch who tended to treat her and others of her class with a barely disguised dismissal. As she approached the counter Mr Fraser-McCulloch looked at her and sniffed, having taken in her bearing, clothing and general appearance and recognising her as someone with little money to spend and therefore of little account. He said, in what Màiri regarded as a rather superior tone

-"Yes, can I help you madam". It was said curtly while looking down his rather large, lumpy nose at her.

–"Nae ye cannae thank ye. I will wait until Mr Johnstone is ready. I prefer tae be served by someone who values ma custom" Màiri said simply and evenly.

Mr Fraser-McCulloch bristled with indignation.

–"I assure you madam .." he began

-"Assure away Mr Fraser-McCulloch" Màiri interjected spiritedly "but I prefer to wait until Mr Johnstone is available thank ye" and she turned away pointedly inspecting a display of soap powders, cutting the conversation short.

Mr Fraser-McCulloch glowed redly with barely suppressed fury, his fat moustache bristling wickedly and he hissed a face-saving "Well really!" before marching to the other end of the counter as the doorbell rang and another customer entered.

–"Ah Mrs McDonald!" Mr Johnstone called out cheerily as he finished totting up some figures in a small notebook "It's a great pleasure to see you again" he said as he looked up. "I hope I find you well?"

Màiri turned back to the counter and smiled warmly.

–"Well enough I suppose Mr Johnstone. I trust ye and yer wife are well?"

–"Mrs Johnstone is very well thank you, save for her feet as usual. Puir Mrs Johnstone is a martyr to her feet. And myself? I am very welltoo thank you, especially for having seen you" he said with a broad smile.

Mr Johnstone liked to "banter" as he put it wth all his customers and made no distinction. He was also also fond of a little light flirting with the younger, married women.

Mr Johnston and Mr Fraser-McCulloch were opposites in every way. Mr Johnstone was a cheerful and unaffected man of generous and open nature; Mr Fraser-McCulloch was a class conscious, mean-spirited, social climber who resented being "in-trade" and wished for something grander. He despised most of his customers, although he was happy to take their money. He had never knowingly committed a generous act in the whole of his life, unless it was towards someone he saw as a social superior, who just might influence his standing in the town. The two men hated each other even though they were partners who had bought the lease on the shop between them some years ago. They rarely spoke to each other except to argue and were each now trapped with the other every working day, their relationship one of mutual loathing and contempt.

Màiri stretched her tight budget to a tin of treacle with an emotional sting as she realised it would never be used again as a treat on Hamish's porridge. Otherwise her purchases were basic and uninteresting; potatoes, cabbages, flour and salt, tea and a little sugar to supplement her honey, along with a large bar of multi-purpose carbolic soap; a ten inch, hard, fat slab of pale, yellow, translucent beeswax which would have to last the winter. She reflected that one of the things about being poor was the grindingly boring nature of it, hardly lit by any material highlights unless you grew, or made them yourself.

The shop presented her with all sorts of temptations which harshly reminded her of their poverty. For adults such reminders might be the want of a tin of biscuits or a new scarf or some other unaffordable treat; for children it would be gazing, nose pressed against the toyshop window yearning after the wonderful, colourful, shiny creations that may just as well be as unreachable as the moon but tantalisingly visible, just beyond one's nose in the shop window. Or perhaps it was having to walk by, eyes averted as you passed a sweet shop; bars of chocolate, whopping great sugary gobstoppers and lollies and fat penny chews. It all left a bit of a dry taste in the mouth and even; despite knowing one's intrinsic worth, feeling somehow a slightly lesser being than those who could afford all these things. The well-off of course took such things for granted as if they were of right, too often mistaking their good fortune for virtue.

Màiri loaded her purchases into her large wicker basket and placed its woven handle over her arm before heading off to the hardware store to purchase nails, candles and a new scrubbing brush. She sold the proprietor two jars of honey, meaning that, with the money for her eggs and butter she had made a profit of one pound, five shillings and tuppence over and above her purchases which went some way to making up for her enforced restraint over her groceries.

When they were a safe distance from the hardware shop and no one else was looking Màiri stopped, took her purse out of her basket and removed two, large, silver half crowns and asked Callum to open his hand. He held out a hand, palm up, a little mystified. She placed the two shiny coins in his hand. She hadn't wanted to embarrass the young man by giving him money from his mother's purse in public, after all he was a working man now.

-"It's no meikle reward for all yer hard work son but now ye're working full-time I must give ye something when I can manage it. Callum looked at the money in his hand; five shillings! The most he had ever had in his hand before had been a small, silver sixpence. He was open mouthed with astonishment but managed to stutter a thank you before carefully putting the two large silver coins in his pocket, after checking he had no holes for them to fall through. They were far too precious to lose. A man's full wage on a farm might only come to ten or thirteen shillings for a whole week. He kept his hand in his pocket, his fist tightly grasped around the two fat, shiny coins.

Màiri couldn't afford it but what with Mr Fraser-McCulloch sneering and her feeling guilty about all Callum's hard work for little reward except his keep, she was determined he should have something to cheer him. There would be precious little to give him now until spring at the earliest.

When they came near the little sweet shop, further along Main Street Callum took off at a run, Jess bounding after him. Callum's heart was pumping with excitement and anticipation. As a child he had until now only been able to press his face against the small, square, bottle top windowpanes, now he jauntily walked in, proud as a farmyard coileach. He spent an age, dazzled by the choice of brightly coloured sweets; a king's ransom's worth to him. In the end he bought tuppence worth of sweets; shiny pink and green lollipops, two sherbert dips, with a liquorice straw for sucking up the sherbert which fizzed and danced on the tongue; a bag of shiny, brown aniseed balls, gobstoppers, one blue, one pink, for Dougie and him and two white chocolate mice for Jeannie. Then he bought a large sixpenny bar of milk chocolate for his Ma. Then the thought occurred to him to get something for Pa before he remembered and the pain slashed at his insides like a blunt, rusty knife, bringing his excitement grinding to a cold, shuddering halt.

The large, severe looking, white-haired lady with the pale face behind the counter took his half crown, half in amusement and half in suspicion and then gave him his change, clearly having decided that he looked like a boy who had come across his wealth honestly. Without a word she handed him a free farthing chew, it was enormous. Màiri was delighted with her present and didn't stop grinning all the way back to where Ian was waiting at the station with the wagon and horses. Callum had taken his mother's arm as they strode brightly down Main Street as if they hadn't a care in the world, happy for the first time in weeks.

Ian smiled to see them looking so cheerful, with Jess pulling ahead on his lead, tongue hanging out and feathery, white and black tail wagging madly. If dogs could smile that was what Jess was doing, picking up on the mood of the moment. Màiri and Callum were rather like two people recovering from a serious illness together, trying to find their feet again and venturing out into the world. They were tentatively trying to feel their way in this new, harsher emotional landscape without a guide to rely on.

When they returned home Callum proudly laid out his bounty on the table, a child's treasure haul and then called Dougie and Jeannie who were just back from being looked after by Isla. They stood dumfounded, unbelieving, gazing at the shiny bright, riches, not daring to approach. Callum was beaming from ear to ear.

–"Help yersel'" he ordered brightly.

They both just gazed at him in stunned, silence, disbelieving the evidence of their own eyes and ears; the white paper bag full of shiny, little aniseed balls, the lollipops and sherbert fountains in bright yellow tubes were spread temptingly before them. Callum handed Dougal the blue gobstopper and he slowly and suspiciously forced the huge shiny ball into his mouth, it was all he could do to fit it in. Then Callum gave Jeannie her two white-chocolate mice. She was almost overcome with wonder. She placed one in her flowered apron pocket with great care and then, as if testing to see if were real, poked out her small, pink tongue and tasted it. She sat down cross-legged on the rug in front of the glowing range carefully sucking it gently to make it last, lost in a sugary, creamy reverie.

Màiri tried to add a little reality to the sudden air of excitement,

-"Ye'll hae tae make the sweeties last children - there wont be any mair fae a while I'm afraid".

But they weren't listening, they were in their own honeyed paradise. Callum popped his gobstopper in his mouth and marched chirpily outside to catch up on his work with a large bulge in one cheek, as if he had toothache.

Not long afterwards, one wet morning in early January, when the New Year had slipped by in grey cloud and mist, a young minister of the kirk made his tentative way up the track, passing the other lonely, far-spread croft houses and up the steep muddy hill to Màiri's cottage. He was tired and footsore and had already come a long way. He knocked quietly at the door. Màiri opened it, surprised that someone was knocking; neighbours would usually just walk in and announce their presence.

-"Good morning madam" the young man said hesitantly and then "are ye Mrs Màiri McDonald?"

Màiri invited him in, it started to rain and he was already wet through. She ordered the young man to take off his thick, wet coat, hanging heavy round his shoulders and she spread his dark jacket on a drying frame by the range and sat him down in the warm of its glow. She hung up his coat on the back of the door to dry. She got him a hot cup of tea; black as he requested, with no sugar and she sat on a dark, bentwood chair opposite him.

-"Now what is it you wish to say?" she asked guardedly.

He was a serious looking, pale faced young man, dark haired with a long, pointed nose, quite thin and ascetic looking with long-rangy limbs on closer inspection. He was even younger than she had first thought, probably still not twenty yet and already well on his way to ordination

–"Well actually" he began nervously "it was your husband I wished to speak to Mrs McDonald but I am -" he hesitated "one of your neighbours, who kindly pointed the way here said that he had died recently. If that's so then I'm sorry to hear it" he said carefully.

–"That's correct minister" Màiri said curtly "so if ye're looking to have him back I'm afraid ye're tae late. Not that he would have gone anyway" she finished with a sigh.

She was suddenly very weary, she didn't wish to explain anything about Hamish to this young man and she was sure he wouldn't have understood anyway.

–"No" he said carefully "and I am very sorry to hear of his death. No, a man must come to us out of conviction, out of a calling, of his own free will…"

Màiri cut him off – "I'm sorry, I dinnae wish tae be rude Minister…"

But he in turn cut in

–"Please call me Daniel, from the Bible," he hesitated awkwardly – "Ah, sorry, I don't want to bring ye mair sad news which may be a little upsetting for ye. The minister, I mean Mr McDonald's father, is seriously ill. I'm afraid he may not last much longer. I have, – –" he stumbled, not knowing how to proceed.

-"Minister", she paused, took a deep breath and softened her tone a little as she spoke, quietly and deliberately "we hae never had anything tae do with that wicked man, nor should we want tae. If ye came here looking for us to visit him before he breathes his last and descends into the deepest hell where he most surely belongs then I'm afraid ye've had a wasted journey and I'm sorry fae that,"

He was struck be the vehemance and bitterness of her tone.

–"I see, um. And I'm... I'm sorry to have bothered you I..." the young pastor obviously didn't know how to proceed. – "I'm afraid I don't know the Reverend McDonald, the older Reverend McDonald that is. I'm here at the request o' the Bishop ye see" he offered by way of explanation.

–"Ye'll stop and eat with us minister, before you begin your return journey. Ye've fulfilled yer duty" Màiri said.

It was a command not a request and, as she had intended it had the effect of ending the conversation, much to the apparent relief of the young man.

He sat and drank his tea a little self-consciously while Màiri went to fetch Callum from outside in the yard. She asked him to show the young man around the croft while she prepared a meal for them. She felt sorry for the Minister, having come all this way for no purpose and warned him not to tell Callum his reason for coming. She didn't want him to remind him of his father.

Callum lent the young man an oil-skin coat of Hamish's in case the rain returned. He enjoyed showing this grave, gangly, young man around his croft. The young man appeared to be so much older and more serious than him. Showing this young city dweller around the croft, explaining to somebody completely ignorant of the animals and the countryside made him realise how proud he was of the croft and of their livestock and how much he cherished this land and way of life. He had never realised this about the croft and the animals before; just how close he was to them and how much he was a living part of it all. Seeing it through the eyes of a stranger, answering his questions and comments made him realise just how much he had taken all this for granted. And why wouldn't he? He had been born to it and knew nothing else. The essence of this place flowed in his veins, a rich, life-giving matter-of-fact.

They stopped and sat for a while on a large boulder on the lower slopes of the Ben. They were both silent at first and then Callum asked the young man how he came to be a minister. He told Callum that he was only in his second year of study 'for the cloth' and was finding it hard, though he was clearly dedicated.

-"It was ma ane choice ye ken" he said "to become a minister" he paused. "Father wanted me to go into his business, to help in his printing shop. He's had a hard time of it these last few years, but I had a vocation, well, I *have* a vocation, I was called to it. That might be hard to understand but, I just knew it was right. It's no about the cassock or the rituals or anything like that." He paused and looked out at the view for a minute.

-"Look!" he continued, "I've seen some terrible poverty growing up in Edinburgh: people think that Edinburgh is a rich city and it is, even noo, but there's plenty live in abject poverty and the spread of disease is awful. The puir are kept away from the business districts, pushed out to the edges of the city, oot o' sight, oot of mind.

The church should be doing more for these people, oor people! Our Lord said blessed are the poor, for they shall inherit the earth: not in oor ruddy lifetime they wont! Is it too much tae ask that people desperate for work be able to lead rewarding lives, be properly educated? It's a moral duty Callum, a Christian duty no' out of some sairt o' charity but because as fellow human beings we have a duty to help people when they're in trouble, when they have nae work." He looked off over the loch, considering his thoughts, rehearsing them.

-"It'is what a civilised society does, not to kick people while they're doon and blame them for things oot of their control. Ach! It was nae the puir who caused this wicked Depression Callum, why should they be the only ones to suffer? Ministers have a particular duty to see that justice is done and to remind our parishioners, especially the better off, that their wealth and guid fortune is no a virtue, but fae the Grace o' God…" and then he paused. "Sorry, I'm preaching tae ye like you're a congregation:. But that's pairt of my calling. It's the work our Lord Jesus called on us tae do and as a Minister, if I'm blessed to become one I shall make a point of telling the congregation so." He smiled "I have an idea it will no make me very popular with some but it's what we should be doing. It's what the kirk's fer." He stopped and looked out over the scene, feeling a little foolish for getting carried away.

They both looked into the distance, letting the thoughts Daniel had expressed hang in the air.

After a while Daniel said,
-"It must be terrible here in winter sometimes Callum."

Callum nodded and agreed heartily. They sat again for a while looking out over the scene below them. The clouds cleared a little and weak sunshine played across the loch. Callum was impressed with this serious young man's passion. It's how his mother felt about religion. She couldn't do with the idea that that we were 'saved by faith alone': being a Christian also meant being a good person, helping your neighbours, whether you thought they were deserving or not.

-"But ye ken there's plenty of poverty in the glens as well" Callum said, "aye and plenty of injustice. Folk who were pushed off a land that was rightfully theirs were left to fend fae themselves on hard land." He swept his arm round to encompass the whole lands along the lochside "This is a wonderful land and very beautiful and all that but it's fair harsh; a hard land tae work. It can take only a couple of bad seasons and a croft can go right doon". Callum paused, a little embarrassed by his speech, even though he meant it.

He had seen his parent's struggle to make a living, heartbreakingly backbreaking. All their hard work could be undone by a ruined harvest, it could break the spirit.

-"I'd no want tae live in the city though" he continued "I could nae imagine being cooped up all day in an office or in a shop, living hug a mugger wi' yer neighbours, kenning everything ye did. I need the fresh air and the wild creatures, the space." He paused a minute and both looked on, their thoughts occupying their attention.

-"Here I'll show ye something!" Callum said getting up.

He was getting a bit uncomfortable with all this serious talk.

He led Daniel down the hill back to the croft, pointing out plants and barely discernible signs of animals; foxes, hares and the hoof marks of a small group of red deer.

–"Ye can hear the stags roaring jest now over the other side of the hill if ye listen fer it" Callum pointed out. "It's ruttin' time. Ye ken what rutting means do ye no' Daniel?" Callum asked, not sure if a man from the city would understand such natural behaviour.

But the young man knew all about rutting and, as he put it "the sins of the flesh."

–"Animals are innocent Callum. They dinnae ken what Adam and Eve learnt by plucking the apple. They dinnae ken about nakedness and wickedness." Daniel said gravely in a hushed voice.

–"They're no naked Daniel, they've nice warm, waterproof coats" Callum said, rather missing the point that Daniel was trying to make.

–"Ah, ye'll no ken aboot carnal sin yet Callum" stated Daniel.

–"Oh I think I ken about that Daniel" Callum replied readily, the ministers are forever banging on about it at the kirk" he said, not wanting to appear ignorant of such things. He thought it had to do with what he saw the male and female animals doing, but between people, something to do with "relations outside wedlock". It was supposed to lead to "fornication" which apparently was a terrible sin but he wasn't exactly sure what that was either though he didn't want to admit it to Daniel. He sensed this wasn't the time or place or the right person and through experience at the kirk he knew it was something that seemed to get ministers all hot under the collar.

When they reached Màiri's small plot of a garden Callum led Daniel to her collection of white painted hives.

–"Are these beehives?" asked Daniel delightedly "I've seen pictures of them but never for real" he said looking interested. "Shouldn't we be wearing face masks or something?" he asked a little hesitantly as they got close up to the slatted hives.

–"Naw" said Callum" a little dismissively "they're pretty dopey this time of year, they only come oot when the weather's warm. They live on the honey they store during the summer, after the males leave and die"

–"But doesn't your mother collect the honey?" Daniel asked.

–"Aye but she always leaves some tae keep them going. A lot of them die off in autumn so they dinnae need sae much and she gives them sugar water if they're gettin' short. Ye've tae look after yer bees if ye want to get any honey" said Callum seriously, removing the top frame to expose one or two lethargic honey bees crawling about the wax comb.

–"There's probably a lesson there fae us all Callum. Something we could learn from the bees and from looking after them" Daniel said.

–"Oh aye, there's a lot tae be learnt frae studying bees" Callum agreed. "I've watched them when they've been oot foraging, communicatin' wi' each other; I'm no sure what they're sayin' but they talk tae each other sure enough"

Daniel was saved from explaining what he had meant by learning moral lessons from bees by Màiri coming out to call them in for their meal.

When the meal was served Callum prepared to dive straight into his mutton stew as usual. He was always hungry; as a growing lad of nearly fourteen, working outdoors all day he had a huge appetite. Plain though the food might be Màiri did her best to fill him up and he had as much fresh food as he could eat with plenty of tasty fat to keep him warm and give him energy, and plenty of "packin'" as Màiri would have called it, barley and potatoes and herby, oatie dumplings to fill his stomach. As he went to tuck into is plate of mutton stew and vegetables, Màiri pointedly cleared her throat to attract his attention. Daniel was waiting to say grace. Shamefaced and a little self-conscious he put down his fork and bowed his head while he waited for Daniel to finish and then gave a quickly mumbled 'amen' before tucking into his meal hungrily.

After a while concentrating on eating Daniel paused and said to Màiri

–"I can see it would be a hard life up here Mrs McDonald. It's a wild enough spot but very beautiful too"

–"Aye but its beauty is deceptive Daniel." Màiri said "When ye see it in the summer sunshine and there's a wee breeze to keep the damned midgies frae eating ye alive I dinnae think ye'll find anywhere mair beautiful and tranquil on airth", she said with conviction "but in a howlin', freezing gale, straight off the Atlantic, that's tearing the roof off and threatening to wash the stock away and yer hoose wi' it, it can be a different matter then. Like the night young Callum was born" she chuckled to herself remembering now the dark, howling night and her joy at the sight of him, so skinny and white.

-"God Almighty! - I hope ye'll excuse me takin' the Laird's name in vain Daniel but it was a fierce night! And ye should hae seen the wee scrap; ye would nae believe it was the same big lummox that's tucking into his tatties and mutton right there" she said with a smile

-"Ma!" said Callum in rebuke

-"Ah, he's grown into a fine wee mannie Daniel, I'm very proud of him. Sae was his Pa" she said wistfully.

Callum shifted uncomfortably in his seat and Màiri changed the subject.

-"So what led a bright young man like ye tae want tae become a minister Daniel?" Màiri asked.

-"Oh it's simple Mrs McDonald," Daniel explained, warming to this uncomplicated pair, finding that he liked them, finding it easy to feel comfortable in this house, at ease with them. They weren't what he expected to find; he had heard tales of Highland people being austere and tight-lipped. Rather than go into detail about his reasons for wanting to become a minister he simply answered that he had a vocation for it and decided to change the subject.

-"I'm very grateful for your generous hospitality Mrs McDonald, it's been a great pleasure to meet ye both, ye've both been very kind tae me, especially since I have come at such a difficult time" he stopped, not knowing if he should mention their bereavement in front to Callum.

–"Ah well ye dinnae want tae believe everything ye hear about us Highlanders," Màiri said almost as if she had read Daniel's thoughts. "Hospitality tae strangers is important tae us, as I believe it is tae most people who live in wild, oot of the way places elsewhere."

–"Well ye certainly made me feel welcome and I thank you." Daniel answered with clear conviction.

They ate in silence for a while. When they had finished Daniel said conversationally.

–"I noticed yer wee kirk on my way down the path into the village yesterday, it's a fine building".

–"Aye our grandfathers built it when they first arrived in this glen as young men with their elders and families in tow, kicked off their fertile lands further inland by a so-called "Laird"; some greedy foreigner who thought he could get mair money oot of sheep than the people who rightfully held the land. It was a statement of their resistance. They had their backs tae the sea, there was naewhere else fae them tae gae except emigration across the Atlantic. The buggers would have cleared them all oot if they'd a chance, shipped oot tae America or Australia,. The English, aye supported by oor ane countrymen frae the cities, had finally beaten us and grabbed oor country, the Highlands and Islands. They treated us nae better than the black folks of the countries they've also stolen frae their rightful owners".

–"Ye're no supporter of the Empire then Mrs MacDonald?" Daniel asked.

–"I am not Daniel, we have nae more business takin' over other people's countries than them bluidy

Sassenachs had taken over oor land." Màiri paused, a little self-conscious about putting her views so forcefully to this polite young man.

Callum excused himself, having finished his meal he had more jobs to do before it got dark.

–"Oh, I'm sorry! said Daniel "I hadn't realised it was so late – I must be off. I need tae walk back to town to catch a train or I'll no get back to Inverness tonight. I'm going to stay with an aunt. I told her I might be visiting."

–"Ye're going nowhere tonight Daniel" Màiri said firmly "that road is no place fae a stranger in the dark and ye'd no make it back before nightfall; and mair heavy rain on the way too by the look of it. Ye'll stay here the night and there's nae arguin'" she said with finality.

–"But I cannae ask you to do that Mrs McDonald, that would no be right, I'll be fine really" Daniel protested.

But Màiri would have none of it.

–"Anyway" she said "if ye left before young Dougie and Jeannie get tae see ye they'll never forgive me. It's rare enough getting a visitor come this way and I assure ye ye're very welcome. Now if I get ye a pair of trews and a shirt o' Hamish's tae put on I'll hae those ye've got on. Ye've got mud on the cuffs and on your seat and that shirt is in need of a guid iron. I'm no having anyone say ye weren't properly looked after while ye were here in my hoose. Come on, ye can tak yer trews off in the boys room if ye're shy!" she said

Daniel tried to protest again but when Màiri had her mind made up it was best to give in gracefully.

Dougal and Jeannie, no one ever called her Jean, except Màiri when Jeannie was naughty, were indeed delighted to see the stranger. For them it was really exciting to have someone from the city come to visit. Flora had brought young Jeannie home, she had been looking after her for the day, she was also very excited to meet this curious and good-looking young man. She already knew he was there of course, no stranger could visit the little community without everybody knowing about it within about half an hour. Jeannie was bold in asking Daniel lots of questions while Dougie was a little shy and reserved though still fascinated by this young man. He seemed to have a way with children, he gently teased Jeannie and treated Dougal with respect and talked to him like an older brother would. When Màiri intervened and said that they were becoming a nuisance he would have none of it, he said he missed his own little brothers and sisters, which Màiri insisted on knowing all about. Then he volunteered to help Dougal feed the chickens, a job he had partly taken over from Callum and he invited Jeannie along with him so she wouldn't feel left out.

They had a supper of nourishing soup made with the remains of an earlier stew, with extra barley added and plenty of slices of home-made bread and home produced butter. Daniel said a short prayer with the little ones before they went to bed. Dougal was moved to Jeannie's tiny little room and complained about it and Jeannie was placed in Màiri's bed which pleased her no end because she got to stay in the warm room and could hear their conversation over at the table and because she got to share a bed with her Ma which made her feel special. Daniel would share with Callum which made Callum feel more grown-up.

After supper, when Màiri had put the dishes to soak in the stone sink in the flagged scullery at the back of the house, they sat around the table and talked over a mug of home-made ale; Callum, Màiri and Daniel.

–"This is fine heather ale Mrs McDonald. I don't often drink but I know a guid ale when I taste it." Daniel said enthusiastically.

–"Thank ye Daniel, I made it fae the harvest and I had a small batch left over, I'm glad ye like it."

Callum was feeling very priveledged indeed, being allowed to have a pewter mug of ale with his Ma and this young man.

–"I didn't notice Mrs McDonald, I could nae see a sign in your wee kirk, is it Church of Scotland?" Daniel asked conversationally "Not that I mind of course, for me a Christian is a Christian" he added quickly, knowing how fierce the issue of religion could be in Scotland, especially this far North.

–"Being such a wee community as we are we share it" she said.

Daniel was astonished, he had never heard of such an arrangement before, not that he disapproved, he was fully in favour of religious tolerance and ecumenicalism but he knew how explosive an issue this would be in most places.

–"We've always had a mixed community here. We've even had services with some o' the Catholics from doon the loch" she said with a smirk, hoping to shock him "and we've had a Wee Free who attended at the same time, although he made a fair old fuss about it, but then he likes tae make a fuss!" She was talking about John Fraser of course, who was a member of the strict Free Presbyterians who broke from the main church of Scottish Presbyterians. The "Wee Frees" were sticklers for observing the Sabbath and many other strictures. Working on the Sabbath was deplored and the Wee Frees often pried on those who might do so, thinking them wicked and denouncing them.

Daniel asked Màiri if she didn't feel a little cut off here, living in the wilds. He asked if it was more difficult to believe in God in a place where nature could be so cruel.

-"We've had many different gods in these hills over the centuries Daniel." Màiri began reflectively. "We dinnae ken what the old ones worshipped, the ones who left the rings of stane in the high places; there's one up on the moor near here. The Celts who came over frae Ireland, the original Scots, had their ane gods, the gods of the rivers and streams, they saw the other animals they lived with as their brothers and sisters, the dòbhran, the selkies, the wolves and bears and the eagles, they all had their place as did the trees. They revered certain plants for their special powers. And then, when Christianity came to Ireland, and then was brought over here by Columba and his followers at the monastery over on Iona, they brought these beliefs with them, nature was still a pairt of it all. Ye ken they still have a colony of white doves at the old monastery? I believe they're going to restore it noo, the symbol of the Holy Ghost, living in that sacred place all this tame. Then of course there were the war gods o' the Vikings but they revered the natural world tae, the ravens and their hunting dogs. They still believed that the land was a pairt of it.

Of course the Church of Rome would hae none of it, pagan nonsense they said, and we lost oor connection wi' it all. That's how we come tae treat nature sae cruelly, dinnae care fer it as we should, try and control it all but, oot here on the edge o' things, a lot of the auld beliefs are still jest below the surface. In the Gaelic there are plenty of words for the natural world that we still ken." Màiri paused and Daniel and Callum stayed silent, waiting respectfully.

They could see you she was trying to work something out, to think it through. Màiri continued, slowly and thoughtfully. She said

"There's nothing of people beyond here,not until ye get tae the sea or over the hills and the empty glens. There used tae be people here, before the Clearances, jest ghosts noo and tumbledown hooses. When ye stand in those great, empty glens ye feel sae small, the mountains sweeping up on either side, the huge sky, surrounded by nature, present but silent except fer the sound of the breeze in the cotton grass. Ye realise we are jest tiny, insignificant beings, jest a small wee pairt in the great scheme o' things, whatever that is. Sae no Daniel, I dinnae find it hard tae see the hand o' God in the fury o' the storm or the power of the sea, or in the wild creatures we share this place with." She paused again.

-"Ma àthair used tae say that, some days, when he stood up there on the moors he could hear God breathing in the breeze" she stopped, her eyes far away, looking up towards the hill, seeing her beloved Pa again with the little Shetland pony they had then in the village, loading up the dry peats into the pannier baskets to bring home and then standing and stopping and hearing the breath of God and wondering.

-"Aye and sometimes when I'm doing something ootside, workin' in the yard, seein' tae the beasts I think I hear Hamish's voice in the breeze. Ah weel, he's at peace noo..." She trailed off looking into space, no tears left now, she had cried herself dry these last few weeks.

Callum swallowed hard and then stood up and and said quietly that he would get off to bed. Daniel too, quietly took his leave and thanked Màiri again. He called out quietly "Good night, God bless" from the doorway. They left Màiri in the pale lamplight, sitting motionless at the table with her thoughts. Jeannie breathed softly in her sleep tucked up in the corner bed and a wind blew gently up on the moor, winding its way through the heather and the cotton grass.

CHAPTER 10

THE GOOD SHEPHERD

Màiri missed the idealistic young man after he had left: he had reminded her of something she had glimpsed in Hamish when she had first met him, but, in Hamish's case it was a spark too soon extinguished. Out of his father's reach and influence Hamish had made a bid for freedom and Màiri had given him the strength to do it. But he had found himself lost and purposeless, without the emotional resources to cope and had begun a painful decline. She had seen occasional flickers of his true self, his inner core, but he had been too badly damaged to allow it to flare into a steady flame. She sighed with huge regret for the loss of what might have been and she tried to turn and face the future alone and to make better lives for her children, to help them develop and fulfil themselves.

Callum also missed the young man, he had stirred something in him that his senior school had almost crushed, his thirst for life and love of learning, for ideas, for making something of himself in the world as Daniel was. He felt he wanted to set himself ideals to live up to, to live a life that was worthwhile, to make something of his talents. He didn't know what it was that he wanted to do but Daniel's appearance had awakened the first intimations of a terrible thirst, that would need to be quenched somehow. Perhaps it was seeing a young man not much older than himself trying to take life by the horns and make something of it. Perhaps it had been seeing the example of a young man, not so different from himself studying and engaging with ideas and the wider world. Perhaps meeting someone near his age from somewhere different had stirred the pot of restlessness that lay within him, and revived an itch in the belly. He had a nagging thought that he was slipping into adulthood without having had a chance to be properly formed, to be moulded and to mould himself before being cast in the shape and constraints of his adult self. He wasn't fully able to articulate all these thoughts as yet, just to feel their bite.

Had he known it, his life was soon to take a very unexpected turn that would change its trajectory out of all recognition and little could he have realised then that the steps he would soon begin to take would, within a few short years lead to him being swept up on a tidal wave of events that would engulf him and his family in such a devastating storm that he or they might not survive it.

But all that was in the future. In the meantime Callum enjoyed the next three years working on the croft hugely, in spite of his newly aroused restlessness. It left him with a deep sense of fulfilment that he would carry with him ever after. Despite, or maybe even because of, the heartbreaking loss of his father and even the circumstances of that loss, he plunged himself, with a renewed vigour into his life of the croft. Even as the harsh snowstorms and bitter winter gales of late January and February that year virtually closed down the work of the croft and at times even closed off the little glen from the rest of the world for weeks at a time, Callum and Màiri began to make plans and prepare for spring.

Without the active strength of a full-grown man to run the croft it could so easily become a disaster. It was hard enough as it was to make a worthwhile living from such a small patch of land. And what land, so harsh and demanding, so unyielding that without a strong man to run it could seem impossible to glean a living. But that would be to underestimate the strength and resilience of a Highland woman, and one born to it, and her son who, though still young, contained the seeds of her resilience and strength.

Somehow they brought their small flock of pregnant ewes and the last few cows safely through the harsh winter. So cold and painful were the icy conditions at times that Callum could have just sat down and wept. He battled to get hay and grain to their cattle and hay out to the suffering sheep who had been brought down into the safer paddocks of the in-bye land. Getting the water to them before it froze was a nightmare. Hardly had you lifted the bucket from the stream than a film of ice began to develop. When the watery, wintry pale sun finally showed it gave some cheer but little warmth and was soon lost again behind dark clouds. Their tiny northern spot on the planet circled at such an angle to the sun that it hardly rose before rapidly sinking to the horizon again.

But, little by little the meagre daylight increased and their world slid on icy tracks towards what seemed an impossibly far off spring. And of course when it did happen, it all came in a rush. But they were prepared for it. The temporary lambing shed, a lean-to next to the old barn in one of the paddocks, had been constructed from pieces of wood, nails and old tarpaulin sheeting. The sheltered space was arranged into comfy pens with boards and string, fitted with a deep litter of barley straw for beds, for use with newborn lambs with enough room for them to practice their obligatory, oddly gaited strutting walk. It was a safe playpen where they could bond with their mothers in peace.

There was little peace for Màiri and Callum though during their first lambing season alone. With the coming of the pale warmth of the spring sun and the lengthening of the days they all began to give birth together for once. A grim, unspoken determination set in not to lose a single lamb if it were humanly possible. There would be no sacrificing of the weaker to save the strong, they would save them all, whatever the effort. They were, each in their own way and for their own reasons, determined to prove they could do it on their own.

They were barely into April and beginning to have up to four or five ewes in various stages of giving birth at the same time. Their pens were set up for two or three giving birth at any one time. Now they had to set up half a dozen new, makeshift pens in the open paddock, giving as much shelter as possible and constructed from anything available. Ideally the newborn would be given a couple of days in the relative warmth and isolation of the pens before going out into a paddock but they now had less than twenty four hours.

In the end Callum spent any time not lambing or having a quick meal or a couple of hours sleep constructing makeshift windbreaks in odd corners of the spare paddock and stuffing them with straw so that those ewes with lambs more than a day old could keep themselves out of the wind. They prayed that the weather held: heavy rain was the worst fear, the newborn lambs had not yet had time to build up their coats or to acquire a good level of lanolin oil in the fleece to keep the coat waterproof. Snow now would be a problem but a lesser one for these tough little lambs once they had weathered the first few days.

The two weeks Màiri and Callum spent lambing, turn and turn about, day or night in the cold damp of early spring, the morning mists and evening showers passed in a haze of tiredness. A rush of births would be followed by long spells of trying to stay awake and keep a wary eye out for signs of a ewe newly going into labour, or waiting for one already in labour to start showing the characteristic behaviours of imminent birth; stargazing, head pointed up, constant turning and restlessness, interspersed with sitting and straining.

An eye also had to be kept open for a labour going on too long, a possible lamb stuck in the birth canal or presented the wrong way, unable to exit smoothly without getting stuck, risking both lamb and ewe. In such cases there was no option but to push a hand into the cervix or birth canal and feel for the lamb, then do whatever was necessary to bring it out safely, including if need be pushing it back in against the efforts of the straining mother in order to manipulate it around for a re-presentation. All this would have to be done fast enough for it not to end up drowning in placental fluid. Long periods of exhausted attention and waiting followed by bursts of frantic and nerve racking activity wore them down.

To keep himself awake Callum engaged in constant activity on his watch, fussing over the new lambs in the paddock, checking on lambs rejected by their mother, usually a first timer and adopting them onto another ewe who had newly given birth to a single lamb; a time-consuming and delicate task. He spent hours constructing shelters and new pens in the open paddock, frantically dashing from one activity to another. To his credit, he never lost concentration long enough to miss a possible emergency and when one came along, he handled it competently and calmly enough; he had become a shepherd.

Màiri was inordinately proud of his efforts. She, being much more experienced, knew to pace herself, to go steady, not to rush but to stay alert despite the tiredness. Màiri used to sing to keep herself awake, she found that her soft, lilting voice calmed the sheep, they had to be Gaelic songs of course, for the sheep were Gaelic sheep and could not understand English, or so she liked to believe. To see her shepherding her ewes as they gave birth to the new year's lambs was to witness a timeless vision of nameless shepherds of ages past, calmly tending their ewes at this fraught time, seeing them through the birth of their lambs with a practised, easy competence. Reassuring and efficient, but tender as well as practical. There had been sheep in these hills for thousands of years, since before the dawn of history and shepherds tending them just as Màiri was now. They, like Màiri would have learnt to deal calmly with emergencies, keeping the panic in abeyance as she desperately tried to rescue a birth gone wrong, she gave confidence to the new ewes, she knew them as individuals, soothed them and helped them feel safe in her careful hands.

Callum had his own way with the ewes, he talked softly and calmly to them and they responded, they recognised his youth and inexperience but seemed to feel secure in his efforts to help and not harm.

Màiri was tending a young ewe giving a difficult birth late at night, lit only by a pall of yellow light from the lamp hung on nail on the lean-to wall, when Isla sought her out. Màiri's calm, lean figure was stooped over a struggling ewe.She took charge, holding the ewe down with her body and kneeling carefully with one knee to keep just enough of her weight on its ribs to prevent it rising. She leaned over and slid her hand with practised ease inside the ewe. Her long dark hair covered her face but Isla could see she was concentrating hard by the taut line of her curved back and the tension in her smooth shoulders stretching the thick grey linen of her dress. Her front was covered by a rough sacking apron. Her concentration in that moment was total. Still softly singing, unconscious of the repeated phrases, the tuneful chant would break off for a second as she pushed hard against the squeezing walls of the ewe's uterus and then resume again, the note picking up from the last. Isla recognised the tuneful, lilting song of lament for a lost love at sea and felt a spasm of sadness take her.

–"There now my precious!" Màiri hushed in Gaelic to the ewe as she pulled hard to drag the limp body of the lamb out by its feet, whereupon it flopped in a soggy heap on the straw. She immediately broke off her song, as she scrubbed its little body hard with a handful of straw to massage the life into it and reached into the throat with her long fingers to clear the slimy birth fluids from its airway.

–"There mum, yer bonny wee lamb, safe and sound!" she announced to the ewe as she laid the floppy creature in front of the ewe. With a look of confused surprise the mother hesitated for a moment before automatically beginning to lick the little creature with a rough tongue. The lamb sneezed and coughed and tried to rise but the ewe flattened her again with her now enthusiastic licking tongue. Màiri reached back for the second lamb she had felt when she had probed for the first, she caught it in her arms as it slid smoothly onto the layer of straw and firmly dealt with it as the first.

Isla remained silent as Màiri leaned back on her heels, still unaware of the others presence and Isla gave her a moment of triumph at the successful birth of two healthy lambs. Isla knew that feeling herself having helped with lambing and calving at their own croft but she still admired the calm skill of this woman, her firm friend who such a short time ago had laid flowers on the waters of the loch for her drowned husband.

–"Màiri!" Isla called softly, so low she didn't hear her at first.

Isla called her name again, Màiri turned round suddenly, shocked.

–"God woman! ye scared me oot o' ma wits. What brings ye here in the middle of the night?"

–"Ian asked me tae come,we've been up all night with Hecuba in such a state he fears fer her life".

Màiri looked confused. Her mind slowed by tiredness.

–"Ian asked me to come' she repeated, he's at his wits end" Isla said by way of extra explantion. "He wants me tae fetch Callum. He's been up all night with Hecuba in the stable, she's got colic and he can't calm the beast. She's in agony and frightened something awful. She's kicked the stable half tae pieces wi her thrashin' and he and fears fae her life." Isla said in a worried, distracted tone.

Mairi's brain, in a fog of exhaustion was failing to take in the implications of what Isla was saying.

Isla paused, realising she wasn't being clear yet.

-"Callum's the only one who can calm her while Ian tries tae get some medicine intae her. I'm sorry Màiri, I ken ye're up tae yer eyes in it and puir Callum must be exhausted. But we cannae jest let the puir beast die" she paused, and she let out in a sigh of frustration and defeat.

-"I'm sorry, I should nae hae come. It's just that Ian's frantic wi' worry."

Màiri deduced that it wasn't just Ian who had been up most of the night trying to calm the great horse. Isla also looked at her wits end.

–"But isn't it awfully dangerous Isla?" Màiri asked anxiously "Ye say she's thrashin' about wi'those great hooves of hers? I canae let Callum risk that!" She looked, dumbfounded at Isla, not knowing what to say or do.

–"Nae, nae ye're right Màiri, I'm sorry" Isla slumped down over the wooden rail of fence next to the paddock.

Màiri stood and came over to her, placing an arm around Isla's shoulder and pulling her to her.

–"It's all right." she said quietly resting her head against her friend's in an intimate, soothing gesture. She lightly kissed her forehead "Take over here while I gae and talk tae him. But he's no going in that bay, where Hecuba is. I cannae bear the idea of him being hurt, especially not now. Not after..." She left the words hanging and handed over her rough apron to Isla in case it was needed while she was away.

–"Thanks Màiri , ye ken Ian would nae let any harm come to him, he looks on Cal mair like a son" Isla reassured her.

–"I ken that, of course I trust ye and Ian, absolutely. It's Callum, he can be so headstrong and he'll dae anything fae those beasts!" She sighed "But he'd never forgive me if I didnae tell him and he'd never hae forgiven ye or Ian if you hadn't let him ken."

In a short while they came back to join Isla, Callum, hollow eyed, bleary with sleep, dark rings etched under the his dark lashes. Nonetheless he seemed keen to get off.

–"Aunt Isla, Ma says Hecuba's ill?" he said looking worried.

Isla realised that this could be a terrible mistake. She had only been thinking of saving the horse and what it meant to the village and especially to Callum but having him see his beloved great horse as she was now and if, as looked likely, they lost her, what effect would that have on him, so soon after losing his Pa.

–"She's really poorly Cal, I dinnae ken if we can save her, she warned him plainly, trying to prepare him for the worst. "I'm no sure now if..." She looked to Màiri.

–"Go on Isla, take him, quick, he'll no rest now."

She grasped Callum firmly by the shoulder and turned him to face her.

-"Now, nae heroics Callum! That horse will be very dangerous the state she's in. Dae not go in there with her! Ye can try and calm her from over the rail. Please!" She spoke each phrase emphatically, hammering in her concern. She looked at Isla pleadingly.

Isla said "I'll see he takes care Màiri and turned withCallum to set off for the stable. Callum realised there was no point in telling his Ma not to worry and turned his attention to Hecuba's plight.

–"What's wrong with Hecuba Aunt Isla?" he asked

–"Oh I'm sorry Callum, did your Ma no say. She's got a bad case of colic and that can easily kill a horse."

–"Dae ye really think she will die?" Callum was appalled at the thought.

–"I dinnae ken Cal. Sometimes a horse will recover on its own but she is in such a state." She looked at him askance as they strode down the main track.

–"I really dinnae ken Cal" she repeated "I'm no very hopeful I'm afraid"

Callum was thoughtful for a moment as they walked under the moonless sky. He became aware of the cool chill of the spring night air, he was only wearing a thick shirt over his woollen underwear and had on a thick pair of his father's old trousers. The Ben loomed over them, an invisible black mass of deep shadow, invisible but ever present. In the silence of the night their footsteps rang out, the crunching of gravel and the clink of disturbed pebbles sounded sharp in their ears. Callum shivered slightly, his eyes felt gritty with a lack of sleep.

That extra stillness in the deep night time can be disquieting but also has a particular quality of depth and peace to it. At the farthest extent of its northern range a long eared owl barked its mating call in the distance, startling them and leaving a harsh echo in the thick dark. Callum heard tiny stirrings in the bushes as they passed, feathery little ghosts ruffling and shifting in their sleepy hideaways; a small, sleek ball of fluff shot across the path in front of them, a nervous, scuttling creature on its secret, nighttime prowling. He felt as if he were encroaching on a forbidden world, a little guilty in this mysterious and foreign land that his daytime world had become. Its stillness contrasted with the tension he felt over what lay ahead.

They hurried on their way as they reached the gate to Ian and Isla's paddocks where the small, makeshift stables were located. Callum thought he heard a faint winnying in the cold night air, then he heard the rustle of movement and the slapping of loose skin and the snorting of a horse shaking its head close by. The great dark shape loomed up to the fence on their left. It was Hector, he was clearly restlessly pacing. Ian had taken him out of the stables, not without great difficulty, the huge beast hadn't wanted to leave his mate. Ian had placed him in the paddock with the little Shetland to keep him company. He hadn't wanted a disturbed Hector to cope with as well as poor Hecuba. In another week or two they would have both been in the newly green field which would have hugely compounded the problem; at least, as it was, Hecuba was confined.

Isla and Callum had agian quickened their pace and, as they reached the stables, they were virtually running. Isla burst open the door and they were stunned by the noise after the still peace of the night. Callum hadn't known what to expect but he certainly hadn't been prepared for the terrible, deafening sounds coming from Hecuba's stall. He heard the crashing and splintering of solid wood and the whinnying and shrieking of the great horse. The noise was bouncing off the enclosed stone walls, shattering the peace of the still night into splintered shards. The small stables seemed ablaze with light after the velvet darkness outside. They had to blink and wait a moment to adjust their eyes to the brightness of the two flaring oil lamps hanging from the wall, gently hissing amongst all the din. Ian towered above them.

-"I'm sorry to drag ye oot Callum, were ye sleeping?" he asked with a strained smile.

Callum noticed that his uncle looked awful, white-faced and drawn with exhaustion and deep furrows of worry on his face. Ian grasped his shoulder with a large firm hand.

–"I'm glad ye're here. I dinnae ken if ye can help but I could nae think of anyone else who stood a chance of calming her. Ah'm black and blue frae trying tae get tae her head and feed her some medicine. It should help calm her if nothing else. I need tae get her up, off her side, if she stays as she is her gut'll become twisted and then it'll be the shotgun I fear." He looked beaten, dejected, trying to hang on to this last strand of hope.

Callum knew his uncle loved this horse as much as he did. He was horrified, to shoot her was unthinkable? He was stunned but he knew his uncle wouldn't do unless it was absolutely the last resort. It forced the urgency of the situation into his tired skull.

–"Look, Cal," Ian strained to make himself heard "she kens yer voice, ye have a way with her. I'm hoping, if ye call tae her, she'll respond enough fae me tae nip in past her and get tae her head without being kicked half tae death." It was obvious to Callum he was trying to keep the desperation out of his voice, it was also clear this was not going to work. They couldn't see the struggling horse from where they were, just hear the terrible cacophony pounding their eardrums. Ian was having to shout at the top of his voice to make Callum hear him.

–"All right!" Callum shouted back and they moved cautiously towards the stall at the end of the row of three.

What Callum saw deeply shocked and distressed him. The huge, proud horse was reduced to something, ugly, contorted, lying flat on her side, her huge powerful legs flashing wildly in the air and striking the walls and sides of the pen. Her skin streamed with the gleam of sweat in the harsh lamplight. Her eyes bulged, large and white, the lids pulled back, she was frothing at the mouth, screaming in a rictus of pain and fear. He didn't think, he just threw himself over her thrashing back legs, leapt again over her forelegs, one great hoof clipping his shin with with an electric shard of pain which he hardly noticed. He couldn't bear to see this huge, beautiful beast in such distress, he had to get to her.

-"No Cal!" Isla screamed but it was too late, Ian reached a huge arm out to catch him and pull him back but he missed. The two stood frozen, shocked. Callum had tucked himself in the corner, grabbing the thrashing muscular neck of the horse and laying his whole weight on it, trying to still her wildly straining head. He turned to look at Ian on the other side of Hecuba's wildly lashing feet

-"I'm alright uncle Ian, really! She cannae reach me with her feet frae here, I'm a lot smaller than ye. It was easier for me tae get in here." he said as he tried to rationalise his desperate act.

He could see his Uncle trying to somehow get in and reach him to pull him out, ready to launch himself regardless.

-"It's alright, stay back, I'm fine" he called out again while pushing down his own fears and trying desperately hard not to panic.

-"If ye can come in at the back and reach across somehow with the medicine I can try and get it intae her" Callum pleaded.

Isla was frantic, she fervently wished she hadn't brought him here, imagining all sorts of appalling outcomes and feeling completely helpless.

–"Callum, ye cannae dae this!" shouted Ian, getting frantic himself now.

Callum looked back over his shoulder, worried but relatively calm. Ian realised there was no point in doing anything than what Callum had suggested now. If Callum couldn't calm the horse he couldn't get back now anyway, so, feeling a terrible weight of responsibility he stepped forward and pushed the cork tight into the bottle of thick, white liquid. He wasn't sure what was in the bottle, apart from a heavy dose of kaolin and morphine but he had nothing else; the horse would surely die if he did nothing. He struggled to get his great muscular legs in between the horse's heaving back and the stone wall of the end gable of the stable and reached in as far as he could. His long reach wasn't quite enough to make it and he swore. He had to stretch up and grasp a low rafter and lean perilously out across the vast, frantic bulk of the heaving horse.

He noticed the rippling, spasming muscles of the chest glistening deeply with running sweat. If they didn't stop her soon she would die of exhaustion, let alone anything else. She had been like this for over six hours now. It was a testament to her huge strength if nothing else. Another fiercely sharp splinter of stable divide skimmed off his forehead cutting deep. Isla winced and she instinctively reached out for him. She loved both these people dearly and hated what was happening to them with a sort of suppressed fury of frustration and helplessness.

Just as he was at its furthest stretch and about to lose his grip and unbalance, Callum, reached out, still clutching Hecuba's neck and got his fingertips to the bottle and snatched it.

–"How much?" He shouted out to Ian.

–"Hell give her the whole damn bottle Cal if you can get it doon her, I dinnae think anything else will dae it!"

Callum knew he had to attract Hecuba's attention somehow, distract her from her panic and calm her if only for a moment. He held on even tighter and bit her right ear as hard as he could; he didn't know why, it just seemed the only option. He tasted the salt of blood on his lips and with his mouth right to her ear, tried to get her attention.

–"Shush my pet, hush Hecuba, its me Cal, yer friend and ye're going to be okay! Shush noo!" He kept repeating the mantra as he held on tight.

The huge chestnut horse leaned its head back and was silent for just a moment as if only just noticing Callum clinging to her neck, the huge whites of her eyes swung back in her head to try and see him.

–"Shush Hecuba!" Callum soothed and, as she opened her mouth to breathe he pulled out the cork with his teeth and tipped the bottle up deep inside her froth, filled throat. She snorted and gulped and it was gone. He barely managed to pull his hand, still holding tight to the bottle, back out of her mouth before she clamped down, grazing the skin of his knuckles and drawing blood. She started to kick again but with a little less force. She still screamed harshly and deafeningly in pain but the terror was beginning to leave her eyes. He hoped fervently that this was a good sign and that she wasn't just giving up as many animals did in extremis, as he had sometimes seen a sheep or a cow do.

Callum hung onto his beloved horse as she continued to buck and scream for what seemed like an age. Eventually, very gradually, she began to calm and breathe a little easier, her breath still coming in deep gasps but no longer harsh and rasping. Her staring eyes began to blink and all three of her human carers breathed a huge sign of relief. Ian pushed his way back in behind the huge weight of the horse.

–"Isla!" he whispered hoarsely, hand me them sacks;" he gestured to some huge sacks of grain in the corner of the stable.

It was all he had to use as padding to hold the great weight of the horse upright. He was straining to push the huge beast up on to her front but even Ian's great strength was insufficient for the task. Isla pushed in beside him, hauling the sacks closer for him to lift.

-"Get away love" he yelled at her "if she starts up again like before ye'll be caught".

Isla acted as if she hadn't heard and pushed hard against the horse, her thighs braced alongside Ian's much broader ones.

-"Are ye goin' tae push or what?" she asked, chuckling a little with frantic tension. Using all his great power Ian got his knees in behind the horse's straining side. He heaved again and pushed two more sacks in closer behind the horse and then repeated the action. They both strained, Isla adding her much slighter weight to Ian's great power, veins standing out on their foreheads, cheeks bulging. Ian got onto his knees and shoved another sack behind the horse. After an exhausting ten minutes of heaving and pushing, propping the horse further and further up onto her knees she suddenly started to roll over.

-"Cal watch oot!" Ian bellowed.

But Callum was ready and rolled with the horse, ending up on his back, completely defenceless, and for a brief moment the horse looked down at him, the look in those huge dark eyes was fathomless and unknowable. She blinked and huffed a bit and he gently stroked her muzzle, soothing her as he did so.

–"Will ye get oot o there noo" Isla pleaded urgently.

-"She's alright noo Aunt Isla, she's calmed doon". He stayed a moment more, just stroking her long, bony head.

Her ears were twitching, eyes searching around, beginning to reorient, still breathing heavily, puffing with exhaustion, her long, pink tongue lolling out of the corner of her mouth.

As Callum stepped out past the now still, exhausted form of the horse Isla grasped him and pulled him bodily away from the stall, clinging to him tightly.

-"Oh Cal, Cal my love, I was frightened somethin' desperate! What the hell am I going tae tell yer Ma?" A great rush of relief poured out of her.

–"Ach! I'm fine Aunt Isla, really" he said; a little embarrassed at the drama he had caused and at the obvious affection in her grasp as she tightly clung to him, enveloped him in her arms. Callum was now just about as tall as she was.

Ian grasped his shoulder, an exhausted smile on his lips.

–"I'm mighty proud of ye young man" Ian said "that was incredibly brave and wildly foolish! Please never dae anything like that ever again" he reprimanded with emphasis and obvious relief.

–"Dae ye think she's going to be alright now Uncle Ian" Callum asked worriedly looking back at the horse.

–"I'm no sure Callum, I sincerely hope so. But without ye she wouldn't be, I dae ken that" he replied.

"And ye two" Callum said insistently. "Ye did most of it."

They walked slowly out into the night air; dawn was still a couple of hours away.

It was bitter cold and cellar dark after the warmth of the lamp-lit stable. They stood for a moment, waiting for their eyes to adjust as Ian pushed the door of the stable firmly to. It was so peaceful now that poor Hecuba's raging had calmed.

–"I'll give her half an hour or sae before I look in again but my guess is that ye gave her sae much jollop frae that bottle Cal it'll keep her calm till noon at least. It's the best thing for her, she was doing herself more damage than the colic. Now it'll either right itself or not, at least she's no in bad pain any more thanks to you Cal."

Callum just said "Ah weel!" shyly and shrugged.

–"I'll get ye a mug of tea and a bite when I get back love." Isla offered affectionately, touching Ian's arm. I hae tae get this one back hame first before his ma comes after me!" She smiled at Callum and they set off back down the path.

Callum was feeling drained and a bit shaky now that the rush of adrenalinehad had drained away.

–"Thanks again Cal" Ian called after him, "well done man!"

Callum inwardly swelled with pride, there was no one, apart from his Ma whom he respected more than Ian McDonald.

Isla put her arm around Callum's waist and squeezed tightly.

–"I'm sae proud of ye Cal but I dinnae ken what I'd hae done if anything had happened tae ye tonight" she said with great affection.

Callum smiled a little awkwardly and they walked back to the croft relaxing and listening out for the small night sounds going on around them.

–"Cal!" Màiri cried out to him as he and Isla rounded the corner of the barn where she had been sitting fretting, keeping an eye on the sheep.

She had been tortured by worry, imagining Callum crushed by the great, thrashing hooves of the Clydesdale. She rushed across and flung her arms around his neck. He stood waiting awkwardly, wishing that everyone would stop making so much fuss of him, while secretly half enjoying the attention.

–"Are ye all right," she demanded worriedly, studying him carefully.

-"I'm fine Ma" he answered casually.

She spotted his bady scraped, bleeding knuckles.

-"I dinnae call that fine!" she said bringing them to his attention "what other wounds have ye?" she demanded to know."Isla, how could ye let him?" she asked, exasperated.

Isla looked shamefaced.

–"I'm sae sorry Màiri, if I'd hae kenned what he was going tae do…"

Màiri took a deep breath and closed her eyes,

–"Aye well, I suppose ye brought the daft wee Mannie back more or less in one piece. Ye can tell me aboot it over a cuppa; I need one and it's all quiet here fer noo."

When they got back to the little croft house Màiri got tea things out and Isla took over making the tea after persuading her to sit down. She got her a small bowl of water with a dash of disinfectant in it and a scrap of clean cloth for her to bathe Callum's knuckles with.

"Ouch!" Callum cried out when Màiri dabbed the disinfected water onto his reddened, scraped knuckles.

–"After what ye did tonight Cal and noo ye're squealing like a wee babe over a small sting!" Isla chided.

Callum grimaced.

-"And what exactly did ye dae tonight Callum?" Màiri asked accusingly.

Màiri sat, open-mouthed and wide-eyed as Isla recounted what had happened, leaving nothing out and finishing by saying

–"I'm sae sorry Màiri, I should never hae let him dae it, I expect ye're justifiably angry with me noo!" She stood, braced for Màiri's fury, she knew how formidable she could be.

Even if she herself was capable of similar ferocity she was anxious she may have wounded their friendship. Màiri took a breath and thought a moment before answering.

–"I'm astounded, she pronounced "Ach! I'm no angry with ye Isla. Ye nae doubt did yer best. God almighty Callum, what were ye thinking of?"

Callum sat still as she poured a florid, eloquent tirade upon his head, battering him with her pent-up relief in a fury of words; Scots and Gaelic curses and imprecations poured out in a powerful torrent. Callum stooped forward in his seat and bent his head as if facing into a fierce wind until she had finished, when he opened his tightly closed eyes and just said

–"It was nae that bad Ma!"

–"Ach!" Speechless Màiri sat, gaping at him.

Even Isla had been impressed with the furious verbal battering Callum had received and she was a grand mistress herself for delivering the furious invective. Callum smiled smugly at his mother, totally unconcerned now that the blast was over. He sensed she had extinguished her anger and pent-up fears for him. Màiri just slowly shook her head.

–"I despair!" she said, exasperated.

–"I'll gae and get a couple of hours sleep now Ma, unless ye want me to take over from ye ootside right now?"

–"Nae, ye've done mair than enough tonight Callum MacDonald" Màiri said archly "Gae on, get to bed and don't disturb Dougal, he's tae go tae school in the morning."

When he had gone Màiri looked at Isla desperately

–"Oh Isla! she wailed "I was imagining all sorts. Ye dinnae think I was tae hard on him dae ye, after all he's done tonight?"

–"Oh nae, I dinnae think it will dae him any harm Màiri and mebbe dae him a wee bit o' guid." She said smiling and then she said

–"Ye should be really proud of him Màiri. What he did may have been foolhardy but it was a wonderfully unselfish thing tae dae and incredibly brave."

–"I ken Isla but I dinnae want him tae be brave or take risks. I cannae bear the thought of anything happening tae him! But I ken I've got tae start letting gae. It's hard, sae hard!" she said, looking imploringly up at Isla standing over her.

Isla grasped Màiri tightly around the shoulders and placed her head close against hers.

–"I ken love" she said quietly "I ken it's hard fae ye, especially jest now and she held her tight for a while before she got their tea. Then Màiri returned to the lambing pens and Isla dragged her weary body back home to comfort Ian and perhaps to feel him close to her so that he knew she cared for him and he for her.

Callum immediately sank into an exhausted sleep, as soon as he had got undressed and into bed, not even bothering to unbutton his shirt before dragging it over his head. Just as soon as his head rested on the pillow he was snoring loudly.

Three hours later he was lambing again; having risen, washed and had a bowl of heavy, steaming porridge with honey; Callum was no purist when it came to porridge, he liked it salty and sweet. He washed it down with a mug of hot, strong tea before taking over from an exhausted Màiri. Drained emotionally and physically she had to get the two little ones up, got Dougal off to school and, as it would have been unfair to ask Isla to take Jeannie after last night, she had to care for her while catching up on her chores.

Callum was in trouble almost straight away. A ewe was straining and straining and getting nowhere, obviously distressed and in a state of panic. She was an experienced ewe, a fine sheep, he couldn't make out what was wrong. He felt inside, there was a lamb, in the right position and obviously ready to come out. He got a grip of the lamb's feet and pulled, he coaxed the mother and encouraged and heaved and still the lamb was stuck. After an hour he was really desperate, there was blood coming from inside the ewe, something had ruptured and she had almost stopped pushing. His stomach felt leaden, he was going to lose this lamb but even worse he was going to lose the ewe. He had to get his mother, something he had vowed not to do, especially today.

He ran the couple of hundred yards to the house, burst through the door and shouted "Ma!"

Màiri was just putting a coat on Jeannie, so that she could take her round to Nellie's and ask if she could take her for a few hours.

–"I'm in trouble Ma, I've a ewe who is desperate and I cannae get the lamb oot – it's stuck and – I think we're going tae lose them both." His tone of voice immediately communicated the urgency to Màiri.

Màiri dashed out, telling Jeannie to follow, Callum led the way to the paddock.

The ewe was still lying on her side where Callum had left her but she wasn't moving. Callum's heart flipped over. Màiri immediately knelt down and felt inside.

–"It's my fault Ma, I should hae come and got ye sooner, I've messed it up!"

–"Nae Cal, it would nae have made any difference" said Màiri quietly "I ken this one well, she's a fine sheep but small and this lamb is huge, nae wonder ye could nae get it oot".

She stopped and came round to the front end of the sheep, she knelt down again and began talking gently to the ewe. She pulled back a closed eyelid: her shoulders slumped.

–"It's nae guid Cal, we're going tae lose her. I've seen that look before. We need tae try tae get the lamb oot and then make her comfortable – come on."

Màiri quickly pulled down a length of cord from where it was hanging on a nail on the barn wall. It was looped in a coil with a slipknot at one end. She expertly felt inside the ewe and located the lamb's feet, slipping the cord round its legs and tightening it, high up, where it wouldn't come off easily.

–"All right Cal, ye come round the back and get yer hand inside, before the walls of the uterus close, can ye dae that?" She looked at Callum, concerned, she realised how hard this was, he had never lost an animal before and the first time was desperately hard. Not that it ever got much easier reflected Màiri.

–"Right Ma" Callum said quietly, he was subdued now, deflated but determined at least to save the lamb.

They both pulled as hard as they could and eventually managed to get the lamb out.

Màiri scrubbed at the lamb hard with a handful of straw and cleared its throat and then, lifting it up by its back legs, stood and swung it from side to side. It took a while but eventually it choked weakly and she gave it to Callum to tend while she went to see to the ewe. The ewe was exhausted, weak and had lost a lot of blood, she had gone into that state of shock and stupor from which animals rarely recover, however good the care. Màiri propped her on a pile of straw and held her around the neck, cradling her on her lap and then singing softly to her. No longer the good shepherd she was now simply comforting a dying animal, but maybe that's what being a good shepherd was about sometimes. She smoothed the ewe's head and then closed it's eyes. The life had left it.

She sat there for a moment, cold, still and empty. Callum stood watching, feeling useless and clumsy and blaming himself. He had lost his first animal and felt defeated, a failure and he felt desperately upset, guilty and ashamed. After the triumph of last night this was shatteringly cruel.

Màiri quietly stood up, stooping and sapped of strength, she put her arms carefully and softly round his shoulders, told him he had done just fine, it would have happened if she had been here, it couldn't be helped. Then she laid her head on his shoulder, so desperately tired and racked by the emotions of the last few hours and then she wept. She wept with great racking sobs, shaking and howling and pouring out her grief and sense of exhaustion while Callum held her tight and rocked her gently in his arms. Jeannie stood wide-eyed and frightened at her mother and Callum; she wasn't sure what was happening and awkwardly went over to them. Callum reached out and included her in his embrace.

–"It's alright Jeannie, dinnae worry" he said "we are just sad at the loss of a ewe wee lass."

Màiri looked down and saw Jeannie and, feeling guilty at her weakness, dried her eyes and picked the small girl up. Jeannie buried her head in Màiri's long, dark curls.

Màiri looked shamefacedly at Callum, concerned for him.

–"I'm sorry Cal I should nae hae broken doon like that," she paused. "I had just reached the end of a long rope". She smiled wanly. "Thanks fae everything" and then she added with a smile of quizzical amusement. "I'm sorry that I gave ye such a hard tame last night; it was only because I was sae worried!"

–"I ken Ma. It's fine. Ye take Jeannie tae Aunt Nellie's and I'll bury the ewe and see if I can't adopt this troublemaker ontae another mum; there's a couple ready fae that."

–"Thanks Cal," Màiri said with a huge sigh of relief. "What would I dae wi'out ye?"

–"Aye well, I suppose that cuts both ways Ma, dinnae worry, ye gae and get some rest."

–"Call me if there is anything else; promise noo!" Màiri said and then, worried that Callum might think she had any doubt about his ability to cope added "though you're mair than capable noo without me."

It made him feel better even if he didn't believe it.

Màiri felt guilty about leaving him to deal with the dead ewe but she really couldn't bear to do it right right now. She had no strength left. It occurred to her as she walked away that something had just changed between them, a shift in their relationship that she was aware of but couldn't quite pin down, not more distant, closer if anything but they now each seemed to see the other differently. It saddened and pleased her at the same time though she couldn't say why.

That was almost the end of lambing, the orphan lamb was successfully paired off with another ewe who had only one of her own. They lost no more ewes or lambs which they saw as close to a miracle. Callum had grown up a little more and was another step on his way to manhood and Màiri was learning to trust him as a working partner and somehow, an even deeper and subtly different bond was developing between them.

Now that lambing was over and the ewes with their young lambs would soon be going up the hill, they had to turn their attention to the arable land and other produce. Spring was fast catching up with them and would soon be overtaking their efforts. The warm sunny days of late April put new strength into them and brought out the first primroses and the bluebell buds. The upland hedgerows the `stane dykes', soon began to sound with the singing of birds perching on capstones declaring their territories and trying to impress their future mates who were scurrying in and out of cracks building nests. The summer visitors were returning, shrews and mice and other little creatures competed for space. Life was returning to the glens and upland pastures, trailing-tailed swallows began to swoop low across the pastures again and revisit old nest sites in the barns.

Jeannie had just turned five and was pestering to go to school like her older brother, so instead of waiting until after the summer break Màiri asked Miss Pargeter if she would mind taking her now. When she agreed with alacrity both Màiri and Jeannie were delighted; Jeannie would get some new playmates and felt immediately more grown-up because she was going to school and Màiri, though she would miss her presence hugely, miss her quiet sweet nature and her open friendliness she had found that it had become ever harder to keep her occupied while she was busy and when Callum also had so little extra time.

Callum took a very protective interest in his little sister, his wee 'nighean' and was a bit worried about her beginning school. To him she seemed so young and he remembered how rough it could be, but Jeannie was determined and had a quiet, persistent way of getting what she wanted. So Jeannie began school and Callum insisted on taking her on her first day. Jeannie was thrilled. She was so proud to be escorted to school on the first day by her big brother who seemed so grown-up to her. He took her by the hand and gave all sorts of advice and told her to be careful and asked if she was really sure she wanted to go. She quietly sighed and patiently listened but, as with most young children she knew best and said thank you very much for the advice but she would have to learn for herself and yes she really did want to begin school just now thank you.

When he got to the little mown, grassy patch that served as the school playground Miss Pargeter was there to meet him.

–"Callum, it's lovely to see you again!" She said with in her cultured Edinburgh accent.

–"Hello Miss Pargeter, I've brought young Jeannie along fer ye tae take on, I hope it's nae trouble?"

–"No, I'll be delighted to have her, I've a few little ones just now and Miss Fraser and I will be pleased to have another lovely wee lass like Jeannie wont we Jeannie?" she asked as she knelt down to speak to her at eye level.

–"I'm Miss Pargeter Jean, welcome to our wee school. I'm going to be your teacher and I think you know the other teacher, Miss Fraser?"

–"Aye, she's my Auntie Maggie and my Ma has pointed ye oot and told me who ye are when we've come past and she says ye're a wonderful teacher and very pretty and I should feel very lucky to be here and must behave myself properly." Jeannie replied smiling brightly.

–"Gosh!" said Miss Pargeter blushing a little, "well what a lot to live up to. I'm sure we'll get along just fine Jeannie."

Callum looked down at the kneeling young woman with her neatly tied up dark hair and pink lips and he noticed the smooth line of her neck and shoulders and the swell of her breast s pushing at the cotton material of her starched blouse. He looked away discomfited, feeling a little strange and guilty. This was his teacher, Miss Pargeter! She had told him off when he was naughty and been kind to him when he wasn't and she had inspired a liking for learning in him. But she was stirring something unaccustomed in him now and he suddenly felt gauche and awkward.

She stood up, other children were arriving and chatting noisily to each other.

–"Good morning Miss" each of them said as they spotted her. A couple of little girls, one of the daughters of the Fraser's sons and a little plump, gingery girl from the other end of the loch were holding hands. Miss Pargeter called them over and introduced them to Jeannie and asked them to look after her. Callum eyed them suspiciously, he still remembered what little girls were like; they smiled sweetly at him but he wasn't fooled. Jeannie said hello and smiled and told them her name and boldly asked them theirs. It was evident that Jeannie had few reservations, she was confident she could take care of herself.

Callum was still standing, trying not to look at Miss Pargeter and feeling awkward.

–"My you've grown into a fine, handsome, young man Callum. It seems like only yesterday you were starting at the school" Miss Pargeter said smiling.

Callum's dark face turned red from his now rather tight feeling collar, to the roots of his unruly dark hair. Miss Pargeter pretended she hadn't noticed, she was flattered and amused.

–"Are you still getting to the library now that you've left senior school?"

−"I am I er, um ah aye" he stumbed out; what was the matter with him, his brain seem to have turned to mutton jelly? Get hold of yourself he silently rebuked.

−"Ah, well I'm having a look at some poetry by a man called John Clare. He wrote nature poems, a long time ago."

−"Oh Callum that's wonderful! I've read Clare over and over, he's not very well known now. He was able to capture the injustices of the Enclosures with a quiet vehemence and a spirit that takes your breath away." She was obviously enlivened and enthusiasitic about the poet.

−"He's a wonderful poet, naive but with such a brilliant grasp of the language too.." She stopped, it wasn't the time for a literary discussion.

−"Guid! What about further study?" She asked

−"I'd love tae but I cannae see how." he said "Anyway what would I dae, I'm a crofter noo, Ma needs me now that Pa's gone" he said seriously.

−"I was so sorry to hear about your father Callum it was so sad" she looked genuinely sorry and concerned for him.

−"Um, er thank you" he said with a little grimace.

The memory was still raw and, whereas he was pleased people remembered his father, each time he was mentioned it caused a spasm of pain and a feeling in his stomach as if he had just lurched over the edge of a small drop.

He became aware that Jeannie was trying to tell him something

−"What is it Jeannie?" He asked, a little testily.

–Ye've still got hold of ma hand!" she said patiently. "Will ye let gae noo please?" She tugged at his hand.

He had been so engrossed and confused he hadn't noticed that he still had hold of her.

–"Sorry, sorry Jeannie." He let go, flustered and looking embarrassed as she dashed off.

–"Take care?" he called out looking a little like a worried hen watching her chicks loose in the farmyard for the first time and knowing the fox was abroad.

–"She'll be fine Callum" Miss Pargeter said and smiled as she touched his arm in reassurance.

He blushed even deeper and felt a sudden spasm low down in his torso.

–"I'll take guid care of her" Miss Pargeter called as she turned "and we'll have to do something about your studies wont we?" She said cryptically as she walked off.

He couldn't help but glimpse the curve of her rounded buttocks below her slim waist, tight against her black skirt material as she stooped to talk to the three little girls. He dragged his eyes away, ashamed again.

–"Florence! Sorry I'm a wee bit late, Ma was in a right tizz!"

It was Maggie Fraser, hair escaping from its pins, arms and legs akimbo as she dashed awkwardly down the path, one hand holding her small, fashionable but impractical hat on her head as she ran. Callum realised with another little spasm that Florence must be Miss Pargeter's first name, it was like being let into another little intimacy with her.

Maggie dashed past him,

–"'Lo Cal!"

–"Hi Aunt Maggie, I'm just leaving Jeannie at school for her first time!" Callum called out in explanation.

Maggie turned round, walking backwards, a dangerous manoeuvre for her.

–"Aye, she'll be fine that one, dinnae worry." Maggie said kindly.

Then Maggie stopped, came close to him and then she leaned across and whispered.

–"Ye're blushing something awful Cal" and chuckled lightly before turning walking demurely on.

Stinging with shame and confusion Callum angrily stomped back to the croft to get on with his work, feeling distinctly unsettled. He spent the rest of the morning banging and crashing around the croft doing his work in a thoroughly disgruntled and irritated manner.

Màiri had decided to extend her little garden. She was still smarting from having lost most of her vegetables in the previous autumn rains. The ground she had been using immediately behind the house was prone to waterlogging. John Fraser had contributed three large rolls of chicken wire and a few spare posts in return for a few bags of oats for his chickens. She was pleased that she had got the best of the deal but she suspected John Fraser had not been bargaining as vigourously as he would with a man. He still found it difficult to accept her independence and self-confidence despite his wife, Nellie being much the same. John Fraser was an old-fashioned man who didn't really approve of independent women, despite having married one

She and Callum set to and removed the old rusting fence and laid out an extended, nearly half-acre patch of around thirty yards square and set out the posts, dug holes, added a cement mix and packed the soil round the posts, taking a good part of the day to do so. Then they laid out rows of beds over a half of the area, each four feet wide and two feet apart, running the length of the garden and allowing for a path in between. They dug out the paths over the next couple of days, piling the soil onto the lazy beds on either side. All around the edge of the garden they createed a three foot wide path, again using the soil to help build up the lazy beds. It was backbreaking work with spade, pick and shovel, shifting numerous rocks heaved out with a pick axe and piled up around the fence line as an extra barrier against roaming sheep and hungry rabbits who would make a tasty snack of their leafy vegetables. In all, they created eight, twenty eight foot long beds of four feet girth dissected by the two foot wide paths with a wider path around the inside of the fence on the perimeter of the garden. The other half of the garden was to be taken up by fruit and Màiri's beehives and broad flowerbeds.

Finally, once the posts were set solid they nailed up the chicken wire, a five foot fence all around the precious new garden. It was a huge project for the two them to accomplish on their own with just a month in all to complete it if they were to have it ready in time for planting for the new gardening year. Màiri had ordered seeds and fruit bushes and even risked a few late, bare-rooted apple and pear trees, an act of faith so far north, though they had the advantage of a sheltered spot. It called for all the cash she could call on and a bit more.

Although the croft was high above the stone-studded cove and set at the foot of the Ben it was on a sheltered, wide platform where the steep little glen began to open out towards the moors. The platform was a series of hummocks and mounds but where the house stood in its small sheltered hollow, next to a fast running burn, it backed onto a flat area roughly fifty square yards, sloping away slightly to the West and draining all but the area around the back of the house where Màiri had previously tried to grow her vegetables and herbs. There was a natural windbreak to the North from the slopes of the great Ben, Ben Oir, towering up behind the house. The lower slopes of the Ben rose away from the house towards the east creating a further windbreak, protecting it from the most vicious winds. The tumbling burn would take excess water away from the new garden.

The biggest problem with the garden though was the sour, acid soil influenced by the ancient bedrock and igneous intrusions of granite. At least here, unlike with their arable soil they didn't have a pan of clay a couple of feet down to waterlog the soil, so common in Scotland overall. It had taken a special, deep plough, brutally dragged through the soil by Hector and Hecuba to break up the clay and create the precious bounty of ten acres of rough arable land fit for barley and oats but not much else. The other crofters had followed suit, taking advantage of the horses and sharing the expense. The great horses had brought the glen as a whole back from the fear of winter starvation, so often an experience in the previous century or so.

The garden project as a whole had occupied almost every waking hour, alongside the day-to-day work of the croft often in bitter temperatures, freezing rain and sodden, muddy soil. It had occupied their time, imagination and most of their thought, giving some respite from the repetitive realisation of grief which both had suffered in silence and dealt with in their own ways.

Over the next twenty years or more Màiri would battle heroically with the acid soil of her garden in order to produce vegetables, herbs and flowers from her patch. The fruit was less fussy, apples and pears and especially soft fruit didn't mind the soil being a bit on the acid side so long as it was well-drained. Not so most vegetables. The answer was lime and lots of it, and shell sand and seaweed, huge amounts of it. Their carefully built up beds were treated with lime expensively ordered by rail in bags and then carted home and dug in. Sand from a little cove further down the loch was poured into sacks by the two of them and then hauled up the steep, rocky slopes to the croft lashed on to the back of Hero, the tough little Shetland pony.

It also meant a return to the trips down to the cove after every storm, collecting seaweed thrown up on the stones and then hauling huge, dripping sackfuls of it back up the steep climb of the fishermen's path, backbreaking work that set the thigh muscles screaming after a few loads. What the two of them did over those months was to create a new runrig cultivation system in miniature in their back garden, just as Hamish had laboured to do on their small arable patch years before; now superseded by the ploughed fields.

At the end of May they could stand in the warm, bright sunshine and admire their work with huge satisfaction. It had been a Herculean effort for them working on into the gloaming of a crepuscular Highland evening most nights and rising in the morning at first light to start again.

When the early rays of spring sunshine topped the slopes to the east of the croft house reaching Callum and Dougie's bedroom window and bathing them in pale, golden light, Callum would carefully rise, quietly so as not to disturb Dougie. He would wash in a bowl of cold water, scrubbing himself awake all over with a rough flannel and using a thick lump of coal tar soap, then towelling warmth back into his body with a rough square, torn from an old dressing gown. Dressing quickly he would lace his boots and go to stoke the fire in the main room; a signal for Màiri to rise and suffer the cold flag stones round the bed on her bare feet as she placed them gingerly on the floor.

Màiri disliked that first disgruntled, rumpled feel of still-clinging, cloying sleep and would grumble to herself as she padded off to the bare-floored, cold scullery at the back of the house. She would light the fire under the large, round copper boiler and wash herself in cold water. She would drench her face with open palms until she was wide awake and fresh. She would close the door, strip and sluice her whole body in cold, stinging water, standing in a widening soap-sudded pool on the scrubbed stones of the dimly lit scullery. Then she would dress, tie back her long dark hair and, if she were feeling glum add a final touch of the palest pink lipstick from a small secreted tube next to a cracked piece of mirror she kept on the tiny scullery window ledge. She would lean her face up to the pale light of the cobwebbed pane and dab the lightest touch of rose pink to her rounded, generous lips and feel immediately better. No one ever seemed to notice or comment, although Isla once asked if she was wearing some rouge but it made her feel so much better, just that smallest touch of luxury, vanity served, savoured and hoarded from years before when a friend had bought it for her when she was a young woman.

Callum would breakfast on a bowl of steaming, stodgy porridge. Afterwards he would fill the kettle for the young ones breakfast, wait for it to boil and make his first steaming mug of biting, hot tea with just a touch of milk and a spoonful of sugar. That few moments of silence sitting waiting for the kettle was Callum's small luxury, just like Màiri's lipstick. While Màiri washed and dressed in the scullery he sat in a quiet state of reverie, it gave him a deep feeling of content and peace. The slow, solid ticking of the old wooden clock on the shelf beside the range and the pinkling and crackling of the hot peats soothed his mind and created a still, tranquil island at the beginning of his days as his thoughts were gatheringtogether, unpacking the broken threads from the night before and rearranging themselves within the stillness of his head.

All this time Jess, who was now eight years old, middle-aged for a dog, would be curled up on the rag rug in front of the fire, one eye open when anyone came near. Only when Callum had raised himself after his long, lingering moments wrapping his hands round his steaming mug and feeling it warm him through as it slid down into his stomach, would she stir herself. Callum would fill her bowl with scraps from the previous night's meal and a few dog biscuits and crumble in a small Bob Martin's dog conditioning tablet and she would rise, stretch and yawn, try a few steps on stiff legs and then, tail swaying in her own happy reverie make her way over to her food dishes and slurp up her food, followed by water noisily licked and lapped from her accompanying bowl. She was now ready for the early morning rounds of her small queendom, following Callum about as he carried out his early morning tasks; releasing the chickens from their coop to forage before Dougal came to feed them and collect their brown eggs before school. Jess had little more than contempt now for the hens and if they came too close they might find a tail feather nipped off in her jaws, just to ensure they knew who was in charge. Nonetheless, she steered clear of the strutting coiliach; she knew better than to challenge that wily old bird.

Next Callum would bring in their two milking cows from whichever paddock they were in and if either had a calf the calf too. The calf would be tethered while the mother waited to be milked, leaving enough to feed her calf. Currently there were only two grazing cows, one with a calf in tow while the other was shepherding around a young heiffer, one of her older offspring. If they could build up enough offspring then they would separate them into a small beef herd.

The cows would be tied by Màiri or Callum in the scrubbed milking parlour as Jess kept a respectable distance from the bullying cows. They knew her fear and would take advantage if she strayed near. The stalls would have been been prepared with fresh, crunchy, barley straw after the previous day's milking. Callum would fill their mangers with sweet hay to keep them occupied until Màiri came to do the milking. Most days he would then stretch his legs and give Jess a run up on the lower slopes to visit the ewes and lambs and to stand back and watch them all with as expert an eye as age would allow.

Up on these high pastures he always felt invigorated and alert, the air always seemed to have a greater clarity and freshness to it, it was always moving, even on the dullest and stillest of days down below. The bleating of lambs carried a long way up here in this crystal, clear air, reverberating off the upper slopes of the great Ben. The birds up here were more secretive and furtive and dashed between stone walls and raised clumps of bog grasses and flag irises with a scurrying, rushing flight, jerky and edgy in this wide open space. Twites and whinchats echoed little secretive cries of chips and cheeps to each other on the exposed slopes; there was an eerie stillness; even the breeze itself seemed to carry the silence of wilderness within it.

Jess too picked up on the rarefied atmosphere here, quietly and furtively sniffing and exploring, chasing moths and starting up mountain hares in a style more of a stealthy wolf than a farmyard pup; it was a wild, bare and silent place. Higher up the Ben winds could scream like hurricane banshees but on these bare pastures of blanket bog and carnivorous sundews there was a peace, even on blusterv days, which gave them a sacramental, ageless feel that overawed and transported the soul.

The apparently bare, rough, grass slopes with their habitat of reeds, shaking cotton grass and bog plants hid an abundance of life on a small scale; tiny, crawling, flying and specialised creatures amongst the grasses; carnivorous bog plants like sundews and flowering plants like asphodels, ragged robin and lady's smock. On the grazed slopes the vegetation was kept low; diminutive, plants and flowers secreted themselves amongst the grasses, bent low, shirking the constant wind. Callum loved to lay on his belly and study the tiny rainforest of incredible diversity in miniature that existed there, so close to the ground as to be hardly noticed by the casual observer. He knew many of the plants and creatures names and their stories from his mother who also loved to lie probing amongst the grasses and reveal their hidden, delicate beauty.

Callum had developed a keen eye for spotting their sheep and knew all their calls, a note of surprise or distress would catch his ear, immediately he would count the herd, look for particular individuals, pay attention, especially to the lambs. He would pick up on the rich, varied picture of what was happening within the flock, so apparently abandoned up on the high, bare moors but in actuality more at home here than down in the paddocks. This was the natural habitat of the hill sheep, they knew its ways, where to shelter, where to find clear, sweet water, where the tastiest, most succulent grasses and herbs lay and they knew the predators. The lambs learnt to keep close when the eagles flew or foxes trotted by; their mothers would face down their would-be attackers with horn-headed aggression. Seeing nothing untoward Callum would sigh at having to leave the rarefied beauty of the high moor and head down slope to the croft to get on with his work.

During late March and April Màiri had hoarded seedlings in boxes and jars and old saucepans filled with soil, protected on window sills and sheltered outside by the house walls; anything to start her vegetable patch before the ground was ready. They were already late by the time the long, heaped up lazy beds were ready to plant up. As each patch was completed, in went onion sets, early brassica seeds and chitted potatoes. Callum had been sent off to explore the gulleys out of the way of sheep and roaming deer herds to collect willow and hazel poles for her beans. He cut and stacked and bundled them up and hauled them home on his back. Root crops like beetroot, parsnip, swede and turnip were sown straight into the soil as soon the earth was warm enough.

Callum became fascinated by this business of creating a garden; the seeds astonished him, so tiny and yet magically bursting into shoots with hardly a helping hand, a little damp soil in a sheltered spot in the light of the spring sun and within days myriad green shoots sprouted in their containers. How? By what means do these dormant, dead looking little capsules suddenly burst into life? As the first little, round seed leaves dropped and the real leaves developed he was seeing the adult plant in miniature. He would pick up a container and study it closely, trying to see how the bent little green-white stems arched their way up out of the hard seed case where it had split, poked a shoot up, shook off the cuticles of the case and then spread their leaves, like stretching cramped limbs.

Whenever either of them had half an hour to spare from the busy round of running the croft; tending the animals, weeding the oats and barley or milking or mucking out the stalls or the more demanding jobs; mending fences and walls. they would disappear into the garden and plant out seedlings. Màiri had also planted three small, bare rooted apple trees and two pear trees along with gooseberries, red and black currants and raspberries, that Scottish favourite and a few delicate, alpine strawberries. Last of all she planted a large, fat-rooted rhubarb crown rescued from a patch in Isla's busy garden.

Callum enjoyed planting out the seedlings immensely, creating rows of green nodding headed vegetables; to see the long curlicues of beans beginning to wind their way up their long poles and the ferny stems of carrots and parsnips begin to cover the ground and green the bare, clay soil. The glaucus, fat leaves of broad beans stood tall and beefy at the far end of the plot, supported by a net of sticks and strings, they looked like a row of green soldiers growing in an untidy but sturdy platoon. The leaves of cabbage seedlings swelled, multiplied their leaves and settled into a slow development towards fat, round fullness. Potatoes developed and showed their haulms in rows of green and were earthed up on ridges as they began to grow.

Màiri's flowerbeds began to sing with colour, annuals burst into bloom in late May competing with the more subdued, tasteful countryside in their gaudy reds, purples and glowing yellow globes of marigolds, riotous snapdragons, waving lupins with widespread, palm-like leaves and perennials like jasmine and clematis weaving their way decadently round their neighbours like good natured drunks.

The crowning glory in the middle of the biggest flowerbed was Màiri's greatest folly, her leap of faith, an act of eccentricity and crazy optimism; a wonderful moss rose, Eglantyne, a glory of glossy green leaves, a sharply barbed little plant on a windy Highland moor. Though she suspected it would never flower she hoped against hope that it would. She coaxed it, tended it and spread good, well rotted cow manure at its feet. She sheltered it with other hardier plants and watched it sulk and rebel and refuse to grow and then grow a little and then a little more until, finally it forgot it was just a rose out of place on a high, windy Ghaidhealteachd moor and sent out a single bud.

Isla brought presents of herb plants and Màiri created well drained beds for them as close to the kitchen as she dare without them becoming waterlogged; sage and rosemary and mint and parsley and tiny-leaved fragrant thyme. Jeannie and Dougie became caught up in the fever of planting and crossly demanded their own patch of soil to grow flowers and vegetables. First Màiri and then Callum patiently knelt with them on the dark soil and helped their clumsy, inexperienced hands sow seeds and poke potatoes into holes and plant a few bean plants. Callum helped Dougie plant a fat-leaved marrow in the middle of his little plot.

In the middle of a sunny, glorious May day they had a strange visitor who trailed fate on his coat tails and brought consternation and dilemmas to Màiri. He was an old gentleman with swept back, white hair and dark-rimmed, round glasses, bushy eyebrows and a dark suit, shiny with age. He appeared in the croft yard seeking her out by calling out her name in a somewhat querulous voice. He found her in the cow byre sweeping the floor with a stiff broom surrounded by piles of straw and cow muck.

–"Mrs McDonald, Mrs Màiri McDonald?" The old man croakily enquired.

–"Aye, I'm Mrs Màiri McDonald?" she said warily.

–"And are you pray the Mrs Màiri McDonald whose deceased husband was Hamish McDonald, a young minister from Edinburgh?" He asked in a quiet, rolling burr but nonetheless authoritatively.

He used a formal, and quite demanding tone that irritated her and made her cautious of his look and sound of officialdom. Officialdom brought little good and plenty of bad news to the glen.

–"And why might I ask dae ye wish tae ken?" She said by way of reply.

–"Because Madam, if you are she I have news for you" he said noncommittally.

–"I am she and if ye wait a moment I'll take ye indoors and we can discuss this" she said in a slightly irritated manner and laid down her broom and removed her rough, calico apron.

She led him to the house, invited him in and excused herself while she went to wash her hands.

Màiri returned to find him studying two photos on the shelf of a little corner cupboard.

–"My parents" said Màiri shortly, my Mathàir and Athair," aware this man would probably be unfamiliar with the Gaelic, he was clearly a city man.

–"Ah the Gaelic" he said "I regret I never learnt any. It was frowned upon when I was at school, still is I suppose. Such a shame; I believe it to be a beautiful and expressive language." He said enthusiastically.

–"It is!" agreed Màiri, surprised and pleased that a city dweller, and an official-looking one at that, should have a good word to say for the Gaelic.

–"Will ye hae some tea?" Màiri asked, relenting a little as she moved towards the fire, placing the heavy kettle on the range.

–"Very kind" he said "yes please and I'm afraid I have been rather remiss in not introducing myself earlier. I shall do so straight away! I am Mr Gregory Johnstone, clerk to the solicitors Stewart and Westacott, an old established Edinburgh firm. I am charged with the responsibility of bringing you details of the Rev Joshua McDonald's last will and testament." He said clearly and formerly in a courtroom voice.

–"Who?" Màiri asked, not recognising the import of the name the man was referring to.

–"Your husband was a Mr Hamish McDonald, a young Minister in the Church of Scotland?" he asked.

–"Ah!" Màiri said, suddenly realising why the formal looking gentleman was there to see her.

–"Ye are referring to the evil old devil who ruined my husband's's life, his god-awful father, may he receive the worst torments of hell when he gets there, as he will, most assuredly." Màiri said with vehemence.

–"Ah, I fear the essence of the Reverand McDonald senior will have already arrived wherever it is going Mrs McDonald! He was deceased as of six weeks ago. I have had a fair old struggle to find you and, if I may say it is that which occasions me to be so tardy."

Mr Johnstone spoke rather like a Dickens novel thought Màiri, who suspected that he hadn't quite grown used to the ways of the 20th Century yet and judging by his advanced age probably wouldn't do so now.

–"Well I am glad tae meet ye Mr Johnstone and ye are very welcome to our hame but I wish tae ken nothing more of that gentleman other than that he is dead and gone." Màiri said with some finality.

–"Just so Mrs McDonald, just so! But I fear nonetheless that I will have to despatch my duty regardless and tell you what I have been sent to convey he continued resignedly.

–"Alright Mr Johnstone" Mairi said with a sigh "but let's sit doon and hae a cuppa first eh!"

–"With pleasure Mrs McDonald!" The old man said and relaxed a little.

Now that she saw him close up, sitting across the table, she realised he was older than she had first thought, probably in his late sixties. His wiry, white eyebrows curled up at the ends spectacularly and the soft, pale skin of his face was deeply lined. He had small, pink spots on his cheeks and slightly watery, blue eyes, myopic behind thick spectacle lenses. His high, starched, collar was a little ragged around the edges and grubby at the neck and his suit looked quite old and worn. She surmised that whatever else Stewart and Westacott solicitors were they were not overly generous to their old retainers.

During tea they had chatted a little and Mairi had ascertained that Mr Johnstone was an old bachelor who lived with a sister of a similar age and that both depended on his limited salary as a clerk with the solicitors. She had discovered that he liked concerts and enjoyed occasionally going to black-and-white "movies" something Màiri had never seen and could only wonder at. He was looking forward to the promise of what he had heard were movies in full colour, something which meant nothing to Màiri who struggled to imagine what any film, or "movie" as Mr Johnstone referred to them in the American way, would be like. He tried to describe it but to someone who had never even been to a theatre it was impossible to imagine.

After they had finished their tea with which Màiri had served oatcakes with honey, Mr Johnstone prepared to get down to business.

–"The deceased had no property as such Mrs McDonald, as a Minister in the Church of Scotland he resided at the manse. After a few a small bequests to the Church Missionary Society the bulk of his estate reverts to his nearest kin, which as the wife of his only child and indeed only relation, that means you Mrs McDonald and by extension your children. You are the one and only beneficiary of his estate." He finished with a formal flourish, laying a folded document on the table which he had carefully removed from his inside, jacket pocket. It was a long, legal looking document. Perhaps you would care to read the schedule Mrs McDonald; one of my colleagues completed the inventory and added the sum of the deceased's outstanding bank account after duties have been paid by ourselves on your late father-in-law's account, as instructed in his will. You are not named but as his only remaining legal relation that is unnecessary."

He looked at her, she looked at him not quite sure what he meant her to do or say.

–"Ye mean everything he left gaes tae me, but I have already made myself clear I think Mr Johnstone, that I want nothing tae dae with that man, nor anything that was his" she said emphatically.

–"Ah, I do see Mrs McDonald. But I'm afraid whether you want it or not it is yours, there is no-one else," the old man said carefully and sympathetically. "Will you not at least to look at the inventory?" He asked pleading.

In order to make it easier for him she gave in.

–"Mr Johnstone, fae yer peace of mind I will look but I hae told ye that I want nothing from this man, it would burn my fingers."

She looked quickly through the list, it included the usual domestic items; kitchen utensils, pots, pans, bedding, cutlery.

–"Can ye gie all this stuff tae a charity or someone who needs it? she asked him.

-"I can if that is your instruction Mrs McDonald . You are sure you do not want any of it?" He asked.

-"Nary a stick, give it away where it would do the most guid; I will leave it tae yer judgement"

–"Now what about the monies?"

Monies, what monies thought Màiri and why can't these people use normal words like money.

–"It's on the second schedule Mrs McDonald.," said the white-haired old man, leaning over and turning to the second page of the document. "You may just wish to look at the total, at the bottom of the page," he said pointing.

Mairi looked with little interest and then looked again. She flushed hot and cold, looking at the figure in astonishment five hundred pounds five shillings and sixpence. It was a fortune to her, an astronomical sum.

–"Guid God!" was all she could say.

–"It is a reasonably large sum is it not?" Mr Johnstone said quite casually.

–"I dinnae ken what ye would call it where ye come frae Mr Johnstone but I call it a bluidy fortune!" She shook her head, unbelieving. "Nonetheless, I still dinnae want a penny of it" she said flatly.

The old man just raised his bushy, wayward eyebrows and said.

–"Nevertheless, I have taken the liberty of paying it into an account at the Bank of Scotland in Edinburgh. You may of course draw from it at any branch, including the one at Kyle of Lochalsh. Here are the account details and a cheque-book, the bank were kind enough to give to me in your name." He handed over a folded piece of paper and a flat, long flexible book. Màiri had never seen a cheque-book though she knew John Fraser had one for conducting the village business at market but had never seen it.

-"I have so very much enjoyed meeting you Mrs McDonald" said Mr Johnstone, rising from the table. "I will carry out your instructions as regards your generous donations on my return. I must make my way back to town for my return journey by rail. I am so looking forward to the walk back through your most beautiful countryside; magnificent!" he announced and he stood and held out his hand to her.

-"Are ye sure ye'll no stay a little longer and hae a meal?" She asked.

-"No, no. You have been most generous Mrs McDonald and I rarely eat during the day."

She suspected he wouldn't be able to afford to have lunch on his measly salary but she could not persuade him to stay.

-"That money will just lie in the bank Mr Johnstone; are you sure I hae tae have it?"

-"I am quite sure Mrs McDonald," and then he stopped as he reached the door;

-"Mrs McDonald, please forgive me if I am speaking out of turn" he said slowly, appearing to consider his words. "You may feel that the old Reverend McDonald did your dead husband a great deal of harm and by extension to yourself and your family as well, but I wonder", he said pausing and looking her directly in the eye with his own clouded, blue eyes "if this money might not in some small measure be used for your children if not by yourself to provide some small redress for the harm at least. It is after all not a huge amount in the great scheme of things but could make a great deal of difference to their life chances, don't you think?" he finished, smiling in a kindly fashion and turned to walk off.

–"Good day Mrs McDonald" he called brightly and bowed his head respectfully before placing his small, black, pork-pie hat on it and striding, a little stiffly, down the path. Màiri stood watching him go, unsettled and confused by the feelings his visit had aroused and thinking about what he had said at the end.

She wandered round her garden and marvelled at the way everything was so burgeoning; against all the odds her garden was bursting with life. She spotted a small splash of pink in her flowerbed and hurried over to see that her rose bush; Eglantyne had bloomed; one large, round, moss rose. It was a glorious deep pink against the dark glossy vegetation. She plunged her nose into it and thought she had never smelt anything so beautiful. She hurried off to find Callum to share this sudden and unexpected beauty with him.

Callum had spotted the old, white-haired man leaving from way up on the slopes of the Ben where he had been checking on the sheep. He had been curious and had hastened down to find out who it was. When Màiri had explained he just commented;

–"So, the auld de'il's dead. Well we can manage without his damn money!"

He had been angry and disturbed by this raising of ghosts as his mother knew he would be, but nonetheless an idea was forming in her mind. If a delicate pink rose could flower so high up on a Highland moor perhaps other small miracles were possible.

Lightning Source UK Ltd.
Milton Keynes UK
UKHW012109151122
412269UK00002B/21

9 781839 758591